CRUSADER'S TOMB

CRUSADER'S TOMB

A NOVEL

by

A. J. CRONIN

LONDON
VICTOR GOLLANCZ LTD
1956

Printed in Great Britain by Richard Clay and Company, Ltd.,
Bungay, Suffolk

"Not only is fame (and until recent years even liberty) denied to men of genius during their lives, but even the means of subsistence. After death they receive monuments and rhetoric by way of compensation."

CESARE LOMBROSO.

PART ONE

CHAPTER I

Afternoon had turned to evening and all the sweep and movement of the Downs lay still, bathed in pearly light. The drenched grass, silvered as with hoar, gave off a wispy vapour that hung cobwebs on the hedgerows, made lace-work in the hollows of the fields. The dew-ponds, saucers of skimmed milk, held no image of a yellow moon that watched, round and low, like the eye of a great cat, crouched on the hill, ready to lap.

Into this bright stillness, from a stone Norman church so small, so lost in a fold of the weald it seemed—despite the sharp etching of its long and short work, its squat tower, and leper squint—unlikely as a dream, there emerged a shadow, long and dark, which was succeeded, following the thud of oak and the clang of a heavy bolt, by the figure of a man, less long perhaps, but of equal darkness. Appropriately enough, a clergyman, Bertram Desmonde, Rector of Stillwater.

Bareheaded, but with a cape about his shoulders, he threaded the maze of lichened slabs, passed the two great twisted yews, of which the younger had undoubtedly made bows for Sussex archers at least five centuries before, then through the wicket to the lane. Here, caught by the whiteness of the night, by an upsurge of his secret joy, he paused and, with a long breath, drew in the beauty of his glebe, a good two hundred acres, reaching away on one hand to the high beech wood of Ditchley, upon the other to the sandy gorse warren that verged the country road to Stillwater. Distantly the Ring of Chanctonbury was visible against the eastern sky, and lower, amidst trees, an absurd yet friendly turret of Broughton Court. To the west the weald swept on, cut by a chalk-pit—a bloodless wound, by barrows reputed to be Roman, yet more likely the workings of an ancient tile kiln. Then came labourers' cottages, six, like mushrooms, in a row, and faintly, above the rim of the road, the twinkle of the village. Beneath him, bright with lights, stood the Rectory.

Solidly Georgian, with Palladian windows, a spacious portico supported by fluted columns and—delightful thought!—a balustrade coping, it was a real country house, built by his great-grand-father,

Canon Hilary Desmonde, in 1780, of the local white stone—the quarry, quite near, was now fortunately overgrown. Traces of an early Tudor building still persisted in the brick barn and stables, the farm outhouses, in the exquisite old wall of flint and rounded pebbles surrounding the large kitchen garden. Embosomed in soft lawns, bordered by beds of tulips and primulas, the rose garden, not yet awakened, a formal hexagon about the sun-dial, cordons of aged Ribstons and Beauty of Bath standing surpliced with blossom, like ancient choristers, along the south meadow, a giant ilex shading the gravel drive, this house, this little Blenheim, rooted and unchanging, his home, home of the Desmondes for so many years, tonight especially it sent a proud warmth into the Rector's heart.

Almost certainly they had come over with the Conqueror. One of them, the Sieur d'Esmonde, who had gone to the Crusades, lay beneath his marble effigy, the beaked nose broken, alas, by some vandal tourist, in the little Downland church. If the name had been altered somewhat by rustic usage—one could not apply the word corrupted— did not this identify them more completely with the good Sussex earth? They had served their country well in the three professions open to a gentleman: in the Church particularly, but also at the bar and in the army. His brother Hubert, after long and useful work on the frontiers of Afghanistan, was now partially retired to Simla Lodge, some fifteen miles away, with the rank of general, still in touch with the War Office, and devoting his leisure to the scientific cultivation of Jargonelle pears. Only on one occasion, so far as recollection went, had the family stooped to trade: when, in the early reign of Victoria, one Joseph Desmonde, great-uncle of the Rector, had embarked upon the manufacture of ecclesiastical furnishings. But as the business had a flavour of discretion, and as a considerable fortune had accrued from it, the lapse, though regrettable, was less difficult to condone.

"A fine evenin' to you, sir."

In the profundity of his reverie, the Rector had failed to observe the stumpy figure of old Mould, his head gardener, who was also his sexton, limping up the lane to close the church.

"Good evening, Mould. I've locked up, you may turn and go back with me." He paused, not revealing the impulse which, against his habit, had drawn him to the church, yet prompted by the same elation to add: "Stephen comes home tonight, you know."

"As if I'd a forgotten that, sir. And high good news it be. I hope he shall find time to come rabbiting along of me." He added more gravely: "We shall have him in the pulpit soon, belikes."

"He still has some way to go, Mould." As they walked down the lane together Bertram smiled. "Though I daresay you'd rather hear a youngster fresh from Oxford than an old fogey like me."

"No, Parson, you shan't say that. I h'ain't served the Desmondes fifty year without I come to know their quality. And howsoever they may preach, there be none better in the county."

It needed only this touching proof of almost feudal loyalty to set a seal upon the Rector's mood. The clotted scent of primroses was sweeter, somehow, the thin night bleating of the lambs, behind their wattle fences, so poignant it almost broke the heart. Ah, this England, he thought: and here, the very heart of it, precious as a jewel, sailing in the moonlight like a ship of souls, his little parish that would be Stephen's too, inviolate, enduring, timeless and changeless as eternity.

"We shall want help with the luggage. Will you see that Albert is on hand?"

"I shall send him up, master . . . if he be home. I'm 'aving trouble with that boy o' mine. 'E don't take kindly to service. But I shall belt 'im into it . . . I promise you."

"He will settle down in time, Mould," Bertram answered equably. "Don't be hard on him."

He parted from the old man at the squat, bow-fronted gate-lodge and, some moments later, stood in the wide entrance hall of the Rectory, yielding his cape to his daughter Caroline, who, inevitably, was on hand to greet him.

"Not here yet?" He rubbed his hands together: the hall had the defect of its lofty ceiling and tessellated floor—a sense of evening chill, barely relieved by the clank of tepid pipes.

"No, Father. But they should not be long. Claire has gone to the station in her new motor."

"We really should get one of those contraptions." A light of whimsy relieved momentarily the austerity of Bertram's thin features and slightly hollowed cheeks. "Useful for parish visiting."

"You cannot be serious, Father." Her practical mind, entirely devoid of humour, took him literally. "You know how strongly you object to the odour and the dust. And don't I do well enough for you with the pony-cart?"

No doubt the imminence of Stephen's return had put her on edge. Thus, she spoke more forcibly than she intended, her plain, earnest face shiny with feeling. And indeed, before she could regret this, her father's absent look as, with ears attuned, he waited for the sound of wheels upon the driveway, punished her severely. She lowered her eyes, her thickset body, supported by too solid calves, drooped insensibly. Would he never appreciate the limitless depths of her devotion, realize that her one desire was to serve him? —from the first moment which began her day, that long day wherein, after her hasty dressing, without benefit of mirror, she shouldered the burden of his household, conferred with cook as to how he should be fed, arranged the flowers, supervised the garden and the farm, dealt with his correspondence, with importunate visitors, bedridden parishioners, sere archæologists, equally with waggonettes of holiday-makers from Littlesea clamouring to view the "toom", found time even to attend to his linen and knit his woollen socks. And now to make matters worse, she had a bad cold in her head and must blow her sore nose in a sodden handkerchief.

"Is your mother coming down?" He put the question with caution.

"I think not. I bathed her forehead with cologne this afternoon. But the discomfort is still there."

"Then we shall be four at dinner."

"Only three. Claire telephoned to say, so very sorry, she cannot stay."

"A pity. Still . . . there will be other days."

His tone conveyed regret, yet she perceived, despite his high regard for Claire, daughter of Lady Broughton of the neighbouring Court, and his warm approval of the tacit understanding existing between her and his eldest son, that, in his heart, he was glad on this night of reunion, to have Stephen entirely to himself.

With an effort she kept her tone even.

"I've not quite finished typing your notes for tomorrow's convocation. When shall you be leaving for Charminster?"

"Oh, after lunch, I suppose. The Dean is seldom punctual."

"Two o'clock then. I'll drive you over." Suddenly, with jealous, glistening eyes: "You look tired, Father. And you have a heavy day before you. Don't let Stephen keep you up too late."

"Do not fuss, Caroline. And by the bye, I hope you have something good for us to eat."

"There's mulligatawny soup, and the salmon Uncle Hubert sent us from the Test, with cucumber and green sauce of course, then a saddle of lamb with our own peas and new potatoes. For the sweet, Beasley has made that whipped apple charlotte Stephen likes so much."

"Ah, yes, my dear. I remember he always asked for it when he came home from Marlborough. Well done. But wait, isn't that the chug of the motor?"

A feeble, if rhythmic beat was indeed perceptible and, advancing to the door, he threw it open, disclosing a small De Dion coupé, alive and quivering, from which, once the agitation had subsided, by the exercise of some ingenuity two figures emerged.

"Stephen!"

"How are you, Father . . . and you, Caroline? Davie isn't here?"

"Not yet . . . he breaks up next Monday."

The fan of light from the portico revealed a slight figure of less than medium stature, darkly clad and struggling with a leather valise—Mould's boy had not appeared—a glimpse, also, of thinly chiselled features, sensitive nostrils, a narrow, thoughtful, rather too serious face. Then came, with reserve, allowing the family greetings to subside, a tall girl in gauntlets and a long tweed coat. Her motoring bonnet, veil-draped, absurdly like a scone, worn only in deference to maternal urgings, could not quite destroy her air of quiet composure, a sense of inescapable good breeding, confirmed by her voice as she joined the little group.

"I'm afraid we left some luggage behind. My little runabout has no space for trunks."

"No need to worry, Claire dear. We'll send for it tomorrow." The Rector took her arm in a near paternal gesture. "But cannot you stay with us now?"

"I do wish I might. But Mother has some village people coming . . . an agriculture committee . . . tenants . . . who cannot be put off."

"Ah well! One must pay for being lady of the manor. Is it not a sweet evening?"

"Perfect! Coming over from Halborough it was bright as day . . ." Her voice softened as she turned her head, a movement that, dissolving the shadow of the atrocious bonnet, disclosed a pure and even profile. "Wasn't it beautiful, Stephen?"

He had been standing in silence, a constraint from which he now seemed to rouse himself by an effort.

"It was a nice drive." Then, as though he felt he had not said enough, forcing a levity quite foreign to him: "But at one point I thought we might have to get out and push."

"On Ambry Hill," Claire laughed. "I'm not very expert with the gears." Her smile lingered for a moment in the darkness of the porch. "I must not keep you. Good night. Come to us soon . . . tomorrow, if possible. And do be careful of your cold, Caroline."

When she had gone, Bertram put his arm about his son's shoulders, led him into the house.

"It's good to have you home, Stephen. You don't know . . . Ah, well . . . How did you leave Oxford? And how are you? Famished, I'm sure. Run up and see your mother. Then come to dinner."

And while Caroline, her eyes and nose reddened by the night air, heaved in a bag of books which had been left, forgotten, on the porch, he stood while Stephen ascended the stairs, looking upwards with an expression that, in its unguarded fondness, was almost rapt.

CHAPTER II

After their excellent dinner, well served by the two table-maids whom, from their pristine village rawness, Caroline had trained so admirably, the Rector, mellowed, led Stephen to the study, where the drugget curtains were drawn and a fine sea-coal fire burned. The heating of the Rectory might not be modern but the hearths were ample, fuel abundant. And this was a companionable room despite the ornate mouldings, with a cosy, sporting flavour to offset the vaguely parochial air, confirmed by a roll-top desk bearing Pusey's sermons, the Ecclesiastical Calendar, and a folded purple stole. A pair of worn brown leather easy-chairs flanked the hearth-stone, against one wall there stood a glass-fronted gun cabinet, upon another a case of Saxon coins, product of the Rector's archæological researches, and above the Adam mantel, two bone-handled hunting-crops were crossed beneath a mounted fox mask.

Earlier that afternoon, in preparation, Bertram had traversed the passages beneath the house to visit the cellar, and now, with a slightly conscious air, he took up a dusty bottle which lay cradled, whitewash splash upwards, upon the desk, and having inexpertly drawn the crumbling cork, poured out two glasses of port. He was a temperate man who touched alcohol only rarely and, for that matter, never used tobacco, but this occasion demanded to be marked in the true family tradition.

"Your grandfather laid this down," he remarked, holding the dark purplish wine to the light with an assumed critical air. "It's a Graham . . . 1876."

Stephen, who detested port, made a murmur of appreciation from his arm-chair as he raised the glass to his lips. He assumed, like an actor, the part expected of him.

"It seems very sound, sir."

The word pleased the Rector.

"Yes, your grandfather knew what he was doing. It was he who put in these remarkable tile-bins downstairs. They drained South Meadow, you know, in eighteen-seventy-eight, and had half a load of short tile pipe ends left. The old man saw that each would hold a bottle snugly, and had them mortared into the cellar, a perfect honeycomb. . . . Of course, he was not a great drinker. But he liked his pint of claret after a good day with the hounds. He went out, you know, until his seventieth year."

"He must have been a great character."

"He was a good man, Stephen. A true English country gentleman." The Rector sighed. "One could wish no finer epitaph."

"My grandmother, too," Stephen prompted dutifully, for on the journey from Oxford, brooding nervously as the train rocked past meadows, orchards, and winding reaches, he had resolved to be unreservedly filial. "She was not far behind him. Mould has told me many stories of her."

"Ah, yes, he was devoted to her . . . as were all her people. . . . But she kept him upon the run." A slow smile of reminiscence kindled Bertram's eye. "You know that in her later years the old lady became excessively stout. Indeed, she had such difficulty in getting about she was obliged to be wheeled, and Mould, then the gardener's boy, was chosen as the means of propulsion. At an extra sixpence a week. It was a tremendous honour. But somewhat exacting, especially when your grandmother wished to go to the village and had to be pushed all the way up Ambry Hill. One hot summer day, when young Mould reached the brow of the hill he stopped to wipe his face on his sleeve. But as he let go the chair, off it rolled without him, gathering speed, flashing down the hill and round the bend at a breakneck pace. The poor lad was petrified. He saw himself the murderer of his mistress. With a horrified yell he dashed down the hill. When he reached the bottom. . . ." Wincingly, Stephen set himself to laugh; he knew the anecdote by heart., ". . . There was your grandmother, calmly drawn up in the village square, bargaining with the butcher for a side of lamb." Bertram's smile faded. "She was an indomitable woman. Immensely charitable. And devoted to my father. She died just eight weeks after him."

Could it be that the Rector was thinking of his own marriage? Outside, an owl hooted. In the still-room along the passage Caroline was moving earthenware pickle jars with unnecessary brusqueness. Bertram straightened and sipped his port, aware that he must break the silence before constraint fell between himself and Stephen. How strange it was to care so deeply, and yet to sense this embarrassment haunting their relationship whenever they were alone together. Was it because he cared too much? He never experienced such lack of ease in the company of his two other children. Of course he was fond of Caroline, admitted her staunchness, found her a "great stand-by". But her homeliness, dedicating her, he felt, to perpetual spinsterhood, jarred, unconsciously, his sense of family pride. As for David, his youngest child, now nearly thirteen years of age, here, alas, his love was swamped by sadness, by disappointment and pity. To think that any son of his, for that matter any Desmonde, should be an epileptic who, even when untroubled by attacks, was inclined to stammer in his speech!

The Rector suppressed a sigh. To yield to feeling was dangerous. Yet in his present mood there was no escape from it.

"It's good you finished so well at Oxford. You've done splendidly."

"Oh, I don't know. I seemed to lose heart rather at the end."

"I felt like that too, when I came down from Trinity . . . though I loved it just as much as you."

Stephen was silent. How could he tell his father that he had hated the university?—the dryness, the superiority, the sense of being outside of life, the endless preoccupation with sports that held no interest for him, the bloodless study of dead tongues which unutterably bored him, and which had driven him, from sheer contrariness, to perfect himself in French and Spanish, above all . . . his detestation of the career ordained for him.

But the Rector had resumed.

"You have earned a holiday. Claire wants you over for tennis. And Uncle Hubert has asked you to Chillingham. . . . Wasn't his salmon good tonight? . . . Your cousin Geoffrey is there, on short leave, at present."

Again Stephen did not answer. And for the first time Bertram began to question if, beneath his passive manner, his son were not suppressing signs of strain. His natural pallor seemed intensified and his eyes held that enlarged darkness which, diminishing the rest of his face, had since his earliest days been a symptom of emotional or physical distress. He is not strong, I hope he is not sickening for something, thought Bertram, with sudden anxiety, and quickly, protectively, he declared:

"You must certainly have a rest. No need for you to go to the Settlement until July. Allowing five months for London, your

14

ordination would then be at Christmas, a most suitable season of the year."

Stephen roused himself. For how long had he foreseen and dreaded this moment, tried, on his friend Glyn's advice, to hasten it, then nervously drawn back, written a score of letters, and always torn them up. Now that it was upon him he felt sick and hollow inside.

"Father . . . I must talk to you."

"Yes?" Encouragingly, with a nod, and finger-tips compressed.

A pause. Is it money? the Rector thought mildly. Some unpaid college debt? Then, haltingly, the words came out.

"I do not want to go on and take orders."

The Rector's expression did not noticeably change, as though sudden and complete surprise had, like sudden death, fixed his features in a semblance of normality. At last, almost stupidly, he said:

"Not take orders?"

"I feel I am not suited to the Church . . . I'm not good with people . . . I can't organize . . . I couldn't preach a decent sermon to save my life . . ."

"These things will come." Bertram, drawn erect, was half frowning now. "My own sermons are not particularly brilliant. But they suffice."

"But Father, it isn't only that. I have no interest in the work. I . . . I feel I'm not fitted to succeed you here . . ."

Confirmed in his earlier surmise by Stephen's broken voice, the Rector recovered himself, assumed a soothing tone.

"You're tired, and rundown my boy. We all get stale and discouraged occasionally. You'll feel different after a few brisk tramps on the Downs."

"No, Father." Breathing unsteadily, Stephen tightened his will. "This has been coming on for a long time. I can't tie myself up in this little place . . . to a future of blankness and frustration."

What had he said in his desperate groping for words? The shocked look in his father's eyes distressed him. A moment of unendurable silence. Then:

"I was unaware that you looked upon Stillwater in that light. We are a small parish, perhaps. But our worth to the country might be judged by other standards than those of mere dimension."

"You've misunderstood me. I love Stillwater . . . it's my home. And I know how highly you are esteemed for miles around. It's something else . . . surely you understand what I mean . . . what I feel I must do with my life."

The Rector drew back sharply then, with gathering comprehension, gazed in startled fashion at his son.

"Stephen . . . it is not that wild notion again? "

"Yes, Father."

Again a bar of silence vibrated between them. The Rector got to his feet and began, slowly at first, then with increasing perturbation, to pace the room. At last, with an effort, he calmed himself, drew close to Stephen.

"My dear boy," he said, with great seriousness. "I have never tried to bind you to me through your sense of duty. Even when you were very young, before you went to school, I preferred to rely on your natural feelings of affection and respect. Yet you must realize how completely I've built upon your following me here. Stillwater means so much to me . . . to all of us. And the circumstances of my life . . . your mother's invalidism . . . David's unhappy disability . . . the fact that you are my eldest and—forgive me"—his voice shook slightly—"my much-beloved son . . . have caused me to rest my hopes on you. Nevertheless, at this moment, I put all that aside. Upon my honour, it is you I am thinking of and not myself, when I tell you, shall I say beg you, to forget this fantastic dream. You do not realize what it means. You mustn't . . . you cannot do it."

Stephen lowered his gaze so that he might not see the slight twitching of his father's cheek.

"Surely I am entitled to my own life." Through respect there burned an inner defiance.

"Not that kind of life. It will bring you only to disaster. To throw away your brilliant prospects, wreck your whole career, for a mere whim . . . it would be an outrage in the face of God. And there's Claire . . . how, under Heaven, would she fit into such a scheme? No, no. You are very young for your years, Stephen. . . . This mad idea that has got hold of you seems all important to you now. But in a few years you'll smile at yourself for having even thought of it."

Sunk in his chair, with flushed cheeks and downcast eyes, his wits made dull and torpid by the port, Stephen could not find a word to say. At this moment, without exaggeration, he hated his father . . . yet was at the same time vanquished by the shamed consciousness of his paternal affection, by the recognition, in justice, of his point of view, and worst of all by a warm nostalgic tide welling up into his throat, a flood of childhood memories . . . of breezy rides to Ambry in the pony-cart, his father idling with the reins, Carrie in clean white pinafore, Davie wearing his first flannel shorts; of water picnics on the Avon, hot sunlight on cool water, and a widgeon rising from yellow reeds as the punt pushed through; of family carols sung before the Christmas tree, a powder of snow upon the window-panes . . . oh, how could one tear up such tender, binding roots?

Bertram bent forward and laid his hand, not impressively, but rather with touching diffidence, upon his son's shoulder.

"Believe me, it's your happiness, Stephen. You can't . . . you could not find it in your heart to go against me."

Stephen did not dare look up lest he should disgrace himself with tears. He was done for . . . at least for the present. And he had meant to fight so hard, had sworn to Glyn that he would win.

"Very well," he managed to mumble at last, tasting all the bitterness which defeat brings to a gentle yet passionate nature. "If you feel so strongly about it. . . I'll give the Settlement a trial . . . and see what comes of it."

CHAPTER III

BERTRAM WENT UPSTAIRS slowly. Although his sense of relief was deep, it did not diminish the weariness that had suddenly come on him, nor the lingering anxiety around his heart. Outside his wife's bedroom he hesitated, head tilted in an attitude of listening, then, tapping gently upon the panel, he braced himself instinctively and entered.

It was a large apartment, formerly the upstairs drawing-room— the best room in the house, old Canon Desmonde had named it, no doubt because of its fine proportions and eastern exposure which, besides admitting the morning sun, afforded a wide panorama of the Downs. In its conversion to his wife's bed-sitting-room, some of the original furnishings had been retained—the needle-point chairs and Chippendale settee, a broad semi-circle of gesso mirror above the white marble mantel, the red Brussels carpet. Protected by a draught-screen, Julia Desmonde lay reading in bed, beneath the satin coverlet. She was a shapely, well-preserved woman of forty-five, with an easy, intensely indolent air, plump smooth features, and thick chestnut hair which billowed like a cloud across the pillow.

Marking with a blanched fingernail the place in her book which bore a drawing of the sign of the Zodiac, Julia directed towards her husband, from beneath fine brows, an inquiring glance. Her eyes were of a remarkable forget-me-not blue, childlike almost, with pale, slightly drooping, fleshy lids.

"So we have Stephen home with us," he said.

"Yes . . . I thought the dear boy looked well."

She could be depended on to express, in her aristocratic, self-absorbed voice, an opinion exactly contrary to his own.

"How is the headache?"

"Better, thank you. I sat too long in the sun this afternoon. That early spring sun is very treacherous. But I have just had a treatment."

He perceived, from the contraption on the side table, that she had just had her vibrations. On the fender a metal kettle hissed out a jaunty plume of steam, indicating that in fifteen minutes the bran extract would be brought and mixed, the tablets of yeast crushed and swallowed, the yogurt spooned, or was it now dried seaweed? Then the hot-water bag would be refilled, the fire made up for the night, the lights turned low, the eye-pads moistened and laid on for sleep. And again, though he fought the question always with determined Christian charity, the thought assailed him: Why had he ever married her?

She had been, of course—indeed, still was, no doubt—in her statuesque way, something of a beauty, and as an only child, daughter of Sir Henry Marsden of Haselton Park, had been regarded, in the county society of those days, as the "catch of the season". Who could have guessed, viewing her, for instance, as the young swan-like hostess of the Haselton Fête, as the belle of the hunt ball at the Assembly Rooms, surrounded by young officers from the Charminster barracks, smiling yet composed, the centre of attraction, that she would later on reveal such marked peculiarity, prove herself so unutterably useless to him as a wife.

Except for a few garden-parties in their early years of marriage, when, trailing a frilled parasol, she moved gracefully about the lawns, in a large hat, she had, with unruffled resolution, refused to interest herself in the work of the parish. God, she said amiably, had not meant her to carry soup to indigent rustics, nor to strain her nerves sewing baby-linen for the encouragement of rural copulation. Fortunately the Bishop's wife liked her, but she would not meet the ladies of the lesser clergy. She preferred to spend her days sitting, overdressed, by her window, or in the rose-garden, engaged upon an endless embroidery of coloured silk from which she lifted her head repeatedly, to gaze for long periods into space, or to make occasional notes, when they occurred to her, of what she should report to her

18

physician, whom—having long ago exhausted the county doctor—she visited in London twice a month. Her children, whom she bore with absent-minded ease, had been to her no more than momentary episodes. So long as they did not put her to inconvenience she regarded them with remote indulgence. Yet as her detachment grew, more and more, she retreated within herself, creating an existence which involved around her physical functions, a little world of happy hypochondria in which—could he, oh God, have forseen it when, on that rose-scented afternoon twenty years before, he had almost died of her kiss in aromatic pain?—she had no greater pleasure, no keener interest, than amiably to discuss with him the colour and consistency of her stools.

Perhaps the stuffed charger—souvenir of Balaclava—in the parental hall should have warned him, but who, alas, could have foretold that her father, until the age of seventy no more than an amiable eccentric, addicted in his spare time to mechanical pursuits—the electrification of his estate by a chain of canvas windmills, the harmless construction of a quick-firing gun which, refused by the War Office, had no more than winged, in a fleshy part, the family butler—who, in Heaven's name, would have foreseen that this irrepressible crank would, in his dotage, launch suddenly a grandiose project for the construction of a flying machine?—not, mark you, an ordinary machine such as that subsequently flown by Blériot across the Channel, though that in itself would have been ill enough, but a weird contraption with fantastic screws, presumed capable of rising vertically from the ground: a helicopter. Thus, in defiance of the laws of gravity, Sir Henry had defiled his lovely park with sheds and hangar, imported workmen, engineers, a Belgian mechanic, spent money like water, in short, ruined himself, and, remaining earthbound, had died a laughing-stock. Haselton, which might have been Julia's, was now a girls' school, the great hangar a gymnasium, the sheds—fresh-painted horrors—turned into repositories for muddy hockey-sticks and unpaired canvas shoes.

Might it not be, thought Bertram, with fresh despondency, that something of this instability was now manifest in Stephen? No, no . . . impossible. The boy, too closely resembling him in mind and body, was all of him, his other self in fact. Yet because of his anxiety, the cloud that hung upon his spirit, he was tempted, despite his better judgement, to open his mind and seek some sort of consolation from his wife.

"My dear," he said. "While he is with us I feel we should make an effort to take Stephen out of himself."

Julia gazed at him in surprise. She possessed to a remarkable degree the power of distorting the meaning of what was said to her.

"My dear Bertram, you know very well that I cannot make an effort. And why should Stephen be taken *out* of himself?"

"I . . . I am concerned about him. He has always been an unusual boy. He is going through a difficult time."

"Difficult, Bertram? Is he not past the puberty?"

"Of course . . . but you know how it is with these young fellows. They get strange notions in their heads in the spring."

"Do you imply that Stephen is in a state of love?"

"No . . . well, of course, we know he is fond of Claire."

"Then what do you mean, Bertram? He cannot be ill. You said yourself a moment ago that he was extremely well."

"It was you who said that." Despite himself, Bertram spoke with growing impatience. "I think he is far from well. But I see you have no wish to share my anxiety."

"If you wish to tell me, my dear, I have no objection to hearing you. But is it not enough that you are worried without worrying me? I think I did my part in bringing your children into the world. There was, from first to last, little pleasure in the undertaking. Afterwards, you made them your responsibility. I never interfered. Why should I do so now?"

"True." He tried to repress his bitterness. "It would make little difference to you if Stephen ruined his life. Julia, there is something in him, beneath the surface, that I don't understand. What is really in his mind? Who are his friends? Don't you recollect when Geoffrey visited him at Trinity last year he found a most impossible person in his rooms . . . a rank outsider Geoffrey called him . . . a down-at-heel artist . . . a Welshman . . ."

He broke off, gazing at her almost beseechingly, until she was compelled to answer. She did so mildly.

"What have you against the Welsh, Bertram? They have beautiful voices. Did this Welshman sing?"

"No," Bertram replied, flushing. "He kept pressing Stephen, all the time, to go to Paris."

"Young men have done so before, Bertram."

"I daresay. But this was not for the obvious reason."

"Then for what reason, if not to have a French woman?"

"To paint!"

It was said, he had got it out at last; and tensely, yet with some slight sense of relief, he waited, in silence, for her to speak.

"I must confess, Bertram, I see little harm in all this. I remember when I was at Interlaken with Papa I did some delightful little water-colours of the lake. Blue was the prevailing tint. Stephen has always liked to draw. Indeed, it was you who gave him his first box of paints."

He bit his lip hard.

"This is no childish hobby, Julia. Do you know that for more than a year now, without a word to us, he has been travelling from Oxford to attend night art classes at the Slade?"

"The Slade is a reputable institution. Stephen will have ample time to sketch between his sermons. And certainly drawing is soothing for the nerves."

He suppressed his impulses to cry out. For a moment he kept his eyes lowered, then in the tone of one who had conquered, but breathing somewhat quickly, he said:

"I hope you are right, my dear. I suppose I worry unnecessarily. No doubt he will settle down when he gets into the swing of his work in London."

"No doubt he will. And Bertram, I have decided that instead of Harrogate, I shall go to Cheltenham next month. There is a mineral in the waters there which I am told is excellent in promoting the flow of bile. When Dr. Leonard last analysed my urine there was a remarkable deficiency in the biliary salts."

He said good night, in a low tone and quickly, lest he say something worse.

As he left the room he could hear along the corridor the slow ticktack of Caroline's machine as, unsparingly, she typed the notes for his speech next day.

CHAPTER IV

On a grey and drizzling afternoon six weeks later, Stephen, returning from a round of house-to-house visiting, walked slowly along Clinker Street in East Stepney. The sulphurous overcast from the London docks made the narrow thoroughfare more dreary, pressed down suffocatingly upon him. No light, no colour—only the deadness of a row of deserted barrows, greasy cobblestones, a brewer's dray horse steaming in the rain, its driver bowed beneath a dripping sack. A westbound omnibus roared past, splashing him with mud as he turned towards the Settlement.

This red-brick structure, built into the line of broken-down stucco houses which sagged along the street like decayed old men, now more than ever reminded him of a small but efficient penitentiary. At that moment the front door swung open and the Warden, the Reverend Crispin Bliss, came out, umbrella poised, nose turned up to scent the weather, tall, meagre form encased to the heels in a long black mackintosh. A meeting, Stephen saw, was unavoidable; he went forward.

"Ah, Desmonde . . . back already?"

The tone was feebly cordial, that of a man, Stephen felt, who had tried to like him, and could not, despite the best intentions and the urge of brotherly love. Unquestionably the Reverend Crispin Bliss, fellow of St. Cuthbert's, was a devoted clergyman who wrought hard for good in this unfruitful vineyard. A Low Churchman, with strong evangelical leanings, he was a man of sincere yet narrow piety. But religion apart, his manner was most unprepossessing: dry, academic, touchily superior. Equally unfortunate was his way of walking with his head thrown back, the donnish air with which he protected himself, and above all, his voice, cracked, slightly sing-song, always ready, it seemed, to utter cultured contradictions in high falsetto tones. Almost at the outset, Stephen had been unlucky enough to offend him.

In the upper corridor of the Settlement there hung, in heavy gilt, a sanguinary portrayal of the martyrdom of Saint Sebastian which bled afresh for Stephen whenever he came from his room. Since the painting seemed ignored by everyone but himself, one morning, in a moment of loathing, he turned it to the wall. The act apparently passed unnoticed. But at supper that night, with a pained glance which passed over the heads of his two curates, Loftus and Geer, and came to rest on Stephen, the Warden observed, in his most nasal tones:

"I do not object to humour, even in its most misguided form, the practical joke. But to interfere with any object in this house which by its subject or association might be regarded as sacred is, to my mind, an unseemly and irreligious act."

Stephen coloured to the roots of his hair and kept his eyes upon his plate. He had meant no harm, and when the meal was over the desire to explain took him to the Warden.

"I'm sorry I turned the picture. The only excuse I can offer you is that it rather got on my nerves."

"Upon your nerves, Desmonde?"

"Well . . . yes, sir. It's in such shocking taste and so obviously a fake."

The Warden's face lost its incredulous look, stiffened slowly.

"I fail to understand you, Desmonde. The picture is a genuine Carlo Dolci."

Stephen smiled apologetically.

"Oh hardly, sir. Not even that. Apart from the crude brush-work, and the modern pigment, it's on white flax canvas—a fabric which wasn't manufactured until around 1890, a good two hundred years after Dolci's death."

The Warden's expression turned altogether stony. He breathed out quickly through his nostrils, not fire precisely, but the Christian counterpart of wrath—just indignation.

"The picture happens to be mine, Desmonde, and a most cherished possession. I bought it as a young man in Italy, from unimpeachable sources. In spite of your opinion I shall continue to cherish it as an original work of art."

Now, however, there was less hostility than watchful moderation in the Warden's regard as, standing in the rain, he offered Stephen the shelter of his umbrella and inquired:

"You did all of Skinners Row this afternoon?"

"Practically all, sir."

He did not wish to confess that, since he expected a visit from Richard Glyn, he had scamped the odd numbers.

"How did you find old Mrs. Blimey?"

"Not altogether well, I'm afraid."

"Is her bronchitis worse, poor creature?" Then, as Stephen hesitated and looked uncomfortable, he added: "Does she need the doctor?"

"No . . . not exactly. As a matter of fact, I found her very drunk."

There was a distressful pause, then came the somewhat worldly question:

"How did she get the money?"

"I believe I am responsible. I gave her five shillings yesterday to pay her room rent. She seems to have spent it on gin."

The Warden made a clicking sound with his tongue.

"Well . . . you will live and learn, Desmonde. I do not reproach you. But you must not put temptation in the way of God's poor creatures."

"I suppose not. On the other hand, can one blame her for trying to escape from her misery for a few hours? She has a bad chest, can't get sewing work of any kind, owes the landlord for the rent and has pawned nearly everything in her room. I must confess I was almost glad to see her rolling about in a state of happy oblivion."

23

"Desmonde!"

"And what's more . . . I couldn't help thinking that if any of us had been in the same position we might have done exactly the same thing."

"Come, come. That is pushing the case a little too far. We should never, please God, find ourselves in a like predicament." He shook his head disapprovingly and put up his umbrella. "You have the boys' club tonight? I will have a word with you about that at supper."

With a parting nod, somewhat distant, he stepped off, leaving Stephen to go upstairs to his room, a narrow cubicle furnished in light oak, with a Gothic overmantel and a revolving bookcase. The bed had not yet been made. The residents of the Settlement were supposed to do for themselves—in the morning, for instance, Stephen would regularly encounter Geer, the senior curate, a bright and brawny Christian, bearing his brimming chamber-pot to the bath-room with an air of hearty unconcern. However, lest the monastic tradition prove too severe, in the afternoon a little outside maid named Jenny Dill came in from the district, ostensibly to supply the finishing touches, in reality to do most of the work. As Stephen flung himself, still in hat and coat, into a Morris chair, he could hear her moving lightly in Loftus's room through the thin party wall. Loftus, a pretty young man, exacting and self-contained, very elegant in a sacerdotal way, always left her plenty to do in the shape of shoes to polish, suits to brush and put away. Yet apparently she had com-pleted these tasks, for in a few minutes there was a tap on his door and, bearing duster and pail, she came spryly in.

"Oh, sir, I beg your pardon . . . I didn't realize you was in."

"That's all right, you go ahead."

He watched her absently as she began expertly to strip the sheets and turn his mattress. She was a pleasant little thing, with a high colour on her cheekbones as though they had been rubbed with brickdust, bright brown eyes, and a fringe of black hair. She looked, he thought, a typical Cockney girl . . . thoroughly competent and nobody's fool. Yet there was about her something more than or-dinary: an air of willing simplicity, an innocence, an affectionate amiability, and above all, a vigour, as though she could not contain the energy and delight which throbbed in her healthy young body. And as she moved about neatly, her waist trim, her bust small and firm, unconscious of his scrutiny, or at least in no way discomposed by it, instinctively his hand went to the pencil and block upon the desk. With the pad upon his knee he began, attentively, to draw.

Presently she went to the fireplace, bent down, and began to clear out the ashes. At this his interest quickened and, when she made to rise, he stopped her abruptly.

"Please don't move, Jenny."

"But, sir . . ."

"No, no. Turn back your head and don't move an inch."

While, obediently, she resumed, and held, her stooping position, his fingers moved nervously over the paper.

"You think I'm quite mad, don't you, Jenny? All the others in the district do."

"Oh, no, sir," she protested vigorously. "We does think you're a morsel queer of course, giving the lads' club sketching and that like, not like a regular curate what learns them to box. Why, when Mr. Geer 'ad the lads you'd go in the 'all and find them 'arf killing one another. And 'ardly know them for black eyes and bloodied noses. Now it don't scarcely seem natural, like. But all of us thinks that you're a very nice gentleman indeed."

"That's encouraging . . . and in spite of the absence of gore. Tell me, Jenny, if you were a bedridden old woman would you rather have a Bible or a bottle of gin?"

"I 'ave got a Bible, sir . . . two in fact. Mr. Loftus and Mr. Geer each give me one. Mr. Loftus's has nice coloured ribbons."

"Don't equivocate, Jenny. Speak the truth."

"Well, sir, it'd depend how bad I was. I dessay if I were proper bad the gin might come in handiest like."

"Good again, Jenny. You're as honest as the day. Here, what do you think of this?"

Slowly, she relaxed, came over and examined doubtfully the drawing he held out to her.

"I don't know nothing about such like things, sir . . . but it do seem proper clever . . ."

"Why, you silly girl, can't you see that it's you?"

"Well, now you mention it, sir," she answered modestly, "it does seem to be my back view. Only I wish I didn't have on my old wrapper with the burst, just there, so awkward at the placket . . ."

Stephen laughed and threw the block back on the desk.

"It's the old wrapper I like. And the burst. You're an excellent model, Jenny. I wish you could pose for me. I'd give you five shillings an hour."

She looked at him quickly, then glanced away.

"That wouldn't be quite correct, would it sir?"

"Oh, nonsense," he said carelessly. "Where's the harm? But I daresay you're not interested."

"Well, sir"—she spoke awkwardly, and a warmer colour came into her cheeks—"as a matter of fact, if everything was in order, I could do with some extra cash at present."

"Oh?"

"Yes sir. You see . . . I expects to be married fairly soon."

His face lost its look of inquiry, he smiled boyishly.

"Congratulations. Who's the lucky man?"

"His name is by way of being Alfred, sir. Alfred Baines. He's steward on a Orient Line boat. He'll be home the month after next."

"Good for you, Jenny. No wonder you want a little extra pin money. Look here. When do you knock off?"

"Whenever I finish your room, sir. Usually around five."

"Well, then . . . suppose you stay on for an hour, from five till six, twice a week. I could pay you five shillings a time."

"That's more than generous, sir."

"It's very little really. But if you didn't find the work too tiring I could give you a note to a friend of mine who teaches night classes at the Slade. He'd be glad to employ you for a short spell."

"He wouldn't expect, sir . . .?" Jenny blushed crimson.

"Good heavens, no," Stephen said kindly. "You'd wear some sort of costume. Probably he'd only want you for head and shoulders."

"Then I'd be very grateful, sir . . . indeed I should . . . especially to you."

"Shall we call it a bargain, then?" He smiled, that rare smile that lit up his face so attractively, and held out his hand.

Still flushed, she came forward. Her small fingers, the nails ill cut or broken, were warm and dry, their tips seamed with work scars and healed chilblains. Yet it was an extraordinarily pleasant little hand to hold, the pulse of her young body was in it; he barely brought himself to relinquish it. When he did so she turned towards the door. She was rather pale now, and not looking at him she said:

"You've always treated me so nice, Mr. Desmonde, it's a pleasure to do things for you. And I've always gave your room an extra polish. And done your shoes special nice because . . . well, just because it was you, sir." She broke off, and was gone.

To one tormented by moods of self-depreciation these words brought an odd warmth. But soon Stephen's momentary cheerfulness faded, he became again conscious of himself, his surroundings, and the dreariness which stretched ahead. He wished that Glyn might come soon.

Taking up Paley's *Evidences*, which he had promised his father he would read, he tried to immerse himself in it. But it was no use. He had no interest in the book, detested the life he had been leading ever since he came to the Settlement: the visiting, the Bible classes, the club—though he had tried in his own fashion to enliven this— the eternal hypocrisy of feeding words to cold and hungry people, while he, and others of the breed, remained warm and well-fed.

He could understand a man entering the Church who was by nature deeply religious, who felt it his predestined mission to succour his fellow men. But to take up a comfortable living without such a strong vocation, for reasons which were clearly material, seemed to him the worst kind of fraud. And besides, had he not his own vocation, a call which kept ringing with greater insistency in his heart? What a fool he had been to let himself be driven into such a pass, like a stupid sheep penned between gates at a country fair. And now he was in, there seemed no escape.

Just then a rapid fire of heavy boots sounded on the wooden stairs, and a few seconds later a man some years older than Stephen broke into the room and flung himself breathlessly into a chair. He was of more than medium size and thickly built, with cropped red hair and a short bristling red beard, his features strong, his eyes, under well-marked brows, fierce, a trifle wild, yet at the moment full of fun. Dressed in moleskin trousers and a workman's jersey, a red spotted handkerchief knotted round his throat, he had the air of a buccaneer, boisterous, unrestrained, full of a vigorous enjoyment of life. Presently, when his respirations had subsided, he pulled out a gunmetal watch, attached to his person by a piece of frayed green picture-cord.

"Just under the hour," he remarked with satisfaction. "Not bad from Whitehall.

Although aware of Glyn's spasmodic passion for violent exercise, Stephen was mildly surprised.

"You walked all the way!"

"Ran," said Glyn, wiping off sweat. "It was devilish amusing. I had all the coppers on their toes—wondering if I'd robbed a bank. But what a thirst it's given me. I don't suppose you've a spot of beer in this house of God?"

"I'm sorry, Richard. We're not allowed to have it in our rooms. I can give you tea . . . and biscuits."

Glyn burst out laughing.

"You young theologians. How can you wrestle with Satan on

27

biscuits and tea? But if it isn't a bother, bring 'em on." He added more seriously: "I'm afraid I can't stay long, but I did want to see you."

They talked while Stephen boiled a tin kettle on the gas-ring by the fireplace. When the tea was brewed Richard drank four cups of the despised beverage and, in an absent manner, finished a plate of macaroons. Then, somewhat awkwardly, the conversation lapsed.

"Your exhibition has done well," Stephen said at last.

"Well enough," Glyn answered carelessly. "The critiques were so perfectly bloody they actually brought people in."

"But you did sell something."

"One ruddy canvas. And only because I'm Welsh. The Cardiff National Gallery bought it. Fostering native talent . . . miner's son, and so on."

There was a pause.

"However," Glyn resumed, "the cash takes me out of hock. Anna and I are off to Paris tomorrow."

Stephen stiffened imperceptibly, a reflex of all his nerves, not only at the sound of a word which haunted him, but because in this too casual remark he sensed the purpose of Glyn's visit. He tried to keep his voice under control.

"How long shall you be there?"

"At least a year. I'll live cheap and work like the devil. Believe it or not, Paris is a wonderful place for work." He paused, shot a swift glance at the other. "You still aren't coming along?"

Stephen felt his throat thicken. His hands on the arms of his chair showed white over the knuckles.

"How can I?" he muttered. "You know how I'm situated."

"At the same time, I had the impression that you wanted to paint."

Stephen, sitting with lowered head, made no reply. Suddenly he looked up.

"Glyn . . . if I chucked everything . . . should I ever succeed as an artist?"

"Good God, Desmonde." Glyn leaned forward, brows drawn down. "What a bloody idiotic question. Succeed? What do you mean by success? Don't you know that you can't get guarantees in this game, you're out on your own from the word go? And you don't get into it for any other reason than that you damn well can't help yourself. If you're serious you give up everything, starve, steal, cheat your grandmother, break every one of the Ten Commandments, just to get your hands on a tube of colour and a palette knife." Glyn broke off, relaxed his posture, then went on more quietly. "I believe you have talent, extraordinary possibilities, otherwise I shouldn't bother my head over you. I know how hard it is for you—bogged in tradition. You've had all the wrong start. You should have been like me, born in a workmen's row in a rotten colliery town. As it is, you must make your own decision. And if it's no, I daresay you'll make a passable parson." Abruptly he tugged out the nickel watch. "Well, I have to cut along. There's packing to do. And various odds and ends. Good-bye, Desmonde. Write me when you have time."

While Stephen remained motionless, Glyn stood up. As he came forward he saw on the mantelpiece a perforated card in the colours of the Marylebone Cricket Club. It was a rover's ticket for the Oxford and Cambridge cricket match due to be played next month. Following Richard's glance, Stephen flushed.

"I have to go," he said stiffly. "All the family will be there."

Glyn shrugged sadly, gripped Stephen by the hand, and went out.

CHAPTER V

THE MATCH WAS over, stumps had been drawn and, as the low sunlight sent long shadows over the greensward of Lord's, a party of seven could be observed in the fashionable throng—one could not refer to such a gathering as a crowd—moving slowly towards the main gates in St. John's Wood Road. Caroline and Claire were in front with Davie and his cousin Geoffrey, while a few paces behind, Stephen followed with General Desmonde and his wife. A parochial emergency had at the last minute prevented the Rector from attending, and Julia, of course, was an annual absentee. For that matter Stephen had come only that he might be with his brother, and while Davie's enjoyment of the game—the more touching since because of his complaint he was not permitted to play cricket—had in some measure been his reward, it had been a trying day for him, his head still rang with Geoffrey's incessant yells of "Well played, sir!" and, as always, the General's wife—he rarely thought of her as Aunt Adelaide—had exercised upon him that familiar combination of condescension and arrogance which aroused his wildest and most perverse instincts. A cold, thin-faced, overbearing woman, reared in the Army tradition and toughened by the suns of India, she was still handsome in a hard, dashing way, her figure admirable though inclined to leanness, her glance, at times, lethal as a bayonet thrust.

Now, as they left the ground, and stood together rather indecisively while hansoms and carriages pulled away from the kerb, she spoke with rapidity, in her clipped "county" voice.

"Today has been so delightful it seems a pity to let it die prematurely." She turned to her husband. "Have you, by any chance, a suggestion, Hubert?"

General Desmonde surveyed the group. Tall, straight-featured, erect as a ramrod, even in his grey top hat and morning coat he looked a soldier, and a distinguished one. A clipped moustache emphasized the incisive brevity of his speech.

"I thought we might all go to supper at Frascati's."

"I say, what a lark, Pater," Geoffrey said, adjusting his tie, then his embroidered waistcoat, for perhaps the two-hundredth time, as though determined to maintain the satorial supremacy which made him, he felt sure, a conspicuous object of admiration. Style, which he named good form, was indeed Geoffrey's major occupation, whether on the parade-ground or in Piccadilly, and already it had shaped him, at the age of twenty-four, to the pattern of a smart, if somewhat brainless, young man about town.

"Davie must be back by seven," Caroline interposed. "And it's after six now. But none of you need trouble, I'll take him to the train."

"Darling, you are so kind, always so obliging." Adelaide smiled. She did not want Caroline at Frascati's, her face peony-red from the sun, and in that hideous maroon frock which made her look like a parlourmaid on her day off, those legs, too, such a misfortune, like the underpinnings of a grand piano; Caroline to Aunt Adelaide was always a social liability, and annual mortification at the hunt ball when, seated by the doorway, unclaimed, with empty programme, she waited sadly for some elderly gentleman to be led up to her; and now it had been bad enough having her with them all day. "You must come another time."

"I'm afraid I must get back, too," Stephen said. If Davie weren't going, he had no wish to be there.

"Must you?" Hubert raised a good-natured eyebrow—he rather liked, at least tolerated, his young parson-to-be nephew. "So soon?"

"Surely you can stay, Stephen." Claire stood beside him, restrained yet somehow appealing, her soft complexion and well-modelled features shaded by a wide-brimmed hat trimmed with roses. Today, more than ever, in this setting, she looked what she

30

was—a most amiable English girl whose good sense and manners and frank pleasant cordiality made friends for her wherever she went.

"Do stay," she added.

"Darling," Adelaide cut in before Stephen could reply, "we mustn't interfere with rules and regulations. After all, it is, I imagine, more or less a monastic life at the Settlement, is it not, Stephen, and I'm sure a most worthy one. It is a great pity that you cannot come. However, we four must make the best of it ourselves. Geoffrey will take Claire and I shall pretend that Hubert is my beau." Adelaide smiled again, and with satisfaction—she had her own reasons for not wishing Stephen to be of the party.

"Can we drop you anywhere, Caroline?" asked Hubert.

"Oh no, Davie and I will take the tube."

"And I a bus," said Stephen.

Good-byes were exchanged, then, vaguely conscious of the regret in Claire's eyes, Stephen moved away with Caroline and Davie. As they had a few minutes to spare he stopped at the Fuller's in Park Road to give his young brother a strawberry ice and Caroline a cup of tea which, surreptitiously easing her feet from her shoes, she confessed she had been dying for all day. Then he saw them off at the Baker Street Underground and settled himself in a number 23 eastbound omnibus.

As he rattled towards Stepney, despite the relief of again being amongst unpolished people who demanded no more than their share of a hard seat, a slow depression settled upon Stephen. How physically and spiritually diminished, how utterly different from the others he had felt during the promenades round the wicket, the meetings and greetings, the luncheon in the Guards Club Marquee —"odd little devil"—he could almost read the thought behind the indifferent glances directed towards him by his cousin's friends, as with Geoffrey they discussed the newest musical comedy, the West Sussex point-to-point, and the latest fancy for the Cambridgeshire. In this mood he reached the Settlement. In the hall, still redolent of the midday odours of boiled beef and cabbage, he passed Loftus, who was going out, and gave him "Good evening." The junior curate barely answered and as he glided past, discreet and elegant, his eye held so noticeable a glint of malice and amusement that Stephen instinctively drew up.

"What's the matter, Loftus?"

Already at the door, the other half turned, his lips twitching with restrained, ecclesiastic humour.

"Don't you know?"

"Of course not, what is it?"

"Nothing much, I suppose. Except that the little Dill seems to be rather in a pickle."

What on earth is he talking about? thought Stephen. But he shrugged it off and, having seen that there were no letters for him in the rack, went upstairs. And there, seated upright in a hard chair in the centre of his room, wearing her outdoor clothes, a flat straw hat with a narrow ribbon, and white cotton gloves, was Jenny.

At his entrance she rose immediately, but with composure, and while he gazed at her in surprise, since she did not normally come to the Settlement on Saturday, she began:

"I apologize for the liberty, sir. But I did want to make sure I'd see you. And there didn't seem no other place for me to wait."

"That's all right," Stephen said, uncertainly. "Won't you sit down? That's better. Now what is it?"

While he went over to the fireplace she reseated herself on the edge of the chair, her gloved hands neatly folded.

"Well, sir, the fact is, I'm leaving today, rather unexpected like. And you been so good to me I felt I 'ad to say good-bye."

"Oh, I'm sorry, Jenny. I didn't imagine you'd be going so soon."

"Nor me neither, sir. But the truth is I'm found out."

"Found out?" he repeated, bewildered.

"Yes, sir." She nodded, frankly, in her practical way, quite without embarrassment. "It's all my own fault, being silly enough to come yesterday without my stays. I didn't realize I was beginning to show. But there's no deceiving that cook. She ups to the Warden like a shot."

"What on earth are you talking about?"

"Don't you see, sir, I'm going to have a baby."

He was so utterly taken aback he could think of nothing to say. At last, feeling that his position demanded some moral reflection, he stammered:

"Oh, Jenny . . . how could you?"

"I suppose I got carried away, sir."

"What!"

"We all have our feelings, sir. You can't get away from that. Oh, it's quite respectable, I assure you. Alf's a steady feller. A ship's steward, like I told you. We'll be married when he gets back."

There was a brief pause, while Stephen studied her with rising sympathy.

"I suppose you're in love with him."

"I suppose I must be, sir," A faint, wise smile passed over her fresh young face. "He's a lot older nor me, of course. And I will say this, but for them two beers I 'ad at the Good Intent I wouldn't have gave in. But then again, I might have done worse. He's decent, is Alf. And accomplished too. He likes music and 'as taught himself to play the mouth harmonica."

Another pause.

"Well . . . we shall miss you, Jenny."

"I shall miss you, sir. I must say you've been more nor kind to me. Not like some of them others."

"What others?"

"Well, chiefly the Warden, sir. I must say he give me a regular going over before he let me have my notice."

"So you're not leaving of your own accord?"

"Oh, no, sir. It don't suit me at all. . . . I'm on my own, you see, and don't have my parents living. But the Warden couldn't have the place contaminated, he said, with three young curates around, and sacked me on the spot."

Stephen bit his lip. Gazing covertly at the girl, he perceived that beneath her usual expression of serenity and good temper, she looked pale and out of sorts. He would swear there was not an ounce of harm in her.

"Jenny," he said impulsively, "I don't want to interfere. But I hope you've made arrangements to be taken care of . . . to go to hospital . . . and that sort of thing."

"I shan't go to hospital, sir. I have my own room. And I shall bespeak Mrs. Kettle. She's the midwife, sir, and highly recommended."

"You're sure you'll be all right?"

"Oh, don't worry about me, sir." For the first time a note of distress crept into her voice. "I only hope I haven't brought trouble on you. It's all come out about you getting me the job at the art class. And the Warden seemed terrible upset."

Stephen was somewhat disconcerted by this news. However, his genuine concern for Jenny, the admiration he felt for her courage and common sense, and his indignation at the treatment accorded her made him careless about himself. He had grown fond of her within the past months, and could not let her go without some expression of his good will. He turned sideways, fumbled self-consciously in his wallet, then took a step towards her.

"Look, Jenny . . . I've no wish to offend you. But you've done so

B

much for me here . . . and you really will need something to see you through. I'd like you to have this."

Awkwardly he put in her hand a five-pound note, which, to conceal its high denomination, he had folded small. But to his surprise, she would not have it, rose abruptly, and backed away.

"No . . . I won't take it."

"But Jenny . . . you must . . ."

Tears did not come easily to her, but she had been through a good deal that day, and now they flashed hotly into her eyes.

"No, sir, I couldn't . . . what I done for you was nothing . . ."

At that moment, while she retreated and he followed, tendering the money, the door opened and the Warden came into the room. There was a mortal silence while, for a moment, he stood in stony observation. Then, in a controlled voice, he said:

"You may go now, Dill."

As Jenny turned and went out, devastated, with tears streaming down her cheeks, Stephen, despite his flushed and guilty look, was calm enough to take advantage of her distress and press the note into the pocket of her jacket.

"Good-bye, Jenny," he murmured. "And the best of luck."

Her answer, if she made one, was inaudible.

Still in that detached manner, the Reverend Crispin closed the door behind her; then, with a quick glance at Stephen, compressed his lips and fixed his eyes upon the ceiling.

"Desmonde," he said, "I surmised that your conduct had been seriously indiscreet. But I never dreamed that it had gone as far as this. As a friend of your dear father, it grieves me more than I can say."

Stephen swallowed the dry lump in his throat. The colour had drained from his cheeks, but there was a spark in his dark pupils.

"I don't quite understand you."

"Come, come, Desmonde. You cannot deny that you are, and have been for some time, on terms of most improper intimacy with that young person I have just dismissed."

"I've been friendly with Jenny. She has done lots of little things for me. And I've tried to help her in return."

"Ah!" said the Warden in a significant tone. "And your idea of help was to have her frequently with you, alone, in your room."

"She came to do my room. And occasionally I made some sketches of her. That was all."

"Indeed! So you thought it part of your duties, as a candidate for ordination, to make a model, furtively, out of one of the servants of this house of God. I have made it my duty to examine some of the drawings which resulted from this illicit collaboration and I must confess they strike me as questionable in the extreme."

The blood mounted to Stephen's forehead. His eyes flashed angrily.

"From what I know of your taste, sir," he answered, trembling slightly, "I'm not surprised you failed to understand them."

"Indeed!" said Bliss, with that acid calm which he felt suited him so well. "It does indeed appear as though my standards, particularly those of morality, differ from your own."

"They certainly do." Stephen flung caution to the winds. "I should not have thrown that poor girl into the street because of one mistake."

"I daresay not. That precisely was what I feared."

"What do you mean?"

Up until this time the Warden's manner had been studiously controlled, but now his nostrils narrowed and something not unlike a scowl settled upon his lofty forehead.

"Although Dill has given a name to her guilty partner, I am not altogether convinced. It is at least my firm belief that in your conduct towards this unhappy girl, by the manner in which you utilized her for your so-called artistic ends, you are responsible, or at least indirectly to blame, for the state of depravity into which she has fallen."

Breathing quickly, Stephen stared at Bliss with a wicked look upon his face. He burst out:

"I never heard such rot in my life. Or such cant either. Jenny isn't depraved. She's got a sweetheart and he's going to marry her. Is it your idea of Christian charity to vilify her, and me, without proper cause?"

"Be silent, sir. I will not have you speak to me so. Indeed, if I were to take a strict view of my duty I should ask you to leave the Settlement at once." He paused to recover himself. "But out of regard for your family, and also the future which may still lie ahead of you, I am disposed to be more lenient. I must give your father some idea of what has occurred. And *you*, of course, will give *me* your written pledge to abandon, once and for all, this obsession you are pleased to call 'art', which is wholly incompatible with your vocation as a clergyman. There will, moreover, be some further restrictions which I feel compelled to impose on you. Come to my study after evening prayers and I will advise you of them."

Terminating the interview, without giving Stephen an opportunity to answer, he swung round and went out of the room.

"Oh, go to the devil!" Stephen exclaimed violently. Unfortunately, the door was already shut.

For a few moments Stephen stood tensely, with clenched fists, his gaze fixed on the panels of varnished oak. Then, with an abandoned gesture, he sank into a chair by the table, drew writing-paper from the drawer and seized a pen.

DEAR FATHER,

I have done my best here and made a complete failure of it. I do not wish to hurt you, nor to take any final decision against your wishes, but under the circumstances I feel that I must go away for a while—a year, at least—which will give me time to see things more clearly, and also to test my abilities in that particular field which is so distasteful to you I shall not even name it. I realize what a blow this will be to you, and my only excuse is this —I simply cannot help myself.

My love to all at Stillwater and to Claire. I shall write you again from Paris.

STEPHEN

CHAPTER VI

PARIS WAS UNKNOWN to Stephen, and although its first heady breath exhilarated him like wine, he entered it nervously—as though fearing those satirical glances which all true Parisians must bestow upon a stranger. Thus he clung to the name of a hotel he had heard his father mention in a tone of mild clerical approval, and giving it to the driver with as much assurance as he could muster, was swept from the Gare du Nord at a reckless pace through Sunday afternoon streets, surprisingly empty, to the Clifton in the Rue de la Sourdière.

This seemed a quiet place, not particularly exciting perhaps, yet respectable, opening through a narrow entrance to a square glassed-in courtyard, around which the rooms were arranged behind flaking cast-iron balconies. In the sleepy office—the tone was set by a tortoiseshell cat drowsing upon the desk—they were not surprised by the sudden materialization of a young Englishman. Indeed, when Stephen had been shown upstairs to his room, which was darkish and fusty, with faded wallpaper and an enormous red-curtained bed, the aged concierge, unstrapping the luggage from his shoulder in exaggerated breathlessness, startled him slightly by inquiring if he required tea.

"No, thank you." Stephen smiled, thinking what superb values this dim interior gave to the water-eyed old man with his sagging, red-veined cheeks, his yellow-and-black-striped waistcoat. "I want to get out . . . to look around."

"Not much to see today, Monsieur." The porter shrugged amiably. "Everywhere is closed."

But Stephen could scarcely wait to unpack his valise and fling his things into the dusty amoire. Then, excitedly, he left the hotel and made his way into the streets, walking at random along the Rue du Mont Thabor and through the Place de la Concorde. His immediate thought had been of Glyn, but in that strained moment of parting, he had forgotten to ask for Richard's address, and in the interim no word had come from him. Stephen felt sure, however, that in the circle he proposed to frequent, he would meet with him soon.

The weather was mild and bright, the pale sky ribbed with glittering clouds. When he saw the long line of chestnut trees, now in full foliage, by the river, Stephen almost cried aloud. Stirred by the breeze, the leaves flickered light and dark, softly, meeting his eye like a caress. Across the avenue he came upon the Seine, steel-grey and polished, shimmering past a row of black moored barges. On one of these a young woman, plump-breasted and yellow-haired, was stringing pink washing on a line. A little white dog capered at her ankles. A man in a singlet and billycock hat smoked placidly, bare-armed, on an upturned bucket.

In a kind of singing rapture Stephen slowly walked along the bank, across the Pont Royal, past the line of shuttered bookstalls, back over the Pont Neuf to L'Ile de la Cité. There he stood, watching the play of colour upon the water, the darkening of shadows upon the masses of stone. Only when the light faded did he turn away, with a besotted sigh, and start back towards his hotel.

Now the city was stirring from its Sunday torpor. In the side streets north of the river, the little corner cafés had begun to fill up in discreet yet lively fashion. Provision shops were opening, middle-class families began to take the air, stout men in carpet slippers appeared in doorways. Outside a baker's shop, not yet unshuttered, housewives, gossiping quietly, were gathering to buy bread. I am in Paris, thought Stephen giddily, at last, at last.

By way of contrast, the Clifton, bathed in a dim religious light, wore a solemn, near sepulchral air. Indeed, for a moment Stephen was tempted to turn back and go out for supper to Maxim's, or the

37

Café Riche, or one of those gay restaurants he had read of so often. But he was tired, and shy of going alone. Besides, he had made up his mind to practice a reasonable economy. Out of his annual allowance, one hundred and fifty pounds remained, and this must last him for a full year.

So he went into the chilly dining-room and ate in solitude—except for a remote, spinsterish gentleman in a drab Norfolk jacket who read continuously during and between the courses, and two whispering elderly ladies in mauve, all unmistakably British—a table d'hôte meal of soup, mutton, and sour stewed plums which, while perfectly wholesome, demonstrated conclusively the fallacy of the contention that in France, French cooking is a universal art. Yet nothing could damp his spirits. He climbed the stairs whistling, and slept like a top in the canopied bed.

Next morning, without delay, he set out for Montparnasse. After considerable reflection, he had resolved not to enroll in the Ecole des Beaux Arts but to seek the more personal attention provided by Professor Dupret, in his renowned academy in the Boulevard Seline. He found the studio without difficulty, having equipped himself, from the hotel letter-rack, with a folding map of Paris. It occupied the top floor of a queer barracks of a building that stood behind high spiked railings, guarded by two empty sentry-boxes, well back from the boulevard. A lingering smell of tan bark indicated that it had once been an armoury, and a great shindy coming from above suggested to Stephen, for one startled moment, that the troops were still in occupation. When he went up, after completing the necessary formalities of admission with the *massier*, a burly, flat-faced character in grey sweater and canvas trousers who had the appearance of a retired prize-fighter—and who, indeed, was there to prevent flagrant disorder—he found that the class had begun.

The large, light room, heated by a huge Dutch stove, with walls which seemed all windows, was crowded with perhaps fifty students, as strange a company as he had ever seen. For the most part they were men, between twenty and thirty years of age, dressed in a variety of taste, from many nationalities—bearded Slavs, a dark-skinned Indian, a group of blond Scandinavians, several young Americans. The few women were as oddly assorted. Stephen's eye was caught by an elderly female in a mouse-coloured blouse, peering at her canvas through gold-rimmed pince-nez, like a schoolmistress at her blackboard in a country kindergarten.

The din, at near hand, was deafening—a continuous babble of conversation, loud snatches of song, in competitive tongues, boisterous remarks shouted across the room. It seemed as though the tumult might permit Stephen to make his entry unobserved. But as he stood, hesitant and rather pale, upon the threshold, wearing his dark clerical suit, stiff white collar and black tie, the regulation attire of the Clinker Street curates, there came an unlucky lull during which the attention of the class was directed towards him. Then, in the silence, a falsetto voice exclaimed:

"*Ah! C'est Monsieur l'Abbé.*"

A howl of laughter greeted the remark. Entering in confusion, Stephen found a stool covered with dried palette scrapings, but no easel, squeezed with difficulty into a place and set up his portfolio of Ingres paper upon his knee.

The model, an old man with long silver hair, who had the appearance of a decayed actor, was seated in a conventional attitude upon the central raised wooden platform, leaning forward slightly, chin resting upon the back of his hand. Stephen did not like the pose, and the ancient's expression was bored and indifferent, but, taking his charcoal, he set to work.

At eleven o'clock Monsieur Dupret appeared—a man of about sixty, handsome in a theatrical way, with bushy head of hair, an erect, dignified carriage, and mobile hands. Despite the slight bagginess of his trousers, his tight-fitting frock coat gave to him a correct, distinguished air, intensified by the ribbon in his buttonhole. His entry, which was impressively abrupt, caused a cessation of the worst of the noise, and in comparative calm he began slowly to make a tour of the room, pausing here and there to scrutinize a canvas with narrowed eyes, to utter, with a flowing gesture of the hands, a few curt words, rather like a surgeon making the round of his wards.

As he drew near, Stephen prepared himself for some words of greeting, of civil interrogation, but the professor, with impersonal aloofness, said nothing whatsoever. He glanced once sideways at Stephen, half curious, half indifferent, then at his drawing, and the next moment, without the flicker of an eyebrow, he was gone.

At one o'clock a bell rang. Immediately a yell went up, the model rose as though released by a spring and shuffled off the platform, while all around the students flung down brushes or charcoal and began piling towards the door. Disturbed and disappointed, Stephen was swept off, against his will, by the pushing throng. Suddenly, at his elbow, he heard a pleasant voice.

"You're English, aren't you? I noticed you come in. My name's Chester."

Stephen turned his head and discovered a good-looking young

39

man of about his own age smiling down at him. His hair, cleft chin, and blue eyes shaded by long dark lashes gave him an air of frank and engaging charm. He was wearing an old Harrovian tie.

"I'll wait for you downstairs," he called out as an eddy of the crush took him away.

Outside, Chester offered his hand.

"I hope you don't mind my speaking to you. In this rabble we fellows from across the Channel ought to hang together."

After his depressing reception, Stephen was glad to find a friend. When he had introduced himself Chester paused for a moment, then exclaimed:

"How about lunching with me?"

They set off together along the boulevard.

The restaurant they entered was quite near, in the Place Seline, a narrow, low-ceilinged room, almost a cellar, opening into a dark little kitchen half a dozen steps down from street level, with a charcoal fire and roasting spit, filled by the clatter of copper pans and an agreeable aroma of cooking. Already the place was crowded, mainly by Dupret students, but Chester, with easy assurance, led the way through to a little yard adorned by tubs of privet and, calmly removing the card marked RESERVED from a table at the far end, skilfully ringed his hat upon a peg, and invited Stephen to be seated.

Immediately a stout, red-faced woman in black bustled out of the kitchen in protest.

"No, no, Harry . . . this place is reserved for Monsieur Lambert."

"Do not agitate yourself, Madame Chobert." Chester smiled. "You know Monsieur Lambert is my good friend. Besides, he is always late."

Madame Chobert was not pleased; she argued and grumbled, but Harry Chester's charm—though she clearly tried to harden herself against it—was in the end too much for her. With a shrug commiserating her own weakness, she raised the slate which hung from her aproned waist and offered the menu chalked upon it for their inspection.

At Chester's suggestion they ordered *potage maison, boeuf bordelaise*, and a Brie cheese. A carafe of frothy yellow beer was already upon the table.

"Not a bad old bird," Chester grinned when she had gone. During the meal he kept up a lively flow of talk; commentating with an unflagging supply of bandinage and ready-made phrases upon their neighbours. He pointed out Biondello, the Italian, who had actually

40

exhibited at the Salon last year, and Pierre Aumerle, a hopeless case, who drank a bottle of Pernod every day, lunching with a raddled-looking woman in a large hat, regarding whom Chester raised his eyebrows with a smile. In between he sounded out Stephen with a few pleasant questions; then, after the *café filtre* was brought, he paused, with a somewhat conscious air, and seemed to find it necessary to explain himself.

"Queer, isn't it," he commented, drawing patterns on the chequered cloth, "how you can always tell a 'varsity man? Philip Lambert is one too. After Harrow"—he shot a quick glance at Stephen—"I should have gone to Cambridge myself . . . if I hadn't thrown it up for art."

He went on to reveal, with a deprecating smile, that his father had been a prominent tea-planter in Ceylon, while his mother, now a widow, had come home to inhabit a large, overstaffed mansion in Highgate. Naturally she spoiled him, gave him a generous allowance. He had been in Paris eighteen months.

"It's tremendous fun," he concluded. "You must let me show you the ropes."

"What do you think of Dupret?" Stephen asked.

"He's the soundest teacher around. You know he has the Legion of Honour."

Jarred slightly, Stephen made no reply. Chester puzzled him, as he might be puzzled by an unfamiliar design which, while agreeable, held intricacies foreign to his taste.

They had finished their coffee. People were beginning to leave.

"Your friend Lambert doesn't seem to be coming," Stephen said at last, to break the silence.

Chester laughed.

"Philip's an erratic beggar. You never quite know when he'll turn up . . . or with what attractive pettitcoat."

"Does he attend Dupret's?"

"He works at home . . . when he *does* work. He has private means, you know, and has knocked about all over Europe, studied in Rome and Vienna. But now he and his wife have rented a little apartment near the Esplanade des Invalides."

"Yes." Chester nodded. "And I can tell you, Desmonde, Mrs. Lambert is a smart one. But of course, a perfect lady."

Here again was a remark that grated on Stephen's ear, and he looked at his companion oddly, wondering how he could use so unfortunate a phrase. But before he had time to answer the question, Harry Chester sat up.

"Here's Philip now."

Following Chester's gaze, Stephen saw entering the restaurant a slim, affected-looking man of about thirty, dressed in a short brown surcoat, with a low collar and a flowing tie. His face, pale and deeply shadowed beneath the eyes, wore a look of languor. His glossy black hair was parted neatly in the middle, but on one side a lock had escaped and fell in a little curl over his white forehead. His manner, indeed his general appearance, conveyed the impression of mannered indolence, of boredom and conceit.

When he came over he put his cane under his arm, began peeling off a lemon-yellow glove, meanwhile contemplating Chester with slightly contemptuous amusement.

"Thank you for keeping my table, dear boy. But now you must clear out. I'm expecting a guest at two o'clock. And I shan't need a chaperon."

"We're just going, Philip." Chester's tone had taken on a submissive inflection. "Look here, I'd like you to meet Desmonde. He joined us at Dupret's today."

Lambert took a look at Stephen, then he bowed politely.

"Desmonde just came down from Oxford last term," Chester threw out quickly.

"Indeed!" exclaimed Lambert. "Which college, may I ask?"

"Trinity," said Stephen.

"Ah!" Lambert relaxed into a smile, showing even white teeth, and, removing the second of his tight kid gloves—a lengthy operation which he performed in silence and without turning a hair—held out a small hand to Stephen. "I am happy to meet you. I myself was at the House. Pray do not inconvenience yourself by hurrying. I can easily find another table."

"I assure you," said Stephen, rising, "we've quite finished."

"Then come to tea at my house one day. We are at home most Wednesdays at five. Harry will bring you along. Then we shall be two men from Oxford and one"—his smile flickered towards Chester—"who so nearly went to Cambridge."

The bill, swiftly presented by Madame Chobert, now lay upon the table. Since Chester did not appear to see it, Stephen picked it up and, despite Harry's sudden and energetic protests, paid.

CHAPTER VII

UNDER THE SPELL of his new freedom, Stephen fell quickly and with delightful ease into a most agreeable routine, the more so since, a week after his arrival, a letter came from Stillwater which greatly relieved his mind. While stressing the pain occasioned by Stephen's sudden departure, the Rector had, in a sense, condoned it. Obviously, he wrote, the inclination (the word temptation had been crossed out) was too strong to be resisted. It might therefore be "all for the best" if, as Stephen had himself proposed, this interim of a year be regarded on both sides as a "proving ground". Meantime, he approved Stephen's choice of lodging, knew him too well to have need of exhorting him to virtue, and wished him to lack for nothing befitting his position.

In the morning it was a sensation which never palled to awaken to the knowledge that he was in Paris, actually pursuing his "artistic career". He rose, dressed quickly, and as breakfast at the Clifton had nothing to recommend it, went out to a little *crèmerie* round the corner from the hotel. Here, for thirty sous, he was served a jug of steaming *café au lait* and two flaky *croissants* still warm from the batch just brought in by the baker. His walk to the studio through the fresh streets was always a delight. The hurrying crowds and blue-cloaked policemen, the early housewives with arms crooked on laden baskets, a Zouave soldier in scarlet trousers, two concierges gossiping across their brooms, an old street-cleaner sending a swirl of water along the gutter, pushcarts of fresh vegetables clattering from the Halles—all this entranced him, cut by sharp, sudden cries, the chatter of many tongues, a slow chime of bells against the background of the soft grey buildings, the graceful white bridges, the lovely river, already beginning to sparkle in the sun.

At the studio, it is true, he did not yet feel at home. The lack of order and perpetual noise made concentration difficult. It seemed as if many of the students had come less for work than for sheer diversion and a wild display of animal spirits. They laughed and sang, played rough practical jokes, held endless loud discussions in the cafés, argued and quarrelled, affected an exaggerated bohemian-ism in their dress and manner. They spoke the argot of the quarter, were all-knowing on the subject of the latest "movements", ac-knowledged Manet, Degas and Renoir as their masters and aped them painfully, despised Millet and Ingres, were critical of Dela-croix, yet had little, or nothing, to offer of their own.

Of course there were others who did apply themselves. Next to Stephen was a Polish youth from a small country town near Warsaw who, fired by ambition, had come penniless to Paris. To pay his fees at Dupret's he had worked for twelve months as a porter at the Gare Montparnasse. The intensity of his effort was frightening, yet he was entirely without talent. Often, when Dupret made his daily round, Stephen hoped he would, with a single word, mercifully end this futile striving. But the professor said nothing, did nothing beyond correcting a line, or pointing, with a blank expression, to the lack of balance in the composition. His attitude towards Stephen remained equally impassive, although once or twice, after studying some piece of work, he glanced at him in a curious manner, almost covertly, as though seeing him, examining him, for the first time.

More and more, beneath Dupret's aloofness and grand manner, Stephen began to discern a worm-eaten core of disappointment, the galling bitterness of a man who in his heart knows that he has failed to fulfil his youthful expectations. To have won recognition in official circles, to exhibit annually at the Salon (a safe, carefully executed picture which was always well hung), to sit upon boards and committees, to represent "art" in white gloves at government receptions—did these distinctions mean anything to one who had wished to rock the world with a tremendous masterpiece? Dupret had no real interest in his studio and still less in his students except when, with a stab of jealousy, he came upon evidence of a talent that might surpass his own. Behind the façade he was a hollow man, a man driven by the man he was supposed to be, a man more worthy to be pitied than despised. Indeed, as the professor strode impressively into the room, Stephen had a queer vision of him, at the end of the day, slowly removing the tight frock coat and shiny button boots, easing his corns by wriggling his crushed toes, then, seated hunched before the stove in his showy studio, turning to the half-finished canvas *A Breton Wedding*, thinking with a shudder: *Mon dieu*, must I go on with this?

At lunch-time Stephen usually went with Chester to Madame Chobert's, but occasionally he escaped from Harry's effusive friendship and wandered alone along the quays, munching a *petit pain* in which lay a slice of ham, enlivened by yellow mustard. Then, with quickening steps, he sped to the museums, to the Louvre or the Luxembourg. It was almost dark when, with eyes not yet reattuned to the realities of the street, he left the long galleries and walked back to the Clifton.

To Chester, and the few other acquaintances he made at Dupret's,

44

it seemed extraordinary that Stephen should spend his evenings alone, and several times he was pressed to join them in a visit to Montmartre. Upon one occasion he accepted, accompanied some half a dozen others to a café concert at La Toque Bleue, near the Moulin de la Galette.

But he was dreadfully bored by scenes which were presumed to be vivid and exciting but were, in fact, stupidly futile. The dance-hall was a mass of stamping, pushing, circling humanity, semi-intoxicated, magnified and distorted by scores of mirrors, twisting themselves into uncouth shapes, to the blare of cheap brass. Surely nothing could be more frighteningly sad than the faces of the older habitués—hollow-checked and dead-eyed, strangely forbidding. Some of the well-known cocottes whom Chester pointed out to him were frankly hideous, their male escorts, dressed in tight black, sinister and degenerate.

Later, several young women became attached to the party, which had now reached a boisterous stage. Stephen gazed at them curiously. Their raucous voices and gross camaraderie, their flinging of arms around necks and loudly whispered endearments, aroused in him a chilly distaste. As he sat there, pale and silent, like a fish out of water, one of the girls bent towards Chester, who had drunk a good deal, and with her eyes on Stephen, giggled and murmured something into his ear. Immediately Chester broke into a fit of laughter.

At the time Stephen made no comment, but on the way home with Chester he brought the matter up.

"It was nothing, old boy. She merely said"—Chester, with a note of apology, modified the original unprintable remark—"that you were a queer one." He added, as Stephen turned away, "I'm sorry you didn't enjoy yourself tonight. Don't forget we're going to Lambert's on Wednesday. Call for me, at my place, beforehand."

On that day, towards four o'clock, Stephen set out for the Rue Bonaparte, where, at number 15, Harry had a lodging on the top floor. After a sharp climb of three flights of stairs, he became aware of a loud altercation going on inside, and pushing through the half-open door he found Chester arguing with a short man in a square black hat and drab overcoat who, quite unmoved, stood superintending the movements of a subordinate busily engaged in stowing into a capacious burlap bag the mantel clock, a pair of china vases, and other articles which decorated the room.

"Now, if you please, your watch, Monsieur Chester."

"Oh, hang it all, Maurice," Chester pleaded, "not the watch. Not this time. Give me to the end of the week and you'll be squared."

At this point Chester saw Stephen. For a moment he looked foolish; then, approaching, he forced a confident smile.

"Isn't it idiotic, Desmonde? I've just run over my allowance. And these wretched duns are stripping me. It's practically nothing. A couple of hundred francs . . . and of course I shall have my cheque from the Mater at the end of the month. Naturally, I wouldn't dream of asking you, still, if you could by any chance . . ."

There was a slight pause; then Stephen said, willingly:

"I'll be glad to oblige you."

"Thanks awfully, old man. You shall have it back, with interest, the first of the month. Here you are, Maurice, you thief. Now *foutre le camp.*"

He folded the crisp notes, which Stephen extracted from his wallet, and tossed them over to the bailiff, who, after counting them twice with a moist thumb, nodded silently, emptied the contents of the satchel upon the table, and, with an enigmatic bow, followed by his companion, slid out of the room.

"Well! That's over!" Chester laughed cheerfully, as though at an excellent joke. "I should have missed my old pots. And of course there's this . . ." Placing the vases back upon the mantelpiece, he absently snapped open a small flat case and exhibited a round silver medal attached to a blue silk ribbon. Lowering his eyes, he hesitated, then added in a rather shamed fashion, which was quite charming:

"One doesn't mention these things, Desmonde. But since you've caught me off guard, so to speak . . . it's the Albert Medal. I'm afraid they gave me it a couple of years ago."

"What for, Chester?" Stephen could not help feeling impressed.

"Oh, saving life at sea, they called it. A silly old woman fell off the Folkestone steamer. Couldn't blame her, it was rough as the devil . . . and winter. I happened to go in after her. It was absolutely nothing. We weren't in the water more than half an hour before the steamer swung round and got a boat to us. But let's forget it and get a move on. If we don't hurry we'll be late for tea."

With his good humour quite restored, Chester led the way downstairs, talking and laughing all the way to the Lamberts' apartment, which was situated in a cul-de-sac well back from the Avenue Duquesne. Here, in a cobbled courtyard, stood a little grey stone pavilion—brightened artistically by an apple-green door and window-boxes of the same colour—which had once served as porter's

46

lodge for a great house in the days of Henri Quatre. Within, smelling of lunch and a recently burned pastille, the small, rather dim interior was made equally artistic by a few scattered rugs, beaded curtains, and bamboo chairs. A Spanish shawl was draped on the upright piano.

Driven by Chester's impetuosity, they were early. Lambert, drowsing in an easy-chair by the ashes of a wood fire, still seemed sunk in an after-luncheon lethargy, and barely lifted one heavy eyelid as they came in. But Mrs. Lambert was there to welcome them. She was tall and slender, older than Stephen had expected, with large green eyes, features inclined to sharpness, sandy hair, and the milky skin which goes with it. Her afternoon dress, cut round at the neck in an arty fashion and with long full skirts, was of white brocade.

While she and Chester talked, Stephen watched as she sat there, poised, with arching neck, against a lacquered screen, until, as if conscious of his scrutiny, she glanced towards him with an arch smile.

"I hope you approve my dress?"

As she seemed to invite a compliment, he said:

"I'm sure Whistler would have wished to paint you in it."

"What a charming thing to say." She added, confidingly, "I made it myself."

Presently she went out and brought in tea, on a silver tray, with many cups, thin watercress sandwiches, and *petits fours*. When she began to pour Lambert yawned and stretched.

"Tea!" he cried. "I can't live without tea. Blessed, nourishing tea. Strong, Elise." Accepting a cup, he balanced it airily. "This may even come from your extensive family plantations in Ceylon, Harry. Is not that a stimulating thought? Tell us if you recognize the flavour." He gazed at Stephen. "Well . . . what have you been doing with yourself in the naughty city, Monsieur l'Abbé?"

Stephen reddened. He saw that Chester had been talking about him.

"I daresay it strikes you as ridiculous. A would-be parson turning to art." In a few words he went on to explain some of the circumstances of his coming to Paris.

When he finished a slight pause followed, then Lambert exclaimed, with his usual irony:

"Bravo, Abbé. Now that you've made your confession you have our unconditional absolution."

And Elise, leaning a little towards him, with her flattering smile, murmured:

"You must have wanted terribly to paint. Now have some more tea."

As Stephen rose to hand over his cup his eye was caught by three fans, painted on silk in the Japanese manner, arranged upon the wall. He paused, struck by the delicacy of the work.

"Who did these attractive things?"

Lambert's eyebrows lifted. He lit a cigarette before answering, almost too casually:

"As a matter of fact, dear Abbé, these are mine. If it won't bore you, I'll show you some more of my work."

He put down his cup, and from a little side passage brought several canvases, then in a fatigued manner stood them, one after another, so that they caught all the light, on a tall chair by the window.

Most of the paintings were quite small, and slight in subject—a spray of cherry blossom in a blue bowl, two willow trees over-hanging a stagnant pool, a child in a straw hat seated in an arbour by a river—yet each had a decorative prettiness that enhanced the mere design. It was a quality which seemed to infuse the pale forms with a fastidious and elusive charm.

When the paintings had been shown—they were few—Stephen turned to Lambert.

"I had no idea you could paint like that . . . these are delightful."

Lambert pretended to shrug, but he was clearly gratified, while his wife, reaching out vivaciously, pressed Stephen's hand.

"Phil is really a genius. He does portraits too." Her green eyes lingered brightly. "If anyone you know should be interested in buying . . . I am the business partner."

After this, the doorbell rang and, in quick succession, a number of other guests arrived, all singularly appropriate to this atmosphere of refined bohemianism: a young man in white socks with a manuscript under his arm, another man, less young, but square-shouldered and well-groomed, from the American Embassy, a model called Nina whom Stephen had seen occasionally at Madame Chobert's, a stout elderly Frenchman with an eyeglass who kissed Elise's hand with touching gallantry and upon whom, as a potential purchaser, she turned all her blandishments. Fresh tea was brought, Lambert poured whisky, the sound of conversation deepened, and presently Stephen, who on his first visit did not wish to stay too long, rose to go. Both Philip and his wife pressed him to come again. Indeed, Mrs. Lambert broke off a conversation to accompany him to the door.

"Come with us up the river on Sunday. We're picnicking at

Champrosay." She paused, wide-eyed, with the air of delivering a compliment. "Philip has really taken to you."

On Sunday, then, and on other days thereafter, Stephen accompanied the Lamberts, sometimes alone, sometimes with Chester or others of their friends, to those lovely reaches of the Seine between Châtillon and Melun. They took the *bateau mouche* from the Pont Neuf to Ablon, where they hired a skiff and pulled with leisurely strokes against the slow green stream, winding placidly between banks made glorious by the Forest of Sénart until, mooring at some riverside inn, they disembarked to lunch at a wooden table in the open air.

The weather was superb, the foliage at its moment of most mature beauty, the hollyhocks and the sunflowers in full bloom. The sparkling sunshine and caressing air, the exercise, these congenial friends, the dazzling newness of every sight and sound, the hoot of a barge, the colour of a workman's blouse, the pose of the lock-keeper's wife as she stood against the sky, all of which awoke in him a quivering ecstasy, above all the belief that he had, at last, "found himself" in the "artistic life", acted like a drug on Stephen. Lambert, save for some moody hours, was in his most winning humour, teasing them all occasionally, exhibiting his brilliance, dropping a witticism here, an epigram there, reciting long passages from Verlaine and *Les Fleurs du Mal*.

"More sacred than the Indus," he would murmur, pausing to catch his breath, trailing his long fingers in the cool current, his narrow chest heaving, the lock of hair drooping over his damp brow. "These water-lilies . . . chalices of purest alabaster . . . translucent pink . . . and cold . . . cold as the breasts of floating water nymphs . . ." And so on.

His eye for beauty was not confined to nature, and whenever the woman who waited on them at their inn was passably well-favoured he would, despite the sharp look in his wife's eyes, flirt with her outrageously.

At first Stephen brought a sketch-book with him, he longed to make a record of everything he saw, but Lambert discouraged him with a whimsical smile.

"You must store it all here, dear Abbé." He tapped his forehead gently. "Later on . . . in solitude . . . it will be born again."

One Sunday evening, after an excursion of more than usual delight, Stephen took leave of the Lamberts and two others who had made up the boating party, and set out from the landing-stage on the Quai St. Bernard for his hotel. The sun, now sinking behind the dome of the Trocadéro, had blazed in the sky all day long. Enticed by the heat of the day, they had bathed in the pool below the weir at L'Hermitage, eaten a special lunch of cold trout and pâté, enriched by the noble Chambertin, then fallen asleep afterwards on the warm grass beneath the Sénart beeches.

How well he felt! . . . skin scorched by the sun, lungs full of country air, body tingling from the sharp river water . . . a kind of god-like satisfaction suffused him.

Suddenly, as he crossed the Rue de Bièvre, a man stepped out of a narrow entry just ahead of him. He wore heavy boots, a pair of stained moleskin trousers, a patched blue porter's blouse. About his neck a red kerchief was carelessly entwined. He looked like a labourer going home after a stint of hard and heavy toil, yet something in the set of the shoulders, the defiant carriage of the head, made Stephen start. He hurried forward.

"Glyn."

Richard Glyn swung round, his face set and lowering, then, as he gazed, the frown which so deeply creased his forehead gradually lifted.

"It's you, Desmonde. . . . So you managed to get over."

"Five weeks ago." Stephen was smiling with pleasure. "And I've been hoping I'd run into you ever since. Look here, I'm just going back to the hotel. Do come and have dinner with me."

"Well," Glyn considered, "I'd be glad of a bite. I've had nothing to eat all day."

"Good heavens, what have you been doing?"

"Painting . . . since six this morning," Glyn answered, with a kind of gloomy violence. "I'm apt to forget about lunch when I'm working . . . especially when I can't master my cursed tone values."

As he spoke his agate-yellow eyes sparked with a sudden harsh impatience, the strain of a prolonged and passionately creative effort. Taking Stephen's arm, he set out with him along the street.

CHAPTER VIII

GLYN'S APPEARANCE, IN red neckerchief and hobnail boots, caused a mild stir in the Clifton dining-room. The ancient head waiter, reared in the tradition of English *milords*, did not like it, and the two spinster ladies, who had hitherto regarded Stephen with sympathetic approval, fluttered in shocked surprise. Richard, however, did not seem to mind and, settling himself in his chair, glanced round with visible curiosity.

"Why in Heaven's name do you stay in a place like this, Desmonde?"

"Oh, I don't know . . . I'm used to it, I suppose."

Glyn tasted the soup, made, as usual with flour and greasy water.

"Perhaps you like the cooking?" he suggested.

Stephen laughed.

"I know this isn't up to much. But the meat course will be good."

"It had better be." Richard broke another roll. "I told you I was hungry. Some evening I'll take you to a real eating-house."

"Madame Chobert's?"

"Good God, no! Not that artistic hash shop! . . . I hate sham in cooking as well as in painting. A cabman's *bistro* near my place. You can always depend on a pub where the cabbies go. They have a rabbit pâté there that's out of this world." Glyn paused. "Now tell me what you've been up to."

Willingly, indeed with enthusiasm, Stephen began a full account of all his recent doings. He spoke of his morning "grind" at Dupret's, glowed over his friendship with Chester and the Lamberts, grew lyrical in describing the expeditions to Champrosay. At first Glyn listened with a half-sarcastic, half-indulgent smile, but gradually his expression turned serious, he glanced askance at his companion.

"Well!" he exclaimed, when the narrative concluded. "You seem to have been busy. Perhaps you'll take me up to your room afterwards and we'll see what you've done."

"Oh, I haven't much to show you," Stephen answered hurriedly. "Only a few sketches. I've been concentrating on line, you see."

"I see," said Glyn.

In complete silence he chewed upon the tenacious *pouding à l'anglais* which constituted the Clifton dessert. He did not speak for a good five minutes. Then, from beneath knitted brows, he turned upon Stephen a steady gaze which held also a glint of extreme disfavour.

"Desmonde," he said. "Do you want to paint? Or fool your life away like one of these fancy characters in *La Bohême*?"

"I don't understand."

"Listen, then. There are perhaps ten thousand blasted impostors in this town who imagine they are artists because they study a little, sketch a little, and sit on their arses in the cafés all night gabbing about their stillborn masterpieces. You're almost one of them. You're bloody well wasting your time, Desmonde. Painting means work, work, and still more work. Hard, hellish work that pulls the guts out of you. Not drifting down the Seine, lying on your backside in a canoe with some half-baked poseur who spouts Verlaine and Baudelaire at you."

Stephen flushed indignantly.

"You're unjust, Glyn. Chester and Lambert are very decent fellows. Lambert certainly has great talent."

"Bosh! What has he done? Some *japonaiseries*, painted fans, fragments . . . oh, pretty enough, I grant you, but effeminate little things . . . affected . . . and all so small."

"Surely it's a sign of vulgarity to produce large canvases."

In his resentment Stephen had quoted a favourite remark of Lambert's and Glyn was quick to scent its origin. He laughed harshly.

"What about Rubens, and Correggio, and del Sarto, with their terrific conceptions, and old Michelangelo, covering the ceiling of the Sistine Chapel with his tremendous vision of Creation, working so hard that for days he didn't even take his clothes off? Were they vulgar? No, Desmonde . . . Lambert is a gifted amateur, a minor artist, who'd never be heard of if he weren't pushed from behind by his shrewish wife. I've nothing against the fellow, it's you I'm thinking of, Desmonde. You have something that Lambert would give his soul to possess. I won't want to see you chuck it away through your own damned foolishness. As for Harry Chester," Glyn concluded, "are you so unutterably green that you haven't tumbled to him yet?"

"I don't know what you mean," Stephen answered sulkily.

For a moment Glyn thought of enlightening him, but he contented himself with a scornful smile.

"How much has he sponged off you?"

Stephen's flush deepened. Chester had on several occasions borrowed additional sums until he now owed him more than five hundred francs, but had he not given his word of honour that he would faithfully pay them back?

"I tell you, Desmonde," Glyn went on more quietly, "you've got off to a false start, landed in bad company, and worst of all you've been slacking abominably. If you don't take yourself up you'll have dug your own grave. The lowest pit in hell is occupied by the artist who does not work!"

A long, cold silence fell. Although Stephen had defended himself, as he contrasted his own useless day with the hours of concentrated effort given out by Glyn, a slow shame spread over him.

"What am I to do?" he said, at last.

Glyn's drawn brows relaxed.

"First of all, get out of this damned Anglican home of rest."

"When?"

"Now."

Stephen's look of consternation seemed to amuse Glyn immensely, but in a moment he was serious again.

"I can't ask you to dig with me. But I know a man who'll be glad to have you."

"Who?"

"Jerome Peyrat's the name. Papa Peyrat. He's an oldish chap, not well off, wants someone to share expenses. A queer fish but, by heaven, a real painter, different from your fake bohemians." Glyn's grin was disconcerting, but it vanished quickly as he concluded. "You're finished with Dupret, of course. You can use my studio. And I'll introduce you to my colourman, Napoleon Campo. He gives credit . . . sometimes. Now let's go."

Stephen's nature was not adapted to sudden changes and abrupt decisions, yet there was an overwhelming force in Glyn's arguments, an irresistible compulsion in his manner. He went, therefore, to the office and, to the surprise and mortification of the director, asked for and settled his bill. He then packed his bag and had it brought downstairs, atoning for the unexpectedness of his departure by an indiscriminate distribution of gratuities.

Glyn, standing by in the passage, and plainly regarded by the Clifton staff as the demon of the piece, was chilly towards this tipping, and commented grimly:

"I advise you to hang on to your cash, Desmonde. You may need it before you're through. Come along."

"Wait, Glyn. They'll have to get us a cab."

"Damn the cab. Are you too weak to walk?"

Picking up the suitcase, which was no light weight, Richard swung it on to his shoulder and strode out of the hotel. Stephen followed, into the luminous dusk of the street.

It was a considerable distance to Peyrat's lodging, but Glyn, who took a savage satisfaction in exacting the utmost from himself, traversed it at a rapid pace, without once faltering or setting down the valise. Finally in a dark little side street on the Left Bank, in the triangle formed by the meeting of the Rue d'Assas and the Boulevard du Montparnasse, Glyn turned into a crooked extrance next to a pastrycook's shop which, though feebly illuminated by an overhead lamp, was scrubbed clean, and began ascending the stone stairs three at a time. On the second floor he paused, knocked on the door, then, without waiting for an answer, turned the handle and led Stephen in.

It was a three-room apartment, and in the living-room, furnished with bourgeois neatness, there sat by an oilcloth-covered table a slight, round-shouldered man of about fifty, with a flat, furrowed face and an untrimmed beard, who wore, despite the warmth of a stove in full blast, a dilapidated black overcoat turned up at the collar and a hard black hat and who, while a thrush with half its feathers gone piped an accompaniment in a cage by the window, was practising softly on the ocarina. At the sight of Glyn his eyes, which were clear and youthful and filled with ingenuous audacity, lighted up. He put down the instrument, and rising, embraced Richard with affectionate formality upon both cheeks.

"Peyrat," said Glyn briefly, when he had disengaged himself, "I've brought you your new lodger. He's a friend of mine. Stephen Desmonde."

Jerome Peyrat's gaze travelled from Glyn towards Stephen and rested upon him thoughtfully—a scrutiny both innocent and amiable.

"If he is your friend, *mon vieux*, then he will be mine. Forgive me for receiving you like this, Monsieur Desmonde. Richard knows how subject I am to draughts."

"I hope we are not disturbing you," Stephen said awkwardly.

"Far from it. In the evenings I am in the habit of contemplating my own soul. Sometimes I find it splendid, sometimes hideous. To-night"—he smiled gravely—"I welcome any distraction."

"Desmonde is a painter, Peyrat. He's going to work with me—and you."

"Good." Peyrat expressed not the slightest surprise. "I make you welcome to my apartment. . . . At least temporarily it is mine since it belongs to Monsieur Bisque, the pastrycook. No matter. Here we renounce the beauty of women and the brilliance of contemporary fame in order to produce masterpieces that will be acclaimed a thousand years after we are dead."

"What a hope!" exclaimed Glyn with ironic indulgence.

"It is that hope which alone keeps us alive."

"What about the blessed Thérèse?"

"Ah, yes. Truly, one is sustained by the example of that noble soul." He turned to Stephen. "Have you visited Spain?"

"No."

"Then some day we may make a pilgrimage together. To Avila de los Caballeros . . . lying behind its granite ramparts, baked yellow by the sun in summer, frozen by the Castilian winter, standing like a great crown amidst its wilderness of rock against the hard blue of the Gredos Mountains."

"You have been there?" Stephen asked politely.

"Many times. But only in spirit."

Glyn burst out laughing.

"I warn you, Desmonde. This madman, who never goes to church and says disagreeable things about the Pope, has an absurd veneration for Sainte Thérèse."

Peyrat shook his head in reproof.

"My friend, do not take in vain the name of that sweet and obstinate woman from Old Castile, who restored the original discalced order, abandoned in the easy, gossiping life of the Carmelites. She fought her campaign with wit, charm, humility, prayer, argument, the patience of a saint and the temper of a sea captain. She was a poet too . . ."

"I'm off," Glyn said with a grin, going to the door. "I'll leave you to get acquainted. Be at my studio at seven tomorrow, Desmonde. Good night."

He went out. Peyrat, after a moment's silence, came forward and held out his hand to Stephen.

He said simply, "I hope you will be at home here."

CHAPTER IX

NOW THERE BEGAN for Stephen, under the influence of Glyn and Peyrat, a new existence, filled with unremitting work, flatly opposed to his recent interpretation of the artistic life. Jerome Peyrat, known all over the Plaisance district as "Papa Peyrat", was of humble origin, his parents, now dead, no more than simple country people—though he spoke of them with pride—working a few hectares near Nantes. For thirty years, as a government clerk, model *petit fonctionnaire,* his days had been passed in paper cuffs and an alpaca jacket, making entries in dusty ledgers at the Palais de Justice. Only once had he been out of France, when, as third clerk to a judicial commission, he had gone to India. Here, he had spent all his leisure a naïve and fascinated spectator of the animals ranging behind bars, beneath the tall palms and carob trees of the Calcutta Zoo. Some months after his return, the personnel of the ministry was reduced and Peyrat was retired with a pension so minute it barely kept him in bread. Then, unexpectedly, never having manifested in the faintest degree any interest in art, he began, prolifically, to paint. Not only to paint, but to regard himself, calmly, as a painter of genius. He had never had a lesson in his life. He painted the portraits of his friends, he painted streets, ugly buildings, wedding groups, factories in the *banlieue*, bunches of flowers grasped by disembodied hands, he painted jungle compositions—a naked female form, prodigal of breast and thigh, bestriding a snarling tiger amidst a tangled undergrowth of palms, creepers, fern fronds, orchids of chromatic hues, a forest of the imagination, lush and stupendous, peopled by snakes, and climbing apes interlocked as though in mortal combat, during the execution of which he trembled, sweated and, lest he faint, was forced, despite his dread of catching cold, to open the window for fresh air.

The neighbourhood shrugged and smiled at these pictures, which were displayed for sale at the price of fifteen francs, in the window of his friend, Madame Huffnaegel, a respectable widow who kept the millinery shop a few doors down the street and for whom he cherished a temperate regard. Except for Napoleon Campo, the colourman, who had taken canvases in payment for materials obtained by Peyrat —and whose attic admittedly was stored with junk from struggling artists—no one bought the pictures which became, to the neighbours in the Rue Castel, a standard subject of hilarious, if affectionate, mirth. Yet, complacently, Peyrat went on painting, often sorely in need, yet eking out his meagre pension by various devices. In addition to the ocarina, which he played for his own pleasure, and the French horn, he had a limited knowledge of the violin, and clarinet. He therefore drew out a number of handbills which, in his best clothes, he distributed from door to door throughout the district.

Notice

JEROME PEYRAT
Painter and Musician

COURSES FOR CHILDREN IN MUSIC,
HARMONICA, AND SOLFEGGIO

Saturday afternoons from 2–5 o'clock. Rapid progress guaranteed. Parents may be present at the classes. Monthly fee for each student 5 francs. The number accepted will be limited.

Also, in the summer, he turned his skill upon the French horn to good effect by playing every Thursday afternoon in the orchestra which charmed the nursemaids and their charges in the Tuileries Gardens. And when necessity pressed too hard upon him there was always the friend of his boyhood, Alphonse Bisque, now the Plaisance pastrycook, stout, middle-aged and completely bald, who, out of sentimental recollection of their distant schooldays in Nantes rather than because of the pictures which, from time to time, Jerome pressed upon him in payment, could be relied upon, in a crisis, to provide a meat pâté or a mutton pie.

In his habits and the general manner of his life, Peyrat—Stephen soon discovered—was as ingenuous, as strikingly original as his pictures. For all his simplicity, he had an active and inquiring mind which, stuffed with the fruits of his researches in abstruse volumes bought second hand on the *quais*, frequently erupted in naïvely erudite discourses upon history, mediæval theology, or subjects so irreconcilable as Cosmas of Alexandria, who in the year 548 denounced the doctrine of the rotundity of the earth, and Sainte Thérèse of Avila, whom he, an atheist, had calmly appropriated as his patroness.

Despite these eccentricities, he proved himself, in his favourite phrase, *un brave homme et un bon camarade*. Early though Stephen rose, Peyrat was up before him to take in the milk and new-baked bread which Alphonse's small boy delivered every morning to the door. Their simple breakfast over, he would put on an apron and wash the dishes; then, having given water and seed to the thrush, which he had found in the street lamed by a cat and proposed to release when its wing had mended, he girded himself for the day's work, shouldered his easel and paint-box and, with a great rusty umbrella to protect him from the elements, set off on foot to some remote corner of the suburbs, to Ivry, Charenton or Passy, where, undisturbed either by the ribald comments of passing spectators, or the practical jokes of the children who tormented him, he lost himself in the wonder and mystery of projecting upon canvas some celestial vision of a railway siding, a tramcar, or a chimney-stack.

Stephen set out at the same hour, hurrying every morning towards the Rue de Bièvre to utilize the clear north light which, after dawn, streamed through the leaded skylights of Glyn's studio. Richard, who never spared himself, was merciless in his attitude, a surly, and often savage, taskmaster.

"Show me what you can do," he said grimly. "In six months, if you don't satisfy me, I'll return you to the Lord."

Glyn's model, Anna Montel, was a woman of thirty, tall and vigorous, with black hair and a gaunt, gypsy look. She was a

Cinzany Romany, her forbears must originally have been Hungarian, though Glyn had met her in a remote part of North Wales. Her skin was rough, and as she went always bareheaded, in a dark skirt and green blouse, without gloves or coat, her hands and cheeks were chapped by the sharp autumn breezes which swept up the street from the river. But the planes of this windswept face, with its firm eye-sockets and high cheek-bones, were flat and strong. Moving about the studio in her list slippers, reading Glyn's wishes by a glance, she was the most silent person Stephen had ever known. She would pose at all hours, and for long periods at a stretch, then without a word would slip out of the studio to the Halles and, returning with an armful of provisions, go over to the tiny stove to make a goulash, or brew coffee in that speckled blue enamel pot with the broken spout which figured, later, in one of Glyn's best-known paintings: *Le Café Matinal.*

Although he never attempted to instruct, Glyn was incessant in his demand for originality, insisting that Stephen discard his preconceived notions, encouraging him to look at objects, not as they were seen and represented by tradition, but with his own eyes.

"Do as Peyrat does!" Glyn would exclaim. "Make every painting absolutely your own."

"You think highly of Peyrat?"

"I think he's great." Glyn spoke with complete conviction. "He has the direct original vision of the primitive artist. They may laugh at him for a damned old fool as much as they please. But in twenty years they'll fall over themselves scrambling for his stuff."

It was hard work—and cold. The studio was frigid, and as the weeks advanced became more frigid still, for Glyn held a Spartan theory that no one could do his best in an atmosphere of comfort. Gone for ever was Stephen's earlier idea that painting was a soft, seductive art. Never in his life had he known such a rigorous regime. And Glyn was insatiable in his demand for greater, and still greater, effort.

One day, when Stephen's head was reeling and he felt he could go on no longer, Richard, with a deep breath, threw down his palette.

"Exercise," he declared. "The top of my head's coming off. Can you use a bicycle?"

"Of course."

"I suppose you did the curate's crawl around Oxford. Four miles an hour."

"I believe I can do slightly better than that."

"Good." Glyn's lips drew open. "We'll see what you're made of."

They left the studio and crossed the street to the bicycle shop of the quarter kept by Pierre Berthelot, an old racing cyclist who, though now incapacitated by a Pernod-damaged heart, had in his day finished third in the Tour de France. It was a small, broken-down establishment with a row of *vélos* strung up to the ceiling in front and a dark repair shop in the rear. They went in. The place seemed deserted.

"Pierre!" Glyn shouted, rapping on the counter.

A girl of about nineteen appeared from the back. She was rather short, wore a black sweater and black pleated skirt, her bare feet in low black slippers.

"It's you," said Glyn.

"Who did you expect? The Queen of Sheba?"

"Why aren't you with the circus?"

"Laid up for the winter." She spoke briefly, ungraciously, hands on her hips, legs planted apart.

"Where's your papa?"

"Sleeping it off."

"Huh! Stephen, this is Emmy Berthelot." As she looked from one to the other in a bored manner he went on. "We want two machines for the afternoon. Good ones, now."

"They're all good. Take the two at the end."

While Glyn lowered the pulley ropes. Stephen watched her as she caught each machine in turn and spun the wheels expertly. She had a pale, sulky face, a low, slightly bulging forehead, well-marked eyebrows, a wide, thin-lipped mouth. Her nose had a good line but had that slum-quarter tilt at the tip which gave her away. Except for her breasts, conspicuous under the tight jersey, she had the figure of a young, well-developed boy. Turning unexpectedly, she caught Stephen's eyes on her. Under her cool appraising stare he felt himself reddening—there was an insolence in her manner that wounded him. Richard was wheeling the cycles to the door.

"Like to come with us, Emmy?"

"How can I? Got to watch the shop. Thanks to that old soak."

"Another time then. We'll be back before dark."

Stephen followed Glyn out to the street. They mounted and, bent double over the downswept handlebars, Glyn in the lead, moved off through the traffic along the Faubourg St. Germain to the Porte de Versailles. Outside the city gates they sped along the flat, straight road towards Ville d'Avray. Richard, with occasional backward glances, set a blinding pace. St. Appoline, Pontchartrain, and Meul flashed past, then Juziers lay behind them, and Orgeval. At last, when in a circular sweep they had covered about thirty kilometres, Glyn drew up sharp at a *buvette* in the little village of Louveciennes. Breathing deeply, he looked critically at Stephen, stained with dust and sweat, completely winded. He smiled.

"Not bad, my boy. You don't like to give up, do you? It's a quality that may serve you. Come in and have a beer."

In the dark, low-ceilinged bar they each had a cool bock, which slid deliciously down their parched throats. Glyn sucked the froth from his beard and sighed.

"Good painting country around Louveciennes," he meditated. "Renoir and Pissarro used to hang out here. Sisley too. But we'll push further out next time. We'll get Emmy to set the pace. She can really go."

The recollection of the encounter in the bicycle shop still rankled with Stephen. He said stiffly:

"That young woman struck me as a rather disagreeable person."

Glyn gave a shout of laughter.

"Moderate your language, Padre." Then, after a pause. "As a matter of fact, she is a cheap little slut . . . your friend Chester could tell you that. . . . And a tough one. Practically brought up in an *équipe* on the *circuit de France*. Hangs around with a lot of the young pros. Tours six months of the year with the Peroz outfit."

"Peroz?"

"Adolf Peroz. Used to be Peroz Brothers. Adolf is the survivor. I've met him. Quite a nice bloke. He runs a pretty decent circus. Emmy does a trick-cycling act. Supposed to be extremely risky. She gets high billing, and lets you know about it. She has no use for us, really, knows we don't make a bean. But she's incredibly vain, and wants me to paint her."

"Shall you?"

"Not on your life. I don't deal in gutter types. But it amuses me to put a spoke in her wheel. She is really such a perfect little bitch." He finished his beer. "Come on. Let's get cracking."

They rode back slowly in the cool of the evening. Glyn was in great spirits, purged of his nervous tension, giving out snatches of Welsh folk songs, ready for the next day's work.

Outside the bicycle shop he looked at his watch and gave out a whistle.

"I'm late. I have to meet Anna. Take this in for me like a good chap." He turned over his machine to Stephen and rushed off.

With some difficulty Stephen manœuvred the two cycles into the shop. As before, it was empty. He knocked on the counter, then, as no one appeared, he pushed through the door that led to the back premises and, in a dark little passage, bumped straight into Emmy, who had been coming towards the shop. The outer door swung shut leaving them together, confined in the darkness, in a space no greater than a cupboard. Quite disconcerted, he could find nothing to say, and all at once his pulse began to beat like a hammer. As she stood beside him, so close that he could feel her warmth, a sudden strange emotion made his throat tighten. She was watching him unmoved, without surprise, but as though his inner turmoil were perfectly apparent to her; she gave him a cool, critical smile.

"*Que veux-tu?*"

The double meaning in the question sent a wave of heat over him. There was a pause during which he heard the quick loud bumping of his heart. In an unnatural voice he answered:

"I wanted you to know. . . . I've brought back the machines."

"Did you have a good ride?" Still observing him through knowing, narrowed eyes, half amused by his emotion, though not partaking in it.

"Yes . . . thank you."

Again silence. She was making no attempt to move. At last, with a great effort he forced his hand to the door behind him and thrust it open.

"I hope," he stammered like a schoolboy, "I hope I shall see you again."

Shamed and overstrung, he tried without success to dismiss her from his mind.

But she grew upon him every time he saw her—occasions which became more frequent since, with the coming of the spring, Glyn insisted on regular weekly exercise. Emmy attracted and at the same time repelled him. He longed to ask her to sit for him, yet could not bring himself to do so. A favourable opportunity seemed never to arise. She remained, like an unsolved puzzle, a meaning sought for and not found, a strange irritant at the back of his mind.

And time was passing with disconcerting rapidity. As the days lengthened, and the chestnuts broke into bloom again, he realized that his year of grace would soon be up. More and more the letters from Stillwater, from his father, Davie, and from Claire, began to anticipate his return, to demand it, indeed, with increasing urgency.

July came, and from brassy skies a stifling air pressed down upon the city. Glyn, who hated hot weather, endured it for two weeks, then suddenly decided to go to Brittany with Anna, to wander round and paint Calvaries. The Lamberts had already departed for La Baule and now Chester left to join them. Even Peyrat spoke of deserting Paris. The lease of the apartment was up in August and he planned to go to an uncle in Auvergne.

Both Richard and Peyrat pressed Stephen to accompany them. But he could not accept—a final letter, tinged with severity, had arrived from the Rector in which he hoped that Stephen would not "go back upon your pledged word" nor allow himself to be detained by "the gaieties and distractions of Paris."

After he had read it, Stephen threw down his brushes and went out into the streets. He could have gone to the Bois, where there is always shade beneath the trees, but his mood, depressed and irritable, forbade it. Instead, despite his fatigue, and a sense of being utterly rundown, he walked straight across the city, through miles of monotonous streets. Shops and cafés all the way, large at first, gradually growing smaller. All nearly empty. In one, deserted, a waiter, his head on his arms, asleep at a table. He went under railway bridges, passed the snake-like tracks of the great Termini, crossed canals, finally passed the *octroi* and stood in a dusty wasteland outside the barriers of Paris. By this time he was dripping with perspiration and kept repeating to himself: "My God, what a life. . . . And Father thinks my days are a round of pleasure!"

When he got back he stopped at the Plaisance post office and wrote out a telegram.

DESMONDE, THE RECTORY, STILLWATER, SUSSEX.
CROSSING MORNING BOAT TOMORROW JULY NINETEENTH.
STEPHEN

CHAPTER X

NOTHING, THOUGHT STEPHEN, exceeds the joy of revisiting loved, familiar places, half forgotten, now seen to be more beautiful than before. Stretched on the grassy bank of Chillingham Lake, a fishing-rod beside him, warmed by the afternoon sunshine, he was watching Davie cast a silver minnow, still awkwardly but with an earnestness that brought improvement, amongst the flowering lily-pads, beneath whose coolness lay the shadowy pike. The air was clear and golden, wild flowers were everywhere, the trees wore their fullest, most tender foliage; upon the briars, dog roses, of a delicate pink, breathed out their perfume which mingled with the heady scent of meadowsweet. Pigeons flew over head and distantly, from the home farm of Broughton Court, he heard the clucking of fowls.

It was difficult to realize that he had been home two weeks. From that moment when, at Halborough Junction he had been met by Davie and Caroline—a combination chosen with exquisite discretion—everything had gone so smoothly, time had been made to fly. Yes, it was good to be back—if only they would not treat him like the returned prodigal who was now forgiven and must at all costs be secured by kindness. Breakfast in bed, his father's *Times* unbroken on the tray—until he had protested he would rather rise and take his coffee downstairs with Davie; his favourite dishes at lunch and dinner, Beasley working overtime in the kitchen, Mould bringing in baskets of the choicest fruit; his wishes deferred to, excursions planned; clearly, all the members of the household were united in a diplomatic effort to disarm him.

The subject of his painting was not discussed—it had been dead since that first evening when, at the Rector's request, he had displayed his canvases. With a contraction of his brows, between a frown and a smile, he recollected how honestly yet vainly his father had striven to approve his work, nonplussed by all that he saw, his bewildered eye coming to rest, in particular, upon a scene of the *banlieue* which displayed a woman pegging a string of washing across her back yard on a windy day.

"My dear boy . . . do you think this . . . beautiful?"

"Yes. It's one of my favourites."

"But I don't understand. Why, of all things, should you paint a clothes line?"

"It's the interplay of brilliant tones, Father . . . against the drab background, the old woman's grey-and-black dress . . ."

He had tried to explain the basis of his idea, how the raw colours were put on with a palette knife. Yet it was plain that the Rector remained perplexed and unconvinced. A long pause followed. At last, after a final survey, his father turned doubtfully yet inquiringly towards him.

"I suppose an expert might appreciate this."

"I think he might."

Thereafter consideration had supplanted criticism. Caroline, much softer in her manner, had pressed his suits, sewed buttons on his shirts, and his mother, prodded from her own solitary and peculiar world, had suddenly discovered, and declared that she would use, a hank of wool from which, while he was at Oxford, she had proposed to knit him socks.

They had been, for the most part, a self-contained family group—rather to Stephen's relief General Desmonde and his wife were in Scotland with Geoffrey, for the shooting—but this afternoon, aware that Davie and he were to be at Chillingham, Lady Broughton had invited them for tea. With a glance at the sun, now slanting across the crest of the Downs, Stephen judged they had better be off. He got to his feet, strolled along the bank and stood behind his brother, who, though showing signs of fatigue, still perseveringly cast his line upon the unresponsive water. The catch, so far, had been a poor one—three yellow perch so small they would fail to satisfy the Rectory cat. Aware of the passionate ardour which Davie had for this, and indeed for every outdoor sport—a feeling so contrary to his own indifference, so touchingly incongruous, too, when one considered the boy's delicate constitution and far from robust health—he wished that a large and worthy trout might even now impale itself upon the hook. He could well visualize the joy and triumph which such a capture would provoke.

But although he waited patiently, with an occasional word of encouragement, no such stroke of fortune occurred. Davie, he reflected with momentary sadness, never had any luck. And as his young brother reeled in his line, he put his arm about his shoulders and by praising his advance in skill, condemning the unfavourable elements of heat and light, finally, by magnifying the size and virtue of the three small fishes now curled dryly in the basket, he brought him back to cheerfulness.

"I do think I have improved," Davie answered hopefully. "I've tried terribly hard. And, as you say, these perch aren't half bad. Do you think they'll make good eating?"

"Excellent."

"Of course . . . they are rather small."

"The smaller the sweeter," said Stephen wisely.

As they set off through the meadows, avoiding the long way round by Foxcross Corner and, since it was so dry, cutting across the lower sedges into the Broughton coverts, Davie chattered away with that eager animation which was the keynote of his character. He had grown lately, seemed tall for fourteen years, and his limbs had the nervous inco-ordination of his difficult age, making him appear to move by fits and starts. Yet the expression on his thin face was less feverish than before, and his attacks, Stephen had learned from Caroline, while no less severe, showed a steady diminution in frequency. Listening with sympathy, watching the play of light upon those clean-cut features, Stephen was conscious of a deep surge of affection for his brother. They had been together almost continuously during the past two weeks.

Breaking out of the woods, they climbed the iron rail that fenced the park, where cattle were placidly grazing, and presently reached the avenue which, skirting the formal garden that fringed the lawn, brought them eventually to the mansion itself, a Victorian pile of massive red sandstone, bedevilled with towers and turrets, which Lady Broughton proudly contended to be the highest house in Sussex.

It was she who received them, reclining on a chaise longue by the open French windows in the south drawing-room, asking to be excused for her apparent indolence—her doctor had lately been ridiculously severe towards her—making them immediately at home with the quiet warmth of her welcome.

"So you are back, Stephen." Still holding his hand, she looked him up and down. "Full of the knowledge of beautiful things. I am sorry you have no beard. Yet I believe Paris has improved you. Can you kiss my wrist like a Frenchman?"

"I have not been studying that art."

"What a pity." She smiled. "Isn't it, Davie?"

"It will only be a pity if my brother goes back, Lady Broughton."

"Well said. You see how glad we are to have you home again, Stephen. In proof, I shall give you Sussex johnny cakes for tea. Don't you remember how you liked them when you were Davie's age?"

"I do indeed. I still like them. And Davie does too."

Lady Broughton smiled, and continued her flow of amiable banter. Yet, listening quietly, Stephen was conscious of the change in her. He had always liked this short, high-coloured, completely undistinguished-looking woman, whose energetic good nature and sound common sense were apparent in all her actions. And now it pained him to observe her passive attitude, that quick catch in her breathing, the faint purplish tinge in her already vivid cheeks.

"Claire should be here soon," she now remarked. "I daresay she wishes to make her entry with a large hat and a basket of roses, like something by Gainsborough."

Almost as her mother spoke Claire entered, not from the garden and without flowers, bareheaded too, looking unlike a Gainsborough and rather like a Burne-Jones in her linen dress square cut at the neck and of a russet colour that matched the red gold in her hair. Although he had doubtless forgotten, Stephen had once told her that she suited this rich Pre-Raphaelite shade.

Her bearing was admirable. One would never have guessed how

C

fast her heart was beating or how long she had looked forward to this moment.

"Claire." Stephen went towards her.

"It's so good to see you." She smiled. "And you, Davie." She hoped the faint flush she felt rising to her cheeks would pass unnoticed. To see him again, to feel the touch of his fingers upon hers, tested her composure more than she could have believed.

Just then tea was brought in, no meagre repast of dry biscuits and thin bread and butter but a regular schoolboy spread of boiled eggs and crumpets, sandwiches and johnny cakes, with strawberries and whipped Sussex cream, all arranged upon a wheeled satinwood table.

"We thought you'd be hungry after your fishing," said Claire, looking at Davie.

"We are," he agreed enthusiastically. "We hadn't much lunch." He took the cup that Claire poured and carried it politely though rather shakily to Lady Broughton before sitting down.

"Thank you, Davie." Breaking the slight constraint, she went on, in her teasing manner, "Claire, don't you think Stephen has acquired quite a Parisian air?"

"He is thinner, perhaps." What a stupid answer. But he was home—the disquieting sweetness of the thought bathed her eyes in light.

"I don't think French food is particularly nourishing," Davie ventured seriously. "At least I shouldn't care for snails and frogs' legs and that sort of thing."

Everyone laughed, and after that they were a merry party. Davie, as though to prove the virtue of an Anglo-Saxon diet, had two helpings of johnny cake, then entered into a lively discussion with Claire upon the methods of catching pike, at the end of which they both agreed that on such a day as this a mayfly would have far surpassed a silver minnow.

"I believe there are some flies in the billiard-room," Claire reflected, after a moment. "Would you like to have them?"

"Oh, I say," Davie murmured. "Don't you want them for yourself? I mean . . . are you serious?"

"Of course. No one uses them. Come along and we'll take a look."

Asking if he might be excused, Davie rose with alacrity, held open the door for Claire. They went out together.

When they had gone, Lady Broughton gazed meditatively at Stephen, whom she had always sincerely liked and, indeed, admired. It did not in the least distress her that he had given up the Church—

with a nature so sensitive, passionate and shy she considered him not cut out to be a country parson. Nor did his recent artistic adventures cause her deep uneasiness. These she regarded merely as a passing fancy, a temporary tendency which derived no doubt from certain freakish traits on the distaff side—she well remembered how as a child she had been petrified by the colourful eccentricities of Mrs. Desmonde's worthy father—and which in no way detracted from the essential fineness of Stephen's character. Yet it was less this genuine regard than her knowledge of Claire's feelings which made her wish to say something compatible with good breeding which might bring the matter to a head. In these past months she had observed with sympathy her daughter's indifference and absent-mindedness, noted too, not without misgiving, her occasional efforts to break these pensive moods and find distraction in pursuits quite foreign to her. Recently Geoffrey Desmonde had been a persistent visitor and, if only for the way in which he drawled his sentences, Lady Broughton detested him. She regarded him as stereotyped and commonplace, a spoiled, conceited and affected young fop, and having herself been married to a man whose bumptious dullness had for more than twenty years made her life a penance, she desired no such fate for Claire.

Without doubt, it was this train of thought which caused her to remark:

"You haven't seen your cousin since you returned?"

"No. All the Simla people are in Scotland."

"Geoffrey has been shooting here a good deal."

"He'd enjoy that. Has he been hunting?"

"Claire and he have been hacking on the Downs quite a bit. They're very often together. I think he took her to Brooklands the other day . . . for the motor racing."

"I didn't know Claire cared for that sort of thing."

"I don't think she does . . . but she isn't good at refusing." Lady Broughton smiled. In the pause which followed she leaned slightly towards him and continued in a tone which, while confidential, she kept deliberately casual. "I do worry about her a little, Stephen. She is such a quiet person—introspective, if you like—friendly, yet not good at making friends. To be happy she needs the right kind of companionship—shall I go further, and say the right kind of husband. I needn't tell you that I shan't be here for ever. Fairly soon Claire may be alone. And although she loves this place there are many responsibilities—she may find it rather difficult to look after."

She had said nothing definite, nothing which could in any way embarrass him, yet there was no mistaking her intention. And indeed, before he could speak, she resumed, placing her slightly swollen, veined fingers upon his sleeve.

"I think you were wise to have that spell in Paris. And your most excellent father was wise to let you go. In my days young men always made the grand tour. Not only was it regarded as a virtual necessity, it got the thing out of their system. They came back, settled down as good landlords and raised a family. That precisely is what you ought to do, dear Stephen."

"But supposing. . . ." He avoided her gaze, a faint colour in his cheeks. "Supposing I felt I ought to go abroad again?"

"Why?"

"To continue studying . . . and working."

"At what?"

"Painting."

She shook her head, indulgently patted his hand.

"My dear boy, when I was young and romantic I thought I could write poetry, and I did, to my shame. I got over it, however. And so will you."

The argument seemed conclusive, she settled back on her cushion. Before Stephen could answer Davie re-entered the room with Claire, carrying a japanned metal box.

"Look, Stephen, what Claire has given me. All these lovely flies. Ever so many swivels and traces. And this waterproof case."

"Don't forget," Claire smiled, "we shall expect lots of fish."

"Why, with this tackle—I wish school didn't take up so soon."

"Isn't winter the best time for pike?"

"Yes, it is. I say, I shall look forward to the Christmas holidays."

"Well, mind you come for tea whenever you're at Chillingham."

Stephen stood up in preparation for departure, touched by Claire's kindness to Davie, by the quiet thoughtfulness, apparent through her reserve, in every word and gesture. The last glimmer of the afternoon gilded the long pillared room, not beautiful, but warm, lived-in, charming with the sentiment of an old country house. Through the windows were the exquisite lawns, dim but still visible, shaded by the great cedar tree, the beech woods with red roofs of cottages above, and beyond, rolling away like the sea, the green Downs.

On the way home Davie found his brother unusually silent. After glancing at him once or twice he said:

"It is jolly at the Court. Don't you wish we could be there oftener?"

But Stephen gave no answer.

CHAPTER XI

ON THE FOLLOWING Thursday, luncheon at the Rectory was almost over. It had been a somewhat oppressive meal, for Davie, already formally attired, was due to return to school that afternoon. Yet, glancing around, Stephen was conscious of a tension greater than that demanded by the occasion, a general air of collusion and expectancy. He sensed an intensification of that intangible coercion which, disguised in a smother of affection, had been brought to bear upon him from time to time during the past two weeks.

The Rector, who had looked at his watch three times in the past five minutes, now did so again, finished his coffee and, with his gaze on no one in particular, remarked:

"It happens that Mr. Munsey Peters is in the neighbourhood. Unfortunately he could not come to lunch. But I have asked him to call in the early afternoon."

"How interesting, Father," Caroline murmured with her eyes upon her plate.

"Do you mean," asked Mrs. Desmonde in the tone of one coached for the question, "*the* Munsey Peters?"

"Yes. You know Mr. Peters, Stephen?" Inattentive, carving a face for Davie on a strip of orange peel, Stephen now looked up, conscious that his father was addressing him. "He is a well-known member of the Royal Academy."

There was a pause. Arrested, his expression suddenly fixed, Stephen waited for Bertram to spring the trap.

"We thought he might care to see your pictures."

Again there was a silence which Caroline broke hurriedly, with an air of brightness.

"Isn't that fortunate, Stephen? Now you can have the benefit of his advice."

"I believe," said Mrs. Desmonde, "if my recollection serves me, that there is a Peters landscape in the Pump Room at Cheltenham. It hangs above the Chalybeate Fountain. A view of the Malvern Hills with sheep. Most life-like."

"He is in the first rank," agreed Bertram.

"Wasn't there a book too, Father?" Caroline interposed. "*Raphael to Reynolds*—something like that."

"He has written several books on art. The most popular is entitled *Art for Art's Sake*."

"I must ask for it in the library," Caroline murmured.

"You don't mind if we show him your paintings?" The Rector turned to his son with a new firmness. "Since the opportunity has arisen it might be wise to have his opinion."

Stephen had gone quite white. He did not answer for a moment. "Show him anything you like. His opinion is valueless."

"What! Munsey Peters is a famous R.A. A regular exhibitor for fifteen years."

"What does that mean? Anything more deadly, more vulgar and stupid than his pictures I can't imagine."

Abruptly he broke off, sensing that they would think him envious and afraid. Then, as he turned away, he heard the sound of wheels and, through the window, saw the station fly draw up at the front door. A short man, made shorter by a broad-brimmed black sombrero and a black Inverness cape, descended briskly from the cab, surveyed the scene and rang the bell. Bertram rose and, followed by his wife and Caroline, went into the hall. Stephen remained seated at the table, only too well aware now of how prearranged was the situation. Peters, from his attire alone, was not visiting in the country but commissioned, no doubt at a fee—had come specially from London like a surgeon called to see a patient dangerously ill, his diagnosis a matter of life or death.

A reassuring touch on his shoulder recalled him. It was Davie.

"Hadn't we better go in now? Don't worry, Stephen, I'll bet you come out on top."

In the drawing-room, originally built as a square parlour and subsequently made ugly by a Victorian bay window thrown out on the west side, Munsey Peters was seated on the sofa, plump, smooth-cheeked, briskly officious, already the centre of an intelligent audience.

As Stephen entered he swung round, extended an amiable hand.

"So this is our young gentleman. Pleased to meet you, sir."

Stephen shook hands, telling himself, despite the conflict of emotions in his breast, that he must entertain no rancour towards this unwelcome visitor, who no doubt was an honest and estimable person acting in perfect good faith. Yet knowing Peters's work, which always received prominence in the press and was often reproduced in the better weekly periodicals, those woolly landscapes and bituminous interiors, reeking with sentiment and full of that chiaroscuro which Glyn had profanely described as burnt sienna and *merde*, Stephen could not repress an instinctive aversion, enhanced rather than diminished by the little man's smug appearance and assured manner which, while somewhat less than assertive, was odiously self-

70

satisfied. He had refused lunch, having "satisfied the inner man"—his actual phrase—in the Pullman dining-car which was always attached to the noon express, but on being pressed, consented to take coffee. And, balancing the cup upon his knee, bespatted boots crossed, he directed towards Stephen a series of agreeable inquiries such as a distinguished academician might employ in putting a nervous neophyte at ease.

"So you've been in Paree, eh?"

"Yes, just under a year."

"Working hard, I hope, in the gay city." This with a glance of veiled humour towards the others; then, as Stephen did not answer: "Who did you study under?"

"In the beginning—Dupret."

"Ah! What does he think of you?"

"I really don't know. I left him after a few weeks."

"Tut, tut! That was a mistake." In a puzzled tone: "D'you mean you've been mostly on your own? You can't have picked up much that way."

"At least I have learned how much will-power, discipline and intense application are necessary to make a good artist."

"Hmph! That's all very fine. But what about being taught?" The chill in Stephen's voice was provoking. "There are certain essentials. I've stressed them over and over again in my book. I daresay you've studied it."

"I'm afraid not. I've been studying at the Louvre."

"Oh, copying," Peters exclaimed crossly. "That's no good. An artist wants to be original above all things."

"Yet all the great artists have influenced one another," Stephen argued flatly. "Raphael derives from Perugino, El Greco from Tintoretto, Manet from Franz Hals. The Post-Impressionists all helped one another. One could continue the list indefinitely. Why, if you will forgive me, one sees traces in your own work of Leighton and Poynter."

The mention of these two artists, so famous in the Victorian era, now forgotten, brought to the face of Munsey Peters a mixed expression, as though he scarcely knew whether praise or insult were intended.

Mrs. Desmonde, for once tactful, broke the silence.

"Let me give you more coffee."

"No thank you. No." He handed over his cup. "In point of fact I am pressed for time, I have kept my conveyance waiting. Shall we proceed to the serious business of the day?"

"By all means." Bertram, an apprehensive observer of this clash of temperaments, gave a sign to Davie, who immediately jumped up and left the room. Almost at once he returned carrying the first picture, a view of the Seine at Passy, which he set up against a high-backed chair already placed in a good light opposite the sofa.

Imposing silence with a finger to his lips, Munsey Peters adjusted his pince-nez. He studied the painting intently and at length, leaning forward, inclining his head to various angles; then, dramatically, he made a gesture to Davie, who removed it, placed it by the window, and brought in the next. For Stephen, standing in the background with a wooden expression and a painfully thudding heart, it was an excruciating experience, a raw exposure of his delicate sensibilities. He looked round the domestic circle—his father, seated stiffly erect with finger-tips pressed together, legs crossed, one foot swinging in nervous suspense; Caroline, on a low stool by the sofa, a frown of concern furrowing her brow, staring now at Peters, now at the floor; his mother, dreamily comfortable in an armchair, perfectly detached; and David, in his stiff clean collar and dark grey school suit, his hair brushed back, eyes shining, not quite comprehending the issues, yet full of confidence that his brother would be justified.

It was over at last, the final picture shown.

"Well?" exclaimed Bertram.

Munsey Peters did not immediately reply, but rising, made a further survey of the paintings arranged against the oval sill of the bay window, as though to remove any impression that his judgement was hurried or unconsidered. One canvas in particular, the woman at her clothes line, seemed especially to disturb him; time and again, almost stealthily, his eye came back to its bold contrasts and vivid colours. In the end he let fall his pince-nez, secured by a watered silk ribbon, took his stance on the hearth-rug.

"What do you wish me to tell you?"

Bertram drew a sharp breath.

"Has my son any chance of becoming a painter . . . shall I say . . . the first rank?"

"None."

There was a dead silence. Impulsively Caroline threw a glance of sympathy towards her brother. The Rector bowed his head. Stephen, with the shadow of a smile, continued to look straight at Munsy Peters.

"Of course," he now resumed, "I could be polite. But I have

gathered that you want the truth. And in these canvases, which while they have, perhaps, a certain crude *brio*, completely ignore our great traditions of painting, traditions of propriety and restraint, I find only . . ." he shrugged his shoulders . . . "a matter for condolence and regret."

"Then," said Bertram slowly, as though determined to be convinced, "if they were . . . for example . . . submitted to the Academy, you think they would be rejected?"

"My dear sir, as a member of the hanging committee, I do not think. I am sure. Believe me, it pains me to extinguish your hopes. If your son wishes to continue this as a hobby . . . a pastime . . . that is a matter for himself. But professionally . . . ah, my dear sir, painting is, to us who live by it, a cruel art. It has no place for failures."

Compassionately, Bertram stole a glance at his son as though expecting him to protest, at least to offer some defence of his work. But Stephen, with that same shadowy smile, that air of proud indifference, kept silent.

"And now, if you will excuse me," said Peters, bowing.

The Rector got to his feet.

"We are very grateful to you . . . even though your verdict has been unfavourable."

Again Munsey Peters bowed and, as he left the room in a grave and polished manner, he accepted nimbly, yet without appearing to see it, the envelope which Bertram, after a murmured apologetic word, slipped into his hand—a transaction accomplished with such dexterity no one seemed to notice it but Stephen. Presently came the sound of a wheezy vehicle. The professor had gone.

As though to spare the others, rather than himself, embarrassment, Stephen went outside. And there, pacing up and down, bareheaded, was the Rector. Immediately Bertram took his son's arm, a sympathetic pressure, and after traversing the flagstones several times remarked:

"I have to go to the vestry. Will you walk with me?"

As they went up the lane together Bertram continued, sombrely, without a trace of self-justification:

"Stephen, that was a painful experience for you and, in no less degree, for all of us. But it was imperative for me to know the truth. I hope you do not reproach me."

"Of course not." The calmness of his son's voice caused Bertram a sharp surprise, followed by a feeling of rebuff.

"You take well it, Stephen—like a true Desmonde. I feared you might feel angered at me for having thrust this test upon you without warning. But then, if I had told you beforehand, you might have refused . . ."

"Yes, I think I should."

"You do realize that there was no question of undue influence, that Munsey Peters's opinion was completely his own?"

"I'm sure of it. I daresay our little argument at the outset ruffled his plumage slightly. But there's not the faintest doubt—he hated my paintings like poison."

"Ah," murmured the Rector condolingly. "Poor boy."

They had now reached the church and, pausing in the chancel, outside the vestry door, Bertram rested his hand upon the effigy of the crusader, a familiar gesture of support, and faced his son.

"At least the way is now clear . . . and there is nothing to prevent your returning to take orders. I don't mean to press you. There is the bar—the services if you wish. Nevertheless"—he gazed around —"your true place is here, Stephen."

A barely perceptible pause.

"I'm afraid you don't understand. I am not giving up my painting."

"What on earth do you mean?"

"Simply that I have made up my mind, irrevocably, to devote my life entirely to art."

"But you've just had the opinion . . . utterly damning . . . of an expert."

"That idiotic nonentity . . . eaten up by secret grudges! The fact that he vilified my work was the highest compliment he could pay it."

"Are you mad?" Anger and dismay brought the blood to Bertram's brow. "He is one of the best painters in Britain and might even be the next president of the Academy."

"You don't understand, Father." Despite the tensity of his features, Stephen almost smiled. "Peters cannot paint for little apples. His work is conventional, sentimental, and without a trace of originality. He's only succeeded through a crashing mediocrity. Why, even that old fake Dupret, with his *peinture léchée*, was more tolerable. Weren't you disgusted by his frightful clichés, his affectations, his podgy little hands? He runs with the herd. The true artist can only fulfil his destiny alone."

During this speech, which struck him as mere ranting, Bertram's face had gradually hardened. He steeled himself against the pain in his breast, and an overwhelming longing to take his son in his arms.

"To any normal person the evidence is plain. You must accept it."

"No."

"I insist."

"I have a right to my own life."

"Not if you are bent on ruining it."

Neither of them raised his voice. The Rector was very pale but his eyes never left his son's face. Beneath his agitation there was a firmness Stephen had never seen before.

"In common justice, do you not owe me some return for all that I have done for you? No doubt you affect to despise anything so sordid as money. Yet I have devoted to your education—the finest any son could wish for—an amount of capital which I could barely afford. We are much less well off than we were, and it is with difficulty that I maintain at Stillwater the standards to which we are accustomed. I had hoped all along that this step would be unnecessary. Nevertheless, for your own sake I must bring you to your senses. Your allowance is stopped, as of this hour. And I fear you will find it impossible to continue without it."

A bar of silence throbbed in the little church. Stephen's gaze fell, dwelt for a long moment upon the stony effigy of his ancestor, who, in the half-light, seemed to smile cynically towards him. Gazing at the sword, the great mailed gauntlets, a phrase of his boyhood reading reoccurred to him: the iron hand in the velvet glove. He sighed.

"Well, Father, that would appear to settle it."

Bertram secured his day-book from the vestry—his hand shook so badly he could scarcely hold the volume and was obliged to press it against his side. They left the church in silence.

For the remainder of the afternoon Stephen was a model of complaisance, heartening the others by his liveliness and good spirits. At six o'clock he insisted on driving with Davie to the station, saw him to the train, sped him on his way with cheerful affection. Then, turning, with an altered look, he went to the cab rank, where the taxi-man had kept his bag, previously secreted amongst Davie's luggage. From the time-table pasted outside the booking-office he saw that a coastal train was due to leave in about an hour. He bought a ticket and set himself to wait.

PART TWO

CHAPTER I

DOVER, IN THE rain, was a mean back-door through which to steal away from England. As the cross-Channel packet left the grimy harbour, muddy streets, yellow hillside buildings, putty-coloured cliffs alike were merged in the greyish deluge.

In the steerage the limited space below was densely crowded, and Stephen, turning from an air thickened by damp and noisy good-fellowship, regained the dripping, rope-encumbered deck. He stood solitary in the bows, sheltering, as best he could behind a tarpaulin-covered winch, his eyes on the amorphous shore, his thoughts so balanced between bitterness and sadness as to fix him in an attitude of utter immobility.

Presently he moved and, seating himself on an arm of the winch, unmindful of the heaving of the ship, of the wind and spray which whistled past this slight protection, took his sketch-book from his pocket. The movement was reflex, an outcry from the heart. Yet once his pencil had begun to travel over pages whipped at their edges by the gale, he lost himself, drew, with great rapidity, phases of the agitated sea, waves strange and ominous, which he imbued with a quality of life, seeing in their fretted contours, in the lashing intricacies of their crests, wild human faces, tormented heads and writhing torsos, the figures of men and monsters, with streaming hair and straining limbs, all lost and swept away by the unconquerable forces of the sea.

It was perhaps a kind of madness, a vertigo which left Stephen limp and spent. He shivered as the steamer slackened its plunging motion to edge warily into the arms of the Calais breakwater and, conscious of his streaming face and sodden clothing, pocketed the sketch-book with a furtive air. Ropes were thrown, gangways rolled, the *douane* was quickly passed. But some slight mishap on the line had held back the Paris train—it had not yet arrived.

Stephen shivered again as, stamping up and down the platform, he strove to restore his circulation. Although the rain was less relentless on the land, the breeze, scouring down the curving tracks, seemed sharper, more cutting than before. Most of his fellow passengers were making use of the delay by taking the à la carte luncheon in the station restaurant. But, faced by a future of sheer uncertainty, a closer view of the state of his finances held him from this luxury. He had, to be precise, five pounds nine shillings remaining from the original ten pounds which had been in his possession when he arrived at Stillwater.

At last the train steamed in and, after many conferences and much gesticulation, shrill whistling, crescendos of steam, and the melodious notes of a horn, the engine was reversed, steamed out again. For Stephen, huddled in the corner of a draughty compartment, it was a wretched journey. He shivered repeatedly, knew that he had caught a chill, and blamed himself for a fool.

At the Gare du Nord he hesitated, then on an off-chance, and not without a melancholy recollection of his previous light-hearted entry of the city, he took the Métro to the Rue Castel. In his present mood he longed, above all, for the simplicities and sustaining friendship of Peyrat. But the new tenant of the apartment, uncomprehending and suspicious, appeared at the door, answering that there were no letters, no messages . . . he believed Monsieur Peyrat would be at Puy de Dôme in the Auvergne till the end of the year, beyond that he knew nothing.

Stephen's next steps bore him to Glyn's studio. It was closed. Similarly, the Lamberts' pavilion provided, with its shuttered windows, a further disappointment. In desperation, Stephen turned to Chester's lodgings. Although he had kept no exact record of the debt, he knew that Harry, through repeated borrowings must own him at least thirty pounds, a sum which now assumed a significance far greater than before. But this room, too, was closed, secured, in fact, by a padlock. However, as he descended the stairs, Stephen was recognized by the concierge and obtained from him Chester's forwarding address, sent on a picture postcard only two days before. It was the Hôtel du Loin d'Or, Netiers, Normandy.

Encouraged, Stephen entered the nearest *bureau de poste* and sent off a telegram, explaining his situation and requesting Chester to wire, if not all, at least part of the money to him at once, in care of Alphonse Bisque in the Rue Castel. When the alpaca-clad young woman behind the grill had achieved, in ink, a complicated addition, a process which occupied her for several minutes, Stephen paid the charge and made his way to a neighbouring Duval's where he ordered hot chocolate and a brioche.

After this light meal, as the rain had come on heavier and the gutters were awash with mud, he decided to find, as quickly as possible, a lodging for the night. Because of its convenience rather than the hope of comfort, he put up at a cheap hotel nearby, the Pension de l'Ouest, which he had often passed on his way to and from Glyn's studio.

Reached by uncarpeted stairs, his room was no more than a narrow cubicle, but it was dry, and the bed, though its linen showed grey, had an ample supply of blue-stamped blankets—those coarse coverings used by the conscripts during army manœuvres and sold thereafter by the government contractors. After some preliminary rigors, he warmed up, and slept heavily. Indeed, when he awoke next morning he felt better, although he was not surprised to find himself with an aggravating cough. He breakfasted on coffee and a roll, again at Duval's, then, at eleven o'clock, made his way towards the shop of Monsieur Bisque.

Here an agreeable surprise awaited him. The pastrycook received him with cordiality, his full moon-face wreathed in smiles, and having chided Stephen for failing to visit him on the previous day, produced with the air of a conjurer Chester's answering telegram. This, though it conveyed no actual cash, was of a nature to enliven its recipient.

DELIGHTED HAVE YOUR WIRE. JOIN ME HERE. WEATHER AND HOTEL EXCELLENT. FINE PAINTING COUNTRY. BEST RE-GARDS.

HARRY

The prospect opened by this friendly invitation, the thought of standing with palette and brushes, before an easel, in the Norman sunshine, brightened Stephen's eyes.

Bisque had a time-table which, though its tattered sheets were rather ancient, seemed to prove that the Granville *rapide*, the one train of any directness, had already departed—at ten o'clock, to be exact, that morning. And as the worthy pastrycook was pressing in his hospitality, Stephen decided to postpone his journey until the following day. He spent the afternoon at Napoleon Campo's, where, in addition to reclaiming his easel and stored equipment, he purchased varnish, new tubes of colour and a number of fresh canvases. On these he made a down payment of fifty francs, promising Campo that he would remit the balance whenever he arrived at Netiers.

Next morning brought a clear blue sky and Stephen set forth with his belongings for the Gare Montparnasse. The *rapide* on Quai 2 was not crowded and he secured an empty compartment in the front section of carriages without difficulty. He could not say that he felt well as they started off, for his head was stuffy and he had a sharp stitch in his right side. Nevertheless, once the train had bored its way through the tunnels and dark walled cuttings that gave egress from the city, he lost his lassitude in watching the flitting landscape: vast fields of yellow stubble holding pools of rain-water, flanked by long lines of poplars—interminable sentinels; a distant spire, slender, graceful; teams of great horses, with attendant crows, dragging upon the plough; old farm buildings, ochre-tiled, the gables splashed with enamelled signs—Byrrh, Cinzano, Dubonnet.

At noon he ate an apple and a slab of chocolate. Gradually the complexion of the countryside had altered. Struggling against drowsiness, he noted with deepening pleasure the winding lanes and small hedged orchards, a draggle of geese in slow procession towards a muddy pond followed by a bare-legged girl with a hazel switch, a row of willows close pollarded, then an aged dame tending one cow by the roadside grass, standing the while, white-coifed, to knit. Even the nature of the drink was changed. *Attendez*, cried the signs, *buvez le cidre moissoné!*

Towards three o'clock the train reached the summit of a long incline and ran into the little station of Netiers. Hastily, Stephen collected his things and jumped from the high footboard. A quick survey showed that Chester was not on hand to meet him. Reasoning that Harry could not well have foretold the time of his arrival, Stephen began to walk in the direction of the town, which could be seen further down the hill, about a kilometre away. The prospect, as he drew near, increased his eagerness—he passed a moated wall with fortifications, entered crooked cobbled streets so narrow the sharp-pitched greystone houses seemed to meet above his head. Then, in the heart of the market-place, opposite the faded terra-cotta façade of the ancient *hôtel de ville*, he discerned the gilded sign of the Lion d'Or.

The inn was massive, solidly comfortable, of an excellent class. Stephen took this in at a glance as he made his way to the reception desk situated in the alcove underneath the oaken staircase.

"Yes, Monsieur?"

"My name is Desmonde. Will you be kind enough to let Mr. Chester know that I have arrived?"

A pause.

"You are calling upon Monsieur Chester?"

"Yes. He is expecting me."

The clerk, a high-shouldered young man with a cropped head, studied Stephen for a moment, then said:

"Have the goodness to wait, sir."

He disappeared behind the curtain which shrouded the back of the *bureau*; then, after a short interval, returned with an older man, a substantial, thick-necked figure attired in a striped business suit.

"You are seeking Monsieur Harry Chester?" The tone, though polite, had a formidable quality.

"Why, yes. I am his friend. Is he not staying here?"

A chilly pause.

"He *was* residing here, Monsieur. Until yesterday afternoon, when we presented his bill. Since that time we have seen nothing of your famous Monsieur Chester."

Stephen gazed at the proprietor, stupefied. Had he not come, expressly at Harry's invitation, spending his last sou upon the railway fare? Then a thought struck him, crushing as a blow. Chester, once again in financial straits, had asked him down solely in the hope of borrowing a further sum.

"If Monsieur is indeed Monsieur Desmonde"—the sarcasm was cutting—"here is a letter his friend has left for him."

An envelope was tossed, like something obscene, across the counter. It had been opened.

DEAR OLD BOY,

They may not give you this. If they do, it will let you know, with my regrets, that I have been obliged, *encore*, to shoot the moon, I thought we might make a go of it together —on the principle that two heads are better than one—but the bookkeeping department here got just one step ahead of me. I'll probably bum my way South, stay in Nice for a while, try my luck at the tables. At any rate I shall certainly see you sooner or later. Frightfully sorry and all that . . . but needs must when the devil drives.

Yours,

HARRY

P.S. No decent women in the town. But don't fail to sample the local cider. Quite excellent.

Stephen crushed the note, hastily scrawled in pencil, between his tense fingers. He had known that Chester was unreliable, but now, beneath the charm, the gaiety, the effusive friendliness, he sensed the core of utter selfishness.

The innkeeper and his clerk were looking at him from behind the barrier with unconcealed contempt. Then came the final insolence.

"Of course Monsieur realizes, without asking, that we have no accommodation for him here."

"Quite," said Stephen, and swinging round, he went out into the street.

CHAPTER II

STANDING THERE, PENNILESS and alone in the market-place of this strange French town, Stephen became disquietingly aware of his situation. Never before had he been without money. His allowance, like the coming of the dawn, was something which he took for granted, the natural consequence of his position in society, in fact his birthright. Now, with a bitter twist of his lips, he perceived how powerful was the weapon his father had used. Nevertheless, his native obduracy stood him in good stead. He set out, at once, to find some temporary shelter.

This, in a town much patronized by tourists, was less difficult than he had feared, and before the afternoon was far advanced he was installed in a little top room in a back courtyard of the Rue de la Cathédrale. As he had baggage the landlady, a decent elderly woman, made no advance demand upon him and, since the rent was only twelve francs a week, he resolved, come what may, that he would place himself in a position to satisfy her before many hours had passed. He had wisdom enough to know that he could not, in this locality, gain an immediate livelihood by his art. Yet his education, his university training and bachelor's degree, must surely fit him for some modest position wherein he could earn sufficient money to set him on his feet. Why, might he not even save enough to discharge Chester's bill—the inn proprietor's final shaft still rankled—and return to Paris, join Peyrat there, with a comfortable sum, before the winter. If only he felt less confoundedly seedy! This cough which, since the Channel crossing, had settled in his chest was a great nuisance. But a fierce desire to prove himself sent him out again to the centre of the town.

Here he made a prospective survey of the main thoroughfare, the Rue de la République. Most of the shops, though small, had that look of solid prosperity associated with a thriving agricultural district. Spades, and hayforks, scythes, zinc buckets, a red-toothed harrow, all these and more were ranged in the hardware store; there were niceties, too—delicious *petits fours* and sugar almonds, contrived like bridal bouquets, adorned the window of a trim *pâtisserie*; while in the corner creamery a great mound of Norman butter stood yellow on its china slab flanked by two brimming bowls of milk.

Outside a stationer's, he saw displayed, on cards in a glass case, a number of advertisements written out in ink. Carefully, he read them through, then turned away. He could not tune pianos or mend basket chairs, had no need of a seaside semi-villa on the cliffs at Granville. Further down the street he came upon the office of a weekly journal, *Courier de Netiers*. Within, the current number was available for inspection. But its meagre columns, devoted mainly to the phases of the moon, the sale of lime and livestock, the servicing of cows and mares, the times of the tides at Mont St. Michel, offered him nothing.

What next? Clearly he must ask advice. On an impulse, he entered the *mairie*, and selecting a clerk with a sympathetic air, sounded him discreetly on the possibilities of employment in the town. The youth, though startled by this inquiry, was well-meaning and intelligent. He thought deeply, then slowly shook his head.

"It is very difficult . . . in a small community like this, the people . . ." he smiled, deprecatingly, straightened his paper cuffs . . . "are not amiable to strangers."

For another hour, Stephen combed the town without success. As night fell he returned, tired and discouraged, to his lodging. Searching in his pockets he counted up the sum of his resources—one franc, fifteen sous. The sight of these few miserable coins resting in the palm of his hand sent a wave of pride over him. He could not, he must not surrender.

Next day, in the hope of finding manual employment, he made a tour, on foot, of the neighbouring farms. Altogether he must have tramped a distance of twenty kilometres. And in vain. There was no scarcity of agricultural labour. At several places he was taken for a tramp and the dogs were set upon him. One charitable country-man forking hay in the yard seemed to hesitate, moved perhaps by the intensity of Stephen's appeal, but in the end his Norman hard-headedness prevailed. He made a gesture of refusal.

"You are not strong enough, *mon petit*; small . . . oh, altogether too small. But wait." He called into the kitchen. "Jeanne, bring this lad a bite to eat."

A comely woman with red, bare arms clattered to the back door in wooden clogs. Presently, having surveyed Stephen, she brought him a hunk of pasty and a mug of cider. As he ate this repast, seated on a low milking-stool beside the porch, the farmer and his wife, watching together, discussed him in low tones, while a small boy in a black pinafore peered at him curiously from behind his mother's skirts. Stephen was paralysed with shame. Oh my God, he kept groaning to himself, I'm exactly like someone in a Cotman print . . . have I actually come to that! But the pie was good, with rich strong gravy, and the sour still drink put new heart in him for his long walk back to Netiers.

It was dusk when he reached the Rue de la Cathédrale. And now, though he had kept his spirits up well enough throughout the day, a frightful despondency fell upon him. The deadly strangeness of this narrow little room, smelling of old wood, mildew and camphor, creaking at his every step; the sense of being so utterly alone, deceived by Chester, trapped in a hopeless future; the suspicion, too, that his landlady had begun to regard him with dubiety—all this rose up and overcame him. Without warning he flung himself upon the bed and, turning his face to the whitewashed wall, cried like a child.

The bout was over soon, but unluckily it had started off his cough. Throughout the night it troubled him severely, since in his anxiety to avoid disturbing the household, he suppressed the spasms and so increased their frequency. At last, towards dawn, with his head beneath the covers, he fell asleep.

It was late, nearly eleven o'clock in the forenoon, when he awoke —first to a brief moment of restful brightness, then to the dulling consciousness of his predicament. He got up, dressed without shaving, and went into the town. The agitation of his mind imparted a queer weakness to his legs. He was walking without purpose or objective. Suddenly, as he began, for the second time to traverse the market square, he heard someone running after him. Then a hand was laid on his own. He started almost out of his skin and swung round. It was the clerk from the *mairie*.

"Excuse me, Monsieur." The young man paused for breath. "I have been watching for you during all my lunch hour. You see, since our meeting, I have made some inquiries on your behalf. And Madame Cruchot who with her husband keeps the *épicerie* there," he pointed across the street, "has two little daughters whom she wishes to be taught English. It is possible you might suit her. In any case, it is worth your while to try."

"Thank you," Stephen stammered, overcome. "Thank you very much."

The young clerk smiled.

"Good luck." He pronounced the words between his teeth, carefully, in English, then, as though pleased by this achievement, he shook hands, raised his hat, and stood watching as Stephen hurried across the street.

The Cruchot grocery, occupying a prominent position in the square, with double plate-glass windows and a glittering sign-board which read ALIMENTATION DE RENNES, gave every indication of a prosperous establishment dealing in a large and tempting assortment of foods. A constant stream of customers passed in and out of the doorway, narrowed by hanging hams, nets of lemons, a tree of bananas and various baskets of choice vegetables. Inside, the shelves were heavily stocked with the generous produce of land and sea, with sausages and goose liver, sardines and anchovies, lard, olive oil, cheese, with fruits in syrup, old brandy too, cordials and wines, coffee, spices, tripe and trotters, the bowls and bottles glittering upwards in shiny pinnacles above the sawdust-strewn floor.

Entering, Stephen was held back less by his own nervousness than by the noise and movement, the shouted orders, the bustling of two white-coated assistants: a heavy-shouldered Norman girl and a lame, harassed-looking man.

It was not long, however, before he felt himself singled out by a voice of penetrating timbre.

"M'sieur desires?"

Presiding at a small desk, controlling the commotion, it seemed, by the fullness of her bosom and the boldness of her eye, there stood a yellow-haired woman of thirty-eight with a curved, well-covered figure, smooth complexion, and pink ears supporting heavy gold drop earrings. She wore a mauve dress of the latest provincial fashion—inset at the neck with a square of lace—several rings and bangles, a large cameo brooch.

"I beg your pardon." Edging forward, Stephen spoke in a low voice. "My name is Desmonde. I understand you might require an English tutor for your children."

Realization that he was not a customer had driven the mechanical smile from Madame Cruchot's lips; her eyes narrowed with the cold appraisal of one who, in the market, could gauge to a hair's-breadth the weight and quality of a grunting porker as she inspected Stephen. But the word "tutor", which by good fortune he had used, flattered the vanity that ranked high amongst the many strong characteristics she possessed, which was indeed the main motive behind the notion that her two little daughters should be taught the English tongue. Also this young man before her looked personable, "refined", and diffident enough to give no trouble.

"M'sieur can offer me some account of himself?"

Quite frankly, Stephen did so.

"So M'sieur is a student of the college of Oxford." A gleam illuminated Madame's china-blue eye, but in the interests of bargaining was quickly concealed. Doubtingly, she shrugged. "Of course we have only M'sieur's word for that."

"I assure you . . ."

"Oh, la, la . . . I am prepared to trust you, M'sieur. But naturally, considering the tender years of my little ones, I demand the highest standards of conduct and morality."

"Naturally, Madame."

"Then what . . ." She broke off, in a shrill command, her words rattling out with the sound and fury of a salvo of small artillery. "No, no, Marie, not these eggs, stupid, they are already commanded by Madame Oulard . . . and Joseph, must I always tell you to take the sugar from the open sack? What salary would you require, M'sieur?"

Hurriedly Stephen tried to calculate the barest stipend which would support him.

"Should we say, with daily lessons, thirty francs a week?"

With a gesture of dismay, Madame Cruchot raised her plump, ringed hands. Then she smiled gently, flashing a gold tooth at him like a bullet.

"M'sieur amuses himself."

"No, really . . ." Nudged and elbowed by the milling crowd, Stephen turned a dark red. "I am quite serious."

"We are honest people, Monsieur Cruchot and I, M'sieur, but far, oh, very far from rich." She touched a note of pathos. "The utmost my husband empowers me to offer is twenty francs."

"But Madame . . . I am obliged to live."

Madame Cruchot shook her yellow chignon sadly.

"We too, M'sieur."

Stephen bit his lip, rage and pride swelling in his heart. The weekly rent of his room was twelve francs. How on earth could he keep himself on the eight francs that would remain after he had settled with his landlady? No, whatever his extremity, he could not submit to such an imposition. He half turned to take his leave. But Madame Cruchot, who did not wish to lose him and who, in the interval, had from the corner of her eye probed him through and through, arrested him with a delicate gesture.

"Perhaps . . ." She leaned forward, spoke with an air of solicitude. "Perhaps if luncheon were provided here for M'sieur it might somewhat aid the situation. A good, substantial repast."

Brought up short, Stephen hesitated. Abased beyond endurance, he could not lift his eyes. He muttered:

"Very well . . . I accept."

"Good. Our bargain is made. You will start tomorrow. Come at eleven o'clock. Do not forget that I shall require instruction of the highest class. And doubtless in future M'sieur will not neglect to shave."

Stephen inclined his head. He could not speak. Yet despite his humiliation, ignominious though his position might be, he could not but experience a sensation of relief. With twenty francs and a daily lunch, for the time being at least he was saved.

As he left the shop he heard Madame Cruchot's voice loudly proclaiming to the regions in the rear.

"Marie-Louise . . . Victorine. . . . Your kind Mamma has just engaged an English tutor."

CHAPTER III

Now, in the stifling dullness of this small provincial town, there began for Stephen a strange existence. Every morning he was awakened by the great bell of the cathedral, which swung thrice, heavily, at the Elevation of the seven o'clock Mass, sending the pigeons flying, breaking the ecclesiastical silence of the empty cobbled square. When dressed he clattered downstairs—at least he could leave the house without fear of meeting his landlady. Crossing the square to the Café des Ouvriers, which stood a stone's throw from the high-walled convent garden, he encountered always the same scattering of pious black-garbed women, and a few nuns, in pairs, emerging—floating, it seemed, upon the wide wings of their wimples —from the church. The café, marked by a withered branch of box above the lintel, was not an especially reputable place, no more than the stone-flagged kitchen of a low dwelling furnished with a rough table and some backless wooden benches. Here for five sous he took the usual breakfast of the house: a cup of black coffee full of grounds, chased down by a tot of white wine served in inch-thick glass, a combination amazing in its restorative power. Often there was a paper of the night before, *Intelligence de Rennes*, which kept him occupied for half an hour. Or he might talk for a while with Julie, the quiet, dark-eyed *fille de comptoir* who served the primitive bar with discretion and who had apparently other functions of obligement, or with another of the customers, perhaps a travelling packman, a railway porter, or a man delivering charcoal.

Punctually at eleven he presented himself at the Cruchot home, situated behind the shop, and approached by a walled side door. Here, in the trellised arbour which adjoined the enclosed patch of lawn, or, on wet days, in the stiffly ornate room referred to by Madame as the "salon", Stephen gave his attention to the little Cruchot girls: to Victorine, aged eleven, and Marie-Louise, who was only nine.

They were, on the whole, not disagreeable children, a trifle spoiled, but with all the attraction of their tender years. Sometimes, indeed, they were very sweet in their ways, especially the younger, a pretty little thing with brown curls and apple-red cheeks. Stephen did not find them difficult to manage and soon grew fond of them. Yet already the parental attributes were manifest—they knew the price of everything, figured like mathematicians, could glibly recite moral aphorisms on the virtue of thrift. Each kept a small metal savings bank, shaped like the Eiffel Tower but actually a cash register, of which the key was worn adjacent to a holy medal on a ribbon around the neck. Often they would repeat, quite innocently, remarks which they had overheard.

"Monsieur Stephen"—he had insisted they call him by his Christian name—"Mama said to Papa that you must be extremely poor."

"Well, Victorine, I must confess she was right."

"But Papa said at least you were not a drunkard."

"Good. . . . Papa is my friend."

"Ah, yes, Monsieur Stephen. For he also said that although you had certainly done some wrong at home and run away, it was not likely to be a serious crime."

Stephen laughed, somewhat wryly.

"Come along then . . . it is time to commence our reading."

So rapid had been the progress of their agile little minds that he had actually brought them on to *Alice in Wonderland*, and their interest in the story was making even the hard words possible.

Monsieur Cruchot, though occasionally in a proprietary fashion he put his head round the door, did not come often to the lessons. He was a man of medium size, with a restless manner, darting coffee-coloured eyes, the corners injected with yellow, and a heavy, black, up-curled moustache, who wore spats and, without and within, except in the sacred precincts of the salon, a hard, shiny straw hat. His place, of course, was in the shop, but two days a week he spent buying in the market at the neighbouring city of Rennes, whence, indeed, both he and his wife had originally come. Linked to Madame by an ostensible felicity, by the two pretty tokens of her affection, and above all by their mutually passionate desire for gain, Albert Cruchot had nevertheless an air, at certain moments, as if the physical proportions of his spouse, her shrill laugh and penetrating voice, were an oppression greater than a man of his stature could reasonably sustain. He did not shrink exactly, yet his bespatted feet would move uneasily and in the pupil of his *café-au-lait* eye there flickered a restive gleam.

In plain truth, behind her smile, her amiable attitudes and the specious glitter of her gold tooth, Madame Cruchot was a bully. Every day she came to witness "for herself" the conduct of the lesson, sitting erect, in a posture of supervision, her eyes uncomprehending yet alert, travelling from Stephen to the children, upsetting them, causing them to make mistakes.

"You understand, M'sieur . . . I desire them not merely to read, but to speak colloquially . . . and to recite poetry . . . as one does in the best society."

In answer to her repeated demands Stephen taught the children the first stanza of *To a Skylark*. Then, on a day appointed to demonstrate his pupils' progress, Madame appeared with three of her intimates, wives of prominent shopkeepers, members of the *haute bourgeoisie* of Netiers, who arranged themselves expectantly on the factory-gilt chairs of the salon.

Marie-Louise, chosen first for the test, was placed alone on the island of fake Aubusson.

"*Hail to thee, blythe spirit! . . .*" she began, then stopped, glanced round, and suppressed a titter.

"Begin again, Marie-Louise," said Stephen in a kindly manner.

"*Hail to thee, blythe spirit! . . .*" Again the child broke down, blinked, twisted her sash, and glanced timidly at her mother.

"Go on," said Madame Cruchot in a strange voice.

Marie-Louise cast an imploring look at her teacher. A light sweat was breaking on Stephen's forehead. In a tone of cajolery which disgusted him he said:

"Come along, my dear. *Hail to thee, blythe spirit!*"

A brief silence, during which Madame Cruchot seemed turned to stone; then, without warning, she reached forward and slapped the child's cheek. Immediately Marie-Louise burst into tears. In the moment of consternation which followed, indignant glances were bent on Stephen, the sobbing child, now clasped to the maternal breast, was comforted with a praline, and Marie's voice was heard calling loudly from the shop.

"Come quickly, Madame . . . the liver is here from the slaughter-house."

In the confusion accompanying Madame Cruchot's departure Stephen stood helplessly, foreseeing with sardonic fatalism the possibility of his dismissal. Yet when her mother reappeared, Marie-Louise ran across the room, took hold of his hand and burst forth instantly with the poem, which she recited completely in a single breath. Victorine, not to be outdone, followed, of her own accord, with a perfect performance.

Immediately the complexion of the gathering changed, there were little cries of acclamation, smiles and nods were bestowed on Stephen, Madame Cruchot glowed with pardonable triumph. Indeed, after she had shown the ladies out, she came back to Stephen in a mood of odd indulgence. Instead of the usual thin slice of ham, she gave him for lunch a plate of hot meat ragout, garnished with carrots and Bordeaux onions. Then, seating herself opposite at the table in the pantry, she remarked:

"Things went well, after all."

"Yes." Stephen did not look up. "It was only stage fright at the beginning."

For a moment Madame Cruchot continued to watch him eat.

"My friends were much pleased with you," she said, suddenly. "Madame Oulard . . . she is the wife of our first *pharmacien*, a lady of some position in the town, though, naturally, she cannot afford a tutor for her children . . . considers you *très sympathique* . . . a most gentlemanly type."

"I'm very grateful for her good opinion."

"Did you think her a pretty woman?"

"Good gracious, no," said Stephen, absently. "I scarcely noticed her."

Madame Cruchot patted her pads of yellow hair, and having pulled down her corset, stroked her firm haunches with a conscious gesture.

"Let me get you more ragout."

In the days which followed, the quality and, indeed, the quantity of the English tutor's midday meal mysteriously improved, and in several other ways the mistress of the household continued to demonstrate her altered attitude, one might even say, her favour. It was a fortunate change for Stephen, upon whom lack of adequate nutrition and that persistent, harassing cough had wrought considerable physical damage. He began to feel stronger, new currents of life moving slowly in his veins, and as the weather was unusually fine, he experienced suddenly, one day, for the first time since his coming to Netiers, a burning desire to paint.

The impulse was irresistible and, on leaving for the grocery, he took with him a block of India paper and a handful of coloured chalks. When the lesson was almost over he set the two children to read from the same book, together, in the arbour, then with all the longing of a pent-up passion, with swift, sure, happy lines, he made a pastel of their heads. The thing was done quickly, so fierce was the inspiration—in a matter of less than half an hour. Never had he achieved anything so vivid, so fresh in its impressionistic composition. Even he, who always underrated his own work, was moved, startled, and excited by this lovely thing which had sprung to being, mysteriously, out of nothing, at his touch.

As with head to one side he sat pointing the background with a yellow crayon, he heard a sound behind him: Madame Cruchot, over his shoulder, was gazing at the pastel.

"Did you do that, M'sieur?"

Her expression of stunned incredulity made him smile.

"Do you like it?"

Perhaps she did not fully understand the picture. But she saw her two children there, beautifully suggested in a few lines, a few shades of pure and brilliant colour. She knew nothing of art. Yet her astute commercial instinct made her instantly, if subconsciously, aware that here was something rare and fine, something of the highest quality. Immediately she coveted it. But beyond that, she experienced a singular quickening of her feeling for this strange young Englishman, that emotion which had begun when, on the day of the recitation, the fog of her indifference had lifted and she had seen him, through the chatter of her friends, as he really was, a most attractive young man, with his slight figure and sensitive face, his dark eyes and delicate pallor. The little girls were still spelling out their book. She came round to the front of the settee and seated herself beside him.

"I did not understand"—she spoke in a confidential undertone—"that M'sieur was truly an artist."

"But I told you so when you engaged me."

At the mention of that first interview, when she had used him so sharply, a deep blush spread over her smooth complexion, extending beyond her round, solid chin into the column of her muscular neck.

"Ah," she said, lowering her eyes, "I did not greatly heed what was said at that time. I had not then the pleasure of knowing

M'sieur as I do now . . . after these weeks of pleasant intimacy, when he has taught my children, associated with me in my household, and always with that politeness and reserve which come only from true distinction. M'sieur Stephen . . ." it was the first time she had addressed him by his name and as she did so an extraordinary thrill made tense the skin of her substantial breasts . . . "even if you had told me nothing, I would know from this picture that you are highly gifted."

Her fulsome words were embarrassing, but he said pleasantly:

"Perhaps you would care to have it?"

The question, with its implications of purchase, made her withdraw slightly, but only for an instant. She answered earnestly:

"Yes, M'sieur Stephen, and I shall speak of it to my husband this evening. Of course it is possible he will argue that the work was done in the hour of teaching, for which you are already paid, in which case . . ."

"My dear Madame Cruchot," Stephen broke in hurriedly, "you completely misunderstand me. I offer you the picture as a gift."

Her eyes glistened, not, for once, from cupidity, but with a softer, a more confused emotion. She suppressed a sigh, gazed at him with tender meaning. "I accept, M'sieur Stephen. I assure you that you will not regret it."

The novelty of sitting so close to him was actually making her head swim, a sensation quite different from that afforded by the proximity of Cruchot. But the little girls were beginning to clamour for attention, she became afraid of committing herself further. With a sidelong glance, fleeting but intense, in which she tried, though vainly, to lay bare her fast-beating heart, she rose, bade him *au revoir*, and made her way back to the shop.

CHAPTER IV

AFTER WEEKS OF clouded apathy, Stephen found that he could paint again. It was like awakening to a new life wherein he discovered himself possessed of greater power, more discerning vision than before. The little town, with its drab inhabitants, hitherto a desert of sterility, became suddenly transfigured, a teeming source of inspiration. He painted the *hôtel de ville*; the parade-ground of the barracks; a view of the rooftops of the town, seen from his window, strangely effective; a lovely composition in grey and black of the convent sisters returning in the rain beneath umbrellas from their Mass. The canvases he had bought from Napoleon Campo were one by one transformed, stacked in the corner of his attic bedroom.

There were letters too, from Peyrat and Glyn, to cheer him. Jerome proposed to remain in Puy de Dôme for the winter and Glyn would return to London for a brief stay in the autumn. Both pressed him to join them. But of course he could not. He was painting here, and happy. In this state of resurrection, the daily lesson to the Cruchot children lapsed to its normal perspective of necessity. Often, indeed, Stephen found it a considerable trial to lay aside his brushes and hurry off to the grocery just when the light was at its best. And although, in the idiom of the establishment, he continued to give value, his mind was not wholly upon his teaching, nor after the instruction was he actuated by any other thought that that of getting away.

Because of this abstraction he remained more or less oblivious to the changes, ever growing, in Madame Cruchot's attitude towards him. The vast improvement in the cuisine was, naturally, apparent, but he put it down to his employer's gratitude for the present of the picture. To this also did he attribute those other marks of attention which were bestowed upon him. It had now become Madame's custom to preside at his luncheon and to press her hospitality upon him. Indeed, her devotion went further.

"M'sieur Stephen," she reflected one day, in an accent of solicitude, "I am concerned about your comfort. You cannot be well looked after at Madame Clouet's."

"Oh, I am," he answered. "She's a very decent soul."

"But it is such a poor room."

"Do you know it?"—in surprise.

"Well," she blushed, "I have passed it outside many times . . . on my way to church, of course. If only someone of taste were to add a few things . . . and arrange them for you, how much more agreeable it would be for you."

"No, really," he smiled. "It suits me as it is . . . bare and airy."

"But that is not good for you," she persisted. "I cannot but notice that your cough still troubles you."

"Oh, it's nothing . . . I only get it in the morning."

"My dear M'sieur Stephen." She gazed at him with tender reproach. "Do not obstruct me at every turn. If I cannot come to improve your room at least let me restore your health."

Next day, to his embarrassment, a bottle of *sirop pectoral* from the establishment of Monsieur Oulard stood upon the table beside his plate and Madame, measuring a tablespoonful, administered the dose with her own hands. Victorine and Marie-Louise were much amused that their teacher should be made to swallow physic. And, in the end, Stephen laughed too.

When the children had run into the garden to play, Madame Cruchot, after a lingering glance, emitted a sigh.

"Of course . . . one thing is quite apparent to me. . . . You have found in the town some wretched girl who attracts you."

"What!" he exclaimed. "In Netiers!"

"Why not? Don't you go every day to the Café des Ouvriers and that Julie Grosette . . . they are not altogether above board there, I can tell you . . ." She did indeed know all the gossip, slanders, and petty intrigues of the little town. But his look of astonishment was so acute it drew her up short. She forced a laugh. "Do not gaze at me like that, my friend. I am thinking only of your welfare. And after all, though I am a good woman, I am also a woman of the world. So you have no one?"

"No," he said shortly.

The look of suspense, of jealousy, faded from her eye and was replaced by an air of coquetry.

"Tell me, do you like my dress?"

She postured slightly from the hips, displaying her new gown, of a somewhat startling green, with a yellow braid, worn low, which gave an effect of youthfulness. And her hair, freshly bleached, had been waved to a more metallic sheen. She had a fondness for dress, was a regular customer of the Galeries de Rennes, and lately had exhibited for his benefit the most elaborate of her *toilettes*, which, alas, he never seemed to notice. It was this indifference which increased her longing, this completely unawareness of her as a woman, perhaps his unawareness of any woman, comparable to the innocence of a young curé who had once served the parish and whom from a distance she had admired, dreamed of at nights while at her side the grocer, his flesh appeased by her unresponsive buttocks, snored unmusically. But that had been nothing, the merest breath of a butterfly's wing beside this desire which now coursed in her veins, made her burn to press Stephen in her arms and cover him with her kisses.

She was blind to the comedy of her situation: that she, a woman almost forty, wrapped heart and soul in the throes of petty business, tightfisted, and a tyrant who spent her life, shrill-voiced and brazen, sanding the sugar, watering the cider, extorting the last sou from grudging peasant palms—that she, of all women, should be softened,

94

liquefied by this devastating passion for a stripling who could perhaps have been her son. She lost interest in her children, her friends, the pursuit of wealth. Her husband became obnoxious to her. His bourgeois mannerisms, way of eating, of breaking wind gently after his bock, aroused in her a storm of loathing.

"*Je te défends de passer le gaz en bas!*" she would cry, enraged. And with all this, her own refinement grew. She bathed often, used a stronger perfume, sucked scented cachous, changed her linen more frequently. If she could not have him, she felt she would cease to exist.

Suddenly there came an answer to her unspoken prayers, an idea of startling brilliance. Why had she never thought of it before? As Stephen entered that day she intercepted him in the passage.

"My friend," she exclaimed gaily, "I have good news for you . . . in short, a commission. Monsieur Cruchot insists that you must paint me."

Taken aback, Stephen stared at her in silence.

"Yes," she nodded. "Cruchot is filled with enthusiasm. He spoke of nothing else last night. Full length . . . in oils."

"But, Madame." Stephen frowned and hesitated, seeking an excuse. "I . . . I do not undertake portraits. . . . I am working on another subject . . ."

She smiled at him reassuringly.

"Do not worry, *mon petit*. I shall see that you are paid. On Thursday, then, we shall begin. It is understood."

Before he could protest, she patted his arm and, with an arch glance over her shoulder, hurried away.

Thursday was the tradesmen's half-holiday. Then it was always quiet since the shop closed down at noon. Yet the moment Stephen arrived he sensed, in the shuttered establishment, a preternatural stillness. Madame Cruchot received him at the door.

"No lesson today," she announced effusively. "The little ones have gone to the country with Marie."

As she led him into the house she explained that the servant paid a visit to her parents at St. Vallé once a month and sometimes, as a great favour, was allowed to take the children.

"And of course," she added, in an off-hand manner, "my husband is at Rennes, for the market. We shall not be disturbed."

Again the unusual silence troubled him: no rumblings from the cellar, where Joseph, the assistant, normally spent two hours overtime taking stock. The house, but for themselves, was empty. But it was the table, in the dining-room, set for two, with stiff napery and the best cutlery, adorned with a vase of red roses, which brought him up short.

"You don't mind if we have lunch together. It will be so much more convenient."

Talking volubly, in that same casual style, she produced from the pantry a roast *poulet de Bresse*, with mushrooms and salad, a Strasbourg *pâté*, peaches in syrup, and a bottle of champagne. Only when she had heaped his plate did she permit herself to look at him, unable to prevent a fond smile from breaking the plump contours of her cheeks.

"We are quite cosy here, for our first artistic meeting. Is it not agreeable, to lunch *tête-à-tête*? You see, you must eat before your labours." She glanced at him coyly. "Let me give you some champagne. It is the best we sell. Five francs the bottle."

He felt confused, baffled, and uneasy. But in his impoverished state he had developed towards food a kind of opportunism. He ate what was placed before him, aware that he was in no position to refuse it, becoming, however, more and more conscious of those languishing glances which lighted upon him. Her bust too, which rose with an effort each time she drew breath, causing her bosoms to bounce and her chin to sink into her neck, seemed to draw nearer to him with every respiration. Contrary to her usual custom, she was not eating, having helped herself with an air of refinement only to a wing of the chicken, but now she poured herself a second glass of wine. Her little round eyes were bright, like marbles. She had an overpowering impulse to reach across and press his hand. Would he never guess what exquisite favours she was prepared to offer him? The less he understood the more he seduced her.

"My friend," she exclaimed, "have you any notion of what my life has been, here in Netiers, for the past fifteen years?"

"Unfortunately I have not known you so long." He forced a polite smile.

"No," she reflected, in a suppressed voice. "Nevertheless it is you who have shown me the emptiness of my existence."

"That would be a poor return to make you, Madame . . . if it were true."

"It is true." As he did not answer she nodded her head in emphasis. "Yes, it is you, my friend, who have opened my eyes to new horizons which I did not even dream of before. Oh, do not misunderstand me. Monsieur Cruchot, although without excessive tenderness or delicacy, is a worthy man. And of course I am a virtuous woman. But there are moments when loneliness seizes the heart, when one has need of a confidant. Ah, my friend, when the heart calls," she sighed, "should we deny it? Is it wrong to seek fulfilment . . . provided one is discreet?"

As he sat silent and constrained, a wild explanation of her behaviour did in fact cross his mind. But he dismissed it as absurd. However, he felt obliged to get the sitting under way without delay and to make it as brief as possible. He pushed his plate away.

"And now, Madame, if you are agreeable, we may begin. I think it best to make a preliminary sketch. Where shall you sit for me? In the salon?"

She gazed at him, took a convulsive breath.

"No," she replied in an indistinct voice. "It is a better light upstairs." She rose from the table and moved towards the door. "I shall get ready now. Finish your wine. Then come up."

He had never been upstairs before. After waiting for five minutes he went towards the staircase. It was dimly lighted and the boards, thinly carpeted, creaked under his feet. The odour of the cheeses that were kept to ripen in the passage cupboard filled the air. On the landing the door facing him was ajar. He imagined it gave access to the sitting-room, but before he could knock, she called to him:

"Enter, *mon ami*."

He went in.

Madame Cruchot was standing by the double bed, inviting his approbation. She had taken off her dress and wore a peignoir which, in a raffish pose, with one hand on her hip, she kept half open, revealing shiny striped knickers with a heavy lace flounce which fell below her thick knees, and a pink camisole, damped by a spot of scent she had just put on, still creased by her stays.

A cold sweat broke over Stephen. His retina was seared by every detail of the showy, yet slovenly bedroom, the ornate rug and draped curtains, the stained commode, the china utensil under the bed, even Cruchot's nightgown tucked away hastily beneath a pillow. He turned white. Misreading his dilated eye, she hung her head, pretended to shiver, then, with terrible coquetry, came towards him. It was too much. He backed away with an expression of disgust, infuriated at himself for having fallen into such a situation, which, while it partook of the elements of farce, was nevertheless abjectly humiliating. Without a word, he swung round and rushed out of the room.

That evening, as he sat in his attic, he heard a loud knocking at the front door, followed by heavy ascending footsteps, then without warning Monsieur Cruchot burst in. The grocer, still wearing his best suit, was in a state of manufactured rage.

"How dare you make advances to my wife . . . miserable wretch . . . the instant my back is turned. I have a mind to go directly to the police. I always knew you as a little English snake. But to sting the hand which fed you . . . a pure-hearted woman . . . a mother. What an outrage . . . an atrocity. You are dismissed of course. Never show your sneaking face in my establishment again. But beyond that there should be damages . . . compensation . . . at the very least a picture."

Stephen knew that Cruchot disliked him, yet plainly this display was at the instigation of Madame—the husband was the emissary of the spiteful wife. And with a swelling bitterness, as Cruchot continued to threaten him, Stephen stripped a page from the block on the table before him, handed it to the grocer. It was a sketch he had just made from memory of Madame as she stood, obese and smirking, in her underclothes in the bedroom.

Monsieur Cruchot, silenced by the abruptness of the gesture, stared at the deadly drawing. His face turned livid. He was about to tear it up when, with native shrewdness, he considered it again, rolled it up carefully and put it inside his hat. Then, with a furtive glance, he turned and went out.

CHAPTER V

NEXT MORNING STEPHEN packed his rucksack, roped his canvases together and, shouldering the load, departed from Netiers on foot. His objective was Fougères, situated on the *route* nationale, thirty kilometres distant, and towards five o'clock in the afternoon, after a sweltering cross-country tramp, he reached the town, built on both sides of a hill and bisected by the main road to Paris. Here he found a cheap restaurant which seemed a likely stopping place for commercial drivers. The waiter, whose aid he enlisted, was confident that an opportunity would arise and indeed, just before nine, a *camion* of the Compagnie Atlantique with a trailer attached drew up and two men in overalls descended, entered the bar. A few minutes later the waiter beckoned, there were introductions, volatile explanations, a general shaking of hands—it was arranged. Stephen's things were stowed beneath the seat and they set off.

Night fell warm and still. They drove through sleeping villages, deserted towns where only a few lights flickered, through Vire, Argentan, Dreux. The hot air whistled past them, cobblestones roared and rumbled beneath, the moon sank damply behind misted avenues of poplars. Finally, as dawn broke, pale and streaky, they crossed the Seine at Neuilly, entered Paris through the Porte Maillot, drew up at Les Halles. There, Stephen thanked his two friends and left them.

The city, not fully awakened, had a grey and haggard air, yet as Stephen strode across the Pont Neuf he breathed the dank air deeply. He was back in Paris. After Netiers he felt stronger, above all suffused by a hard determination to demonstrate his talent to the world.

When the *mont-de-piété* in the Rue Madrigal opened its doors he was waiting outside. Entering, he pawned his watch and chain—a present from the Rector on his twenty-first birthday—for which he received one hundred and eighty francs. Next, after a considerable search and much bargaining, he found a lodging in a side street near the Place St. Séverin, a section frequented by artists as a last resort. It was a poor quarter and a poorer room, barely furnished and dreadfully dirty, but from its situation on the top floor it had a good light and was cheap—only ten francs a week. Immediately he set to work and, borrowing a brush and bucket, scrubbed out the place. He even washed the walls, so that they looked creditable, though some of the bug-stains remained.

It was now past two, but without thought of food he selected four of his paintings and hurried along to the *quais* to Napoleon Campo's shop. The colourman was seated on his customary box behind the counter, his short legs dangling, wearing a blue pilot coat and yellow knitted cap, his chapped ears protruding, purple cheeks unshaven, hands folded across his stomach. He greeted Stephen amiably, as though he had seen him only the day before.

"Well, Monsieur l'Abbé, what can I do for you?"

"First of all, let me settle what I owe you."

"Good. You are an honest man." He took the fifty francs Stephen gave him and slid them into an old leather purse.

"And now, Monsieur Campo, I want a specially large canvas, two hundred centimetres by eighty."

"Ha! So a great work is in prospect? Of course you can pay?"

"Not money, Monsieur Campo. These."

"Are you crazy, Abbé? My God, my cellar is stuffed with paintings, rubbish unfit even for the dustbin, that I took through the softness of my heart."

"Not all rubbish, Campo. You took paintings from Pissaro, and Boudin, and Degas."

"Are you a Degas, my little Abbé?"

"One day, perhaps."

"*Mon dieu*, it is always the same fairy-tale. So your specially large canvas is to hang in the Salon, with crowds gathered before it. You are to have fame and fortune overnight. Bah!"

"Then take twenty francs down and these paintings as a pledge against the balance."

Napoleon's pinpoint blue eyes searched the pale, serious face before him. So many, many faces had passed through his store in the past thirty years they swamped his recollection. He was a phlegmatic man, not easily moved, and age had rendered him more stolid. But occasionally, though rarely, there had been in the manner and appearance of some needy aspirant, as there was now in the features of this curious little Englishman, a quality of intensity which impressed him. He hesitated, then got off his stool and, grumbling, began to rummage in his shelves. When the canvas that Stephen wanted—a fine linen of close grain—lay upon the counter there was a pause.

"Twenty francs, you said."

"Yes, Monsieur Campo." Stephen counted out the coins.

Napoleon Campo took snuff, meditatively dusting his fleshy nose with the cuff of his pilot coat.

"And now, naturally, you will starve."

"Oh, not quite. Anyhow, now I have this canvas I don't care."

Another pause. Suddenly Campo pushed the coins back across the counter.

"Return these to your offertory box, Abbé. And give me your wretched daubs."

Surprised, Stephen handed over his paintings. Without even a cursory glance Napoleon thrust them under the counter.

"But . . . don't you want to look at them? . . . They are . . . the best I've done."

"I am not a judge of paintings but of people," Campo retorted gruffly. "Good day, Monsieur. And good fortune."

Stephen got back to his room with the canvas at three o'clock, and without delay immediately set off for the bicycle shop in the Rue de Bièvre. So far things had gone well, but as he drew near the Berthelot establishment he felt nervous and unsure of himself, yet filled with a quick anticipation that made his heart beat fast. Often during the past months he had thought of Emmy, the recollection of those moments in the darkness of the narrow passage had come to him from time to time without warning, yet with a queer insistency.

He found her in the yard behind the workshop, bent over a nickel-plated, reinforced bicycle enamelled in red and gold. It gave him a warm feeling inside to see her again. She looked up as he appeared, accepted his greeting without surprise, then went on oiling the hub bearings. His pulse was still absurdly uneven, yet from their expeditions together he knew her well enough to damp down all evidence of emotion.

"That's a nice-looking machine," he said after a few moments.

"It's mine. I shall be using it soon." She straightened, thrust back a lock of hair. "So you're in town again."

"Since this morning."

"Want to hire a wheel?"

He shook his head.

"I've more important things on hand."

There was a pause. She had always been mildly curious about him and now, as he had intended, her interest was aroused.

"What are you up to?"

He took a quick breath.

"Have you heard of the Prix de Luxembourg, Emmy? It's a competition open to all artists who've never been in the Salon. I mean to have a shot at it." Then, as she turned away indifferently, he added, "That's why I came round. I want you to sit for me."

"You mean . . ." arrested, she stared at him, her expression altered . . . "do my picture?"

"That's it." He made his tone casual. "You've never been painted, have you?"

"No. Though I ought to have been, long ago, considering who I am."

"Well, now's your chance. It might do you a bit of good. All the best entries will be exhibited at the Orangery. You'd be sure to be recognized."

He could see that her vanity was flattered, but she hesitated, looking him up and down as though estimating his capabilities.

"You can paint, can't you? I mean, you could do a good likeness?"

"You may depend on me. I'll put everything I've got into it."

"Yes, I suppose you would, for your own sake." A thought struck her. "But I'm going on tour next month."

"That's time enough. If you come every day for three weeks, I can work on the detail after you've gone."

Again he could see her mentally debating the possibilities.

"Well," she said at last, in her ungracious style, "I don't mind. I don't suppose I can lose."

He suppressed an exclamation of satisfaction and relief—not only had he wanted to paint her from the beginning, she would be perfect for the subject which in these last few hours had taken command of him. Quickly, he gave her his new address, asked her to be there at ten tomorrow, wearing her black sweater and pleated skirt, then before she could change her mind, he took his leave.

Tramping back along the boulevard, he felt excited at what he had accomplished that day. Only then did he realize that he had not eaten since he shared a sandwich with the driver of the *camion* on the previous evening. Hunger struck him like a blow. He dived into an *épicerie*, bought a long loaf and a *tranche* of sausage. He could not be still. Strolling through the darkening street past the Jardin des Plantes, he bit alternately the crisp bread and the succulent *pâté* encased in its soft white coat of lard. How good it tasted. He felt happy, free, and strangely exalted.

CHAPTER VI

ON THE NEXT day he was ready and waiting impatiently, his canvas set up, when she arrived some twenty minutes late.

"There you are!" he exclaimed. "I thought you were never coming."

She did not answer but, from the doorway, gazed round the wretched little room with its bare boards, broken cane chair and sagging truckle bed. Finally she looked at him, cruelly.

"You're broke, aren't you?"

"Practically."

"You have a nerve. Getting me up to a *trou* like this. Not even a place to hang my things."

He had reddened, but he forced a smile.

"I admit it isn't the Elysée, but it's not a bad place to paint in. Just give me a chance and I promise you won't regret it."

Her lips drew down in a kind of grimace, but with a shrug she came in, permitted him to take her coat and to pose her by the window.

The light was good and, filled with a sudden surge of power, he began to outline the conception which now obsessed him. As the rules of the competition demanded a "classical" painting, his theme was to be allegorical, though modern in composition, the subject: *Circe and Her Lovers.* Could it be that his absurd adventure with Madame Cruchot, working deep in his subconscious mind, had ignited a spark which flamed to this strange vision? Symbols and images filled the screen of his sight, captivating his senses. In his imagination pleasure fought with virtue, and lust stood revealed in the shape of prowling beasts. All as yet was a mirage; nevertheless, within the intimate and mysterious recesses of his soul, he felt the power to make his dream exist.

Although he could have gone on all day, warned by her expression he did not dare to keep her long, and towards noon suggested that she might have had enough for that day. Immediately, she crossed the room and examined the canvas, where already, using charcoal, he had made a preliminary sketch of her, full length and fairly complete. Her frown lifted, the sulky look left her face as she saw herself occupying the centre of the canvas, legs apart, hands planted on her hips, an attitude which was all her own. She said nothing as she allowed him to help her on with her coat, but at the door she turned and nodded.

"Same time tomorrow."

During the afternoon, while the light lasted, he worked on the background. And on the next day, and the days which followed, he went on, not always in an elevated mood, but with a purpose which carried him through momentary despondency to fresh intoxications. At the same time, as the sittings progressed and he was brought more closely in contact with Emmy, he could no longer blind himself to the deepening of his feeling for her. Every day after the sitting was over he found himself missing her, more and more. In the absence of Peyrat and Glyn, he was lonely. But did this explain his constant desire for her companionship? Angry at his weakness, he reminded himself of how much he had disliked her at their first meeting, of how so often she still irritated him by her rudeness and lack of consideration. When she was in an ill humour and he tried to talk to her, her responses came in monosyllables, and when he told her she might rest she would often ignore him, sprawl on her stomach on the bed, light a Caporal and immerse herself in a crumpled sports magazine. He realized that it was not regard for him but vanity alone which brought her regularly to his room. A dozen times a day she would take stock of the progress of the work, and while never praising it would congratulate herself:

"I'm coming out well, amn't I?"

The legend from the Odyssey, of the daughter of Helios and the ocean nymph Perse, which he explained to her, tickled her fancy. The idea that she should possess the power to change human beings into the forms of animals brought out her smile.

"That'll teach them, for trying it on."

The vulgarity made him wince. And yet it was no deterrent. What was it about her that provoked this pressing interest? He tried to analyse it. What did he really know of her? Little enough, except that she was common, cheap and tough—a little nonentity, unintelligent, without imagination, completely callous. She knew nothing of art, had no interest in his work, and when he spoke of it was bored. But her figure was exquisite—was he not reproducing every subtle line of her strong slender limbs, flat stomach and firm breasts?—and above all, she was small. While he could admire on canvas the voluptuous flesh of Rubens's women, his taste had always been for a less rounded perfection. And she had that physical neatness, a figure which he compared always to that of Goya's La Maja. Yet no one could call her beautiful. She had a gamin prettiness, but her lips were thin, her nostrils a trifle pinched, and her expression, when not alert and watchful, was almost sullen. Strangely, all her imperfections were apparent to him. Yet they made not the slightest difference to this strange emotion that, despite all his efforts to suppress it, grew within him.

He longed to be with her and felt restless and miserable when she had gone. Inordinately affected by her variable moods, he responded to them in a manner that made him despise himself. On the rare occasions when she was agreeable his heart lifted. Sometimes, in this talkative humour, she would question him on that subject which of all others connected with himself, alone seemed to interest her.

"It is true that your parents have a *grande propriété* in Su-ssex, with many acres of good land?"

"Not so many." He smiled. "If Glyn told you that he was exaggerating."

"And you were to be a little priest . . . until they sent you from the seminary."

"You know I left of my own accord."

"In order to live in a room such as this?" She spoke unbelievingly.

"I quite like the room—when you're in it."

She shrugged, but without contempt—flattery always gratified her. This affability, while it afforded him no respite, was in pleasant contrast to the mortifying indifference with which she usually met his attempts to please her. And while she posed, indolent as a cat, he began to tell her, not ceasing to paint, stories of Stillwater which he felt might entertain and amuse her. When he finally ran dry she reflected for a few moments, then declared:

"Of course I have lived with, or rather," she corrected herself, "amongst artists all my life. I am myself an artiste. I understand some giving up all for art when their all amounts to nothing. But you are in a different category. And to give up your *bonne propriété*, which you could inherit . . ." she paused and shrugged . . . "it was *imbécile*."

"Not altogether," he smiled, "since otherwise I should not have met you." A sudden surge of longing overcame him. He paused, dared not look at her. "Don't you realize, Emmy . . . I've grown terribly fond of you?"

She laughed shortly and raised a warning finger.

"None of that, Abbé. It's not in our arrangement."

Defeated, he resumed work. And all that evening he felt the sting of the rebuff. If only he might take her out in the evening—she was fond of entertainment of the raffish variety—he felt that he might win her favour. But his lack of means precluded it. He was living on little more than half a franc a day, subsisting on a roll or an apple until six o'clock, then taking his solitary meal at the cheapest café in the district.

One afternoon, when her sittings were nearly at an end, she was later than usual. On her arrival she seemed in excellent spirits. She was wearing a new yellow *fichu* with a short red Zouave jacket trimmed with braid, and her hair had been freshly washed.

"You're looking extremely nice," he said. "And I'd almost given you up."

"I had an appointment with Peroz. His office is quite far . . . in the Boulevard Jules Ferry. But I got the contract I wanted."

"That's good." He smiled, although mention of her departure depressed him. "When do you leave?"

"The fourteenth of October. It's put back two weeks."

"I shall miss you, Emmy." He leaned towards her. "More than you think."

She laughed again and he noticed that her teeth were sharp and regular, with definite spaces in between. Then, with vivacity, emphasizing her remarks, she began to describe how she had got the better of Peroz in arranging the terms of their agreement.

"They say he's good-hearted," she concluded. "I think he's just a *gobeur* . . . a soft touch."

Knowing that his conversation usually bored her, he encouraged

105

her to go on talking about herself. Then, as the light failed, he put down his brushes.

"Let me walk back with you," he said. "It's a lovely evening."

"Well," she shrugged. "If you like."

When she had put on her things they went downstairs and presently came out to the Boulevard Gavranche, where a warm darkness cast a halo around the street lamps, investing the muted city with a mysterious beauty. Couples were moving slowly, arm in arm, along the quiet pavements—the night seemed made for lovers. In a side street near the river they passed a café where, to the music of an accordion, people were dancing in a little arbour, under Chinese lanterns hung from the branches of plane trees. The scene was full of light and gaiety, and he could feel her glancing towards him inquiringly.

"Don't you like to dance?"

With a slow flush of embarrassment, conscious of his ineptitude, he shook his head.

"I shouldn't be much good in there."

It was true. She gave her familiar shrug.

"You're not good at much, are you?" she said.

They reached the cobbled shadows of the *quais*. The Seine flowed without sound, a smooth green tide, beneath the low span of the Pont de l'Alma. As though bored by his silence, walking a little in advance, she had begun to hum the tune played by the accordion at the cabaret.

"Wait, Emmy." He drew up in the shelter of an archway. She looked at him sideways, over her shoulder.

"What's on your mind, Abbé?"

"Can't you see . . . how much you mean to me?"

He put his arms round her and held her close. For a few moments, unresponsive as a lamp post, she permitted him to embrace her, then, with an abrupt movement of impatience, she pushed him away.

"You don't know the first thing about it." There was contempt in her voice.

Hurt and humiliated, weak with frustrated emotion, feeling the truth of her remark, he followed her towards the street. They walked towards the Rue de Bièvre. Outside the bicycle shop she glanced at him as though nothing had happened.

"Shall I come once more tomorrow?"

"No," he said bitterly. "It won't be necessary."

He turned away, furious with her and disgusted with himself.

"Don't forget," she called after him, "I want to see it when it's done."

He hated her for her hardness, her lack of common decency—she had not even pitied him. He told himself he would never see her again.

Next morning, when he awoke after a restless night, he threw himself passionately into the completion of the picture. So far, only the central figure had taken form, there was still the theme to be developed. The weather had turned wet and dismal, the light was poor, his makeshift studio swept by draughts, but no difficulty seemed too great for him to overcome. In his search for realism, he went every forenoon to make studies at the Zoological Gardens; then, returning to his room, he transferred to the abject creatures upon the canvas something of his own sadness and subjection. At the end of that week his money ran out—searching for a coin to buy his daily *petit pain*, he could not find a single sou. Undeterred, he continued to paint all that day with a kind of fury, in bitter protest against the difficulties that hampered him.

On the following morning he felt weak and faint, yet still he forced himself to resume work. But when afternoon came a shaft of reason struck through the mists that now befogged his brain. He realized less that he must eat to live than simply that he would never finish the *Circe* unless he could find some means of sustenance. Seated on the edge of the bed, he considered for a while, then, rising, he went to the corner where his Netiers pictures stood and selected three that were especially bright and colourful. They were good, they satisfied him, gave him confidence. In Paris, the most artistic city in the world, there must be a market for such beautiful things. He wrapped them in brown paper and, with the package under his arm, set out across the Seine, along the Champs Elysées towards the Faubourg St. Honoré. It was an act of courage. Yet the time for half measures had passed. He was resolved to offer his work to the best art dealer in France.

At the corner of the Avenue Marigny, a thoroughfare mainly given over to smart apartment buildings and sumptuous establishments of the *haute couture*, he paused outside a rich though restrained façade of Palladian pillars and cut white stone. Then, gathering himself resolutely, he passed through the gilt Venetian doorway and entered a marble-floored vestibule, panelled in rosewood and hung with red velvet, where he found himself confronted by a young man in a cutaway coat, seated at a Louis XVI lacquer and ormolu desk. Through the portières behind, a large salon was visible, equally splendid, embellished with great sheaves of lilies in alabaster vases and hung with paintings, beautifully lighted, before which a number of fashionable people moved and mingled, consulting their catalogues, conversing in subdued voices.

"You have a card for the *vernissage*, Monsieur?"

Stephen returned his gaze to the sleek young man, who, beneath his professional smile, was viewing him with extreme wariness.

"No. I was not aware that you had an exhibition. I called to see Monsieur Tessier."

"And your business, Monsieur?"

"A personal matter."

The smile, of ineffable politeness, did not waver.

"I am afraid that Monsieur Tessier is not in the house. However, if you will take a chair I shall inquire."

As Stephen seated himself the young man rose gracefully and glided off. But almost at once a side door opened and three persons came into the entresol—a woman, very chic, in black, with a dashing little plumed hat, and a cascade of bracelets on her gloved wrists, carrying a miniature beribboned poodle, fantastically clipped; her escort, an elderly man, bored and distinguished, impeccably dressed in brown from shoes to hat; and Tessier, whom Stephen recognized at once, a suave figure, dark, shaven, with a protruding lower lip and a hooded bistre eye. The dealer was talking, reasonably, with reserved animation and restrained movements of his hands.

"I assure you, it is a perfect gem. The finest which has come my way in several years."

"It is lovely," said the lady.

"But the price!" her companion interpolated, somewhat moodily.

"I have already told you, sir. At one hundred thousand, this is unquestionably an occasion. But if you do not wish me to reserve it for you, you have only to let me know. Virtually, I am committed to another client."

There was a pause, a touch on the escort's sleeve, a murmur of intimate conversation, then:

"You may consider the picture sold."

An inclination of the head, not obsequious but gravely approving such good taste, was Tessier's sole response. He did, however, conduct them to the door and, when he turned, in a meditative manner, his head bowed, hands clasped behind his back, Stephen stood up.

"Monsieur Tessier, I apologize for this intrusion. Will you give me just five minutes of your time?"

The dealer looked up sharply, disturbed in his train of thought, which was almost certainly a calculation, and his hooded eye, with immediate comprehension as of something encountered with distaste on previous occasions, took in the shabby figure before him, from the sodden, mud-splashed shoes to the ill-wrapped bundle beneath the arm.

"No," he murmured. "Not now. You see that I am fully occupied."

"But, Monsieur," Stephen persisted, shakily yet with determination. "I ask you only to view my work. Is that too much for an artist to request of you?"

"So you are an artist?" Tessier's lip drew back. "I congratulate you. Do you know that every week I am besieged, waylaid, and importuned by self-styled geniuses who imagine I will swoon with ecstasy when I behold their execrable efforts? But never did I know one with the effrontery to approach me here, at the very peak of my autumn exhibition."

"I am sorry if I disturb you. But the matter is somewhat urgent."

"Urgent to me . . . or to you?"

"To both of us." Stephen swallowed convulsively. In his agitation he spoke wildly. "You have just sold a Millet for a considerable sum. Forgive me, I could not help overhearing. Give me the opportunity and I will show you work as fine as anything that came from Barbizon."

Tessier glanced at Stephen, noted his distraught appearance, the dilation of his eye.

"Please," he said in a fatigued manner, relinquishing the argument. "Another time, I beg of you."

He stepped aside, entered the salon, and a minute later was lost to view. Stephen, who had begun, with nervous haste, to undo the package, stood for a moment very pale, then, with a strange expression, he moved towards the door. As he came into the street, the string, half untied, slipped from his grasp, and the three canvases dropped to the wet pavement and slid into the gutter.

He picked them up carefully, with a tenderness almost ludicrous. The mere act of stooping made his head swim. But stubbornly, with an almost fanatic intensity, he told himself that he would not be defeated. There were other dealers in Paris, less arrogant, surely more approachable than this insufferable Tessier. Slowly he started across the street, through the traffic, towards the Rue de la Boétie.

Two hours later, wet through and still encumbered with the three paintings, he was back at the Place St. Séverin, so exhausted he could barely climb to his room. Indeed, half-way up the stairs he sat down to recover his breath. As he did so the door on the half landing above swung open and there appeared, dressed for the street in sabots, collarless shirt, and a threadbare black overcoat, a man of about thirty, thin and dark, with a sallow complexion and sunken, Semitic eyes. On his way down, almost stumbling over Stephen, he drew back, studied him with a peculiar, bitter smile.

"No luck?" he exclaimed.

"No."

"Whom did you try?"

"Most of them . . . from Tessier down."

"Salamon?"

"I can't remember."

"He is not bad. But none of them are buying now."

"I had one offer. Two hundred francs to fake a Breughel."

"And you accepted?"

"No."

"Ah! Life has its little vexations." Then, after a pause: "What's your name?"

"Desmonde."

"I am Amédée Modigliani. Come in and have a drink."

He led the way back to the landing and threw open the door of his room. This was an apartment identical almost with Stephen's, but perhaps more squalid. In one corner, beside the unmade bed, stood an untidy stack of empty bottles, and in the centre an easel bearing a large painting, almost finished, of a reclining nude.

"You like it?" Pouring two Pernods from a bottle he had taken from the cupboard, Modigliani inclined his head towards the canvas.

"Yes," Stephen said, after a moment. There was in the painting a personal style, marked by its efforts in arabesque line, something monumental and pure.

"Good." Modigliani handed him the drink. "But it will bring the police commissioner after me. Already he has proclaimed that my nudes are scandalous."

The absinthe, fortifying Stephen, clearing his brain, evoked a note of recollection.

"Didn't you exhibit at the Indépendants? *Le Joueur de Violincello?*"

The other made a gesture of admission.

"It was not my best work. But it sold. Now they will buy nothing. Indeed, were it not for my talent as a *plongeur* at the Hôtel Monarque, I should have obliged my critics and ceased to exist."

"A *plongeur*?" Stephen did not understand.

"Yes. Would you care to try the job? I am going there now. It is a fascinating employment." A faint, saturnine smile flickered across his impassive, olive features. "And they are always agreeable to taking on a new man."

Stephen was silent. Then, with sudden decision, he stood up. "I'll try anything," he said.

They went out together and began to walk in the direction of the Etoile. The Grand Monarque, one of the most famous Parisian hotels, was an immense palatial building in the style of the Third Empire, occupying an entire square just off the Grands Boulevards. Imposing and dignified, if a trifle old-fashioned, its marble steps, red-carpeted, the vast public rooms hung with glittering chandeliers, a bevy of liveried attendants hovering behind the polished brass doors as though alert to receive the ambassadors, foreign dignitaries, and native princes who were amongst its visitors, it conveyed a sense of opulent magnificence. Modigliani, however, when they reached the central portico, did not attempt an entrance, but led the way round the corner and through a dark alley to the back premises, where, flanked by a row of battered garbage cans, a steep flight of littered steps admitted them to the basement.

It was less a basement than a huge underground cellar, the ceiling damp and dripping, crossed by a maze of iron pipes, the walls scaling, patchy with mildew, the broken stone floor ankle-deep in slops, the whole feebly illuminated by a few naked electric lights, filled with steam, noise, and a confused babel of many voices. Here, at the long stand of wooden tubs, a row of men, assembled, it seemed, from the slums of Paris, were feverishly washing dishes which a relay of scullions kept rushing in, in arm loads, from the adjoining kitchens. Now, thought Stephen, as he adjusted his sight to this nightmare vision, I know what is meant by a *plongeur*.

Meanwhile Amédée had approached the *contremaître*, who, with an indifferent glance towards Stephen, handed out a metal disc stamped with a number, and chalked a time opposite that number on the slate that hung above his cubicle beside a notice which warned that anyone caught removing broken meats would be summarily prosecuted.

And now, imitating his companion, Stephen stripped off his jacket and, taking his place in the line, began to wash the dinner-plates piled above the sink. It was not easy work, stooping over the low tub, and it went on without a break. The smell of the scummy water, never changed, foul with grease and remnants of food, was nauseating. Periodically this pulpy debris clogged the drain and had to be removed by thrusting the hand into the outlet pipe. It was strange, during this process, to hear faint wafts of polite music coming from the orchestra in the palm court overhead.

Towards eleven o'clock the pace slackened, and before midnight there was a definite lull which indicated that the ladies and gentlemen above had been fed. Amédée, who, all along, had not uttered a single word, put on his coat, lit a cigarette, and with a motion of his head drew Stephen towards the door where the foreman, after a glance at the time-slate, paid each of them two francs fifty.

Outside, still in silence, he slouched off through the darkened streets and five minutes later led the way into an all-night *bistro*. Here, while Amédée drank several Pernods, Stephen consumed a large bowl of *pot-au-feu*, thick with good vegetables and shredded pieces of mutton. It was his first satisfying meal in several days and he felt the better for it.

"Don't you want anything?" he asked.

"This is meat and drink to me." Amédée gazed with a hard indifference at the greenish, opalescent fluid in the glass which he held in his nicotine-stained fingers. "It has been my diet for quite some time."

Seated there in the deserted café, the lights half dimmed, the billiard table in the rear shrouded for the night, the solitary waiter half asleep, with his serviette over his head, behind the bar, Amédée revealed something of himself in brief, laconic phrases.

Born in Italy, he came of a family of Jewish bankers, had studied, despite interruptions due to illness, in Florence and at the Academy of Venice. For the past seven years, inspired by the primitives and Negro art, he had worked in Paris, sometimes with his friend Picasso, and occasionally with Gris. He had sold practically nothing.

"So now," he concluded, with his gloomy yet reckless smile, "you see me, enfeebled by poverty, excess of alcohol, and the use of pernicious drugs. Alone, except for a young girl who has the misfortune to be devoted to me. Devoid of all reputation." He tossed off the last of his drink and got up. "But rejoicing in the fact that all my life I have never debased my art."

He said good night, without further communication, on the staircase of their lodging.

Brief though it had been, this strange encounter was a providential one for Stephen. Now, by enduring every night five hours of sweated labour in the steaming cellars of the Grand Monarque, he was able to survive and, what seemed to him of greater moment, continue to work with all his powers upon the *Circe*.

At last, some three weeks later, one cold, dry afternoon, it was finished. There she stood, in that familiar attitude of careless insolence, indifferent yet alluring, with her pale face and enigmatic eyes, this modern daughter of Helios, her background not the palace of Aiaie but a Parisian slum street wherein were grouped those vanquished lovers, changed and degraded to the form of beasts, and who, tamed and broken, looked up at her in servile longing as though still thirsting for her caresses.

Exhausted by his final effort, Stephen could not appraise the value of this work, which had taken its fantastic shape under a compulsion he had been powerless to resist. He knew only that he could do no more to it and, in a spasm of nervous haste, he wrapped it in the same creased brown paper that had served him before, and carried it all the way to the Institut des Arts Graphiques in the Place Redon. Here an aged official took his name, laboriously entered all particulars in a book, then, discovering that the canvas was unframed, became reluctant to accept it.

"You see, Monsieur, there is a specification as to *montage*."

"I was not aware of it."

"But it is apparent. Look, Monsieur, every other entry is correctly mounted."

Stephen, glimpsing a long gallery stacked with scores of paintings, experienced a sudden apathy. One way or the other, he did not care.

"I cannot afford a frame. Take it as it is or not at all."

There was a pause, then the porter threw up his hands.

"It is most irregular, Monsieur. But leave it if you wish."

Back in his attic he sat down, supporting his head with his hands, suffused by a post-creative lethargy. And now . . . what was he to do? Impossible to continue at the Monarque—his soul revolted at the thought—yet he was on the verge of destitution. His rent was due on Monday. Except for the clothes he wore, his painting equipment, and fifteen sous, he had nothing of material value. Everything else had been pawned. He got up and looked in the cupboard. It contained half a stale roll, hard as a rock, and a rind of cheese. Downstairs, Amédée had been absent for the last three days, submerged in one of those debauches to which he periodically succumbed, and from which he would emerge, dizzily, in some remote region of the city. Through the matchboard wall the couple next door had begun to quarrel, shouting at each other. Children at play, squabbling on the dirty pavement outside, added to the din. Despite the open window the room was stagnant with the tired air of the city, and from the cracked wainscoting he could see beginning the usual evening procession of cockroaches.

All this was difficult enough to withstand, yet it was nothing compared to the insupportable sense of loneliness and deprivation that racked his breast. No longer dulled by the anodyne of work, his longing for Emmy returned, stronger than ever. Unlike Odysseus, he had no magic herb to protect him from her spell. He blamed himself for not having asked her to view the painting. And next day she would be gone, moving south with the Peroz troupe—he would not see her for at least six months, if indeed he ever saw her again. Remembering the infatuation which Madame Cruchot had entertained for him, he shuddered at the trick fate had played on him—now it was he who had taken over that preposterous role.

He had nothing to occupy him, not even a book to read; he felt too unutterably languid to venture out into the streets. When darkness fell, he lay down on the bed, but could not sleep. The next day was Thursday, and it came with a clear, sweet dawn. He got up and dressed. The thought of the circus vehicles leaving that afternoon for the open country and the sunny Côte d'Azur tormented him anew. Suddenly, out of the blue, an idea came to him. For a moment he stood quite still in the middle of the floor. Could he do it? At least he could try. Snatching his hat, he hurried from the room and set off shakily in the direction of the Boulevard Jules Ferry.

CHAPTER VII

ON A STRETCH of common land just outside the ramparts of the town of Angers, under an afternoon sky brilliant for late October, the Cirque Peroz, ringed by bright red caravans, had raised its canvas city. Already the sideshows were in action, a thin music came from the children's roundabouts, the *aboyeurs* had begun their exhortations upon the few spectators already on the ground.

At his stand, at the end of the line of booths, dressed in a blue blouse, beret, and loose black tie, a costume designed to suggest to the rustic mind the height of Parisian artistry, Stephen took a long breath of the country air, aromatic with wood smoke, orange peel, tan bark, fresh sawdust, and the scent of horses. Beside him stood an ornate easel bearing a sign that extolled him as *Grand Maître des Académies de Londres et Paris* and promised an exact likeness, hand-done, profile or full-face, in high-grade charcoal for only five francs, in rich and permanent colours seven francs fifty, courtesy and service as afforded to the crowned heads of Europe, satisfaction guaranteed.

There came the nicker of a stallion, the sharp blare of a cornet, a low grumble from an aged lioness. With his cough practically gone, Stephen experienced a sudden lift of physical well-being. He did not regret the impulse that had taken him to Peroz three weeks ago. In brief, he was almost happy.

"Walk up, walk up. Come, sir, won't you persuade Mademoiselle to have her pretty face drawn? Don't be modest. Make a record for your grandchildren."

A country couple, arm in arm, wearing their Sunday clothes, lingered before him and now, blushing, the young woman took courage and came forward. She was not beautiful, but with a few swift strokes he drew a pleasant likeness upon the folio sheet that lay on the easel, brought out the fine lace work on her coif, the hand stitching on her cuffs, and taught by experience, did not forget the cameo brooch, an obvious family treasure, which she wore upon her bodice.

Meanwhile a small crowd had collected, there were murmurs of approval for the finished portrait, and soon he was hard at work. It was, for him, no more than a mechanical process executed without thought. Yet he amused himself by giving to certain of his portraits an ironic individuality, dwelling in detail upon a particular feature, an ox-like eye, an outstanding ear, a bulbous nose, and when, as sometimes happened on Saturday nights, his client was offensive, he drew with malice a subtle caricature that, more often than not, provoked the onlookers to laughter.

At six o'clock the crowd thinned, as it always did before the main performance of the circus, and taking down his sign and shedding his blouse and tie, Stephen went through a labyrinth of ropes and canvas to a small enclosure behind the adjoining booth. Here, crouched at a glowing brazier, a shrivelled little man in cracked leggings and soiled corduroy breeches was cooking supper. Bow-legged and close-cropped, he had weathered, sharp features, except for the nose, which was flattened and broken. His eyes were beady, unblinking, and a spark from the brazier gave them warmth.

"What have we tonight, Jo-jo?"

"The usual." Jo-jo looked up. "But also some fresh Angers pork sausage which I picked up in the Rue Toussaint. One of the two things this town is good for."

"And the other?"

"Cointreau, of course, *mon brave*. They make it here."

The sausages, spluttering in a flat skillet, looked plump and promising. Jo-jo, who in his youth had been a jockey, then a tipster, then stable-man, then bookies' tout, and had finally been warned off at Longchamps, was an expert forager. He knew the ropes all over France. No one was more adept at driving a bargain in the market or at picking up a stray chicken from a roadside farm.

"I like these two-night stands." Stephen made room on the brazier for a tin coffee percolator. "We're free tomorrow until three. I mean to have a look at the river."

"The Loire is a good stream," Jo-jo said, with the air of one who knew many things. "A good sandy bottom, with lots of good fish—I shall set night lines if I have the chance. In fact all this country is good for us—Bolis, Tours, and Nevers especially. The wine is a trifle small, but the grub is first chop, and the women . . . these wenches of Touraine, big before and behind . . ." He whistled and turned up his eyes.

As he spoke the flap of the booth opened and a strange-looking man in checked trousers and a khaki turtle-neck sweater came out. He was tall and thin, so painfully emaciated he resembled a skeleton, and his face and hands—the only visible parts of his body—were covered with a thick crust of coppery scales. This was Jean Baptiste, who shared one of the poorest caravans with Stephen and Jo-jo. Mild, taciturn and melancholy, he was an extreme case of chronic psoriasis, a painless yet incurable condition of the skin from which, by exposing himself to the curious as the Human Alligator, product of the union of a ferocious male saurian and a woman swimmer of the River Amazon, he made a modest livelihood.

"Had a good afternoon, Croc?" asked Stephen.

"Not much," said Baptiste gloomily. "Not a single intimate."

It was the most profitable part of the Croc's technique to uncover himself slowly, from the extremities inwards, and when he had reached the navel to pause and, permitting his eye to roam over the audience, exclaim dramatically, with a kind of macabre allure:

"For those who desire more intimate disclosures I shall be available in the small tent at the rear. Adults only. Special admission for these private revelations only five francs."

When the meal was ready they shared it, sitting round the glowing charcoal—a big can of steaming soup followed by the sausages, crisp yet juicy, spicy with country herbs, the gravy sopped up with hunks of fresh bread hacked off with a clasp knife. Only since he had joined the troupe had Stephen learned the savour of food eaten in the open. Afterwards there was coffee, hot, strong and gritty, served in the soup can. Then Jo-jo rolled a cigarette and, with the air of a conjurer, produced from his hip pocket a bottle of the clear local liqueur.

"How about a drop of altar wine, Abbé?"

The nickname had followed Stephen from Paris—he did not mind. They passed the bottle from hand to hand, drinking the clear, warming liquid without glasses. Jo-jo rolled it over his tongue.

"You may have confidence in this. Made from the best Valencia oranges."

"At one time they told me never to eat fruit. At another to eat nothing else." Baptiste liked to reminisce on the subject of his malady. "From first to last I consulted nineteen doctors. Each was more of a fool than the one before."

"Then have another dose of my medicine."

"Ah, there is no remedy for me."

"You can't complain, Croc. Haven't you a rich and interesting existence? You experience the delights of travel. In fine, you are famous."

"It is undoubtedly a fact that people have journeyed fifty kilometres to view me."

"And don't you have a great success with the ladies?"

"True enough. I exert a certain fascination upon them."

At this serious admission Jo-jo gave out a shout of laughter. Then, extinguishing his cigarette, he got up to see to the horses.

It was Stephen's turn to wash up. When he finished, dusk had fallen, lights strung out from the generating engine were glowing like fire-flies over the fair-ground. Gazing, he felt all his senses aroused. He had not seen Emmy all day. But she did not like to be disturbed before the show, and people were already converging towards the big tent. He put away his easel and the rest of his gear in the locker underneath his bunk in the caravan, dressed in his ordinary clothes, and crossed to the back entrance of the arena. Under the terms of his engagement, it was his duty to join those members of the ground staff who showed the patrons to their seats, dispensed programmes, ices, *citronade*, and that brand of Montélimar nougat made especially in Passy for the Cirque Peroz.

It seemed to Stephen an excellent "house"—the circus had a deservedly popular reputation throughout the provinces and in fine weather on the good stands was usually sold out. Tonight tier upon tier of expectant faces rose up from the sawdust ring. Suddenly, on its raised platform, draped with red and gold, the brass band struck into the grand march, the ringmaster, Peroz himself, appeared in top hat, white cords and scarlet coat, a procession of cream ponies cantered with tossing manes into the arena and the performance began. Although by this time Stephen knew the show by heart, crouched by the rail at the back of the aisle, with a sketch-book on his knee, he followed every phase, every movement of the spectacle with absorbed interest, noting, again and again, the rhythms of muscular co-ordination, the play of light and colour tones in the vast shimmering kaleidoscope, even the individual reactions, often bizarre and comic, of members of the audience.

It was fascinating, this new world he had discovered, with its superb, high-stepping horses, ponderous elephants and sinuous, yellow-eyed lions, its tumbling acrobats, deft-handed jugglers, and tight-rope walkers swaying beneath paper parasols. Watching, he thought of the famous circus piece by Manet, *Lola on the High Wire*, and in his present uplifted mood felt he could draw from this field an equal richness. Design, of course, he would have, but above all colour would be the instrument of his expression. He saw on his palette the pure colours, the ultramarines, ochres, and vermilions, saw how he could humanize them without reducing their intensity. He would create a new world, a world which only he perceived, a world for himself alone. Bent in his corner he drew and drew. This was his real work, his daytime portraiture no more than a method of existence, and already in the portfolio in his locker he had scores of studies which he would use in one tremendous composition.

After the interval the more important performers made their appearance—the Dorando troupe of trapeze artists, Chico the sword swallower, Max and Montz the famous clowns. Next a wooden floor was swiftly assembled in the centre of the ring and there came that fanfare he knew so well, which always caused his heart to beat. Then, below, he saw Emmy cycle in, wearing a white satin blouse, white shorts, and long white boots. Once she had gained the flooring she began to execute upon the light nickel-plated machine a series of evolutions that left the spectator dizzy, circling and turning backwards, forwards, always within the confined space, altering her position until she rode upside down beneath the handlebars, finally dismembering the machine while in motion and completing the complex pattern upon a single wheel.

Perhaps these manœuvres were less difficult than they seemed, yet that cult of the bicycle, a national passion which reaches its peak annually in those hectic weeks devoted to the Tour de France, made them popular with the crowd. A burst of applause rattled round the dome, followed by a silence as Emmy walked towards a curious structure at the far end of the arena. This was a high chute, a narrow strip of metal painted red, white, and blue, descending almost vertically from the roof of the tent and ending in a curve that swept abruptly upwards.

By altering its tempo the band exaggerated the suspense as Emmy, slowly climbing the rope ladder, reached the minute platform on top. There, seen dimly through the upper swirls of smoke, she unhooked a heavier cycle from the cleats that held it, tested the frames, stretched her limbs, dusted her hands with chalk. Finally, mounting the machine on the platform, she seemed for a long moment to be suspended, floating almost in the steamy haze. The brass, which had gradually muted to a prophetic murmur, now came to life, supported by a violent staccato of drums which rolled and reverberated, louder, louder. It was the instant which made Stephen wish to close his eyes. Jo-jo had told him that if one were an expert and had nerve the danger was limited, yet the white central strip down which the wheels must exactly travel had less than a six-inch span, and after rain, or when the humidity was high, the slippery surface, despite preliminary rubbing, was treacherous. However, there was no time to think —in a final thunder of sound Emmy let herself go, dropped, it seemed, like a plummet, shot upwards on the curve, flew through the air for thirty feet and landed on the wooden platform with a velocity that carried her out of the tent like a flash.

Under cover of the applause, though he was not supposed to leave, Stephen escaped, went round to the dressing tent. He had to wait fifteen minutes before she came out, and immediately he sensed that she was not in the most amiable temper.

"Well?" she inquired.

"You were good . . . very good," he assured her.

"The chute was wet—a heavy dew—and these lazy *fripons* hadn't wiped it half. Don't they realize it is suicide to skid on a damp track? I almost didn't go down." On several occasions, because of this, she had called the act off—in fact she had an understanding with Peroz which permitted her to do so. Now, however, the complaint left her voice. "I wanted to tonight, though."

"Why?"

She did not seem to hear him. Then, indifferently, she answered: "Because of these military fellows."

"The soldiers?"

"No, stupid, officers, of course. There is a cadet school of the first class here. Didn't you see that group in the front *tribune*?"

"I'm afraid not."

"A smart lot they were, in their tunics. I like a uniform. And were they trying to get off with me. Not that I took notice, naturally. Still"—her sulky expression lifted slightly—"I did put in a little extra for their benefit."

He bit his lip, trying to stifle the jealousy which she had such capacity to arouse in him. After the stuffy heat of the tent the air was soft and cool.

"Let's walk by the town walls . . . it's rather nice there."

"No. I don't feel like it."

"But it's such a lovely night. Look, the moon's just coming out."

"And I am just going in."

"I haven't seen you all day."

Not a muscle of her face moved.

"You've seen me now."

"Only for a moment. Do come."

"Haven't I told you I am always fatigued after my act? The strain is most severe. All very well for you, selling programmes and nougat down below."

He saw that it was useless to press her further. He concealed his disappointment stoically. They reached the caravan which she shared with Madame Armande, the woman who looked after the costumes of the troupe. He had thought of her all day, he was hungry for her company, for a sign of her affection. As she stood there, her taut figure seductive in the moonlight, he wanted to seize her roughly and force kisses on her pale, indifferent face, her slightly open mouth. Instead he said:

"Don't forget about tomorrow. I'll call for you at ten."

He watched her run up the steps and disappear in the caravan.

As he turned away the show had ended, and crowds were pouring out of the big tent talking, gesticulating, laughing. They all seemed happy, pleased with life and with themselves, on their way back to normal, comfortable homes. His own earlier cheerfulness was gone. Restless and unsettled, he could not bring himself to return to his quarters, to face Jo-jo's banter and Baptiste's snores. He set out for the ramparts alone.

CHAPTER VIII

But on the following morning, which came with a mild, grey dawn, she surprised and cheered him by her punctuality. She was almost ready when he called, and shortly after they were on their *vélos*, bound for the Loire, the fine outline of Angers, with its Roman walls, spired Cathedral of St. Maurice and arcaded *préfecture* fading into the luminous mist behind them. As usual, she set a very fast pace, bent over the handlebars, legs moving like pistons, with the fixed purpose of outdistancing him. His machine, bought cheap with his first week's pay, was an old model; however, fresh air and country food had hardened him. Though it cost him a stiff effort on the hills, he maintained his place just behind her shoulder.

Presently they swung through a wood to the left and all at once the splendour of the valley was revealed—the great broad river glinting in the placid light, moving lazily between its banks over shallows of golden sand, past tall banks of osiers, moored flat-bottomed boats and little green islands. On the winding road, thick with sand, they slackened speed. Behind a screen of beeches, Stephen glimpsed the lichened, grey façade and pointed turrets of an old château. The beauty of the countryside was intoxicating to his spirit. Uplifted, he looked towards his companion, made as though to speak, then, wisely, refrained.

Towards noon they drew up at a riverside *estaminet* where above the doorway a monstrous fish, swathed in weeds, swam in a glass case. Stephen had at first proposed a picnic, but this held slight appeal for Emmy, who preferred always to stop at those cafés likely to be frequented by the sporting fraternity, where under an atmosphere of camaraderie there was free companionship, sharp slangy talk, and the music of an accordion. This inn, however, while possessing considerable charm, was at present empty of customers—a fact which did not displease Stephen, who suffered from the too open admiration which his companion chose to provoke. They crossed the clean sanded stone floor, sat down at a scrubbed table by a window hung with box and, after consultation with the landlady, chose a local fish dish which she strongly recommended to them. This arrived after a brief interval on a tremendous wooden platter, a *fritto* of tiny Loire spratlings each no bigger than a whitebait, so crisply cooked they broke at the touch of the fork. With them came *pommes frites* and a carafe of the Bière Navarin that Emmy favoured.

"This is good." Stephen glanced across the table.

"Not bad."

"I wish you'd let me order a bottle of wine."

"I like this beer. It reminds me of Paris."

"On a day like this?"

"On any day Paris is good enough for me."

"Still . . . you don't mind being here?"

"It could be worse."

Emmy was not addicted to superlatives, but for once she was in an excellent humour and presently she broke into a laugh.

"You'll never guess what I got this morning. Flowers. Roses. And in them a *billet-doux* from one of the officers."

"Indeed." His expression had turned slightly rigid.

"Here it is. Embossed monogram and all." With another short laugh she felt in her pocket and brought out a crumpled pink sheet. "Take a look."

He had no wish to read the note but neither did he wish to offend her. Quickly he glanced through it, noting the double meaning in the polite phrases inviting her to take an *apéritif* on La Terrasse and go to supper afterwards at Le Vert d'Eau. He handed it back without comment.

"He's a captain, apparently. I think I noticed him in the group last night. Tall and good-looking, with a moustache."

"Shall you go?" he asked, masking his feelings with an expressionless tone.

"How can I, with the show on, and the move to Tours tonight?"

"But the captain?" he persisted. "And with a moustache."

The cold irony of his manner pierced her self-esteem. She rarely coloured, but now a faint flush showed under her bluish-white skin.

"What do you think I am? I know these garrison towns and what you can get in them. Not for me, thanks."

He was silent. Although he despised himself for it, and vainly tried to combat it, from time to time jealousy would surge over him in an overpowering wave. The mere thought that she might go out alone with this unknown officer caused him excruciating pain. However, she had flatly stated that she would ignore the invitation, so telling himself to be reasonable, he forced a conciliatory smile.

"Let's go down to the river." When they quarrelled it was always he who made the first advances.

He paid the bill and they went down to the water's edge. The sun, unusually warm for the time of year, had broken through and, blinding upwards from the stream in glittering shafts, enveloped them in a bath of light. He loved the sunshine—water and sun were the twin gods he could have worshipped. And while she lit a Caporal and, with shut eyes, relaxed in a posture of ease beneath a shady willow, he sat in the open brightness and began to sketch her. Already he had made scores of drawings wherein was reflected not only his intensity of feeling for her, but also the complex interplay of anguish, desire, and at times near hatred which composed it.

He was not blind to those qualities of selfishness, cruelty and vanity which in another person would have aroused his contempt. He knew that she merely tolerated him—perhaps because her Gallic mind lingered upon the possibilities of the *grande propriété*, but mainly, he felt sure, because his unconcealed desire flattered her, gave her that sense of power which her nature best enjoyed. She brought him more pain than happiness. Yet he could not help himself. He longed for her with a physical need which, since she would not satisfy it, increased from day to day.

Presently, glancing up from his sketch-book, he saw that she was asleep. An involuntary sigh, nervous and irritable, broke from him. Leaving his drawing-block and crayons, he went further down the bank, then, on an impulse, threw off his clothes and plunged into the river. He knew from their previous excursions that she did not care to bathe—she had a feline dislike for cold water—but to him the shock of these spring-fed streams was an invigorating delight.

When he returned she was standing up, shaking the dried grass from her short bushy hair.

"You are a fine one to go off."

"I thought you were asleep."

"What time is it?"

"Still early." He came close and put his arm around her waist. "We have another hour."

"Oh, leave me." She leaned back and pushed her hands against his chest. "You're wet."

"But Emmy . . ."

"No, no. We mustn't be late. You don't want to lose your job. It is so agreeable and convenient for you, is it not?"

"Yes, of course," he answered in a strained voice. As she had already started towards the inn he followed.

Her unusual concern for his welfare puzzled him. Nor was this dispelled by her sprightly manner as they rode back to Angers. In a high voice she sang snatches of the latest music-hall air:

> Les jolis soirs dans les jardins de l'Alhambra
> Où donc sont les belles
> Que l'amour appelle?
> Et le rendezvous, de l'amour très fou.

And, following her habit when she was gay, she left the local inhabitants gaping by a display of trick riding in their swift passage through the riverside villages.

It was not yet three o'clock when they reached the circus and few people were on the ground. He changed and put up his easel. All the afternoon he worked absently, moodily, the line between his brows gradually deepened. Although he struggled against the thought that she had cut short their expedition in order to keep the assignation at La Terrasse, it grew within him. Dusk brought no alleviation, during supper he spoke scarcely a word to Jo-jo and the Croc.

At last, he got up abruptly and made his way to the other end of the field to Emmy's caravan. Madame Armande was seated on the steps with a bucket between her fat knees, washing stockings. At one time she had been part of a trapeze act but a bad fall had broken her hip, and she had walked with a limp ever since. Now, at fifty, heavy and shapeless, with dropsical legs and a double chin, she was known as the gossip of the company. Jo-jo, who expectorated at the mention of her name, swore that during the winter lay-off she managed an establishment of doubtful reputation in the port of Le Havre.

"Good evening." Stephen tried to make his voice calm. "Is Emmy in?"

Madame Armande considered him sideways, with her small eyes.

"But Abbé, you understand very well that she sees no one before the show."

"It's only for a moment."

She shook her head, encased in a spotted handkerchief.

"I would not dare disturb her."

"Then . . ." He hesitated, anxious to believe her. "She's resting?"

Madame threw up her hands.

"What else! *Nom de Dieu*, do you make me a liar?"

Was her indignation real or affected? He wanted to go into the van, but her bulk, and the bucket, blocked the way. He must not make himself completely ridiculous. He forced himself to make a few conventional remarks, then turned away in the darkness.

The crowds flocked in, the show began, roars of laughter and applause filled the big tent. She was late in coming on. Was this mere accident? He could not be certain. He tried to reassure himself. Yet when she finally appeared it seemed to his overstrung fancy that her performance was more dashing, more showily vivacious than usual. Prolonged shouts of "Bravo" from the front *tribune* followed her as she made her exit.

Afterwards, in the bustle and confusion of lifting stakes, he could not see her. Dismally he joined Jo-jo and the Croc and began the task of dismantling the stands. Working heedlessly, he cut his hand on an iron hook. He did not care. A cold wind had risen and whipped across the ground. The generator was cut off, the electric lights died. All around, by the red light of flares, amidst shouts and imprecations, men toiled like demons, uprooting stanchions, hauling on ropes, struggling with the great bights of flapping canvas. As always happened in this first hour of transit, the animals were upset, gave out in every key, from their mobile cages, weird howls of protest. The traction engines, pounding and snorting, with whirling flywheels, added to the tumult. To Stephen it seemed that the scene came straight from Doré's drawings of the Inferno and that he too was suffering the tortures of the damned.

CHAPTER IX

From Angers the Cirque Peroz moved to Tours, then to Blois, then on to Bourges and Nevers. The weather kept fine, business flourished, old Peroz wore his hat at a jaunty angle. After a three-day stay at Dijon they swung due south into the Côte d'Or, making one-night stands in the old stone-walled towns, approached by gateways, strung out between sloping vineyards, along the valley of the Ouche.

Stephen had at first been viewed by the company with reserve. But the weekly "take" from his portraiture was satisfactory, and since a fixed percentage of this sum went into the *tronc*, in which all the performers would share when it was distributed at Nice, he was considered to be pulling his weight. Beyond that, his agreeable manners and quiet disposition soon put him on friendly terms with most of the troupe.

They were a human lot. Fernand the lion-tamer, who strode into the circular iron cage fearless as a hussar in his blue-and-silver uniform, with a sleeve dramatically slashed to ribbons, was the most timorous of men, who suffered acutely from nervous dyspepsia and was coddled on a milk diet by his devoted wife. The lions themselves were harmless as cows, for the most part extremely aged, the males castrated; they roared only because they wanted their supper, and all the business of surrounding the cage with attendants bearing red-hot irons was sheer hocus-pocus.

"We have not had an accident in twenty years," Peroz would remark complacently as he sent out advance notices to the local paper of the next town on the circuit.

NARROW ESCAPE AT THE CIRQUE PEROZ

LIONESS RUNS AMUCK
Fernand Severely Mauled

Max and Montz, both dwarfs, were the two principal clowns, a pair internationally celebrated, whose feature act was known as "The Elopement", a sketch in which Max, garbed in grotesquely outmoded finery, played the part of the elderly bride. The routine, carried out with an antique Panhard motor-car that broke down, refused to start, and finally fell apart, was uproariously comic. Max, with his puckish grin, left the audience helpless from side-splitting laughter. Yet out of the arena he manifested a melancholy more profound than Hamlet's, confided to Stephen, sadly, a frustrated, lifelong passion for the violin.

With such inconsistencies before him, Stephen was less surprised to discover that the Japanese juggler was a devout Christian Scientist, that Nina d'Amora, who rode bareback, was allergic to horses and in consequence endured a chronic asthma, while Philippe, who every night took spectacular risks on the high trapeze, spent most of his spare time knitting socks.

Because he was teamed with them, Stephen saw more of Jo-jo and the Croc than any of the others. Jean Baptiste, beneath his apparent apathy, was a sensitive and intelligent man—Stephen made several striking studies of him standing on his platform facing the gaping crowd. He had been well educated at the *lycée* in Rouen, had passed on to a position with good prospects in an excellent firm, La Nationale. Then this incurable affliction had struck at him, turning him gradually from a normal being to a gruesome freak, breaking up his marriage, causing him to lose his position, sending him to one clinic after another—a hopeless progress—and bringing him in final desperation to a sideshow in the Cirque Peroz.

But it was for Jo-jo that Stephen entertained a particular regard. The ex-jockey was a thorough rogue who stole at every opportunity, cheated his way across the countryside and, whenever he had the chance, drank himself into such a state of stupor that he lay all night on the bare ground, "sleeping it off". Yet in his duplicity there was an oddly human quality which bore out his boast that never in his life had he let down a friend. Often in the evening, after seeing Emmy, when Stephen came in to the converted *camion* where he bunked with the other two, he caught Jo-jo's gaze fixed peculiarly upon him—less in sympathy, an emotion of which Jo-jo was incapable, than with a sort of cynical understanding, mixed faintly with derision.

"Been out with your girl?"

"So it would seem."

"Had a good time?"

Stephen did not answer.

Upon several occasions the ex-jockey had appeared to wish to press the point, but instead, shrugging, he had turned to Jean Baptiste and started a discussion with him which he made deliberately gross.

"What is your opinion of women, Croc?"

"I regard them with tolerant contempt."

"You speak like a husband."

"Yes . . . I have been married. My wife now operates a *passage à niveau* at Croiset on the Chemins de Fer du Nord. It is my fondest hope that one day the Paris express, travelling at ninety kilometres an hour, will strike her in a vulnerable part."

"For myself, though I have never married, I like women. But only to sleep with. Every other way they are a worse nuisance than the clap."

"But one achieves that by sleeping with women."

"Not my women. I never choose tarts. Only good honest country wives I meet in the market who are seeking some slight variety."

"Ah! Variety! That is a true word—to which I owe much of my later successes."

"You! Scaly one!"

"But, certainly. I have made many conquests amongst my intimates through curiosity. Women bored with the marriage bed will do anything for novelty. I have read that a murderer about to be guillotined can have his pick of scores of women."

"*Sacré bleu!* Though you merit it you are not going to lose your ugly head."

"No. But I have equal attraction. Reflecting on the power of the crocodile's tail, women believe me endowed with formidable phallic powers."

"But you disappoint them, *farceur*."

"Only once, Jo-jo. There was a stout one, a spinster, unattached, who for months followed me around in the hope that our repeated congress would produce an alligator. Unhappily the child was normal."

A burst of profane laughter filled the caravan but Stephen did not join in it. He knew that the dialogue was directed at him, less from any malicious intent than as a remedy administered to the victim of a persistent fever. Yet his malady had now progressed so far it seemed incurable, intensified by Emmy's moods and inconsistencies. Sometimes she treated him well, seated on the steps of her caravan, flattered by his attentions, full of her own importance, laughing at him, kicking her bare toes in the sun. And while she was not lavish with her favours, when they strolled together in the darkness sometimes she permitted him to kiss her, before she quickly drew away. In vain he told himself that in a nature so lacking in depth he would never arouse an answering passion. He hung about her like a wasp around a nectarine, but without once penetrating the soft flesh of the fruit.

One wet afternoon when they had quitted the pleasant district of the Saône for the barren territory of the Pays de Dombes, they pulled into the small and scattered community of Moulin-les-Drages. Their destination had been St. Etienne, but the main traction engine had broken down en route, holding up a long line of coupled waggons, and since the repair would take at least twenty-four hours, this enforced halt became necessary. Peroz, much upset at missing an important date, decided after considerable debate to give a show, or the greater part of it, in Les Drages, and so cut some of his loss.

But having begun with misfortune, the day went from bad to worse. No advance bills had been posted; the town, on investigation, proved to be mean and poverty-stricken, its sole industry a decayed brickworks. And the rain steadily increased. When evening came not more than a hundred people were assembled in the dripping tent.

True to the Peroz tradition, most of the artistes went through with their performance in good style, then got back to the big stove in the dressing-room. Emmy, however, was less fortunate. Twice during her preliminary evolutions her wheel skidded, spilling her on to the damp flooring. The first fall raised a laugh from the boorish audience, the second evoked a definite jeer followed by catcalls. As a result, she cut the main part of her act and rode from the ring with her head in the air.

When Stephen saw her afterwards outside the tent she was still pale with mortification. He knew better than to speak, but instead moved off with her along the road towards the common, about a half kilometre distant, where the caravans were parked. To make matters worse, they had not proceeded far when a heavy shower broke, forcing them to run for shelter to a barn that stood in an adjoining open field of stubble.

When his eyes had grown accustomed to the darkness, Stephen looked around, observing that the place was filled with straw. He broke the silence.

"At least it's dry here." He added: "I'm glad you didn't go down tonight. That crowd didn't deserve it."

"What do you mean?"

"Well." He coloured slightly. "They seemed rather an unsympathetic lot."

"I didn't notice it. I always hold my audience."

"Then why didn't you go down?"

"Because the chute was sopping wet. Don't you realize that it's suicidal in the rain?" In a spasm of temper, her eyes sparked at him. "Who are you to stand there and criticize? Don't you know the risks I take every night, while you sit safe on your backside, scratching on a sheet of paper, with no more guts than a louse? I go down or don't go down exactly as I choose. And I won't break my neck for any little half-baked curé!"

He stared at her for a moment, as pale now as she, then, infuriated, he caught her suddenly round the waist.

"Don't speak to me like that."

"Let me go."

"Not till you apologize."

"*Fiche-toi le camp.*"

The next instant they were struggling together. Blind with anger, recollecting all the slights and insults she had heaped on him, he determined to subdue her physically, and locking both arms about her like a wrestler he tried to bring her to the ground. But she fought like a wildcat, twisting and turning in the soft straw, threshing against him with her elbows. She was stronger than he had believed, with short, powerful muscles and a feline suppleness. He began to breathe heavily, to feel the pressure of her body bearing him down. Straining every nerve, he resisted. They swayed to and fro indecisively until, crooking her leg behind his, with a quick jerk she threw him heavily.

"There," she gasped. "Let that be a lesson to you."

He got up slowly. It was less dark than before, through the skylight of the barn the moon was visible behind racing clouds. With an effort, still trying to catch his breath, he made himself look at her, saw, with confused surprise, that she had not risen, but was leaning back amongst the straw, her dress still disarranged from the struggle, watching him through narrowed eyes with an odd, speculative expression, aroused, yet vaguely derisive. On her face, usually of a cold pallor, there was a tinge of colour, on her pale lips a curious, faintly shrewish smile. For a moment she sustained his gaze, then, placing both arms behind her head in an attitude less of enticement than expectation, she made an impatient movement.

"Well, stupid . . . what are you waiting for?"

The invitation he had sought so long was unmistakable, yet it was

E

so blatant, so devoid of the faintest semblance of affection, he did not stir. Frozen and repelled, he stared at her, then spun round and, without a word, walked away. She could not believe it. Her expression altered. Affronted and enraged, she jumped to her feet.

"Softy!" she called after him. "*Espèce de crétin!*"

He walked for perhaps fifty yards before desire surged in him again, more desperate than before. He did not care, he wanted her, and he would have her, anyhow. He turned and came back.

"Emmy . . ." He cringed, weak with wanting her.

But now she was cold and hard as stone.

"Go to the devil," she spat at him. "You'll wait for another chance."

The look in her eyes told him it was hopeless. Again he turned away. Heedless of where he was going, he went straight ahead, with contracted eye and contorted lip. In these past weeks, victimized by his insatiable longing, reduced to a perpetual attitude of propitiation, he had already known himself sufficiently humiliated. But now, wounded in all his sensibilities, he felt that he had reached the lowest level of abasement. He could not, would not submit to it.

His thoughts had not taken coherent form before he found himself back on the circus ground. Since the defective engine would not be repaired till the following morning, nothing had been dismantled, and in the muddy field the great tent stood empty and deserted. Something drove him inside. The moon, shining through the top aperture in the canopy, bathed the arena in a spectral light, revealed the chute, left standing, glistening with moisture. A strange impulse, a sense of duty to himself, gradually took shape in his tormented mind. Gazing upwards, he saw that the equipment was still in place. Unable to repress a shiver, he walked towards the rope ladder, his footsteps leaving imprints in the pulpy sawdust. He took hold of the rope, began slowly to climb, spiralling slightly because he had not the knack of it.

Now he was at the top, edging on to the platform. The smallness of this perch, its height from the ground—far greater from above—made him so dizzy he closed his eyes and clung to the metal support. Momentarily the fit of vertigo paralysed him. The wind at this altitude had greater force, caused the chute to sway, and the damp canvas, flapping and billowing, increased his sense of insecurity. But he compelled his rigid muscles into action. Gazing upwards and using one hand, he unhooked the bicycle from its cleats, then, still hooked firmly to the pole by his other arm, he aligned the wheels. Shakily he mounted the machine, forced himself to look down.

The ring, beneath him, was impossibly small, a distant yellow disc. The chute on which he was poised had no more substance than a tricolour ribbon. Another violent shudder passed over all his body. He was still holding on, he could go back. Fear petrified him. He fought it. Whatever happened, he must go down.

He took a deep breath, firmed his position on the machine, crouched forward. As he did so he was vaguely conscious of a shout, of a dark foreshortened figure waving from below. If a warning were intended it came too late. Focussing his gaze on the central white strip, by a supreme effort of his will he released his hold on the support. There came a split second of flying, incredible descent, an upward surge which catapulted him through the air, then in the same instant with a resounding bounce he was down, shooting at tremendous speed into the field outside, spilled into the soft mud of the boundary ditch.

For a moment he lay there, motionless, surprised to be alive. Then he heard someone running towards him.

"*Nom de Dieu* . . . Do you try to kill yourself?" It was Jo-jo, for once in a state of considerable agitation.

"No," said Stephen, getting up giddily. "But I may be going to be sick."

"You crazy son of a bitch. What got into you?"

"I wanted some exercise."

"You are mad. When I saw you up there I thought you were done for."

"What difference would it have made?"

Jo-jo stared at him.

"For Christ's sake, come and have a drink."

"All right," Stephen said, then he added, "Don't speak of this to anyone."

They went across to the village café. After a stiff glass of Calvados, Stephen's hand stopped shaking. He sat there drinking with Jo-jo, almost in silence, until the place shut down. The brandy thickened his head, made him feel dull and numb. But actually he had accomplished nothing. He realized that he could not break with her. And the pain in his heart was still there.

CHAPTER X

Two weeks later they reached Nice. The city, entered by way of the mimosa-hung terraces of Les Baumettes, was larger than Stephen had expected. The Promenade des Anglais, all the glittering sea-front, with its formal flower-beds and ostentatious hotels, struck a disagreeably pretentious note. But the circus ground was well inland, towards Cimiez, at the back of the Place Carabacel, surrounded by narrow streets filled with open-air markets and little stalls bearing fruit, vegetables, and a profusion of flowers, a network of noisy and colourful passages which had the intimate charm of Paris and the added warmth of the South.

"Not bad, eh?" Jo-jo expanded his narrow chest under the torn singlet. "It is good to be back."

"You like it here?"

"Greatly. And you will also. Look." He made a comprehensive gesture. "There is much of interest for an artist in the Carabacel."

At another time it would have been an entertainment for Stephen to explore this quarter. Now, tense and restless, he felt he could not work. But he forced himself out with his Ingres block and made some studies of the Niçois—an old woman in a white cap selling artichokes, a farmer from the country with a net of live chickens, labourers working on an opening in the roadway. Yet his heart was not in it, and in the heat of noon he went back to his quarters to rest before starting work at his booth.

On the following afternoon, standing at his easel in the fair-ground completing his final portrait of the session, he became conscious of a spectator at his elbow, leaning lightly upon a Malacca cane. Something in the attitude struck a chord of recollection. He glanced round.

"Chester!"

"How are you, old boy?" Harry broke into his infectious laugh, removed a wash-leather glove and held out his hand. "I heard that you'd joined up with Peroz. But where on earth did you get that frightful rig-out?"

"It goes with the job."

"That's one way to attract the natives. But doesn't it make you feel a bit of an ass?"

"Oh, I'm used to it. Hold on and I'll be with you in a minute."

While Stephen quickly put the finishing touches to the portrait, Chester took out his cigarette case and lit up. Dressed in a linen suit, white and tan shoes and a panama hat, he had an air of leisure. His trousers were creased, his shirt was of tussore silk, and he sported a natty bow tie. His face was deeply tanned.

"I can't get over seeing you here," Stephen said. "Though you did say you'd make for Nice. You look well."

"I'm pretty fit, thanks."

Harry smiled good-naturedly and Stephen had to smile in sympathy, drawn by that careless warmth which Chester dispensed so easily.

"I gather you've had some luck at the tables."

"To put it mildly, yes." Chester's smile became a grin. "I was down to my uppers and bet my last fifty francs on double zero. Why? Because I knew I'd have less than zero if I lost. Double zero came up. I left everything on. Why? Heaven alone knows. Up came double zero again. My God, you never saw such a pile of lovely big red counters in your life. I went to lift it. I couldn't. Something inside me said, third time lucky. I left it on. When the wheel spun I nearly died. Double zero came up again. And this time I picked everything up quick and scooted to the cashier's desk. Next day I moved out of harm's way to Villefranche, to a little apartment. I've been living like a lord ever since." He took Stephen's arm. "Now tell me about yourself. How's the work going?"

"Only so-so."

"Let's have a look."

Stephen led the way to his caravan, brought out a few of his canvases and stood them one by one against the hub cap, while Harry, with a professional expression, studied each in turn.

"Well, old boy," he declared at last, "you may have something there, but I can't quite get it. What about perspective? And isn't your brushwork pretty rough?"

"It's meant to be rough . . . to convey an impression of life."

"These horses aren't particularly life-like."

Harry pointed with his cane to a composition in tempera of stallions racing madly in a thunderstorm.

"I'm not trying to express the obvious."

"Obviously not. Still . . . I like a horse to look like a horse."

"And when you see a man on his back, then you're sure," Stephen said wryly, and piled the canvases together, realizing that Chester had not the least idea what he was driving at. "Are you still painting?"

"Oh, of course. In my spare time. I'm doing a bang-up view of the promenade. I go out with Lambert occasionally. You know that Elise and he are here. He's got hold of a rich American widow at the Ambassadeurs and is doing a full-length of her."

As he spoke a step sounded, and from behind the tilt of the caravan Emmy appeared. As she advanced towards Stephen she suddenly drew up, aware of Chester's presence. A queer look came over her face.

"What are you doing here?"

"I usually turn up when least expected."

"Like a bad centime?"

"This time like a good thousand-franc note," Chester answered amiably, not in the least put out. "Didn't you miss me?"

"The deprivation was unbearable."

"Now don't be rude to Uncle Harry. You know his nerves are weak." He looked at his watch. "I have to shove off. I'm due at the Negresco at six. But I want you both to come tomorrow for luncheon at my apartment, 11-B Rue des Lilas—off the Boulevard Général Leclerc. The Lamberts will be there. You're both free? Good. It's only a few kilometres along the Corniche, the tramway goes past my door."

With a smile and a wave of his cane he hailed a *fiacre* at the end of the ground, jumped in, lay back on the plaited straw seat and was whirled off. Emmy followed him with resentful eyes.

"Patronizing *voyou*. Telling us to take the tramway while he drives off in a carriage."

"We mustn't grudge him it. He's had his bad times too."

"I don't believe he made a *coup*. He's living off some old woman."

"Surely not. Chester's just the sort of chap who'd have the luck to win a packet. Besides, he only goes after the pretty girls."

"He'll do it once too often." She showed her sharp little teeth. "Cheap *sale type*. I always hated the sight of him."

"Then you won't want to go tomorrow?"

"Of course I'm going, don't be completely *fou*. We'll make him sorry for his conceit."

He gazed at her in perplexity. She obviously disliked Chester. Why, then, should she accept his invitation? Perhaps she wanted to see the Lamberts. He never knew what was in her mind.

On the following day, when she met him, she was wearing a little yellow dress of embroidered muslin and a ribbon of the same colour round her short bushy hair. She gave him her little tight-lipped smile.

"Can we run to a *fiacre*?"

"I should say so. No tram for us."

She picked the smartest turnout from the line. Settled back comfortably.

"How do I look?"

"Wonderful."

"I needed a new frock. I bought it this morning at the Galerie Mondial."

"It's charming," he said. "And suits you perfectly."

"I like to show these people that I am not something beneath their feet. Chester especially. He is too full of himself for words."

"Oh, Harry's not a bad sort. He can't help being a bit spoiled. He's too good-looking."

"Then you think him attractive?"

"I think a lot of silly women have fallen for his blue eyes and curly hair."

She gave him a sharp side-glance.

"At least I'm not one of them."

"No." Stephen smiled. "I'm really rather relieved that you dislike him."

They drove down the Avenue Raspail, a broad thoroughfare shaded by catalpa trees, along the Boulevard Carnot, then round the curve of the bay towards Beaulieu. The sky was blue, a breeze of delicious fragrance blew from the hills. He pressed her hand happily —she let him hold it for a moment. Lately the attentions that he showered upon her, the little presents he continually gave her, the restraint which by an effort of will he placed upon himself, seemed to have made some impression on her.

"You are being nice to me," she murmured.

The slight remark made him ridiculously happy. Perhaps, after all, she could be taught to love him.

Presently they drove into Villefranche. Chester's apartment in the Rue des Lilas, a street set at right angles to the front, was one of a series of suites opening upon a common balcony around a courtyard and serviced by a small hotel, the Hôtel des Lilas. A little fountain surrounded by cacti trickled in the centre of the courtyard and green tubs of flowering oleanders decorated the veranda. The place looked clean, pleasant and discreet—exactly the right sort of *pied-à-terre* that Chester, with his knack of doing well for himself, would come upon without the slightest effort.

They were the first to arrive and Harry greeted them effusively.

"Welcome to the ancestral château. It's not large, but it has a history."

"A bad one, no doubt," said Emmy.

Chester laughed. He was wearing white flannel trousers and a blue blazer with brass buttons. His thick brown hair, freshly waved, had a lighter streak running back from his brow.

"If that's what you think I must try to live up to it."

While he took Emmy to the bedroom to leave her scarf and gloves, Stephen glanced round the small living-room. It was conventionally furnished, but on the walls were two framed water-colours which he recognized at once as Lambert's work. He inspected them in turn, the one an arrangement of sweet peas in a Ming bowl, the other a group of storks standing in a misty pool, and as he gazed, he wondered how he could ever have been taken in by such prettiness. Beautifully executed, with an almost feminine brush, they were nevertheless empty and insipid, devoid of all vitality or invention, utterly meaningless. They might have been done by a clever art mistress at a superior girls' school. They made Stephen realize how long a road he had travelled since those first days in Paris. If the journey had been hard, at least it had taught him what really constituted a work of art.

"Good, aren't they?" Chester had returned with Emmy. "Lambert rather decently loaned me them. The price is on the back. There's always the chance one of my visitors will buy."

"You haven't shown us your own things."

"Well," Harry parried somewhat consciously, "as a matter of fact, most of them are away. I sent them to Paris. How about a drink?"

He produced a bottle of Dubonnet and poured out three glasses, then handed round a plate of fresh shrimps.

"Can I tempt you, Mademoiselle? *Bouquet de la baie.*"

"You caught them yourself?"

"Sure. Got up before breakfast."

Rearranging her hair, she looked at him, but for the first time with diminished animosity.

"What a liar you are."

Harry laughed heartily.

"I'm pretty good at that too."

The bell rang and the Lamberts came in. They seemed little changed, except that Philip had grown stouter, more languid in his manner. He wore a grey suit with a pink carnation in his buttonhole and carried on one forefinger a cardboard box of *pâtisserie* tied up with ribbon.

"I brought some cakes from Henri's, Chester. We'll have them with the coffee. Of course, you remember my sweet tooth, Des-

136

monde." He stretched out leisurely on the divan, and delicately put his thin nostrils to the flower in his lapel. Elise, who was dressed in the inevitable green and whose smile appeared a trifle more fixed than of old, was talking to Emmy. "Now tell me everything, dear boy."

Stephen began a brief account of himself, but before he had gone far he saw Lambert was not attending, and broke off.

"You know, Desmonde," Philip's tone was light and amused, "I wish for your own sake you wouldn't make such heavy going of it all. You can't attack art with a pickaxe. Why sweat your guts out like a stonebreaker? Do as I do and use a little delicacy, a little skill. I never overwork myself yet I never want for a client. And I do sell. Of course I admit I have talent, which does make it rather easy for me."

Stephen was silent. He could well guess at Lambert's facility. But Chester's announcement that luncheon was ready saved him from a reply.

The meal sent up from the hotel below was admirable, and well served by a young waiter who, in producing the food so hot, must have performed incredible feats of agility on the stairs. A lobster cooked in the local fashion was followed by a chicken *risotto*, then came a cheese *souffle*, and early on, Harry, with an expert touch, had popped the cork from a bottle of Veuve Cliquot. But the gayer the party became, the more Stephen felt completely out of it. At one time he had enjoyed this society, yet now, though he tried hard to attune himself to it, he failed dismally. What had happened to him that he should sit mute with the deadly consciousness that he no longer belonged here? Emmy, drinking more champagne than she should, was giving silly impersonations of Max and Montz which caused Chester, more boisterous than ever, to roar with laughter. Lambert, whom Stephen had once admired, he now saw exactly as Glyn had viewed him—a poseur and dilettante, a feebly endowed amateur. Perfectly mannered, well educated, made safe by his regular little income, refusing to be ruffled or excited, he drifted about, never exerting himself, skimming the cream from life. By cultivating women, he picked up clients who commissioned him for portraits or who paid good prices for his fans and water-colours. Elise, with her fixed smile and sharpened profile, showed the marks of this existence. Her looks were beginning to fade and lines to gather beneath her green, light-lashed eyes, yet while her capacity for flattering him had worn a trifle thin, her inexhaustible devotion made of her more and more a complaisant partner in this game of artistic bluff, the mere thought of which made Stephen move restlessly upon his chair.

After coffee and cakes, of which Philip, excusing himself by delicate literary allusion to Stevenson's young man with the cream puffs, ate five, they sat out upon the balcony. Continuing to monopolize the conversation, Lambert described, with ironic fastidiousness, the facial and social deficiencies of the elderly woman he was at present painting.

"In fact," he concluded airily, "all that one would expect of a Chicago hog-packer's widow."

"I imagine her cheque was good," Stephen said stiffly.

Lambert looked pained.

"Well . . . naturally."

Although he tried to throw off his dullness, time passed for Stephen with interminable slowness. But at last, towards three o'clock, taking advantage of a lull in the conversation, he looked at Emmy.

"I'm afraid we must go now."

"Oh, nonsense," Chester protested. "The afternoon's young. You can't possibly leave us yet."

"If I don't I shall be late for my job."

"Then why don't you stay, Emmy?" Harry smiled genially. "I'll take you back later."

There was a pause. Stephen saw her hesitate, then she shook her head brusquely.

"No. I'll go now."

They said good-bye, the porter downstairs found them a *fiacre*. As they turned the corner of the street, out of sight of the hotel, Stephen leaned towards her.

"It was good of you to come away with me. I do appreciate it."

"I don't care to make myself cheap."

It was not the answer he had hoped for, nevertheless, encouraged by the recent indication of her consideration, he drew closer to her and, under cover of the apron of the carriage, sought for her hand.

"Don't," she said, pushing him away pettishly. "Can't you see how I am?"

And as he gazed at her in surprise she gave, with vulgar frankness, a physical excuse which, if it were true, had perhaps occasioned her premature departure.

CHAPTER XI

AFTER THE RUSH and excitement of cross-country transit, most members of the Cirque Peroz found it agreeable to be settled in their winter quarters on the Côte d'Azur. This was their base; many had relations in Nice, Toulouse and Marseilles, and with more time on their hands were at liberty to visit them. Although business kept steady, the schedule had been reduced to five performances a week and, after the big night on Sunday, Monday and Tuesday were entirely free.

Already Stephen's friends were settled in the new routine. Max had resumed his violin lessons and could be seen, every afternoon, with the black pear-shaped case under his arm, departing at the brisk rolling trot enforced by his diminutive legs. The Croc, on the other hand, spent most of his time in the Bibliothèque Nationale, bowed over thick volumes, returning to expound to Stephen and Jo-jo a novel version of Schopenhauer, while Fernand, looking worn and wistful, went every morning arm in arm with his wife to a Cimiez homeopath for the daily irrigation prescribed for his *flux intestinal*. More practical, Jo-jo had found a spare-time occupation at the Negresco livery stables, where, in the pretence of washing down carriages, he spent most of his afternoons gossiping with the grooms and chauffeurs, making a small book on the local races and commenting satirically, out of the corner of his rat-trap mouth, on the visitors moving in and out of the hotel.

Stephen, on his part, had begun the preliminary design for a painting wherein he meant to utilize the individual studies made in the big tent, and which he proposed to name *Circus*. Such a complex arrangement, a grouping of innumerable figures with their matching and contrasting colour tones, was difficult and, since he had neither studio nor canvas large enough, he proposed to follow the precedent of the old masters and build up his composition, first of all, upon a smaller and less exacting scale. The idea grew upon him as he progressed, he began to feel that such material, the result of weeks of patient observation, must yield a magnificent result.

Since the day of the luncheon at the Hôtel des Lilas the barometer of Emmy's moods had gradually turned fair. Following that event, they had seen nothing of Chester or the Lamberts and it appeared as if the connection were finally broken. At the back of Stephen's mind, perhaps from a remark of Glyn's, there had always been the idea that an attachment had existed between Chester and Emmy. It gratified him that Emmy should accept the abrupt severance of their friendship with so little concern. She, with the others, had found an interest in Nice. Madame Armande's sister, who lived in the outskirts, just beyond the suburb of St. Roch, kept a small millinery establishment devoted mainly to the production and sale of carnival straw hats. Emmy, like most French girls, had a talent for the needle, and every afternoon she went off modestly in the tramcar to earn some pin-money in the workroom of the *Chapeau de Paille*. As a result Stephen saw even less of her than usual. Yet he derived a certain inner comfort from this unexpectedly sedate aspect of her nature. Still, such work must be frightfully dull and he told himself he must try to lighten its monotony. From the *Clarion de Nice* he discovered that a touring operatic company, fulfilling an engagement at the Casino Municipal, was giving a performance of *La Bohême* on the following Monday. This overdone romance of student life in Paris might entertain her, and at their next meeting he brought the subject up.

"Will you come to the theatre on Monday?"

"The theatre?" She seemed slightly at a loss. "Aren't you busy on your picture?"

"Not at night, surely."

"Well . . . if you like."

"Good. I'll get the tickets today."

He walked all the way down to the Casino and booked two seats in the *grand cercle*, then, knowing how much she enjoyed an "evening out", he reserved a table for dinner on the same night in the restaurant. He began to look forward to the event with that anticipation which so painfully affected him whenever he thought of being alone with her.

Monday came. When he had finished his session at the booth he scrubbed up at the tin basin outside his quarters, then put on his suit and a clean shirt he had washed the previous day. Just as he was ready he recognized her step behind him. He swung round, arrested by the expression of regret on her face.

"What's wrong?"

"I can't come with you tonight."

"Can't you?"

"No. Madame Armande's sister is down with *la grippe*. I must go to sit with her."

"Madame Armande can go."

"Ah, but there is a rush order to be got out. Madame is no good for that."

"But surely . . ."

"No, truly, I am completely obligated."

There was a long pause.

"Well . . . I suppose it can't be helped." He was badly cast down but did not care to show it.

"You must take someone else. Don't waste the tickets."

"Oh, blast the tickets. What do they matter?"

"I am sorry." She gave his arm a little condoling pat. "Some other evening perhaps."

Her air of preoccupied concern softened his disappointment. Nevertheless, as he watched her hurry off, then slowly turned and sluiced the soapy water from the basin, his dejection was so apparent that Jo-jo, who had just come back and, leaning on his elbow against the steps, had witnessed the recent scene, strolled over inquiringly.

"How goes it?" He spoke without removing the straw from between his teeth.

"All right."

"You're all dressed up."

"I'm wearing clothes, if that's what you mean."

"Where are you off to?"

"The theatre. Come with me. It's *La Bohême*."

"Vaudeville?"

"No, opera."

"Opera? Not me. But let's go over to the Mas Provençal and have a drink."

They went across the square to a nearby café much patronized by the Peroz ground crew. It was a cheap but pleasant place with long benches and tables running out to the pavement. In the dim interior a mechanical piano was playing, and people were sitting in their shirt sleeves. Jo-jo nodded to some workmen who, on their way home, had stopped in for a bock.

"What's your poison, Abbé?"

"Anything . . . vermouth."

"Vermouth *Quelle blague*. You'll have a *fine*." He called out in a loud voice for Pernod and a cognac.

The drinks were brought by a strapping young woman with bare red arms and round full breasts which swung under her blouse like young coconuts.

"There's a wench for you." With a practised hand Jo-jo filtered the Pernod through the sugar lump, took a comforting gulp of the opalescent liquid. "Name's Suzie. And no *poule* either. Daughter of the house. Why don't you try your luck? These big girls always like little men."

"Oh, go to hell."

Jo-jo laughed briefly.

"That's better. Trouble with you, Abbé, you never let yourself go."

"What do you mean?"

"*Sacré bleu!* You can be less tied up. Don't I know you have guts —that night . . . when you came down the chute. You ought to cut loose once in a while. Fling your weight about. Be gay, get drunk, have a good time."

"I've tried that. It doesn't work with me."

A short pause followed.

"There's a tea-dance every afternoon at the Negresco. Very high class. It might be interesting to go there."

There was an odd inflection in Jo-jo's voice, but Stephen merely shook his head.

Jo-jo threw up his hands resignedly. Then he said:

"What's happened to the bicycle beauty?"

"She had to go to Madame Armande's sister."

"Armande has a sister? Are there two such bitches in this unhappy world?"

"She got a milliner's shop in Lunel, beyond St. Roch. And she's sick."

"Ah." Jo-jo nodded. "An errand of mercy. Mademoiselle Nightingale the second."

A silence followed, during which he continued to regard Stephen with a satiric compression of his lips. Once he seemed about to speak but instead he shrugged slightly, beckoned with a finger for fresh drinks, and began to talk about the next day's races.

At seven o'clock they left the café, Jo-jo went off to feed and water his Arabs, and Stephen was alone. He felt better, warmed and more cheerful after three brandies, but he nevertheless had little inclination to go by himself to the Casino. The evening was delightfully fine—it would be a shame to spend it in a stuffy theatre. Suddenly he was struck by an idea. Lunel was not too far off, only a twenty-centime fare on the St. Roch tram. Why not make the trip, find the Armande shop and, even if he were obliged to wait until she had completed her work, bring Emmy back? With luck they might even be in time to have supper together.

The prospect briskened his steps as he set off across the Boulevard Risso for the Place Pigalle, where, without difficulty, he found a northbound tram. The journey was slow, and longer than he had supposed, but it was not yet eight o'clock and still light when he reached his destination. Lunel, as a place, was surprisingly small and undeveloped, the flat terrain largely occupied by market-gardens, the town little more than a collection of small new stucco villas surrounding a single unpaved street. Twice Stephen went up and down this thoroughfare without finding the Chapeau de Paille. Indeed, of the few stores that were there, not one bore the least resemblance to a hat shop. Puzzled and put out, he stood for a moment in the gusty wind which was blowing the dust around, then came back to the post office which, being attached to the local *épicerie*, still remained open. Here his inquiry revealed that there was no modiste, and assuredly no hat shop of any kind in Lunel.

With a queer look on his face, seated in the corner of an almost empty tram, Stephen rode back to Nice. The bumpy vehicle made his head ring. Had he made a stupid mistake through mishearing the place-name she had given him? No, he was sure she had said Lunel, not once, but several times. Could she have put him off by inventing this excuse on the spur of the moment? That also was impossible—she had been visiting Madame Armande's sister every day for the past two weeks. His expression, if anything, became more fixed. It was quite dark when he got to the Carabacel. Everything was quiet and deserted on the ground. He had an impulse to go to her quarters and find out if she had returned, but pride and a sense of physical weariness restrained him. He had already made himself sufficiently ridiculous without starting a scene at this hour. He went into his caravan, lay down on his bunk and closed his eyes. He would have it out with her in the morning.

CHAPTER XII

On the following day, although he rose early, he did not see her until eleven o'clock, when she appeared on the wagon steps in slippers and a blue-and-white cotton dressing-gown. She sat down on the top step, holding a cup of coffee. He went over.

"Good morning. . . . How did you find your patient?"

"Oh, fairly well."

"Did she have the doctor?"

"Naturally."

"It was nothing serious, I hope."

She took a sip of coffee.

"I told you it was the grippe."

"Isn't that rather infectious?" he said, with solicitude. "You must be careful."

"I can take care of myself."

"Really, I'm serious . . . there's a sharp wind out at Lunel. And one has to wait such a time for the tram."

She looked at him over the rim of the cup in silence. Then she said:

"What do you know about Lunel?"

"I was there last evening."

She looked at him suspiciously, then broke into a laugh.

"Don't pull my leg. You went to the theatre."

"On the contrary, I went to Lunel."

"Why?"

"I thought I might buy you a hat. Unfortunately, I couldn't find a hat shop."

"What are you getting at?"

"Nor for that matter could I discover a sister of Madame Armande."

"Who the devil do you think you are, pushing your nose into other people's business? Setting out to spy on me. You dirty sneak."

"At least I'm not a liar."

"Who do you call a liar? What I told you was the truth. If I chose I could take you to the place. Where you went mooning off to last night I don't know. But it exists. Besides," she added, with a crowning stroke, "Madame's sister is a widow—her name is not Armande. And now perhaps you'll shove off and let me have my breakfast in peace."

With his heart beating like a hammer, he gazed at her between anger and despair. He felt that she was lying—when occasion demanded she could be as slippery as an eel. Her very vehemence was suspicious. Yet it was just possible that she spoke the truth. He wanted with all his soul to believe her. Always ready to impute the fault to his side, he wondered if in the frightful sickness of his heart he had not completely misjudged her. The desire for reconciliation seized and weakened him.

"I was looking forward so much to our evening together . . ." he muttered.

"That's no excuse."

"Anyhow, let's both forget it."

"Only if you apologize for what you called me. Do you?"

He hesitated, biting his lip nervously, his eyes lowered. His pride forbade his accepting this humiliation from her. But his need of her made him abject.

144

"Yes . . . if you like. I'm sorry if I offended you." The words seemed wrung from him, they made him feel contemptible.

He passed the rest of the day torn by indecision, longing to be with her. It was some consolation for him to observe that she did not leave the grounds at all. In the evening she retired to her quarters immediately after the show. But he knew he could not go on like this, it was impossible; one way or the other, he must make certain.

Next day, after lunch, as she went towards the Place Pigalle, he followed. In hearing of such cases, he had always despised the doubting husband or jealous lover who spied upon the woman he suspected. Now he could not help himself. But he was no expert at the business and, in his effort not to be observed, he lost his quarry at the Pigalle terminus. Yet he had seen her take a tram bound for the promenade, and as another was on the point of leaving, he boarded it. In fifteen minutes he was at the sea-front. Hurriedly he looked around, walked the length of the esplanade and back, made a tour of the Casino, but could see no sign of her. Then, as he stood undecided, he suddenly recollected Jo-jo's manner when he spoke of the tea-dance at the Negresco. Although the chance appeared remote, he crossed the street, entered the gardens of the Musée Masséna and gazed over the gilt-tipped railings across the Rue de Rivoli, into the covered terrace of the hotel. At the side, under an awning thrown out from the lounge over a little platform set with tea-tables, an orchestra, concealed amongst palms, was playing a two-step to which a number of couples were dancing. At first he thought she was not there. Then, from behind the screen of foliage, another couple stepped on to the floor. The girl was smiling as, with a practised gesture, she extended her arms while her partner came close and held her by the waist. They glided off together—Chester and Emmy.

Motionless, with a strangely expressionless face, Stephen watched them, observing how gracefully they moved. Their steps matched perfectly. When the music stopped they remained standing together, and as an encore began, started off alone. So expert was their exhibition, they were allowed to monopolize the floor, and when they finally sat down they received a polite murmur of applause.

Stephen tore himself away, walked slowly to the promenade, and sat down on a bench from which he could command a view of the hotel entrance. The pain in his heart was almost unbearable. He winced as he thought of how she had deceived him. How she and Chester must have laughed together at the invention of the fictitious milliner, and at his unutterably fatuous belief that she was modestly, industriously plying her needle, while all the time she had been with Harry. Madame Armande was without question another partner in the burlesque and had undoubtedly spread word of it amongst the members of the troupe. Certainly Jo-jo knew, and while, through compunction, the little man had said nothing, what a fool he must have thought him.

Yet all this was nothing beside the anguish and bitter hunger of the soul that now possessed him. Greater even than his mortification and rage was this frantic intensification of jealousy and desire. Through his hurt and humiliation he still wanted her, through his hatred he still had need of her. And as he sat there with his head between his hands, he tried to find excuses for her, to rationalize her conduct. After all, she was only dancing with Harry, and that surely was no crime. One often heard of dancing partners who cared nothing for each other and were united by no more than a purely impersonal fondness for the art.

The music continued intermittently until six o'clock, then the floor emptied, he could see the musicians carrying out their instruments. A long interval followed. Almost certainly Harry and Emmy had gone into the bar—he pictured them close together on high stools, Harry easy and relaxed, on the best of terms with the bartender.

They were so long in coming out, he began to fear that they had left the hotel by another exit. But at last, as dusk was falling and strings of coloured lights flashed on along the front, they appeared, and after descending the wide portico steps came along the promenade. Talking together with animation, they passed so close to him he could have hailed them. But he kept his lips shut tight, and when they had progressed some fifty yards ahead he got up, almost automatically, and followed.

They did not go far. A short distance beyond the Casino they left the promenade, turned up a side street of the Marché aux Fleurs in the Old Town, and entered a small restaurant—the Brasserie Lutétia. Dinner for two, thought Stephen grimly, and he had a sick, wavering impulse to walk in and seat himself at their table. But he had not the heart for it—instead he buttoned his coat collar and posted himself in the shadow of a doorway opposite.

Not many people went into the *brasserie*—it was one of those quiet places where one could be sure of complete privacy. Once a waiter came out, looked up and down as though hoping for customers, then went in again. A cat padded slowly along the pavement. From the doorway, over the roofs at the end of the street, Stephen could see the dark bulk of the mountains and high pin-points of light that might be mistaken for stars.

He had to wait there until past nine o'clock before they emerged. Only the heavy urgency of his need to discover the truth helped him to maintain that weary and degrading vigil. And the moment was approaching—a tremor went over him as he watched them standing under the lighted marquee. Surely Chester was about to say good night, or at least escort her back to the Place Pigalle.

They were talking to the waiter now, the same one, he had come out with them, and Harry said something which made them all laugh. Then a *fiacre* clattered up, summoned from the line in the square below, a tip was handed, Emmy and Chester got in. Quickly, as they moved off, Stephen hurried down to the rank, jumped into another cab, told the man to follow.

They drove through the deserted Flower Market into a network of old streets, and swung on to the front; then, with a sinking heart, Stephen saw that they were heading directly towards Villefranche. In no time at all they were there. At the end of the Rue des Lilas, Stephen stopped his conveyance and paid the driver. Further along the quiet thoroughfare he could see the other vehicle drawn up. Both of its occupants got out, disappeared into the courtyard. Now the two cabs had driven off, except for himself the street was empty. Instinctively he looked at his watch—the luminous dial showed half-past ten o'clock. Slowly, he came towards the Hôtel des Lilas, gazed up at Chester's balcony apartment. The light in one room was on, he recognized it as the bedroom and could see the two figures moving behind the yellow blind. For some minutes longer the light remained on, then it suddenly went out.

How long Stephen stood there, staring dully at the dark apartment, he could not tell. At last he turned and walked away.

CHAPTER XIII

He was back at the Carabacel before midnight. Through the dull ache that lay behind his forehead he knew that he must get away. Methodically, without disturbing Jo-jo and the Croc, who were both asleep, he packed his belongings in his saddle-bag. Having tied his canvases together, he strapped them upon his back and, with a last look at his companions, pushed off on his bicycle. He rode north at a hard pace on the flat road towards St. Augustin, with the dim intention of striking the *route nationale* which would eventually bring him to Auvergne. He felt the need to rejoin Peyrat—he should have done so weeks before. But mainly he was pressed forward by the desire to escape, to obliterate the memory of these last insufferable weeks.

Towards morning he dismounted, stretched out on a patch of heath by the roadside and closed his eyes. He could not sleep but, having rested till the sun was up, he set off again. And now he saw from a signpost that he was not on the *grande route* but on a subsidiary road which ran along the rocky gorges of the Var and climbed circuitously towards Touet and Colmars. Nevertheless, he would not go back. All that day and the next he toiled on, through small hill villages and remote farm communities, forcing himself beyond his strength in the effort to forget. At Entrevaux he took a wrong turning into a secondary, steeper road that wound up through thick pine-woods towards the mountains. The surface was bad, the going harder here, there was an oppressive roar of rushing water as the stream thundered over its bed of boulders, yet that strange dread of turning back kept him moving forward, snatching a meal when he could and sleeping out on the bare ground, behind haystacks, in deserted cowsheds, with his folded cape for a pillow. A morbid aversion to all human contact kept him from even the poorest inns.

The weather had broken and amongst the hills it was damp and misty. On Sunday morning as he came into Annot, a small agricultural town built on a high plateau, a cold wet wind was blowing from the Alps. He knew that it was Sunday from the ringing of the church bells and the parade of sober, black-clad inhabitants who gazed at him with open suspicion. Sick as he was with fatigue and over-exertion, this hostility nevertheless bore down upon him, and although he felt desperately in need of hot coffee and had meant to stop, he did not, but put his head over the handle-bars and pedalled beyond the walls. Outside the town the rain began to fall. He was obliged to rest. In getting off he almost fell from his machine. Crouched under a dripping hedge by the road, eating the remains of the cold food he had bought the night before, he felt utterly homeless, without place or shelter, unreal and separate as a ghost.

The rain continued but he went on, slower than before and with a shortness of breath that caused him to dismount upon the steeper inclines. His nose began to bleed, intermittently, and although he attributed this to the altitude and gave little heed, it was an odd sensation as the blood flowed warmly to the back of his throat.

Towards noon he began to feel extremely queer and, through the

148

numbness that oppressed him, a shaft of reason penetrated. He would never reach the Auvergne in this fashion, it was lunacy to continue, he must get to a railroad or some convenient centre without delay. Unfolding his large-scale map, and shielding it under his dripping cape, he saw that by cutting across to the west through Barrême he could reach the junction at Digne, not more than thirty-five kilometres distant. Digne was not much, perhaps, but it was on the plain, and would let him escape from these impossible mountains.

He set off on the cross road. This was wilder, more difficult than before, with a covering of sharp metal which made his tyres bounce and skid. He had less power than ever upon the hills and the additional effort started his nose-bleed again. The sky ahead was low and overcast, the rain rapidly increased, and presently a deluge was upon him. Wet through, with darkness rapidly descending, he became alarmed, lit his carbide lamp with difficulty, and again consulted the map.

He had not peered at the sheet for more than a minute before a groan escaped him. Oh, God, what a fool . . . what a blind, senseless idiot. Tracing with his finger, he saw where he had gone wrong. Back at St. André that right turn should have been left. And now—he checked on the sign, *route accidentée, fort montée, isolée*—he was on a dead-end track leading directly upwards to the Col d'Allos.

A fit of nerves, almost of panic, shook him. He held the map closer. There must be a village of some sort in the vicinity. Then, with a relief, he made out the name St. Jérôme. This apparently was only a hamlet, but luckily was marked by a circled red Cross of Lorraine, indicating the presence of a hostel listed by the Touring Club de France as affording lodging for cyclists and where at least he might obtain shelter for the night. If he were not completely lost he should reach it within the hour.

He pedalled off, bent forward against the wind. The salt taste in his mouth increased, and pressing his handkerchief against his lips, he felt it grow thick and sodden. His legs no longer belonged to him, a hammer was thumping in his head, but when he felt that he could go no further he saw in the hollow before him a wavering cluster of lights.

They grew nearer; a large building surrounded by smaller houses dimly took shape ahead. Completely spent, he let his machine fall and stumbled up the path of the first house—it looked like a labourer's cottage. His knock remained unanswered for an interminable interval, then the door was opened by a small child who stared at him, then turned and ran. He stepped into the passage, hearing voices in a room at the back of the house. He was breathing irregularly and, though dripping wet, was dying of thirst. They must take me in, he thought, I am going to be ill . . . in fact I am damned ill.

A workman in a blue shirt came towards him, followed by a woman carrying an Argand lamp and, behind her, the child. He saw their startled faces through a shifting fog. The woman shone the lamp on him, and gave an exclamation.

"Terribly sorry." With tremendous difficulty, as though from some deep well, he brought out the words. "Lost my way. Can you put me up?"

"But Monsieur . . ."

"Please . . . can I sit down? . . . A drink."

Before he could speak again the man drew nearer, waved an arm excitedly.

"Not here," he said. "You must go along."

"Let me stay." Again that fearful problem of articulation. "I can't go on."

"No, no . . . further along . . . not here."

The man took him by the shoulder and steered him from the house. Believing that he was being thrown out on the road, unable to resist or even to protest, Stephen, swept by a final hopelessness, felt a dry smarting behind his eyes. Then, as they reached the wicket gate, he realized that the man had not relinquished his grasp but was helping him, supporting him in a dizzy passage down the street. Indeed, as they advanced, he murmured encouragement.

"See . . . it's not far . . . we are nearly there."

In the end, they reached the large building. There were thick trees on either side. The man rang a bell and, after a moment, a grille opened in the studded door. A brief conversation ensured, then they were admitted to a small whitewashed hall with a bare stone floor and scrubbed benches round the walls.

On the edge of collapse, Stephen gazed giddily about him. Everything was out of focus. The lines of the hall all ran together, then drew apart, like ripples in a pool. Even the porter who had let him in seemed blurred fantastically, dressed in a long coat and hood which gave him the look of a woman. Another man, or woman, had appeared. Then, all at once, the whole distorted pattern dissolved. The workman from the cottage, turning towards this new arrival, misguidedly removed his sustaining arm. Stephen fell forward on his face, the bundle of sopping canvases still strapped on his back.

CHAPTER XIV

THE MORNING SUN, slanting through the single, deep-set window towards the head of the trestle bunk, awakened him. He lay passive, his gaze travelling over the few objects in the narrow hermitage which, during the past three weeks, had become intimate and familiar—the single straw-bottomed chair, the Provençal armoire, the wooden *prieu-dieu* in the corner, the black crucifix on the white wall. Speculatively, he inspected his hand, holding it up to the light, finding the fingers still blanched, but perhaps less translucent than yesterday. It was a test he performed every morning.

A light footstep, grating slightly on the sanded corridor outside, caused him, without moving his body, to turn his head. He was gazing towards the door as it opened and the Infirmarian entered, carrying his breakfast on a tray.

"How did you sleep?"

"Very well."

"Our singing did not disturb you?"

"No, I'm quite used to that now."

"Good." Placing the tray on the chair. Dom Arthaud produced a thermometer from the recesses of his white habit, shook it down and, with a smile, put it between Stephen's lips. "This is no longer necessary. But as you are to be up today we shall make sure."

He was a man of about fifty, of medium stature, sturdy and square-shouldered, with a broad, pleasant face, faintly blue around the chin, and intelligent, bespectacled brown eyes. His cropped head was tonsured, he wore strapped sandals upon his bare feet. At the end of a minute he removed the thermometer, read it, then with a nod of reassurance pushed the chair and tray up to the bed.

"Do not forget your medicine."

When he had taken, through a glass tube, the dark metallic draught, Stephen began his breakfast—a bowl of *café au lait*, fresh butter in an earthenware pot, sliced bread and fruit. The milky coffee was hot, smelling of chicory. As he dipped bread in the bowl he looked up with compunction at the monk standing—he would never sit down—at the end of the cot.

"Won't you share this with me? There's more than enough for two."

"On no account. We have our meal at noon."

"But . . . this is so good."

The Infirmarian smiled cheerfully.

"Yes . . . our food is perfectly horrible. But we're accustomed to it. And then, we have not been ill."

Stephen took another slice of bread.

"That's what I've been meaning to ask you. What exactly was the matter with me? You've never said."

"You had an inflammation of the lung . . . from exposure. In addition, you overstrained yourself. As a result you had the complication of a hæmorrhage. Quite severe."

"I thought the bleeding came from my nose."

"No. It was from your lung." He paused, glancing over his steel-rimmed spectacles. "Have you suffered anything of that nature before?"

Stephen reflected for a moment, then shook his head.

"I had a cold some months ago. Bronchitis, I imagine. But it couldn't possibly have come from that?"

The Infirmarian lowered his eyes.

"It would not be proper for me to answer. I am not a doctor."

"You pulled me through all right."

"With God's help."

"And a lot of skill. I can't believe you're not qualified."

"I studied medicine at Lyons under Professor Rolland. In my final year, no doubt as you were called to be a painter, I had the call to be a monk."

"Very fortunate for me."

Dom Arthaud inclined his head, then, as Stephen had finished, he took up the empty tray. At the door he paused.

"Do not rise just yet. This morning the Reverend Prior is coming to visit you."

When he had gone Stephen settled back, with his hands clasped behind his head. He still felt atrociously weak. Yet his cough was almost gone and he no longer had the stabbing pain in his side. How good the sun felt on his cheek—the stirrings of convalescence had begun. He did not worry about his condition. The Infirmarian's persistence in taking his temperature morning and evening was palpably no more than a kindly routine. Indeed, he wondered calmly if his illness, with its strange depletion, had not been peculiarly opportune. He had heard of blood-letting as a remedy for fever. At least it had cured him of those pangs which had so unendurably tormented him.

Looking back, he was amazed that for all these months, he should have remained in a state of such utter subjection, cast down by a single word, grovelling for Emmy's favour. The mere thought of it made him shudder. He rejoiced that he was himself again, and swore that never again would he submit to such an enslavement—indeed he went further and solemnly vowed that in future no woman would ever have any part in his life. His work alone would concern him now, and to that he would apply himself with rigorous self-discipline.

At eleven o'clock his visitor arrived. The Superior, a tall commanding figure in his white hooded robe, sat down quietly upon the chair, and studied Stephen with a grave reflectiveness.

"So you are at last to leave your bed, my son. I am glad."

"And I am grateful," Stephen answered. "It was a lucky thing for me I found your cross upon my map."

"It is true that we have a cross. But we are not upon the map." The Prior barely smiled. "That mark is for a cyclists' inn in the adjoining valley. You lost your way, my son. Or, since Providence brought you here, could one say you found it?"

An odd inflection in the Prior's tone brought a faint colour to Stephen's pale cheek. Had he given himself away in the early days of his illness?

"At any rate," he answered, "it's high time I was clearing out. I have given you a vast amount of trouble. You must want to be rid of me."

"On the contrary, you are most welcome to stay. You have had a severe turn, and although you are over the worst, Dom Arthaud thinks it will be several weeks before you are fit to travel."

"But . . . I'm afraid I couldn't pay . . ."

"Have we asked you for money, my son? For that matter, who would expect it from a struggling artist? Stay with us for a while. Sit in the sunshine in the garden. When you are stronger life will have a different aspect. You will be better able to face the world."

The Prior let his hand rest on Stephen's arm, then he rose and went out.

Stephen had to struggle to force the tears back from his eyes. He got up. His clothes, washed and neatly folded, were in the armoire with his other belongings. His money, some thirty francs, was in a precise little pile beside his watch, which was going and, he guessed, had been wound for him every day. When he was dressed he left his room and went along an unfamiliar, stone-flagged corridor which took him to the garden at the back.

It was not a large enclosure, a few paths laid out around some straggling rose-beds leading to a grotto, with a statue at the far end. A handball wall broke the contours of the surrounding hedge. Some fields were beyond. From his conversations with Dom Arthaud, Stephen had learned that, following upon the gift of a small country house, the community, devoted to the training of twenty novices, had only recently been established and was growing solely through the efforts of the monks themselves, who had built with their own hands the small chapel adjoining the old mansion. He could see it now standing white and somewhat raw against the fleecy sky.

After he had wandered round the paths he was obliged to rest on one of the benches that flanked the handball court. An old man, in the brown habit of a lay brother, was tethering a cow in the pasture. Presently a service began in the chapel and the low chanting, carried on the soft breeze, was more than he could bear. He got up and crawled back to his room.

There he saw a letter, placed conspicuously for him upon the narrow window-ledge. About a week before, feeling terribly alone, he had propped himself on his pillow and had scrawled a few lines to the tenant of 15 Rue Castel, asking him to forward any mail which might have been sent to that address. This, presumably, was the result. He tore open the envelope. It was from Stillwater, a brief note dated two months previously.

DEAR STEPHEN,

I do not know if this will ever reach you. If it does it will inform you of the death of Lady Broughton, in October. This was not unexpected. Some weeks before, the engagement of Claire and Geoffrey was announced. They are to be married quite soon. There is no other news of consequence to give you except to say that Father continues to be most unhappy at your absence. I beg you to return and accept your responsibilities as a dutiful son.

Yours,
Caroline

Still holding the letter, he sat down on the bed. At another time this word from home might not have so deeply affected him. He had known of Lady Broughton's illness, and his fondness for Claire had never been more than a kind of brotherly affection. Yet here, in these strange remote surroundings, beaten down by illness, the death of the one, the impending marriage of the other—to Geoffrey of all men—seemed to increase his sense of exile, to cut him off more sharply from all that pleasant life which normally would still be his. The tone of Caroline's letter, curt, filled with unspoken bitterness and implied reproaches for what might have been, made him more than ever feel himself a creature apart, whose very nature set him in conflict with family, home, and society.

As the weeks passed he grew stronger. The surrounding country, covered with rocks and stone-pines, unbeautiful and without character, gave him slight incentive to leave the grounds. He made friends with the two children of Pierre, the cottager who had brought him to the monastery, gave them rides, perched high on the seat of his bicycle. He helped old Brother Ludovic in the garden, and played handball with the novices at their hour of recreation. They were a cheerful group of youths, recruited mainly from good bourgeois homes in Garonde and the neighbouring towns. Perhaps because he was a stranger, and of a different race, they went out of their way to show him many small attentions tinged with a proselytizing spirit which, while it left him otherwise unmoved, touched and amused him. Their hearts were bound up in this new little community, and when not engaged in prayer they gave themselves unsparingly to hard manual labour in their endeavours to improve it.

One day, at the handball game, a remark, half laughing, half serious, was addressed to him.

"Monsieur Desmonde . . . since you are an artist, why don't you paint a fine picture for our church?"

Stephen, his attention arrested, gazed at the speaker.

"Why not?" he answered, with a serious air.

The idea, which had not occurred to him, struck him as an admirable way of expressing his gratitude, of making some tangible return for the kindness he had received. Besides, his enforced idleness had begun to weigh oppressively upon him.

That same afternoon he spoke to his friend Dom Arthaud, who received the suggestion warmly and promised to take it to the Superior. At first the Prior hesitated. The chapel, although admittedly unfinished within, was the product of prolonged and arduous effort and dear to his heart. Would it be wise to place this prized and hard-won possession in the hands of an unknown painter whose few canvases, while strangely compelling, gave no evidence of orthodox proficiency? In the end, that faith which was the sustaining force of his existence moved him to his decision. He sent for Stephen.

"Tell me, my son, what you propose to do."

"I should like to paint a fresco above the altar on the end wall of the apse."

"A religious subject?"

"Naturally. I thought of the Transfiguration. It would light up the entire chapel."

"You are sure you could produce something of which we would approve?"

"I would try. I have no pigments, no brushes large enough. You would have to get these for me. You would have to take me on trust. But if you do so, I promise to do my best."

Next morning two of the fathers departed for Garonde, returning in the evening with various brown-paper packages. Meanwhile, the novices had erected a light wooden scaffolding behind the altar. Early next day, with that excitement which he always experienced at the beginning of a work, Stephen took up his brush.

Yet his state of mind was quite unusual. Relaxed in body, not altogether free of the lassitude of convalescence, he seemed bathed in a languid softness. His emotions were still unstable, moisture came readily to his eyes. The atmosphere of the chapel, the intoning of the monks, the sense of being detached from the world, induced in him emotions quite foreign to his nature. Although he had no models, the work came into being with an ease surprising to one accustomed to strain beyond endurance in those first creative hours. Already he had blocked in the central figure of the Lord, clad in white garments, radiant with a cloud of light, and was beginning to outline the features of Moses and Elias.

As he progressed with such facility he experienced odd moments of distrust wherein he wondered if, instead of projecting his own ideas, he was not unconsciously reproducing a composite of the early religious painters. Applied in tempera, his colours, usually so hard, were soft and flat, his forms seemed disturbingly conventional. Yet against these doubts was the growing approval of the community.

In the beginning, he had been watched with anxiety, perhaps even with misgiving. But soon this gave way to open admiration. Often as he turned on the scaffold to clean his brushes he would observe in the eyes of some novice who had come in ostensibly to pray, but actually to incur the sin of distraction, a look of perfect rapture. Was not that reassurance enough? And, after all, had he not pledged himself to please?

The fresco, occupying the entire space above the reredos, was finished within three weeks, and when the scaffolding had been removed all the community assembled, viewed it with acclamation.

"My son," the Prior addressed Stephen, "now I know that your coming here was providential. You have given us a memento of your stay which will endure for good, beyond the lifetime of all of us. Now it is we who are most deeply in your debt." He went on: "Tomorrow we shall celebrate a High Mass to consecrate your work. Although you are not a member of our faith, I hope you will please us by being present."

Next morning the altar was bedecked with flowers, ablaze with candles. The Superior, in white vestments, assisted by Dom Arthaud, sang the Mass while the choir chanted the responses. To Stephen, seated in the gallery, the painting, glowing in the candlelight, made mystical by a fume of incense, seemed a splendid achievement. Never before had he had such a success.

A special repast was served after the ceremony, with a country wine of such surpassing potency that Stephen took a walk to the village to clear his head.

In the afternoon when he returned from the village Dom Arthaud met him at the door with a queer expression.

"There is a visitor to see you. A gentleman who says he has come to take you back to Paris."

Stephen went to his room. There, reclining on the bed, wearing hat and coat and puffing furiously at his pipe, was Peyrat. He jumped up immediately Stephen entered, kissed him on both cheeks.

"What have you been up to? Not once, but a dozen times have I tried to reach you. And now, only by chance, I got your address from the Rue Castel. Why do you bury yourself down here?"

"I've been painting." Stephen smiled, still tingling at the unexpectedness of seeing Peyrat.

"Worse luck," said Peyrat, frowning, with an assumption of fierceness. "While I was waiting they dragged me to the church. What a frightful thing you have done, *cher ami*. Oh, what a miserable copy of del Sarto. What a dreadful rehash of Luini. Although they love it and will go down on their knees before it for centuries, it is inexcusably shocking, and for you, especially at this moment, a disgrace."

"Why at this moment?" Stephen asked, rather out of countenance.

"Because of the announcement made last month which has caused me to chase after you all over France."

"What on earth are you driving at?"

"An announcement," Peyrat continued, undisturbed, rolling the words over his tongue as though he enjoyed their savour, "which will put a medal on your breast, fifteen hundred francs in your pocket, and permit us, I trust, to take our trip together to Spain."

Suddenly he threw his arms round Stephen and once again embraced him.

"Never mind your sickness, or that horrible Moses and Elias. Your *Circe* has won you the Prix de Luxembourg."

PART THREE

CHAPTER I

ON A GREY afternoon early in June, 1914, Stephen came along the Faubourg St. Honoré towards the Place Vendôme. It was a district he rarely frequented, especially at this hour, when the fashionable thoroughfare made him feel strangely out of place. However, he had been to the Salles des Ventes Soulat, in the Rue Heber, had decided to walk off the headache acquired in the crowded auction-rooms and get back to his own less elegant haunts.

The sale had made him sad and angry. In order that he might find his share of the expenses of their Spanish expedition, Peyrat had decided upon that expedient used occasionally by artists of the quarter and had sent in ten of his paintings to the Soulat *vente libre*, held once a month.

Today the feature of the sale had been a large Bouguereau, a diaphanously draped young female, with skin like coloured putty, black hair parted in the middle, and the eyes of a tame gazelle, holding a pitcher, borrowed from Greuze, from which water gushed into an ornamental, rose-embowered well. On the dias, the picture had induced a hush, then a hum of admiration from the assembly and, after brisk bidding, the hammer fell at ten thousand francs. Various lots of antique furniture followed, then some kitchenware—Peyrat's paintings came last upon the list. The first caused a faint titter, the second a decided ripple of amusement, and by the time the final canvas was exhibited the crowd was laughing heartily, encouraged by a shower of witticisms from the back of the gallery. Not one of these imaginative and original works fetched more than sixty francs. There was no reserve—the entire ten were knocked down to the same buyer for a total of four hundred and eighty francs. Who had purchased them? Was it merely some *farceur* who thought to shock and entertain his friends? Curiosity caused Stephen to remain behind and question the clerk in the *bureau* where settlements were made. And there had come the worst moment of all—the entire ten paintings had been secured, practically for nothing, by an agent of the art dealer Tessier.

"Did he buy the Bouguereau?" asked Stephen grimly.

"*Mon Dieu*, no, Monsieur."

"Why did he go after these others?"

The clerk shrugged.

"Surely Monsieur is aware of the tricks and trends of the art world. What one buys today for fifty francs one may sell in ten years' time for fifty thousand . . . if one is Tessier."

Stephen left the office saying some bad words to himself. Yet it was not long before his mood lifted. Exploited though Peyrat was, and must always be, now at least Jerome had almost five hundred francs, which, added to the fifteen hundred he had himself received for his prize, would enable them to set out for Madrid and, with economy, to spend several months in Spain together. Here in Paris, spring had been cold and dismal—the wind blew sharp and dusty on street corners, and the leaves of the chestnut trees were shrivelled at their edges. The prospect of escaping to a sunnier clime warmed Stephen's bones.

At this point he passed the creamery which he had patronized when first he came to Paris, just opposite the Clifton Hotel, and he reflected with a shadowy smile on the changes wrought in him since he had driven up, timid yet entranced, to its stuffy portals. Suddenly, while the thought was in his mind, his expression altered. Advancing directly towards him, accompanied by two men—an elderly French officer wearing a kepi and a much-beribboned uniform, and a younger man, deeply bronzed, also with a military bearing—was his Uncle Hubert. It would have been possible for Stephen, by feigning interest in a shop window, to avoid the encounter. Instead, with features already set, convinced that General Desmonde would cut him, he went on.

However, he was wrong—with a barely perceptible flicker of his grey eye Hubert recognized him, halted slightly, continued for a few paces, then, with a word to his companions, turned back.

"Stephen." Though his voice was quite controlled, he did not extend his hand. "I'm fortunate to have run into you. I thought I might have to reach you at the Rue Castel."

"Yes?"

"I very much want to see you. Will you come to my hotel later? I can't stop now—I'm with these people."

Across his shoulder Stephen was conscious of the two officers, pretending, with perfect politeness, to be unaware of his existence.

"Where are you staying?"

"The Clifton, as usual." The General glanced across the street. "Look here, come to breakfast tomorrow. Nine o'clock."

Stephen hesitated, but only for an instant.

"Very well."

"Good. I haven't a deal of time, so make it nine sharp."

With a brief nod, Hubert swung round, strode off with his friends.

With less military precision, Stephen resumed his way towards the Left Bank. This unexpected encounter, awakening memories both poignant and bitter which he wished to forget, had disconcerted him. There had never been much understanding between General Desmonde and himself—their natures were antipathetic—yet Hubert had always treated him with condescending amiability. And the impersonal coldness which he had just now displayed seemed to presage that the interview tomorrow would not be agreeable. Nevertheless, Stephen's pride, and that ironic humour which had lately reinforced his character, above all, a fixed determination not to be intimidated, made him firmly resolve not to evade the issue. On the following morning at nine o'clock precisely he entered the gloomily respectable, dark maroon lobby of the Clifton.

General Desmonde was already in the dining-room, its solitary occupant, and having acknowledged Stephen's punctuality with a slightly less frigid greeting, he remarked:

"I've ordered bacon and eggs, tea, toast and marmalade for both of us. One thing about this place, you can get a decent English breakfast."

A waiter brought the admirable British food. Buttering his toast Hubert bit into it crisply.

"I suppose," he said, munching, "you'd like news of home."

"If you care to give it me. How is my father?"

"Fairly well, on the whole. They all seem to be. Your mother's been away again. Davie's grown—quite a tall chap now."

Stephen, with an effort, maintained his expression of polite interest. His uncle went on:

"My lot are pretty fit, too. Geoffrey and Claire nicely settled in." He shot a glance under his brows. "Claire is expecting a child in the summer."

"You hope for a boy, of course." Again, politely.

"Oh, either kind . . . I daresay Geoff wants a son to follow on at Sandhurst."

There was a silence. The questions which Stephen wished to ask remained unuttered. In this atmosphere of chill constraint he could not speak with feeling of Davie or his father, but if only to protect himself must maintain, with equal stiffness, this attitude of seeming indifference.

At last the General finished, touched up his cropped moustache, folded his napkin with the calm precision which marked all his actions, looked steadily across the table at Stephen.

"How has your . . . your sketching been progressing?"

"Oh, very much as usual. We have our good days and our bad, you know."

"Hm. You've been away almost two years now."

"Art is long," with an indifferent smile. "Time is fleeting."

"Indeed! I suppose . . . you have . . . no success . . . to show for your efforts?"

"Very little," Stephen maintained his tone of irony.

"Ah, nothing destined for immortality?"

"Not yet, perhaps . . . but who can tell?"

Hubert made a disdainful gesture.

"Why do you go on . . . leading this kind of life?"

"It is impossible for me to explain it to you—thought I daresay I could to a sympathetic ear."

"Is it some kind of idiotic notoriety you are after . . . or mere slackness?"

"Whichever you consider the worse of these motives."

The deliberate satiric lightness of Stephen's manner caused General Desmonde to compress his clean-cut lips. To one who prided himself upon maintaining the highest standards of soldierly efficiency, who set honour, discipline, and self-control above all else, whose cool courage and physical hardihood were a by-word in his regiment, Stephen's present attitude was like a red rag to a bull. He decided, in his own phrase, to stop beating about the bush and got straight to the point.

"You must come home," he said, and paused. "If not for your family . . . for your country."

Astounded, Stephen gazed back at his uncle in absolute silence.

"You may not realize it," Hubert went on. "There is going to be a war. In a matter of weeks, months at the latest, Germany will attack Britain. It will be a desperate business. To achieve victory we shall need every available man we have got."

Again there was silence. Stephen, understanding at last what was in Hubert's mind, experienced a deepening of his resentment. How often in the past had the General given false warning of the imminence of war! For years now he had been voicing suspicions of Germany, distrust of Kaiser Wilhelm and his general staff, gloomy prophecies of the unpreparedness of Britain. Doubtless his profession as a soldier induced such a precautionary view-point, nevertheless, in the family, this attitude of Uncle Hubert's was admitted to be an obsession. To imagine that on such a supposition he would cut short his career seemed to Stephen fantastic.

"I am afraid I must disappoint you. I am not coming home."

A pause followed.

"I see." Hubert's voice was cold as ice. "You intend to continue slouching around here in indolence and dissipation."

"You appear to have some misapprehension of the nature of my activities. Would it surprise you to know that I work twelve hours a day? Indeed, I'll wager I work harder at my art than ever you did on the parade ground."

"Your art!" Hubert's lip curled. "What conceited rot!"

"It is absurd, is it not, to be concerned only with what is beautiful, and not, as you are, with the business of killing people. Nevertheless, despite your opinion of us, we are the only ones who matter. I would hazard a guess that the works of the great artists will be remembered and cherished long after all your bloody conquests are forgotten."

The General, extremely angry, bit his lip. There was a spark in his glacial eye.

"I refuse to argue with you. I repeat—whatever you have done, you are still British and a Desmonde. I won't have our name held up to ridicule and contempt. At a time like this you can't get away with daubing paint on a strip of canvas. You must come home. I insist."

"And I refuse." Stephen got up from the table. "Too bad there's nothing you can do about it."

Still preserving that faint, fixed smile which more than anything enraged his uncle, he spun on his heel and left the dining-room. As he passed through the vestibule, on an impulse he stepped into the hotel office and paid the bill for his breakfast. Then, no longer smiling, trembling a little from the hurts inflicted upon him, he went out to the street.

CHAPTER II

IN THE STRANGE yellow light which filtered through the glass roof, the Biarritz express was on the point of departure, most of the passengers had taken their places, and on the *quai*, where belated travellers were hurrying, porters shouting and pushing their trucks, amidst a final confusion of noise, steam, and sulphurous smoke,

Stephen stood at his compartment, already almost full, awaiting Peyrat with increasing anxiety. Jerome, staying at Louveciennes, had promised to be at the station in good time. All the arrangements for their departure were made. And now the carriage doors were being shut. Upset, reflecting how unwise he had been to rely on anyone so impulsive and uncertain, Stephen gave his friend up. Peyrat was evidently not coming. Then, just as the horn sounded, he observed a familiar figure walking calmly up the platform, wearing a shaggy, dilapidated coat, carrying an easel and a carpet-bag of terrifying antiquity.

They got into the moving train in the nick of time, and after some manipulation Peyrat piled his belongings tenderly upon the rack. When, not without a struggle, they had found places near each other he turned quite at his ease to Stephen, with a smile which, springing from his bright blue eyes, irradiated his wrinkled and unshaven face.

"You must forgive me. I am late. In the Métro I found myself next a young curé who, learning that I was bound for Madrid, engaged me in conversation on the subject of the discalced rule. Our discussion attained such fervour I got carried past my station . . . to the Odéon."

His soft voice and affectionate manner, so polite, gentle and gay, above all that irresistible air of ingenuous audacity which was so much a part of him, made Stephen relent immediately.

"A fine thing if you had been left behind."

Peyrat immediately became grave.

"My friend," he said, "do not reproach me for pursuing so fascinating a subject. I intend to look into the matter by visiting the convents of that order in the province of Andalusia. I have often thought of instituting a barefoot brotherhood, dedicated to art and meditation. This may be my opportunity." He added, after a moment of thought, "Poverty will save the world."

Stephen raised his eyebrows.

"Poverty will not save us. I have got your money from the Ventes Soulat and, as you were roundly cheated, it is little enough. We have no more than nineteen hundred francs between us."

"Divide it equally. I offer no objections," said Peyrat calmly. "Or if you wish, let me have it all. I will be our treasurer." Then, pointing to the moth-eaten carpet-bag, "I've got a Bayonne ham there, weighing not a milligramme less than fifteen kilos, given me by Madame Huffnaegel. We shall not starve."

Whilst the train gathered speed through the outer suburbs, the other passengers having their own preoccupations, Stephen, never any good with money, remembering, too, how excellently Peyrat had managed the housekeeping in the Rue Castel, handed over the packet of banknotes. Accepting this with placidity, Jerome stuffed it in the bulging wallet, held together with string, wherein he hoarded all his precious documents—frayed cuttings from provincial newspapers, dirty and dog-eared cards for past *soirées musicales*, and those complimentary letters which, on the slightest provocation, he would produce and read to chance acquaintances in cafés, public conveyances, and even in the street. Then, having assured himself that nothing was lost, he took out a sealed envelope, already somewhat soiled, and fingering it with an air of mystery not unmixed with pride, glanced several times at Stephen as though hopeful of provoking his curiosity. When this did not succeed he observed:

"You will not guess what this is. A letter of introduction to the Marquesa de Morella. She is old, but of the highest aristocracy, and Mother Superior of the convent in Avila. She will undoubtedly receive me. An ancester was painted by Goya. He hangs in the Prado."

"Then I shall call upon the ancestor. And all the other Goyas."

"Ah, yes, that undoubtedly will be something for you," Peyrat agreed. "Still . . . a marquesa. . . ."

He replaced the letter and retied the string. A silence followed during which he studied his companion.

"You seem depressed, my friend. Has anything upset you?"

"No," said Stephen; then, on an impulse, for indeed the quarrel with General Desmonde still weighed upon his mind, "Someone wanted to make a soldier of me."

Peyrat, master of the *non sequitur*, betrayed not the least surprise. For a few minutes he sucked meditatively at the cold stem of his pipe.

"Enforced military service is a monstrous institution—the greatest evil of our time. Why should men be forced into uniform in order that they may kill each other? In the days of chivalry the knights engaged in battle of their own free will. It was a sport to them— and they were good for nothing else. No one ever dreamed of bolting up a poet or a philosopher in armour and sending him to the battlefield. Even the peasants were exempt. But now we must all be made expert in the methods of slaughtering our fellow creatures."

Stephen, who had listened with a smile, now laughed outright. This Peyrat accepted as a compliment, but suppressing his satisfaction, he pulled a long sigh.

"Ah, poor humanity, what do you not suffer from your masters!"

"At least," said Stephen, quite cheered up, "we are not suffering at present. Moreover, since it is now past noon, we are going to have lunch."

Jerome admitted that he was hungry. He wished to produce Madame Huffnaegel's ham from his carpet-bag, but Stephen, in his uplifted mood, cast economy to the winds. They elbowed their way along the crowded corridors to the restaurant car and, while bushy hedgerows, willows drooping yellow across grey streams, and trees canopied with green flew past them, lunched on sardines, breast of veal, and a rich Brie cheese. Afterwards they lingered over a glass of Benedictine while Peyrat tranquilly smoked his pipe.

Late afternoon brought them to the flat monotony of the Landes, wastes of sand and interminable pines, through which occasionally they caught a twilight gleam of brightness that was the sea. Quickly, evening emerged to night, casting a veil upon the rolling hills and fertile vineyards of the Garonne. When the moon rose, gazing at the shadowed plains beyond which mountains lifted up their crests, Stephen was conscious of a troubling sadness springing from the past. But he shut his mind against it, thinking only of the future and of the splendid adventure that lay ahead.

Except for a faint blue glow the lights were dimmed. In various attitudes of contortion the occupants of the compartment composed themselves to sleep until they should change for Hendaye. Peyrat, seated erect, his head enveloped in his coat, was already breathing deeply. Gazing at that fantastically shrouded form, Stephen was conscious of a warmth in his heart. How good it was to be travelling with a friend so original, gay and gentle, so prodigal of his affection, always naïvely happy, and while sometimes absurd, yet on occasion so profoundly wise. He closed his eyes and, rocked by the motion of the train, shivering a little in the night cold, was soon asleep.

CHAPTER III

THEY REACHED MADRID late the following afternoon and without much difficulty found two modest rooms in the Calle Olivia, near the Puerta de Toledo, a poor neighbourhood adjoining the fruit market some distance from the centre of the city, but convenient to the yellow trams. Peyrat, in bad yet comprehensible Spanish, arranged the terms in a business-like manner and paid for a week's lodging in advance.

166

On the morning after their arrival Stephen rose, much refreshed, and roused Jerome.

"Seven o'clock. Time you were up. We ought to get to the Prado early."

Peyrat, supported by an elbow, considered his companion with indulgence.

"Nothing is early in this country. The Prado does not open until nine-thirty." He added in a reflective manner: "In any case I am not going."

"What!" Stephen paused, incredulous. "Then why have we come to Madrid?"

"To enable you to view the Prado. Go, my friend, and profit by the experience. But there is little point in my going. What others have done does not influence me."

"Not even the great masters?"

"I am perhaps a master myself," Peyrat said simply. "Besides, I am going to Avila."

"Oh confound Avila."

"My friend, do not speak of that chosen city, birthplace of Thérèse, in a tone so lacking in respect."

There was a silence. Stephen, remembering the letter of introduction to the Marquesa, knew that it was useless to debate the matter. He felt annoyed, nevertheless, by this unexpected desertion.

"How shall you get there?"

"By train, eleven-twenty A.M. from the Estación Delicias." Peyrat rolled the words upon his tongue.

A knock on the door eased the situation. The landlady, a little, bent woman who never once raised her eyes, brought in breakfast on a tray of painted wood.

The coffee, thick as treacle and diluted with goat's milk, had a queer flavour; the rolls, oval in shape, with a dusting of sugar, were sweet and heavy.

"Olive oil," Peyrat commented. "An essential of Spanish cuisine. We shall get used to it, after a preliminary period of intestinal flux. The olive," he meditated, "a remarkable tree . . . of great antiquity. First introduced into Spain in the time of Pliny, it sometimes attains an age of seven hundred years. Homer, in the Iliad, speaks of its oil as a great luxury, prized for its value in the hero's toilet. The Roman gourmet was addicted to the unripe fruit, steeped in brine. The Phoenicians used its hard, durable wood . . ."

But Stephen, still rather put out, was paying no attention. He drained his cup and got up.

"I'm off now."

"By the way," Peyrat said mildly as Stephen went to the door, "I shall be absent for some days. How are you situated for money?"

"I have enough . . . about thirty pesetas," Stephen answered shortly. "I don't expect to be dining at the Ritz."

"Then that should suffice till I return." Peyrat nodded gravely. "*Adiós, amigo.*"

Outside, the morning was still, the sky cloudless. The sun, still low, gave promise of a hot day. At a doorway a woman was mashing tomatoes in a bowl with a wooden spoon. Stale smells of frying oil and rank tobacco, of sour, polluted dust and decomposing fruit filled the air as Stephen walked to the corner of the street. But there was life and colour in the market that atoned for the squalor of the district: women bartering in quick voices amongst green piles of melons under canvas sacking, the brilliant reds of pimentos, heaped yellows of squash and maize. At the Calle Salazar he boarded a trancar bound for the Alcalá, and standing on the crowded rear platform, was bounced slowly and with many jolting stops through traffic made tortuous by small, decrepit donkeys weighted with panniers, and high-wheeled, clattering carts, holding the middle of the street, drawn by emaciated mules, carrying oil and wine, charcoal and cork bark. However, at half-past nine he reached the Avenida Calio, his pulse hastening its beat, as though matching his steps when he jumped off the tram. The doors had barely opened as he entered the Prado.

The long galleries were empty except for a few copyists, spreading drop-sheets on the polished floor beneath their easels, preparing to work. An anteroom given over to Flemish primitives led him to a corridor devoted exclusively to Valdés Leal, where the huge agonized figures, the religiosity and contented mediocrity of the compositions, momentarily took him aback, nor was this reaction lessened by a succession of soft Murilos, exquisitely done, yet too sweetly pretty, steeped in sentiment. Then his eye was caught, suddenly, by a small, inconspicuous still life of utter simplicity, three water-pitchers in a row, a Zurbarán, and he felt within him an answering glow which deepened and quickened as he came upon El Greco and Velasquez. But the end gallery drew him. This, he thought, with a tremor of instinctive delight, is my painter, this at last is Goya.

He sat down, steeping his senses in the impressionism of the two *Majas*, in one of which he saw immediately the inspiration of Manet's *Olympia*. Then the *Dos de Mayo* held him for a long time, and *Los*

168

Negritos, those great canvases painted in the last years of the artist's life. Yet it was the drawings, by their superb originality, that most wholly captivated him.

Never before had he seen work of such quality, so passionate, charged with such devastating truth. Here was the human creature stripped naked, exposed in all his petty and ignoble vices. The glutton, the toper, the voluptuary, all were here, satirized and reviled in savage and profane caricatures. Here, too, were the powerful and the wealthy, great personages of court and church, lampooned and castigated, laid bare physically and morally. Here, created by this simple man from Aragon, was an entire world, fantastic yet universal, independent of time or place, filled with intense suffering and misery, with all the terror and frightfulness of human brutality, yet leavened at the same time by tenderness and pity—the compassionate protest of a man appalled by the cruelty and injustice of his day, filled with hatred of its oppression, superstition and hypocrisy. What courage he must have shown, thought Stephen, what contempt of danger, when old, deaf, and alone in the little house called the Quinta de Sordo, he still risked the anger of the Inquisition and the king in the service of human liberty.

Absorbed, he was not conscious of the passage of time—it was evening when he was ousted from the museum. Although the sun still shone, it was declining, the air felt cooler. Deciding to walk to his lodging, he crossed the Plaza to the broad incline of the Carrera de San Jerónimo and advanced towards the Puerta del Sol. The cafés were crowded, the pavements overflowing, the streets, now almost devoid of traffic, had filled with people slowly promenading up and down. It was the time of the *paseo*. The murmur of voices, dry and sustained, fell upon the ear like the hum of innumerable bees, interspersed by the shrill cries of the newsboys, the vendors of lottery tickets. All classes, all ages were there: old men and women, children with their nurses, the rich and the poor, all mingled and annealed in this sacred hour of entertainment.

When he reached the Puerta del Sol, Stephen suddenly felt tired, and observing a vacant chair at an outdoor café, he seated himself. Around him men were drinking iced beer, shelling and devouring platefuls of prawns. He hesitated—the uncertainty of the alien— then ordered coffee and a sandwich. Watching the passing throng, he could pick out individual faces that seemed to come straight from Goya's drawings: a bootblack quick and mischievous of feature, the grotesque foreshortened nose and bossy forehead of a dwarf, another type, tall, dark, grave and proud, then the women, reserved, short and full of figure, with brilliant eyes and skins of pallid gold.

All this life and movement had a strange effect on Stephen. After the emotion and excitement of the day, he was conscious of a slow reaction settling upon him, one of those moods of sadness and self-distrust succeeding an experience of beauty that cast him down to the depths. In this great concourse he felt himself to be unwanted and unutterably alone, a predestined spectator, powerless to share its gaiety or partake of its pageantry. At an adjoining table three men were discussing a performance of *canto flamenco* to be held that evening. As they once or twice glanced amiably towards him, he had a sudden impulse to join in the conversation, even to propose that he should accompany them to the entertainment. But he could not bring himself to do so. And in a flash of self-tormenting thought he told himself how easily and quickly one less inhibited, someone like Harry Chester, would have struck up an acquaintance with these pleasures of the city.

Work, inevitably, was his anodyne, and during the next three days he applied himself with intensity to his study of the drawings in the Prado. Despite his preoccupation he missed Peyrat. It was therefore, with a throb of pleasure that, on the evening of the fourth day, while sketching from memory a detail of *Los Caprichos*, he heard a familiar footstep on the wooden staircase of their lodging. A moment later Jerome entered, dramatically, with the carpet-bag, flung back the woollen shawl, and embraced him.

"Ah, it is good to be back, and to see you again."

Stephen put down his block.

"You enjoyed Avila?"

"Surpassing my expectation. Do you know that, filled with delicious sadness, I stood on the very spot where Thérèse was born? Her family's house was in the ghetto of the town. Indeed, a new and startling theory has presented itself to me—that in the saint's veins there was actually Jewish blood. Torquemada must have burned her ancestors."

On Peyrat's face, which was slightly flushed, a look of triumph, a kind of mild intoxication, was mingled with something that in another might well have been taken for embarrassment.

"You stayed at the convent?"

"Naturally. It is small, falling to pieces, and infested with rats. The diet of these poor sisters is abysmal. However, despite an extreme looseness of the bowels, I was happy."

"And the Marquesa?"

"A noble creature—gracious, practical and brave. She suffers atrociously from gout. But, like Thérèse, she is a soldier, seeking always new conquests for God."

"She has obviously conquered you."

"Do not jest, my friend. That excellent woman is no coquette. She is nearly eighty years of age, crippled, and with a paralysis of one cheek."

Stephen was silent for a moment. Peyrat's manner, less exuberant now, puzzled him. He thought he detected in his friend vague signs of timidity.

"Have you had supper?"

"I was given some provisions of an indescribable nature, which I ate on the train. My appetite has certainly been destroyed for weeks. Ah, it is good to be with you again." Affection, strengthened by an unnatural camaraderie, suffused Peyrat's voice. He put his hand on Stephen's shoulder, at the same time avoiding his eye. "Tomorrow we shall be off again together."

"Tomorrow?"

"Why not?"

"We planned to stay another two weeks in Madrid."

"Ah, what is Madrid! Besides, we have our railway tickets to Granada. And afterwards"—his theatrical air increased "I have devised a wonderful plan. Once in Granada, we shall buy a donkey and a little cart and set out by road for Seville."

"Set out by road?" In his surprise Stephen echoed the words stupidly.

"Assuredly." Jerome made a gesture, expansive yet diffident. "It is the common mode of transport in this country. We shall be pilgrims of joy, troubadours if you like, singing on our way, begging if need be, living off the land, which at this season is rich in the fruits of nature—grapes on the vines, melons in the fields, ripe figs and luscious pomegranates on the trees."

"Are you quite out of your mind?" Stephen said sharply, convinced now that Peyrat had been guilty of some frightful indiscretion. "I refuse to take part in such a crazy expedition."

There was a pause. Peyrat lowered his eyes. In a tone both humble and contrite he murmured:

"My friend, bear me no ill will. What I now propose is sheer necessity. Moved by their poverty and a need so much greater than ours, I have given our money, except for some two hundred pesetas, to the good Reverend Mother Morella in memory of Sainte Thérèse."

CHAPTER IV

I<small>T WAS RAINING</small>. Through the streaming windows of the station waiting-room in Granada, Stephen watched the branches of a row of eucalyptus trees sway and drip in a chilly wind that swept down from the Sierra Nevada. Wet railway tracks stretched into the desolate distance. Peyrat's carpet-bag and his own valise stood in a corner.

They had arrived, after changing twice, by an execrable train, crowded and smelling of the latrine, in the wet darkness, at four o'clock that morning. When light appeared, an expedition to the Alhambra, undertaken on foot, had proved a dismal failure. The marble columns and Moorish arches, swept by the rainstorm, seemed as out of place as a wedding cake at a funeral, the Court of the Lions was under water, the view from the Generalife had been obscured by mist. They returned in silence to the shelter of the waiting-room; then, still filled with justifiable resentment and re-solved to accept no responsibility, Stephen had ignored the other's plea that he accompany him, had let him depart alone for the town market.

Since then more than an hour had passed and the delay had not improved Stephen's mood. What rankled was the thought of having, with so much difficulty, acquired adequate funds for this long-anticipated trip only to find all his careful plans dissipated at a single stroke. He looked at his watch, then noted that the rain, which a few minutes before had begun to slacken, had ceased. Then, through the rear window, he observed a light cart, drawn by a donkey of small stature, approach smartly and come to rest at the station en-trance. He went out. The equipage, better than he had expected, surprised him out of the worst of his vexation.

"Where did you get this?"

"From a *cingaro* in the market. Believe me, I struck an excellent bargain." Peyrat spoke with pride. "As you see, the cart is light and completely sound. The donkey, though perhaps not large, is very hardy. His master wept on parting with him."

There was such obvious desire for a reconciliation in Jerome's voice that Stephen relented slightly.

"You might have done worse."

"And look," Peyrat indicated a number of packages in the back of the cart. "I bought these supplies with the pesetas that were left. Bread, bananas, cheese, wine. With our ham we have enough for a week or so."

At that moment the sun came out, warm and brilliant in the clearing sky. The transformation was miraculous. A sense of light and gaiety pervaded the air, there came a flash and sparkle from the raindrops on the eaves of blue-washed houses. In the eucalyptus trees a bird burst into song. All at once it seemed a gay adventure to set out in this fashion, travelling free and unhampered into the unknown. Stephen's spirits lifted.

"Let's be off."

They piled their possessions into the cart and drove away. The donkey pulled steadily and with a good heart; soon they were out of the town traversing a wide road shaded by peeled sycamores and flanked by patches of maize, sunflowers and tobacco plants. Bougainvillea, mimosa and wild geraniums were everywhere. Then came orange groves, the branches laden with little fruits, green and waxen. Stephen, on the narrow driver's seat, breathed the warm aromatic air with delight, enjoying the passing landscape, the play of light and shadow amongst the trees, the gurgle of clear water in the freshened irrigation channels. Presently he glanced sideways at his companion.

"It is good to be out of these trains. We go by Santafé and Loja, don't we? Then over the mountains?"

"The Sierra Tejea. I studied the map at the *municipio*."

Afternoon passed and twilight came. They had turned from the main road and were now beginning to ascend from the valley of the Rio Genil into the lovely foothills of the Sierra. No human habitation was in sight, but a small ravine sheltered by a clump of pines gave promise of a suitable encampment. They unharnessed the donkey and tethered him in a patch of rough grass where the admirable little beast began quietly to graze. Then, without troubling to make a fire, they ate a good supper of bread, cheese and wine. The night was soft, black and warm; pine needles carpeted the dry sand on which they stretched themselves. Almost at once Stephen was asleep.

The days that followed were delightful, the weather sunny yet temperate, the countryside mellow, fertile, studded with tiny farms on whose pink roofs the harvest of ochre maize-cobs was spread to dry. Pumpkins were ripening in the fields, chaff flew under the threshers' flails. They moved without haste, stopped frequently to make sketches or, shaded by jacaranda trees, set up their easels to paint. The fleeting forms of clouds had infinite grace, bees hummed in the low scrub, in the distance the tiled dome of a village church burned on the horizon like a clear blue flame. The scent of jasmine,

173

hanging in the air, was a perpetual intoxication. At night, after a meal made from the stores they carried, while the crickets sang, Peyrat played an accompaniment on his ocarina, then, watching the milky constellations in a sky that glowed with Arabian blackness, would embark on profound monologues, to which Stephen gave no heed, dissertations ranging from St. James of Compostela to the cultivation of cork trees, from Ferdinand and Isabella to the love-poems of the Archpriest of Heta. Then with a romantic air he would seek repose, quoting the Spanish couplet:

I spread my cloak upon the ground
And fling myself to sleep.

CHAPTER V

TOWARDS THE END of the third week, a change took place. The route diverged, the mountains suddenly loomed nearer, and they were obliged to leave the green foothills behind, striking up by a steep winding road into wild and rugged rock country. There was no cover, not a visible tree in this great barren sweep of burned and tortured rock, buttressed and pinnacled, gashed and furrowed into a thousand fantastic formations. The sun blazed down, the ascent in parts was almost precipitous. To ease their willing little beast they walked beside the cart.

For days the flaming heat continued, even the lizards lay motionless as sticks in the crevices of the baking rocks. Superb colours—red, violet, chrome, sienna, all the pigments of nature, bleached and rusted by the furnace of the sun, gave an appalling magnificence to this primitive and abandoned wasteland.

In the evenings they camped on patches of rocky ground. They slept badly, and when Peyrat rose his joints were so stiff he could barely move. Yet there was no other road, no alternative but to go on, and all that week they struggled forward. A torrid, spiteful wind blew, filling their eyes with grit, swirling up spirals of dust. The donkey was showing signs of the lack of proper pasture; their provisions, even the ham, were at last exhausted. Stephen had become concerned when, past noon on the ninth day, they emerged upon a high plateau where signs of life were visible. They saw a peasant striking his mattock into the lumpy, chocolate-coloured earth. A woman passed, silently, swaying, on a mule, her head shaded by an old umbrella. A man, gathering olives from a stunted tree, observed them covertly. Then a village, white as a heap of petrified bones, was discernible in the distance.

Peyrat had grumbled a good deal during the trials of the journey, but now, as they approached the village, he briskened, became communicative.

"We are certain to find a *fonda* here. It will be a relief to have a roof over our heads again."

They entered the single narrow causeway of the *aldea*, where a few women in black sat on low chairs facing their doorways, crocheting lace in the shadow, their backs turned towards the street. From one of these Peyrat received directions to the inn. This was a low dilapidated house, constructed of loose stones, set in a dirty yard where several donkeys were tethered, on the further side of the village. A few straggling castor-oil shrubs grew outside, their pink spikes withered and covered with dust. Within the dark interior, where wood embers smoked on the earth floor, some men were seated at a table drinking from a black goatskin. Peyrat called the landlord, and a slow, lumpish fellow with small eyes and a long, unshaven chin detached himself torpidly from the group with the goatskin.

"My friend, we are two travellers, artists in fact, and strangers in your country and, unfortunately, in some distress. Will you, of your courtesy, afford us a meal and lodging for the night? In return we will paint your portrait, or that of your good wife."

The man gave Peyrat a prolonged and inquiring stare.

"The Senor is welcome to the best we have. We turn no one from our door. But on the one hand I require no portrait, and on the other I have no wife."

"Then, if you choose, we will make a sign for your inn."

"But I do not choose, Señor. An inn of such quality as mine needs no sign."

"Then you must like music? I will play sweet tunes for you."

"I swear by the Virgin of Guadalupe, Señor, music is the one thing I abominate."

"For the love of the Virgin, then, name something that we can do for you."

"You can enter, Señor, eat well and sleep soft. But of course you must pay."

"I have told you . . . we are poor artists."

Stroking his long blue chin, the man shook his head.

"No one is poor who has good clothes to wear, who arrives with baggage and a fine donkey."

Taken aback, Peyrat nevertheless persisted.

"Yes . . . but we are without actual money."

The man gazed from one to the other, slyly, with a native shrewdness, yet not without dignity.

"Then give something of fair value . . . it need not be great . . . no paintings, however, but perhaps a cloth coat or, for example," his eyes dropped to his own battered espadrilles, "a pair of stout boots."

Jerome was silent, his face a study, then he gave a sign of assent.

"The ruffian is holding us up," he muttered to Stephen. "Napoleon was right when he said, 'Never trust a man with a long chin.' However, we must eat."

"He can have my coat," Stephen said.

"No," said Peyrat, with pertinacity. "I shall give my boots. But only these old ones I am wearing. I have a better pair in my bag."

Despite their lamentable situation, Stephen turned away to hide a smile—Jerome's expression was scarcely that of a joyous troubadour. He went outside, unharnessed and stabled the donkey, rubbed it down, left it with a good truss of hay. Then he seated himself on a bench by the door to endure the interminable wait for supper.

This was not ready until nearly ten o'clock and, served at the table in the smoky room, proved to be as wretched as the inn. They had *gazpacho*, a watery cold soup of tomato and cucumber, swimming with rancid oil, followed by fibrous slices of dry, salted cod tasting of garlic, and a hunk of dark bread.

"In the name of God, landlord," Peyrat protested, "what food is this?"

"It is named *bacallao*, Señor. A rare, delicious fish, coming very far, from the sea."

"Undoubtedly it has come a long way. And such wine . . ." Jerome winced as it passed his lips.

"Ah, it is the choicest in the district. Indeed, without boasting, one might say the finest in Andalusia." And the landlord went on to praise extravagantly the thin watery liquid which bit the tongue like an acid vinegar.

They had to make the best of it. It was a relief at last to be able to escape to the hay spread in a vacant stall adjoining the stable.

In the morning they set off again across the plain that stretched before them in a monotone of parched yellow, relieved only by an infrequent grove of silvery olive trees. Here the sole signs of cultivation were the maize-fields, where, wandering head down amongst the withered stalks, herds of black goats stirred up a steam of dust.

Where were the juicy figs, the luscious grapes and crimson pomegranates that Peyrat had promised when he said they would live bounteously off the land? All that day their diet consisted only of uncooked cobs of corn, and a handful of unripe olives, eaten with the loaf of bread which, unexpectedly, the landlord had given them on their departure. Stephen felt the grim humour of their position. He did not mind the Spartan fare, and always in this strange lunar landscape there was some new vista which thrilled his vision and which from time to time he noted in his sketch-book. But Peyrat, plodding moodily at the donkey's head, victim of his own philanthropy, was plainly losing his earlier *élan*. He talked to himself, brandishing his stick, and, as he could be on occasions, was childish, disagreeable and absurd. And that evening, camped beside a stony arroyo, after a mush of maize cooked in a can picked up by the wayside, he broke a meditative and dejected silence.

"These new boots, made for the pavements of Paris, are hurting my feet atrociously. Already I have a galling blister on my heel." He paused, then went on. "I fear I have led you into an unfortunate situation. I mistook the nature of this countryside which, if one can believe that rogue of a landlord, is equally poor all the way to Cádiz. In such a region we have not even the advantage of beggars, but must always be taken for men of substance." Another pause. "Only one solution presents itself—to abandon the long direct road to Seville. When we reach Lera we will cut down to the port of Málaga. There, almost certainly, is a civilized community where we shall find some respite. And afterwards, if necessary, we may resume our journey."

Stephen considered for a moment this suggestion, the most practical Jerome had made since they entered Spain. It was an annoyance, but obviously they could not indefinitely continue to tramp through this wilderness without means of subsistence. He nodded his agreement.

"It can't be more than a hundred and forty kilometres to the coast."

Peyrat, with his socks off, was tenderly examining his heel.

"How long do you think it will take us to get there?"

"At our present rate of progress, about a week."

A suppressed sigh came from the other side of the dying fire.

"My friend, I may have found my discalced order sooner than expected. I seriously doubt if I shall get these boots on my feet tomorrow."

CHAPTER VI

THREE DAYS LATER, when they were midway between Lera and Málaga, the real trouble began. They had stopped by the roadside in the shade of a clump of cork trees for their customary midday rest. The sun, filtering through the stunted branches, made fitful patterns on the dusty bank. Beside them in the shade of the up-tilted cart, the donkey stood absolutely motionless, passive as a statue shaped in clay. Blackened by the sun, grimed, unshaven, his shirt stained and torn, Stephen had the appearance of a tramp. Peyrat, with one foot bare, had rolled up his trouser leg to the knee. Although he always maintained a sort of spinsterish privacy in regard to his own person, now, after a period of silence, he turned to Stephen.

"My leg pains me. Will you look at it?"

Stephen went over and looked casually at the leg. Then, disquieted by what he saw, he examined it more thoroughly. Although he had known that the excoriated heel was troubling Peyrat—he had on several occasions observed him dispense with the tight boots and limp along in his bare feet in the dust behind the cart—he had never suspected that the condition had become so acute. The right foot was swollen and inflamed, the heel itself ulcerated.

"Well?" Peyrat was watching his expression closely.

"No more walking for you." Stephen assumed a confident tone. "Not for a while, anyway."

"What do you think of it?"

"It's probably slightly infected. Let's see what we can do about it."

He took his spare shirt from his valise and tore off several strips. Moistening these with water, which now they always carried in an old wine-bottle, he cleansed the raw, inflamed area as best he could and applied a loose moist bandage.

"How does that feel?"

"Cool . . . in fact, somewhat easier."

Hitherto Stephen had been content to allow Peyrat a free rein; now, however, he knew he must take the situation in hand, and after briefly considering whether or not to return to Lera, at best only a straggling country town, he decided to press on. Málaga was their safest objective and they must get to it as soon as possible.

He harnessed the burro, assisted Peyrat to the cart and, after settling him in the back, started off. He set a good pace at the donkey's head, but whenever they approached an incline he fell behind, and by pushing hard on the tailboard helped to master the slope. In this fashion they proceeded without interruption, and towards five o'clock in the afternoon drew near to the village of Cazaba.

Here Stephen stopped in the central square, and approaching a young man who stood filling a bucket at the well, asked to be directed to the doctor's house.

"Señor, there is no *médico* in Cazaba."

"None?"

The young man shook his head.

"If need be we are visited from Lera or Málaga. However, there is in the village an excellent *farmacéutico*."

"Where can I find him?"

"I will show you, Señor."

Obligingly, with studied politeness, the youth conducted them through several narrow side streets and halted outside a doorway above which a pole striped in red, white and blue bore the sign: BARBERÍA. Stephen helped Peyrat from the cart. They entered.

A tall, extremely thin man in a grey alpaca jacket, one of those pale, reserved, sad-faced Castilians who look always as though their thoughts were of another world, who seem, indeed, as if they stand waiting to cross the threshold of the next, was slowly cutting a boy's hair.

"My friend has hurt his foot. Will you look at it?"

"Be seated, I pray you."

He went on cropping the boy's skull, methodically and with melancholy dignity. Five minutes later, when he had finished, he shook and folded the sheet, put away the clippers and turned his liquid eyes towards them.

"Now I am at your disposal."

Peyrat unwrapped the bandage of torn shirt and held up his foot. The barber inspected it.

"You are brothers?"

"No, as I have said, friends."

"Not Spanish?"

"No," Stephen said. "I am *Inglés*."

"Ah, *Inglés*. How lucky for you to be in Spain at such a sorrowful time. What do you do? And where have you come from?"

"We are artists . . . painters. And we have travelled from Granada."

"That is a long way. Too long for such a foot as this. And where are you going?"

"Málaga."

"A beautiful city. After my marriage I went there with my wife, who now, alas, has gone to God. I myself am from Saragossa. You do not know that town? It lies on the Ebro. I was born within sight of the river, near La Seo. Ay, ay, doubtless I shall never see it again. Ah, well, it is no matter." He was pressing the leg gently with his thumb. "Does it hurt you?"

"Not badly," Peyrat answered. His face looked white in the dark little room and Stephen knew that he was lying.

"Well . . . let us see what is to be done."

The barber opened a wooden cupboard in the corner and from the shelves, on which stood a number of jars and bottles, selected a yellow ointment. As he began to spread this gently on the ulcerated skin, with a little bone spatula, he said:

"This is a remedy which I compound myself. It is simple, but soothing."

"Then it should help?"

"Would you think otherwise?"

The foot, covered with soft raw cotton, was loosely bandaged with a swathe of lint and, as on the previous occasion, Peyrat emitted a sigh of nervous, yet hopeful relief.

"*Muchas gracias, Señor.* I am a new man."

Stephen rose, hesitated, then said, resolutely, yet with great awkwardness:

"And now . . . I am afraid . . . we are without money. But once we are in Málaga, our circumstances will improve. Name your fee and I will send it within the week."

The barber looked from one to the other, then held up his hand in the manner of a grandee.

"Say no more, friend. For the little I have done you may pay me simply with your gratitude. But I advise you to show the foot at once in Málaga." He looked directly at Stephen and added, in an undertone, as they moved towards the door, "I do not like it. With such a case there are always possibilities which may arise."

For the first time a faint foreboding passed like a shadow across Stephen's mind. Peyrat, on the contrary, seemed reassured. As they took the road out of the village he was loud in praise of his benefactor, and especially eloquent on his skill, which he contrasted, to the disparagement of the latter, with orthodox medicine, in which he professed no faith whatsoever. He spoke of the virtues of salves and unguents, of the use of oil and wine in treating wounds, of balsams, salt and rosemary, of rare herbal nostrums containing myrrh, bergamot, and ambergris that healed overnight, particularly those compounded by alchemists of the East—there was, he interpolated, undoubtedly Moorish blood in the veins of the good barber of Cazaba. Perhaps because he had been silent for some hours, this volubility seemed unnatural, and Stephen noticed with growing uneasiness that Jerome's cheeks were slightly flushed. He realized again, and with greater urgency, that they must push forward with all possible speed.

The road was favourable for the next few kilometres and they made good progress. Then, as the light began to fade and they looked for a shelter for the night, Stephen caught sight of a large outlying barn set on the crest of a field of stubble in which some goats were pastured. It was a fortunate discovery. The barn, filled with fresh hay, promised them not only a comfortable night but fodder for the animal. Stephen brought Peyrat inside, then, after several attempts, spurred by a sense of emergency, he caught and milked a goat. In the cart were some green cobs of maize they had picked some days before. Within half an hour he had prepared a hot dish of corn and milk.

"How do you feel now?" he asked, when Jerome had eaten.

"My friend, I am deeply touched by your care and consideration."

"Yes, yes . . . but your foot?"

"It is throbbing, naturally. However, that I regard as a favourable reaction. After a good night's rest I shall be perfectly recovered."

But Peyrat did not rest well—he could be heard twisting painfully and muttering under his breath, and in the morning, by the grey light of dawn, he looked definitely worse. Stephen, aware now that he had a sick man on his hands, was thoroughly alarmed. He did not dare examine the limb in these surroundings. He filled the cart with hay, supported Peyrat as he hobbled from the barn, made him as comfortable as possible on this improvised couch, and hastened to be off.

The donkey, refreshed and fed, went with a will and, aided by Stephen on the hills, made excellent progress. If only they could reach Málaga before dark—the thought of another night on the road did not bear contemplation—he would go immediately to the consulate for help. There must be a French or British agent in a port of such importance. He drove forward still harder, only stopping occasionally to give Peyrat, who complained of thirst, a drink of water. As he handed the bottle he could feel that Jerome's skin was hot with fever. Then the road became bad again, curving steeply upwards in a series of hairpin bends to a sharp summit from which they were faced, after an abrupt and lurching descent, with yet another precipitous climb. Still there was no possibility of rest. At noon, using sticks and a blanket, Stephen contrived a primitive shade over the cart. Peyrat seemed quieter but confused. He had lost all his earlier bravado, and asked continually if they were not yet within sight of Málaga.

Now Stephen kept looking over his shoulder, as though hoping for some sudden materialization, for a conveyance, even the oldest and most dilapidated *carretón*, for help of any kind that might bring them more speedily to their destination. Yet nothing, no one came.

As the afternoon passed and the granite boulders that studded this inhuman landscape cast shadows on the dusty earth, a sense of helplessness, almost of panic, struck at Stephen. The loneliness of these hills, their absolute and primæval desolation, was enough to constrict the heart and paralyse the will. He felt utterly exhausted, his gallant little beast, flanks sodden and heaving, head drooping, was almost spent. And still they were at least twenty kilometres from the coast.

Another hill, then, over the brow, a collection of houses drew Stephen on. It was a small, miserable settlement, composed of caves and rock dwellings, no more than thirty in number, built into and occupying a cleft in the hills. A few mangy pigs, encrusted with dried mud, were rooting in a heap of rubbish beside a well with a broken coping. The sense of squalor, decay and filth passed belief. Not a human being was in sight.

Stephen stopped beside the well, looking up towards the blank walls of the cave dwellings. All were situated high above the road, on the face of the canyon. I must get help, he told himself. He left the cart and started to climb the sharp slope. There was no path and the surface of the cliff, seamed with gutters and innumerable crevices, was covered with loose, gritty sandstone. Several times he lost his footing, but he persevered and, on his hands and knees, had almost reached the first house when he lost his hold, slid back violently the full length of the slope. As he lay there at the bottom, covered with grit, scratched and bruised, a man came from one of the caves and, throwing down a bucket of refuse, shouted to him to be off.

"They think I'm drunk." He muttered the words hopelessly.

He picked himself up, refilled the wine-bottle at the well, watered the donkey and went on. How far they travelled in the next two hours he could not guess. Now night was approaching swiftly, flinging its banners across the eastern sky. At his wit's end, Stephen gazed desperately about him. All at once, at the end of a rough track, he saw a small white house with a lean-to *cabaña*, roofed in esparto grass, standing in a patch of wasteland. Summoning up the last of his resolution, he went towards it.

As he drew near a woman came out of the low doorway, her head a little to one side, as though listening to his approach. She was about sixty years old, dressed respectably in worn black, with a heavy figure and thickened, dark features, a face almost Negroid in its darkness, its full, bluish lips and flattened nose. Her eyes were prominent, strangely opaque, and Stephen, now close to her, saw suddenly in the centre of each pupil the yellowish blight of trachoma. But it was her expression, the stolid enduring placidity of that sightless face, which most truly revealed that she was blind.

"Señora." The word came raspingly from his dry throat, he had almost lost the faculty of speech. "We are strangers, travelling to Málaga. My friend is sick. I entreat you to give us shelter for the night."

There was a silence. She stood motionless, her hands, on which he could make out the badly broken nails, crossed before her. It was as if, through some strange vibration in the air, she sought not only to establish the truth of what he had told her but to discover, actually, the nature and character of these unknown visitors. A long moment passed. Then, without a word, she turned, led the way to the thatched lean-to, and opened the door.

"This may serve you." She made a gesture with her passive hands. "There is a place for your burro behind."

The shock of this sudden and unlooked-for security after the afflictions of the day was such that Stephen, overcome, was unable to utter a word of thanks. It was a poor room, but clean, the floor of beaten earth. A table and a wooden chair stood under a hanging oil lamp. In the far corner, on a wooden trestle, was a flock mattress.

He helped Peyrat out of the cart and, supporting, almost carrying him, on to the low bed. Then, having taken off his clothes, he washed the dust from his face and got him into a clean shirt. The foot still remained encased in cotton wool and lint. Next he stabled the donkey, giving it fresh water and all the hay that remained in the cart. As he returned from the back of the *cabaña* he met the woman of the house carrying a grey earthenware bowl filled with thick bean soup.

"Take this for your supper. It is not much but it may help your friend."

Again, he was speechless. At last he said:

"Your kindness leaves me without words. Believe me, we had need of your help."

"If you are worse off than I, then you are badly off indeed."

"You live alone here?"

"Completely. And, as you observe, I am blind."

"Then . . . you manage . . . yourself?"

"I manage. I grow these beans. I exist."

A pause followed. Then, as he remained silent, she turned slowly on her broad, heavy feet and left him.

He took the soup to Peyrat and, propping him up, tried to induce him to swallow it. But after a few spoonfuls he was forced to desist. Jerome had turned irritable and in a fretful manner kept pushing the spoon away. Nor would he permit Stephen to examine his leg. The light, faint though it was, hurt his eyes. Only half awake, almost in a state of stupor, he begged to be left undisturbed. What next? thought Stephen. I have brought him so far, I won't, I can't give up now. But he will never be fit to travel in the cart tomorrow, nor will the burro be fit to move. Then he thought: I must not waste the woman's soup. Seated at the table, under the flickering lamp, his harassed gaze fixed on the sick man, who lay muttering in his sleep, he drank the thick soup quickly. It was good, but he did not taste it; all the time he kept thinking what he should do for Peyrat. Presently, with the empty bowl, he went to the door of the house. The woman answered his knock.

"Is it a far distance to Málaga?"

"Yes, it is far. More than ten kilometres."

"Perhaps there is a bus, perhaps a *carretón*, which runs there every day?"

"There is nothing of that nature on the hill roads. Only such *carros* as the one you possess."

Stephen forced his tired brain to think. Ten kilometres . . . He felt sure he could walk that distance in three hours, and by starting at dawn, reach the consulate before nine o'clock.

"Señora, I must go to Málaga early tomorrow. I shall leave my friend, also the burro and the cart. But have no fear, I shall return soon after noon. Is such an arrangement agreeable to you?"

Her head remained averted, yet in some strange fashion she seemed to measure him with her sightless eyes.

"It is agreeable. But do not call me Señora. My name is Luisa . . . Luisa Mendez. And do not speak to me of fear. I have long passed the stage of having fear."

184

He went back to the lean-to and, after a last look at Peyrat, turned out the lamp, around which great moths were hovering in the languid air, and lay down on the beaten floor.

CHAPTER VII

NEXT MORNING, AS he crossed the last summit and came down the steep incline towards Málaga, he felt the dark cloud of his anxiety lightened by a sudden gleam of hope. He was here at last. The town beneath, curving along the bay, sheltered by its long breakwater, shimmering white and gold against the deep Mediterranean blue, the roof of the cathedral glinting in the early sunshine, seemed, after the arid wilderness behind him, a haven of security. Peyrat, when Stephen left before dawn, although still fevered, had been quiet, and apparently in less pain. Now it would not be long before help reached him.

Hastening through the outskirts of the town, Stephen passed along an avenue of palm trees, then entered the Calle de la Victoria. As he made his way towards the main square he began to sense a singular stir in the streets. Men were standing in groups around the cafés talking and gesticulating, and at the corner of the Calle Larios a large crowd had collected outside the offices of the *Gaceta de la Caleta*. Stephen stopped and spoke to a man on the edge of the gathering.

"Friend, what is the reason of this assembly?"

"The reason? Why, man, we are waiting for the next edition of the *Gaceta*."

"And is that usual here . . . in such numbers, every day?"

"No, it is not usual. But then, not every day is there such news."

"What news, friend?"

"Why, man, news of the war."

"War?" Stephen did not understand, thinking that the word *guerra* which the man had used referred to some local disturbance, a strike perhaps. "Then there is a conflict in the town?"

"Not here, thanks to the Virgin of Guadalupe and the natural good sense of Spain. But elsewhere. A great, very great war." He paused, observing the look of stupefaction on the other's face, then politely, with a slight bow, he offered the folded newspaper which he carried in his hand. "This is of the day before. The Señor may see for himself."

Stephen straightened out the sheet, which was dated August 7, his gaze instantly arrested by the smudged grey headlines. They struck him like a blow. In the daze of one long out of touch with the progress and culmination of events, he read on, then, after a few minutes put the paper down, stared blankly across the alleyway, recollecting with a pained constriction of his brow all that Hubert had said to him in Paris.

"You are *Inglés*?"

"Yes." Stephen came to himself, aware of the other's mannerly curiosity. "Can you direct me to the *consulado*?"

"It is quite near. Take the second turning on the left, then again to the left. You will see the flag above the entrance."

With an expression of thanks Stephen hurried off.

The consulate was a villa standing in a small garden near the harbour. The door was open, and as Stephen mounted the short flight of steps and entered, he found the hall and staircase already crowded. From the two rooms on the ground floor came the sound of intense activity. A Spanish clerk, carrying an armful of documents, accompanied by a consular official, passed and re-passed through the hall.

With a sense of urgency Stephen took his place at the end of the line. His need was immediate and, judged by their comments, the people ahead of him had already been waiting a long time. Many of these were tourists, some of them women, all anxious to get home, aggrieved at the unexpected crisis, yet more upset by the interruption of their holiday than by any grave premonition of world disaster. They chattered a good deal, even joked, as the queue moved slowly forward.

He must act quickly. Yet he could not push his way up the jammed staircase. Then, as the official emerged once more from the room on the right, Stephen stepped forward. At the same time he said, rapidly:

"May I speak with you? It's a matter of importance."

"Not now."

"I assure you, I should only take five minutes of your time."

"You must wait your turn."

"But surely . . ."

With an exclamation of annoyance the official looked at Stephen. He was under thirty, with thinning hair and a fair complexion, wearing a light linen jacket, his open and agreeable expression marred by the frown of a man harassed and overworked. His gaze travelled upwards with distaste over the dusty, worn boots and shiny suit, the dingy shirt, last washed in a muddy arroyo, then, with a slow and

186

subtle lightening of his eye, a faint look of recognition appeared upon his face. Pleasantly, with a slightly mannered air, he said:

"Why . . . yes. Come into my room."

He led the way into a small office, bare and distempered, but made personal and human by two tennis racquets in one corner and several group photographs on the walls, and pulled out a chair before seating himself at a littered, varnished desk.

"Sit down, won't you? I'm George Hollis."

"My name is Desmonde."

There was a pause, then suddenly the other smiled.

"Now I remember. Didn't you come up to Trinity in '09?"

"Yes."

"Of course. . . . That was the year before I went down. I felt sure we'd met. How are you?"

Stephen shook the proffered hand. Then, quickly, he said:

"I hate to impose on you at a time like this. But actually . . ."

Hollis waved away the apology.

"I understand. It's perfectly natural. We all want to go back in double-quick time to get into the show. Tell me . . . what are you doing out here?"

"I've been on a painting trip, with a friend who . . ."

"Ah, sort of walking tour. Rough country to get about in. May be a bit rougher, though, when we march on the Rhine. Now, let me see what we can do for you." He consulted a paper on the desk. "As you may imagine, we're practically off our heads trying to get people home. The frontier is closed, so trains are impossible. Shipping is at a premium. There isn't an inch of space. And most of the coastal waters are being mined. But I'll take care of this for you. There's sure to be a freighter leaving soon. By pulling a few strings I'm sure we can get you a berth on her."

"Thank you . . . thank you." Stephen spoke precipitately, desperate to come to the point. "In the meantime, could I tax your goodness further? My friend is ill, seriously, I'm afraid. I must get him a good doctor, in fact get him into hospital at once."

"Well, now . . ." Hollis considered. "That shouldn't be too difficult. Dr. Cabra, in the Calle Estada, would be your man. He's physician at the Hospital San Miguel. Best thing to do . . . I'll give you a note to him." He took a pen and wrote on the consulate notepaper, blotted the sheet, placed it in an envelope and pushed it across the desk. "That should do the trick, Desmonde."

"You are really too kind. I'm grateful." Stephen spoke with feeling. "When may I see you again?"

"Look in any time. I ought to have news for you in a few days." He stood up with a smile. "We might dine together one evening before you go."

Hurrying across the Cathedral Square, Stephen observed, with satisfaction, that it was not yet eleven o'clock. He found the Calle Estada without difficulty and there, on an arched doorway, was a brass plaque: DR. JUAN CABRA, beneath which was added: EQUIPO TRANSFUSIO DE SANGRE. A servant admitted him, accepted his letter, and left him in the hall. A few moments later the doctor appeared. He was a youngish man, small, dapper, with neat hands and feet, and a round, smooth, saffron face in which his sloe-dark eyes seemed to radiate cheerfulness, to twinkle with perpetual good nature. He bowed to Stephen, his manners were perfect.

"I am always pleased to be recommended by the *Consulado Británico*. What can I do for you?"

As briefly as possible, Stephen explained the situation. A pause followed, during which the little doctor looked thoughtful. Then, after questioning Stephen on one or two points, he nodded with decision.

"Impossible to treat your friend at such a distance. Besides, the conditions are too difficult. We must bring him to the hospital."

"But how?"

Cabra smiled, genially self-deprecating, yet with a kind of humorous vanity, his little black eyes disappearing completely in the smooth, creamy folds of his cheeks.

"We are quite up to date in Málaga. The Casa de Socorro has an ambulance. A motor, in effect, for the use of all the *médicos* in town. I myself frequently conduct it. And as I do not consult at the hospital until four o'clock, we shall requisition it and proceed together to visit your friend."

"Then we may leave at once?"

"Whenever I have had breakfast. Come and join me." As he showed Stephen into a small panelled sitting-room where coffee and rolls were set out on a tray, he added: "I have been to a case most of the night. Such fun to bring a fine boy into the world. And such joy for the mother."

"It was a first baby?"

"Oh, no, no. The tenth. And all alive and healthy."

Another cup had been brought and with perfect courtesy he poured coffee for Stephen, proffered the platter of rolls. Then, with relish, he began his own meal, talking almost continuously, deploring the war, but predicting its speedy ending, discoursing on his practice, the beauty of Málaga, the excellence of the climate, all with a kind of natural gaiety, yet from time to time darting towards his guest glances charged with sympathetic curiosity. Finally he said:

"If you had not come to me for your friend I should have suspected that you were the patient. You are much under weight."

"I am naturally thin."

"You have a cough."

"It is nothing."

"So it is nothing. Well, then, smile a little, for a change."

Stephen reddened.

"I daresay I am anxious about my friend."

Cabra did not immediately answer, but as he finished his coffee and got up, he leaned forward suddenly and pressed Stephen's hand.

"We shall do our best for him."

They left the house and in five minutes were at the Casa de Socorro, where the ambulance, a field model with a canvas top secured by straps, stood in the cobbled yard at the back. The doctor put his bag on the seat, cranked the engine, and presently they were moving out of the town at a surprisingly good pace. If Cabra had been talkative before, now he was equally silent. Crouched over the wheel, to which he anchored himself with both hands, like a little bantam cock, he drove with concentrated intensity and incredible lack of caution, taking the curves without slackening speed, sounding his horn incessantly, rocking the top-heavy vehicle until it seemed in danger of turning over. But as the dust-clouds billowed behind them, the long road over which Stephen had tramped that morning steadily diminished. Within the hour they passed the *aldea* of the cave dwellings, turned on to the narrow hill track, and bumped across the wasteland to the house of Luisa Mendez. They went into the *cabaña*. Peyrat was lying on his back, a compress on his forehead. Seated at the table, wringing out a fresh cloth in a bowl of water, was the woman Luisa. Stephen went forward to the bed.

"Jerome, I've brought the doctor. How have you been?"

"I have been suffering of course." His eyes, bright in his furrowed, yellow face, turned suspiciously towards Cabra. His hands were fidgeting with the blanket. "But now I have taken the turn, and am mending rapidly, thanks to the ministrations of this good woman."

"Has he had food?" The doctor put his bag on the table and opened it.

"No, Señor, only water. And that in great quantity."

"Water, spring water, is a purifying agent. Although no longer regarded as an element, as it was in former times, water cleanses the system, purifies the blood . . ."

"And quenches thirst," Cabra interrupted. "You are thirsty?"

"I may have been."

"Your head aches?"

"No. But I admit to a painful ringing in my ears. Indeed, because of that"—Peyrat raised himself, feverishly and with difficulty, upon his elbow, speaking through dry, cracked lips—"I have been reflecting upon the subject of bells . . . their immense variety . . . even when one does not include gongs, cymbals or tinkling ornaments. There are, for example, sheep and cow bells, sleigh bells, harness bells, house bells, bells which summoned the Romans to the public baths, bells which rang the Sicilian vespers when eight thousand French were slaughtered by John of Procida, bells that ushered in the Massacre of St. Bartholomew, curfew bells, wedding bells, passing bells, and of course church bells. In *De Tintinnabulis* . . ."

"*Amigo.*" Cabra placed a restraining hand on Peyrat's shoulder. "I beg of you, no more of bells. Be silent and permit me to examine you."

Peyrat closed his eyes and sank back, exhausted, submitting while the doctor took his pulse and temperature.

"Does your leg still hurt?"

"No," said Peyrat, feebly but with a triumphant air, not opening his eyes. "It is absolutely without pain."

Studying the doctor's face, Stephen saw his expression alter imperceptibly.

"No feeling whatsoever?"

"None."

"Ah, then perhaps we may look at it."

Cabro turned down the blanket and bent over the bed. Standing back at the window, filled with anxiety, Stephen observed only the movements of the doctor's hands as he removed the dressing and made his investigation. This was not unduly prolonged, and when Cabra straightened, there was a false cheerfulness in his manner.

"Well, *amigo*, don't you think it time you were in a comfortable bed? We have one for you at the San Miguel. And I propose to take you there now."

Peyrat moved his lips in protest, but said nothing. Stephen could see that his imaginative, childish soul was struck with fear. Presently he looked up in a pitiful manner.

"My friend, when I gave our money in honour of Thérèse, I did not think she would repay me in this fashion."

Cabra, at the table, was repacking his bag.

"I'll come with you," Stephen said to him.

"No." The doctor was emphatic. He advanced to the window. "You would be useless. Besides, if you are not careful, you too will be ill. Stay here and rest."

"When shall I come? Tomorrow morning?"

"Let us say the day after tomorrow."

"Then you are hopeful?" Stephen asked in a low voice.

Cabra looked away—his eyes were altogether less humorous. He picked a shred of lint from his sleeve.

"From the thigh down the leg is in a serious condition. The foot is probably gangrenous. If he is to live something must be done at once. But rest assured, we shall do it."

On the stretcher, as though to protect himself, Peyrat still kept his eyes tightly shut. From time to time he murmured meaningless, incoherent phrases. But as the moment of departure arrived he signed to Stephen. He was clearly not himself.

"Let me have my ocarina."

He was clutching it as slowly, and with considerable care, Cabra drove off. Stephen stood there a long time, watching. The blind woman, in a posture of listening, stood beside him.

CHAPTER VIII

NEXT MORNING, THE sun broke early out of a blinding sky and struck through a rent in the sacking that served for the window of the *cabaña*. It awoke Stephen, who had slept as one dead. He lay motionless for some time, then, as thought returned, he got up and in a mood of sick wretchedness went from the hut. The old woman was at the dome-shaped oven in the yard, drawing from its blackened mouth a flat loaf of maize bread. As he approached, without turning her head, she broke the new loaf and handed him a piece, still steaming and damp. While he ate, standing, she remained passive, silent, her opaque eyes turned upwards in their orbits, her attitude so withdrawn it seemed as though with every other faculty than sight she saw him, sounded the depth of his distress. Suddenly she said:

"You are thinking of the other?"

"Yes."

"Have you know him long?"

"Not long, but enough to call him my friend."

"He seemed to me a learned man, speaking of many things, but foolish."

"He spoke so because he is sick."

"Ay, ay, he is sick. Of that there is no doubt whatever. I have seen them so before."

"I have much anxiety for him."

"It will pass. Everything passes, love and hate alike." There was a grave fatalism in her voice. Then as she moved away she said: "Work is the best cure for sadness. I have need of brushwood for this oven. Usually I bring it from the clearing beyond the *valle*."

He went to the stable. The donkey was on its four legs, standing solidly again, and glad to see him, rubbing its muzzle against his shoulder. Luisa had given it fresh hay. He saw that it had recovered, harnessed it to the cart, then took a rusted machete from its hook beside the stall and started out across the arroyo to the place she had indicated.

This had once been a wood of chestnut trees, long since cut down, the stumps now rotted and overgrown by a jungle of briars and *avellano* bushes. While the donkey began to nibble the *avellano* leaves, Stephen took off his shirt and set to work. The machete was old and blunt, he was not used to swinging it, but with a kind of desperate intensity, he slashed at the tough scrub, trying to stifle, or at least to deaden, the images that crowded in upon him.

Yet he did not succeed. While he slaved and sweated he thought of Peyrat, self-martyred through a sequence of follies heartbreaking to contemplate. He winced at the recollection of the wild donation of their funds, the inopportune surrender of the boots, the perverse determination to ease the blistered heel in Iberian dust. It was as though by some trick of Spanish sun or air the knight of La Mancha had been reborn in Jerome, had sallied forth again on this most lamentable misadventure.

When, with an effort, he wrenched his thoughts from this sadness, they turned inevitably towards the war. At this precise moment men were killing and being killed. And he too must join in the holocaust, whose only result would be a hideous chaos of suffering, hatred and vengeance. Once again recollection of Hubert's taunt brought the blood rushing to his brow. He must go back, and quickly, if only to justify himself, prove that he was not afraid.

All day he worked, bringing one load after another to the yard behind the stable, where, as shown by a ring of scattered branches, the brush-pile stood. All together he brought eight loads, and as he came over the rim of the arroyo with the final one, Luisa was standing by the door, hands clasped, elbows indrawn, in her attitude of brooding immobility.

"That is a good measure for the last journey."

"How can you tell?"

"By the creak of the cart axle and the breathing of the burro." Her impassive expression did not relax. "Your supper is ready. To-night, if you wish, you may eat at my table."

He bedded down the ass for the night, washed in a bucket drawn from the well, then entered the house. Like the *cabaña* it had only one room and was almost as sparsely furnished, the table and chairs roughly hewn from chestnut wood. A charcoal *brasero* stood at one end of the room and some old copper pans hung on the wall behind it. A brass bedstead, half screened, occupied the other and beneath a coloured lithograph of the Virgin de las Batallas. Some wicker matting, much worn and frayed, covered part of the clay floor.

The woman, with a gesture, bade him be seated, cut a slice from the maize loaf and, from a pot on the *brasero*, served him a heaped dish of beans cooked with pimentos. A moment later she took the chair opposite him. There was a silence, then Stephen said:

"You are not eating?"

She put aside the question with a motion of her shoulders.

"Is the food to your taste? There is more. I am sorry I have no wine."

The beans were coated with oil and tasted of garlic, but he was hungry and their meaty warmth made him feel less tired.

"You worked well today . . . though you are not used to it. I shall not want for brush this winter."

"Is it cold here then?"

She nodded.

"The snow blows across from the Sierras. Often the drifts are of great depth."

"Are you not lonely at such a time?"

"I am used to it." She spoke with complete indifference. "For five years now I have been alone. Since the passing of my husband. We do not wish to die. But we die."

"Have you lived here always?"

"No, man. I am from the town of Jerez. There I was married in the church of San Dionisio. My husband worked with the Casa Gonzalez, a cooper, making hoops for the wine casks."

"That was a good position."

G

"Yes, but it did not endure. Had he kept to the outside of the cask all would have been well. But he went within, and for drunkenness was dismissed. Then my eyes became bad, from the dust of the esparto grass. In Andalusia it is a common thing. The lids swelled and I was without sight. For a time I sat outside the Ayuntamiento selling tickest for the *lotería*. It is a work they give to the blind. But I fell sick and, like my husband, was without work."

"Then you knew poverty."

"Worse still . . . humiliation. In Jerez, there is a strange custom instituted by the rich. When one is destitute, one is given the blue uniform of charity and sent into the streets to solicit alms for the common fund. One becomes officially a worthless person and a beggar who receives a small part of what is collected."

"That was a hard thing to do."

"You speak truly, man. I would lie awake at nights, hungry, longing for a little place in the country where we could grow food for ourselves. In desperation, taking two pesetas I had saved, I bought one tenth of a lottery ticket. With all my strength, with my heart, my soul, my famished stomach, I prayed to San Dionisio that we might have the number."

"And you did?"

"No. Never. But the month after our only son, a boy of fourteen, was killed by a train at the *atajo*. It was a great sadness. We sought no compensation, but it came. The rich people who gave the uniforms saw that it was paid. And with that amount we achieved this small place. We named it Estancia Felipe for our son."

"It is a good place," he said, wishing to praise her.

"It was good. Now it is gone to nothing. How can I maintain it alone? If only some help was possible. But that is like a child wishing for the moon."

There was a silence. He had finished his cup of water and, rising, she went to the dipper in the corner, by the door, and refilled it.

"Are you . . . are you long in this country?"

"Not long."

"And shall you remain?"

"No. When my friend is fit to move we must leave."

"Ah, your friend. Clearly, you are devoted to him. You go to Málaga tomorrow?"

"Yes."

"And return in the evening?"

"If you permit it. I have no other place. I shall do work for you in payment."

She did not answer, and although her sad, heavy face gave no sign he knew he had said a wrong thing. He corrected himself quickly:

"I meant, not in payment, but in gratitude."

"That was well spoken. When one is as poor as I, that word payment has lost its meaning."

"But not so the other word." A sudden thought came to him. He said: "The burro and the cart now in your stable would be of some service to you. As for us, we no longer have use for them. Will you accept them, as an expression of our thanks?"

She did not answer. Yet, behind that stolid exterior, he could see that she was deeply touched. Her thick, seamed lips that looked as though cut strongly from a dark wood quivered slightly, she drew a long sighing breath. Then, unexpectedly, still without a word, she leaned forward and with the forefinger of one hand lightly explored the contours of his face. It took but a moment, and when she had finished she offered neither explanation nor apology. She rose, gathered up the empty dish, the metal spoon and cup.

"For your journey tomorrow you must rest. Sleep well. Then you will better withstand whatever the day may bring."

CHAPTER IX

ON THE FOLLOWING day, shortly after ten o'clock, Stephen reached the Hospital San Miguel, situated in a quiet back street that opened on to the Guadalmedina, where a group of women, kneeling on the stony river bank, were pounding linen. The sound of their laughter came to him as he nervously rang the bell and waited. Presently a sister in the blue robe and winged wimple of St. Vincent de Paul came to the grille, and when he had given his name admitted him to a spacious inner courtyard and asked him to wait.

He sat down on a low stone bench, and looked about him. It was a superb fifteenth-century patio. In the centre stood a statue of Don Miguel de Montanes, the Andalusian noble who, turning suddenly from the frivolities of the world, had devoted his life and fortune to the establishment of the hospital. At the base of the pediment was a time-worn plaque defining the intention of the founder to tend the sick, and to give Christian burial to paupers and executed criminals. Behind the statue a magnificent pillared archway of chipped and faded marble gave entrance to the hospital proper. The right side of the courtyard was formed by an enclosed cloister, from which came the distant droning of nuns, and the left by a small baroque chapel. Beyond the open, nail-studded cedar-wood doors, surmounted by a coat of arms, there was visible the high altar, tiled with *azulejos*, with a gilt *retablo* wrought with profuse and intricate figures.

At another time Stephen would have deeply felt the beauty and touching sentiment of this enclosure, but now, brought to a pitch of uncertainty and suspense, its seclusion and mediæval solemnity served only to increase the tension of his nerves. Why did they make him wait so long? His apprehension grew more acute with every passing minute.

At last there came a brisk step, so sudden it made him start, and from a side door Dr. Cabra appeared, bareheaded, and wearing a short white coat. He came towards Stephen, shook hands, and seated himself beside him on the stone bench.

"Well, here you are. Forgive me if I kept you waiting. We are not supposed to talk here, but it is cooler than my office and the good sisters are indulgent." He paused and, with a sympathetic look, placed a hand on Stephen's shoulder. It was a gesture that filled Stephen's heart with foreboding. The news is bad, perhaps the worst, he thought, as Cabra said: "I want to tell you exactly what has been done for your friend. When I brought him to the hospital I immediately opened the leg and drained it. We then irrigated continuously with Carrel's solution. At the same time we used all the remedies at our command to control the septicæmia. But without effect."

Stephen felt his throat contract.

"I considered then whether the major step should be undertaken. Amputation. As I had warned you. His condition was so poor, the circulation so impaired, I realized that the operation might induce an immediate collapse. And yet without it, he could not survive."

There was a silence broken only by that faint intermittent murmur from the nuns in their choir. Cabra was staring straight ahead, frowning, as though finding it difficult to choose his words. Stephen bit hard on his lip, assailed no longer by misgiving but by a dreadful certainty.

"I had to make the decision. I decided to amputate. I assure you," Cabra placed his hand upon his heart, "I could not have used more care had it been my brother or my sister. The operation went well and was quickly over. However . . ." He broke off with a sorrowful little gesture that hung between commiseration and compunction. "A condition of shock supervened late yesterday evening.

I saw that all we had done was of no avail. Had it been humanly possible to communicate with you at that hour I should have done so." He paused again. "The end came shortly after, at eleven o'clock last night."

Stephen had known even before he spoke, yet, though that pre-knowledge was now confirmed, his mind seemed incapable of accepting it. So soon, so suddenly, and without the chance to see him— the private, impersonal death of Jerome Peyrat. Then, as Stephen sat motionless, without speaking, Cabra murmured: "If I can help in any way, with the necessary arrangements . . ."

Stephen stirred from his lethargy.

"He is here?"

"No. At the *mortuoria de mendigos*. By our charter we are enabled to provide a simple funeral . . ." Cabra shrugged with a sad and charming tact . . . "in certain circumstances. You do not mind?"

"It makes no difference. Peyrat will not be the last artist to die without the price of a coffin in his pocket." He stood up. "Forgive me. You have been kind. When can I go to the mortuary?"

Cabra looked at his watch.

"It is closed now until the afternoon. Best to go late . . . about seven o'clock. Come first to my house. There are some papers which I must sign."

"Thank you. When I come you will tell me what I owe you. Although it may take a little time, I can assure you that you will be paid."

"You owe me nothing. Some day perhaps, you will paint me a picture. It shall be for me the souvenir of a meeting that held both pleasure and sorrow." Then, as he escorted Stephen to the doorway, he continued, in a voice of curiosity: "But tell me one thing. You say that your friend was a solitary man, with no wife, no woman. Why then, all the time, in his fever, did he speak continually the name Thérèse?"

"She was someone . . . he admired."

"An affair of the heart?"

"No, only of the spirit."

"Ah, then, she died before him?"

"Yes," Stephen said, with sudden violence. "Four hundred years ago."

He went out, walking at random, head lowered, the pavement blurred and wavering under his vision. Along the river-bank he went, through the public gardens, under the flowering jacaranda trees, between rows of tamarisks, clipped like umbrellas. A band was playing distantly, in the *paseo*. Then, at a turn of the road, he found himself on the sea-front, moving towards the breakwater. He could not breathe, the need for a freer air drove him out on that long finger of stone, reaching far into the blue water.

A mood of the darkest and most abject desolation was upon him. Used though he was to that pit of dejection into which, self-projected, he would plummet like a damned soul, seldom had he fallen to such depths, or known such despairing thoughts. Peyrat dead. And now, as a soldier, he must abandon his work, a loss worse by far than any ordeal of battle. Was he afraid? The question was so puerile he did not even consider it. He had long since ceased to value his life in terms of physical survival. Did Hubert's scornful attitude bear weight upon him? Perhaps. Yet in reality he cared nothing for Hubert, nor for his family, nor for any man's opinion of his conduct or character. The only thing that mattered was this creative instinct that burned within him. To paint was his passion, the very reason of his existence, a need more urgent than hunger or thirst, an inner compulsion so powerful as to be irresistible.

He was now at the end of the pier, and he sat down beside the lighthouse to rest. On the inner side of the sea-wall a boy was fishing, baiting his hook with fragments of shrimp, and from time to time whipping from the water tiny, silvery fish which one after another he thrust into a canvas bag. As he watched, Stephen's hand went instinctively to his pocket for the sketch-book which he had not used for many days. It was not there. But the longing to work again would not be stifled, it rose and seethed within him like a ferment, activated by his sadness, his loneliness, and the period of aridity he had recently endured. Carried away by this tide of unexpressed sensation, he thought, I must paint, I must, or I shall go mad.

For a long time he remained motionless, made pale and distraught by that frantic desire which was, for him, stronger, more imperative, of greater importance than anything else in the world. Then, all at once, through the tormented effort to grapple with his situation, he was conscious of a moment of illumination. At the same time, through the soft damp air came the creak of oars on wooden rowlocks, the sound of men singing. The sardine fleet, as yet undeterred by the war, was beginning to leave the harbour for the night fishing grounds. Beyond the breakwater they shipped their oars, hoisted lateen sails. Out and away they went, dipping, rising on the quiet swell, hovering between sea and air, disappearing like a flight of swallows into the calm and misty distance. To the landward, the sun was slanting towards the crests of the Sierras, setting the clouds

198

on fire, casting violet shadows on the lower hills, making them vague and infinite. Beneath, the terraced vineyards stood out in pure and firm relief, and lower still the clear-cut outlines of roofs, minarets and towers. Minutes passed. Now the sunset was like a flame in the forehead of the city. The beauty of the scene appeased the anguish of his heart, strengthened the purpose that had formed within him. As greyness was falling like a shroud upon the dome of the cathedral, near which, in the *mortuoria de mendigos*, lay the body of Peyrat, he rose and went with decision towards the town.

He reached the end of the breakwater. Suddenly, as he came past the gates of the harbour, someone hailed him. He swung round and saw Hollis, a portfolio under his arm, hurrying towards him from the docks.

"Desmonde, I thought I recognized you. It's a fortunate meeting." Smiling, he paused to regain his breath. "I have good news for you. The SS *Murcia*, a Star Line freighter, has been cleared for Liverpool, leaving Málaga on Tuesday of next week, and the Consul General managed to save a berth for you."

A pause. Stephen did not speak.

"Not only that. I've got leave to go home and join the show. I shall be on the old tub too." Despite his nonchalant, rather lazy manner, Hollis was plainly delighted, bubbling with enthusiasm. "She's only three thousand tons, with no accommodation whatsoever. We shall probably be in the fo'castle, so bring a blanket if you can and I'll take along a few tins of bully beef. Incidentally, I don't believe she'll have an escort allotted. As enemy submarines are in the Mediterranean, we might have a bit of fun."

Another pause, then Stephen said:

"I'm sorry. I am not going back."

"What's that?" Startled, Hollis seemed to wonder if he had heard correctly.

"I am not returning to England. I am going to stay here."

A silence. Hollis's expression changed, slowly, from stunned amazement, through incredulity, into a final cold contempt.

"And what do you propose to do?"

"I am going to paint."

Leaving the other, he turned and walked off rapidly into the gathering darkness.

PART FOUR

CHAPTER I

On a wet October morning in the year 1920, breakfast at Broughton Court was almost over. Outside, the rain dripped from the yellow beech leaves, spattered on the terrace, the Ring of Chanctonbury was lost in mist and, despite the warmth of the red-carpeted morning-room, the crackle of a good fire and the comforting aroma of coffee, bacon, and grilled kidneys from the silver dishes upon the sideboard, a vague constraint had begun to hover, though it seemed little to affect General Desmonde, visiting for the shooting, and who, erect and clean-cut, spreading Oxford marmalade on crisp toast, was constitutionally imperturbable.

Geoffrey broke the silence.

"Confound this weather. Never saw such rain."

"It may go off before lunch," Claire said, with eyes averted towards the park.

"Even if we go out the coverts will be sopping and the birds won't fly."

Thwarted in his pride as a man of property—he had not ceased to enjoy the demonstration, especially to his father, of the sporting qualities of the acres which had come to him by marriage—Geoffrey lounged back, his long thin legs elongated beneath the table, and moodily turned the pages of the morning paper.

Claire, with an effort, threw off her air of languor and turned towards her father-in-law. Recovering from a recent attack of influenza, she had slept badly and, since she still suffered from recurrent sickness, had eaten almost nothing.

"More coffee?"

"No thank you, my dear." He patted her hand, with understanding. "When are you seeing your man in town?"

"Tomorrow."

"Then tell him he must give you something to make you eat."

Claire smiled.

"I shall be all right. Coffee for you, Geoffrey?"

Geoffrey did not answer. Immobilized suddenly, his attention bent upon the sheet before him, an exclamation broke from him.

"By George! Listen to this." In the voice of one disclosing a sensation he read: " 'Yesterday saw the opening at the Maddox Galleries, New Bond Street, of an exhibition of paintings by Stephen Desmonde. Mr. Desmonde, whose controversial picture *Circe and Her Lovers* was awarded the Prix de Luxembourg in 1913, is the son of Reverend Bertram Desmonde of Stillwater Rectory, Sussex, and has recently returned to England. His younger brother, Lieutenant David Desmonde, was killed in action at Vimy Ridge. In this present collection, introduced to Britain under the sponsorship of Richard Glyn, Mr. Desmonde exhibits, presumably, the fruits of his labours during the war years which, we understand, were passed in the comparative tranquillity of the Iberian peninsula. Despite this advantage, we fear that Mr. Desmonde has toiled in vain. We find his landscapes crude, his figure compositions clumsy and brutal. In his complete severance from tradition he has lost sight of the basic principles of proportion, and is entangled in perpetual eccentricity. Indeed, while they are not without some torrid evidence of atmosphere and imagination, these canvases suggest to us only a perverse, frustrated spirit. We hesitate to use stronger words, but others may have less restraint. In brief, we cannot grasp this *soi-disant* art and cannot like it.' "

A pause of considerable intensity followed this communication, then Geoffrey added: "There's a photograph here of one of the paintings. A half-naked slut surrounded by a gang of the most appalling roughs. The thing looks completely decadent to me."

He flung down the paper. Claire, sitting motionless, with a strained expression, had to curb an immediate and almost irresistible impulse to pick it up. Meanwhile the General had risen and, standing with his back to the fire, lit his pipe with a sort of frowning detachment.

"How will they take this at the Rectory?"

"Badly. It's sure to reopen the whole messy business."

"I suppose he'll turn up at home."

"Bound to. He can't have a bean."

The General's brows drew together reflectively.

"I'm afraid Bertram is not now in a position to subsidize him. Pity . . . great pity! It surprises me the fellow has the nerve to show his face in England."

"Not me. I knew he would sneak back when the fighting was over."

Claire had kept silent during these exchanges. Now she ventured:

"I wonder if the paintings are as bad as they make out."

"Good heavens! Didn't you hear what the chap just said about 'em?"

"I know, Geoffrey. But it seemed to me a rather biased critique. He also admitted he couldn't grasp the meaning of the pictures. He mayn't be qualified to judge."

"Not qualified! Why, he's an expert. Or he wouldn't be on the *Post*."

"Then there's Glyn," Claire persisted, mildly, but with slightly heightened colour. "A well-known artist. Why should he sponsor Stephen's work if it were rubbish?"

"Because he's hand in glove with my heroic cousin, and a damned radical to boot." Geoffrey glared at his wife, unaccountably irritated by her attitude of logic. "I daresay they fixed this thing up together in some rotten dive in Paris."

"However it was arranged," said the General with quiet reason, "it's a bad thing for the family . . . very. When I think of David . . . and this . . ." He moved towards the door. "If you'll excuse me, Claire, I'll telephone Bertram now."

"Do that, Father," Geoffrey agreed with approval, pushing back his chair. "I'll meet you in the billiard-room. We'll have a hundred up, and talk it over."

Alone, Claire took up the paper, found the paragraph she sought, read it through twice, sat for a few minutes, pensive, yet with troubled eyes. Then, abruptly, she rose and went upstairs to the nursery. But Nicholas and little Harriet had already gone out with Nurse Jenkins for their walk to the lodge. Whatever the weather, Jenkins was a believer in the morning "airing", and from the window Claire made out the two small figures of her children, in yellow oilskins and south-westers, plodding forward in their Wellingtons, on either side of the stout blue-coated Nanny, who, more for gentility than protection, carried a tall umbrella. It was a reassuring sight and, without knowing, Claire smiled. Yet almost immediately, she sighed. There was, of course, beyond her concern for the family, no cause for her to be unduly disturbed by the unexpected news of Stephen's reappearance. She had, in Geoffrey's phrase, written him off long ago. Acknowledging his defects, she, like the others, deplored them. Yet there still lingered in her the hope that he would in some way make atonement, less for than through these same lamentable peculiarities. And her sense of justice, so she named it, detected in the review of his exhibition a note of prejudice, a judgment of the man rather than the artist, which made her wish to rise in his defence—at least, she corrected herself, in defence of his work.

The rain continued, the men could not shoot, and in the dull passage of the afternoon Geoffrey's irritability increased. Claire knew that he was cross with her for being out of sorts—as if the fault were hers—and she suspected also that he had an unpleasant settlement day in prospect. But although she was sensitive to his moods, and indeed to the moods of others, upon this occasion her own preoccupation protected her. An impulse, as yet only half formed, was stirring beneath her consciousness.

On the following morning she drove to Halborough Junction and boarded the train for London. Seated alone in the corner of the compartment, wearing a dark grey costume, her small hat drawn back from her fine creamy brow, chin sunk in a brown necklet of fur, gloved hands clasped before her, she gazed with eyes unusually dark and wide at the green, familiar Sussex fields, sodden with recent rain, the clipped hedges and swirling ditches, the chalky Arun, winding between wet grasses, russet sedges, and bulrushes that stood like purple spears.

At Victoria she took a taxi to Wimpole Street, where Dr. Ennis, delayed at the hospital, kept her waiting until quarter past eleven. But the consultation passed off without incident, she was pronounced much improved, rallied a little on her pensive mood, then liberated, with a smile and a paternal pressure of the arm, just before noon.

Slowly, she walked towards the West End, the entire afternoon before her, responding to the movement of unknown people, the gay shop-windows and rushing omnibuses—these days of emancipation were always dear to her. Should she go to her club? No, she decided she was not in the humour for chatter. Unconsciously, perhaps, her steps had taken her through Oxford Street to a little French pastry-cook's at the upper end of Bond Street. Here she ordered coffee and a brioche. Geoffrey, in his role of country squire, demanded such rich and satisfying meals, it was a relief to lunch on less vitalizing fare. Afterwards, quite contrary to custom, as though its purpose was merely to delay departure, she smoked a cigarette . . . Ennis had encouraged her to minor dissipations.

Presently, however, she was in the street again and moving, uncertainly at first, then with a sort of fatalism, towards the Maddox Galleries. Here it was, a narrow frontage, rather in need of paint, pressed between an antique shop and the studio of a fashionable photographer. She entered quickly, with a beating heart, surprised by the modest appearance and by the emptiness of the place. Only two women were present, conversing softly, in the tones of Surbiton, behind a catalogue; a long somnolent youth in striped trousers and black braided jacket, reading at a desk, seemed the sole guardian of the gallery.

As her vision cleared, Claire began to look at the paintings, seeing little in the beginning but an audacious contrast of brilliant colours, yet striving, despite the emotion which troubled her, to evaluate, to understand them. Could she do so? No, perhaps not. She was unqualified, rating herself a very ordinary person, with only a modest endowment of what might be called artistic taste. And, she admitted, she was not impartial, wishing with all her heart to like and approve the pictures. Nevertheless, despite these disadvantages, she was conscious, honestly, of the powerful impact, of a sense of animation, an intensity of life springing from the canvases before her. She saw in them an originality of form and idea. They were not commonplace.

One, in particular, an Andalusian landscape, held her for a long time. She could feel the hard brilliance of the light, the sun beating on arid slopes and stunted olive trees. Then she came upon the figure of a barefoot peasant, an old woman, standing in profile, dressed in a ragged blouse and skirt of sacking, with a wooden *azada* upon her shoulder. There was in this composition such a fusion of sadness and dignity, so poignant an expression of the soul of oppressed and suffering humanity, it touched Claire to the heart.

Suddenly, as she stood absorbed, a voice addressed her. She swung round, and saw Stephen. Immediately the blood rushed from her cheeks—from surprise and shock she actually turned faint. Not for an instant had she dreamed he would be here, indeed, her visit, unpremeditated and impulsive, had all the elements of secrecy. She had thus a sense of being discovered, of having somewhat shamefully revealed herself.

"Claire! How good of you to come."

He took her hand warmly, held it for a moment between his hard thin fingers. He had, she saw through her confusion, become extremely thin, his figure was taut and spare, there seemed not an ounce of flesh upon him. And he had grown a beard, cropped close on cheek and chin, which somehow accentuated the length of jaw and temple hollows, gave the planes of his face bones an almost startling gauntness. Yet he was brown and held himself erect. Dressed in washed corduroy, flannel shirt and blue pilot coat, he had a vital quality which reassured her, corrected an impression that he had been ill.

"How little changed you are," he went on. "Let's sit over here, where we can talk. You are in town for the day, of course. How are the children, and Geoffrey?"

She gave him news of her family, not daring to mention his own people at the Rectory. His manner, direct and friendly, lacking entirely that youthful shyness which had once tormented him, should have set her at ease. Yet, try as she might, she could not fully regain her composure, could scarcely look at him.

"I suppose you've been round the show," he remarked lightly, after they had talked for several minutes. "Do tell me what you think of it."

"I like it . . ." she answered awkwardly, like a schoolgirl.

"Don't be afraid to speak your mind," he reassured her. "I'm quite hardened to abuse."

She flushed unexpectedly.

"We saw the critique in the *Post*. I'm so sorry. It was so . . . so unfair."

"Oh, that! That was comparatively mild. Almost complimentary. You ought to see some of my other notices . . . sheer effrontery . . . aboriginal daubs . . . perverted nonsense . . ." He smiled faintly. "Why, when Peyrat and I held our first exhibition, in a little room off the Rue Pigalle, the solitary critic who came advised us to burn our canvases and start a sausage shop."

The calmness of his tone affected her deeply. Her gaze, downcast, took in a rough darn on the knee of his corduroys, and, more particularly, his boots, well brushed and neatly laced, but coarse, heavy workman's boots, with thick nail-studded soles. She exclaimed, involuntarily:

"Stephen! It hasn't been easy for you."

Instantly he rejected this sympathy. "I've been doing what I wanted to do. The only thing that matters to me . . . without which I couldn't bear to exist."

"But it must be dreadfully discouraging, to meet always with abuse, to be denied success."

"Material success isn't so important, Claire. Usually it's assessed by false standards. It's the work itself, and one's feeling for it, that really matters. Besides, I've had some slight recognition. Two of my paintings are in the Municipal Gallery in The Hague, one in Brussels and another in the Oslo State Museum." Her movement of surprise made him smile again. "Does that amaze you? After all, some countries do buy the works of the younger artist."

The revelation, so unexpected, filled her with pleasure. Her eyes came to rest on the painting of the old Spanish woman.

"I like that . . . very much."

"Lusia Mendez. Yes, she was a good one. When I was down to my last peseta she took me in. She had little enough. But it was clean poverty." He added: "She was blind."

Claire studied the picture and, anxious to show her interest, ventured:

"The rough finish is striking."

He smiled.

"I couldn't afford proper canvas. It's painted on burlap . . . a piece cut from a potato sack."

"Have you just come from Spain?"

"No, I got out eighteen months ago. There was a man in Paris I wanted to work with. Amédée Modigliani. A fine painter. I was fond of him.

"You say, 'was'?"

"He died in January at the Hôpital de la Charité. Next day the girl he lived with killed herself."

The calmness of his tone startled her. What depths had he not sounded in these intervening years? Nervously she stole another look at him. Yes, she could see in his face the marks of hardships and expedients, as though for years he had mixed with the poorest and most wretched of his kind and, driven almost to despair, had escaped, not through cynicism, but by the secret passion that was in him. What a queer fellow he was . . . and yet . . .

A silence followed. Several persons came into the gallery, with the air of investigating a curiosity. The young man behind the desk was sitting up, sweeping back his hair with a pocket-comb. Claire felt his eyes upon her.

"Are you staying in London?" she asked.

"Yes. Glyn's given me a shakedown in his studio. Just off the Fulham Road. He's away for a few weeks. Maddox has been rather decent to me too. By the bye, he'll be here at three. I'd like you to meet him."

She stirred nervously at the thought of further involvement. She could not, must not wait, made a pretence of inspecting her watch.

"I must rush for my train." She began to gather up her things, folded her catalogue, placed it in her handbag. Then forced herself to ask an all-important question. "You will be coming to the Rectory, won't you, Stephen?"

There was a pause.

"It was a mistake for me to go back before. It would be a worse one now. Besides, they can't possibly want me."

"Oh, I'm sure they do. I talked on the telephone with Caroline last evening. They have really missed you."

A longer pause.

"Well," he hesitated, "if I'm asked . . ."

"I'm so glad. We shall see you there, then, Stephen. Good-bye."

Outside, the air was cool upon her warm cheeks, the western sky held a rosy gleam. She walked briskly, lightly even, down the incline of St. James's and across the Mall towards the station, her mind still occupied by her recent brief encounter. It seemed to her remarkable that she had seen and talked with Stephen. The protective instinct she had always had towards him, and which, of course, she still might legitimately feel, was re-aroused, and it its glow she was happy—without knowing it, happier than she had been for many months.

In the train, as it tore through the October twilight, past darkling woods, stark trees, and unseen villages where lights already made frosty haloes in cottage windows, a smile of recollection parted her lips. And suddenly, she had a thought, one might say an inspiration, which caused her to sit up with a stifled exclamation. How splendid, if it could be done! She set herself to consider the possibilities calmly. Inevitably, in the circumstances, there would be difficulties, yet surely, oh, surely she could overcome them. At least she would try with all her heart.

CHAPTER II

STEPHEN HAD ARRIVED in England with less than three pounds in his pocket—a condition of near insolvency that was certainly no novelty to him. Fortunate in having a bed and the use of the small kitchenette in Glyn's unused studio, he had nevertheless to do his own catering, and the post-war price of food appalled him. A quartern loaf now cost one and fourpence, a pound of the cheapest sugar, previously sold for twopence, had soared to one and three. Daily the cost of living rocketed, inflicting suffering upon the wage-earners, and even greater hardships upon those who, like himself, were earning nothing.

Often in those years of absence his thoughts had turned towards London. Now he scarcely recognized it. The process of demobilization, still proceeding, the reshuffling of thousands of human beings, produced a shifting air of dislocation, gave to the city the singular impermanence of a change-house. In the West End a restless gaiety prevailed. Nearly a million young Britons had died in the war, another million had been incapacitated. Was it to forget this fact, or because it already was forgotten, that people flocked to places of entertainment, to the theatres, cinemas, restaurants and nightclubs? Sadness had vanished as though it had never been.

But the river remained unchanged, and Stephen, spurning the busy streets, spent many hours wandering along the Chelsea and Battersea embankments, studying the fluid play of reflections, infinite gradations of grey light, broken by a sudden gleam of pink and pearl—the pale discretion of an October sun. During his brief but eventful sojourn in Stepney, the lower Thames had laid upon him a singular spell, a need, intense and insistent, to paint her there, in all her moods. A reach on the Isle of Dogs not far from Clinker Street he especially remembered and, moved by recollection, a kind of nostalgia, he felt increasingly the desire to renew his impressions of the scene. And one morning, the day before his exhibition closed, having nothing else to do, he took a bus to Stepney.

The weather was fair when he started off, opaque grey sky and a calm still air, perfect for the colour tones he wanted, but unluckily, as the omnibus drew into Seven Sisters Lane, a misty rain swept up the estuary and blotted out the water-front. At the Red Lion he got off the bus and, with a look at the dripping overcast, turned up the collar of his jacket and soundly damned the climate. The day was killed for painting—no one but Monet could have dealt with the prevailing blur. But he was on familiar ground, the sight of the corner fish-and-chip shop and the oil-merchant's store where he used to get his colours restored his spirits. And on an impulse he swung up the Lane into Clinker Street, mounted the steps of the Settlement, and rang the bell.

No one answered for a long time—running true to form, reflected Stephen—then a manservant with the general air of an old drill-sergeant, in discarded clerical trousers, with cropped head and a strip of green baize around his middle, opened the door.

"Yes?" He gazed at Stephen.

"Is Mr. Loftus still here? He was a curate on the district some years ago."

"You mean the Reverend Gerald Loftus? He did used to be here. Got on a treat since. Why, only last year they made him vicar of St. Barnabas."

"Indeed! I'm glad he's done so well. There was another curate about the same time, Mr. Geer."

"Oh, Geer . . . he's gone too. But he didn't amount to much. He's still a curate, I believe . . . mining village near Durham . . . rough stuff."

"I see." Stephen stood for a moment. Then, "You don't by any chance know of a young woman who used to work here . . . her name is Jenny Baines?"

"Mrs. Baines!" the man answered at once. "C'ourse I do. Lives quite near. Seventeen Cable Street. Had some bad luck in her time. But a nice little woman, and doing all right now."

"Bad luck?"

"She had a kid what died. Then lost her husband. Caught a fever in Australia and was buried at sea. Why d'you ask? Friend of yours?"

"Yes . . . in a way." Stephen spoke non-committally, then, as the sergeant's gaze became more searching, he said. "Thank you for your information," turned, and went down the steps.

His interest in Geer and Loftus had been merely academic. Jenny was the one real person of his Clinker Street days, and he warmed to the thought of seeing her again.

Cable Street was on the right, nearer the river, only two streets away. In ten minutes he was there, walking along the slightly curved row of low, one-storey brick houses, noting the numbers on the fanlights—the odd numbers were on the right. He was almost opposite 17 when the door opened and a woman came out, bare-headed, wearing a mackintosh and carrying a string bag. He would have known her anywhere.

"Jenny," he said. "Don't you remember me?"

She looked at him, looked hard, as though confronted by an un-believable circumstance which really startled her. Then in a fara-way voice she said:

"Mr. Stephen Desmonde."

"Yes, Jenny. You look as though you'd seen a ghost."

"Oh, no, sir. You have changed though. You're thinner, but of course you always was small made." The colour had flooded back into her face and, still flustered, she added: "I am glad to see you. I was just going shopping down the street. Come back in the house."

"No, no," he protested. "I'll go along with you."

He took her umbrella and held it over them as they walked along Cable Street.

"How long is it since we last met?"

"It must be eight years and . . . let me see . . . yes, eight years and three months . . . if it's a day."

The exactitude of her reply amused him.

"I sent you a postcard once from Paris. Did you ever get it?"

"Get it! It's on my kitchen mantelpiece this minute. The Eiffel Tower. Been much admired."

"I'm truly flattered, Jenny. So you haven't forgotten me?"

"That I haven't, Mr. Desmonde," she answered firmly.

They were now in the main street and, as the drizzle had increased, he took her by the elbow and steered her into a tea-room that stood at the corner of the Commercial Road.

"We'll shelter here. And have a cup of tea."

"You remember my weakness, sir. I always was a one for tea."

After some delay a waitress detached herself from the little group gossiping in the back premises.

"Tea and hot buttered toast for two."

"And see it *is* butter, miss, if you please," Jenny amplified, dryly adding, later, to Stephen, in a confidential undertone: "I know them here. Give you marge as soon as look at you."

The tea was brought, steaming hot, the toast examined and approved.

"And how have things been with you, Jenny?" He took the cup she poured for him. "I was sorry to hear . . . that you were alone now."

"Yes, I've had my troubles. But you get over them, sir. I never was one to sit and mope. I put Alf's insurance in a nice little house and haven't done too bad."

"You take lodgers?"

"In a very particular way, sir. I have one regular, old Captain Tapley—Mr. Joe Tapley really is his name. Not to mislead you, it was only a barge he had when he retired, and before that a canal boat. But he's nice, sir, though very deaf. Then I have another room I let temporary, mostly on recommendations, ships' officers unloading at the Docks, engineers what come down for a refit. Why, when they're pushed at mission time, I even take a clergyman from the Settlement."

"Good God, Jenny. Clergymen. After all they did to you. You're as forgiving . . . and as cheerful as ever."

"Why shouldn't I be, sir? I like to be busy. I have my independence. And I'm lucky to have Florrie."

He gave her a glance of interested inquiry.

"Florrie Baines. Alf's sister, and one of the best. We're ever so friendly. She has a tidy little business in Margate. I go down a lot to help her."

"What sort of business?"

"Wet fish."

Her choice of an adjective made him smile. "Is there any other kind?"

"Never thought of that," She laughed. "Wet's what they say in the trade. Silly p'raps. Still, I suppose there's kippers and dried salt haddick and that like. But Florrie's mostly in the shrimp line."

Studying her as she sat there, bareheaded, with her arms comfortably on the table, mackintosh open at the neck, breasts rounded under the tight drab bodice, he understood why he had always wanted to paint her. Something in her: a quality of womanhood, the generosity of her wide mouth and full underlip, that too vivid complexion, with the reticulated network of tiny veins on the cheeks, the fringe of black hair, eyes soft yet fiercely independent. He could see her now, reclining, small-boned under her plumpness, on a blue couch, against which reds in her skin would burn and crackle.

"And how about you, sir? Getting along all right?"

"Oh, pretty well, Jenny." He came out of his dream. "I've disgraced myself beyond the hopes of my worst enemies. Dodged the war, rolled in all the gutters of Europe—that's a quote from a recent letter—and come out of them rather the worse for wear."

"That I can't believe, Mr. Desmonde. You was always the gentleman." A pause. "You're still at the painting?"

"It's still at me. Got me by the throat. Won't let go."

"Yes," she agreed with practical complaisance. "If you have to do a thing I suppose you have to. It's like . . . like going to sea, I was going to say, sir."

"Like being thrown overboard, Jenny. And having to swim for it."

"Well," she nodded briskly, "you always liked the water, sir. I remember you had a cold bath at the Settlement every day."

Her dry smile was irresistible. He laughed, and so did she, a joint fit of laughter that caused the waitress to emerge from the rear with a disapproving frown and pointedly lay the bill upon the table.

"Impudence!" Jenny commented, wiping her eyes. "Still, I feel the better for that. Nothing like a good laugh. Have another cup of tea."

"No more, Jenny."

"It is strange to see you in these parts again, Mr. Desmonde." She spoke with rare artlessness. "I suppose . . . I suppose you've come down to see them at the Settlement."

He shook his head.

"Then what?"

"I wanted to paint a bit of the river."

"Oh!" Her eyes fell.

"You know the old Barking wharf?"

"Course I do."

"That's the bit."

"These tumble-down old shacks . . ." She broke off, biting her lower lip, then asked: "Shall you be stopping in London long?"

"I'm afraid not. I'm leaving in a couple of days."

"I see."

A silence followed. He took up the bill.

"I mustn't keep you from your shopping."

"No, I suppose we can't sit here for ever." She drew a quick breath, then asked, with touching diffidence: "Won't you come back and meet Cap'n Tapley? I could give you ever such a nice lunch, sir."

The genuineness in her voice and the thought of a good hot meal enticed him. But he shook off the temptation abruptly.

"Perhaps another time, Jenny. Who knows but what I may be down here again one day."

"Don't forget to look me up if you come, sir."

"I will."

She picked up her bag and umbrella, at the swing doors they shook hands, then she went towards the market while he set off in the opposite direction with the intention of walking back to Fulham. As he reached the street corner something made him turn his head. And she too was looking back, towards him. He hesitated, then waved his hand and went on. The mist, thickening to fog, seemed to accentuate his sense of having lost both warmth and companionship.

CHAPTER III

STEPHEN'S EXHIBITION CLOSED on the last day of November. Charles Maddox, owner of the gallery, fearing that a strong feeling might develop against Desmonde in the press, had undertaken it with reluctance, and only after pressure from Richard Glyn, whom he had represented with considerable profit in the last few years. However, to his surprise—if an art dealer is capable of such emotion— two of the highest-priced pictures, *Charity* and *Noon in the Olive Grove*, were sold to an agent during the final week of the show, so that he more than covered his expenses, while Stephen, after deduction of commission, received a cheque for three hundred pounds. Despite his indifference to material success, it was a relief to be so unexpectedly lifted out of his chronic state of penury and, in addition, this unaccustomed affluence cast a better light upon his prospective visit to Stillwater. A letter, brief but not unkind, had come from his father, inviting him to the Rectory, and he had already written to accept. Now, at least, he would not return a beggar.

Early on December 3 he packed his rucksack, left a note at the studio for Glyn, who was soon due to arrive in London, and entrained for Sussex. An hour later he got off at Gillinghurst, the station before Halborough, so that he might take the long cross-country walk to Stillwater. It was an exquisite winter morning. The pale yellow sun had not yet dispelled the crisping frost which silvered every blade of grass, every hawthorn twig. On the branches of the beeches, prisms of ice caught the light, splintered it into brilliant rainbow fragments. The air was still, but sharp as cider. In the fields cows moved in the vapour of their own breath. How often in Spain, suffering acutely the sickness of exile, wandering through the hot olive-groves in burning loneliness, the thought of England had haunted him; the wet earth and leafless trees, the drenched meadows and osier-hung brooks had called and called to him.

As he tramped through the winding lanes, the hard ground ringing like iron under his boots, every step brought him back to the days when he had scoured these woods and meadows with his brother. On the right was the thicket where they gathered hazel nuts, and further on the coppice which, one June afternoon, had yielded them the rare speckled egg of a golden-crested wren. Another bend of the road and, through the leafless trees, he could see the glitter of Chillingham Lake. How often had they come together to fish for the silver perch that hovered and darted among the lily-pads and beds of water-cress in these clear springs. A pang of recollection made him grit his teeth. That sense of self-reproach which, since he learned of Davie's death, had never quite left him, flared up again in his breast. Suddenly, painfully, he seemed stripped of the faith in his own creative powers which usually sustained him, felt himself worthless, his life no more than a weak and wasted essay in futility.

He reached Stillwater village and, with beating heart, traversed the cobbled streets which wandered between the old half-timbered gables. Yet the place apparently had grown in his absence, a modern note was struck by a number of strange shops, by a red-fronted Woolworth's, a cinema which presented a showy marquee, and a large dance-hall, embellished with neon signs, on the site of the old corn exchange. Then, as he climbed the hill out of the village, he was brought sharply to a halt by a row of new red-brick suburban bungalows, built on the main road above the lane which gave access to the Rectory. Their dreadful style and cheap pretentiousness, even their names—his gaze quailed before such titles as "The Nest", "Cosy-Nook", "Billancoo"—gilt upon the ornate front doors, were an insult to good taste. And this high ridge, offering an exquisite view of the Norman church and the rolling Downs, had been a lovely spot, a warren, wild with gorse and bracken, ever since he could remember.

Saddened, he swung away, and hastened down the lane, cutting to the left through the wicket into the Rectory grounds by the wood-land path known as the Canon's Walk. Here, too, he sensed an air of change, a slight neglect in the wind-blown leaves littering the mossy drive. In the orchard an ancient apple tree lay riven and unstripped where it had fallen across the tiled coping of the stable wall. But after seven years of absence, he was in no mood to linger. The side door, which gave entry through the fern conservatory, stood open. The next minute he was in the house. In answer to his call there was a movement in the still-room. He went in and found Caroline, wearing a stained apron, hair wrapped in a coloured scarf, seated at the table, coring apples.

"Carrie!" he exclaimed.

She turned, gazed at him, dropped the coring knife.

"Oh, Stephen, I'm glad you've come."

Her welcome touched him. Yet he saw that she was put out at being taken unawares and that her eyes had a worried look. He did not press her. After a moment he asked:

"Where are they all?"

"Father has gone to a conference at Charminster. Won't be back till afternoon. We didn't expect you till evening."

"And Mother?"

"Away. As usual. Let me get you something to eat?"

He shook his head.

"I warn you, lunch won't be much."

At this, moisture formed beneath her lids. He sat down beside her, pulled out the red cotton handkerchief he always carried and offered it to her.

"Am I to blame?"

"No, no . . . it isn't you . . . it's . . . it's everything."

"Tell me."

She sighed and unburdened herself. The troubles which afflicted her could be expressed in a single word . . . change . . . change in that splendid world they had known in their youth . . . change which had come with such rapidity it baffled and bewildered her.

The Rectory had never been an easy establishment to manage. But now . . . the difficulties were heartbreaking. Since Beasley died just after the Armistice she had not had a decent servant in the house. Grown women, accustomed to the large wages of the munition factories, had lost taste for domestic service. A procession of girls from the village had passed in and out of the kitchen. Pert, careless, with no interest in their work, they thought of nothing but going off to the cinema or to the new dance-hall which now desecrated the village. Only this morning she had been obliged to dismiss Bessie Gudderby, the thatcher's daughter, having discovered her, late last night, in the servants' hall, sharing a bottle of the Rector's port with a young man from Brighton, in her pyjamas.

"Think of it. Pyjamas!" Caroline declared. "It's the war that's done it, the awful war. If I hadn't taken in an Austrian immigrant straight from the Tyrol I wouldn't have a person in the house to help me. And Sophie speaks no English, can cook nothing but *apfelstrudel* and *wiener schnitzel*!"

Stephen might have smiled but for the drawn expression on Caroline's face. He noticed, too, that her hands were red and chapped, the palms roughened by hard work. He kept silent while she resumed:

"It isn't only inside, it's out as well. Money seems to be scarce with Father. We don't work the farm any more. It's let to Matthews. During the war we were all ploughed up, it was simply too much to get the meadows back to grass, especially since we'd lost Mould."

"What! Is the old chap dead?"

"No. Retired . . . by his remarkable son." As Stephen gazed at her inquiringly she continued with a note of real bitterness. "I suppose you noticed the new bungalows on the warren. Albert Mould built them. Owns them too. Albert has shown himself to be quite go-ahead since last you saw him. During the war he got hold of the old clay pit, worked it at a fantastic profit. Made heaps of money. Now he's in all sorts of business projects—politics too. County councillor . . . quite a force in the district. Of course he hates us, he always has, and last year he had a violent row with Father over the glebe boundary."

There was a pause.

"How is Father?"

"He's well, considering. He can't do so much as he used to, but he's perfectly sound."

"He must miss Davie." Stephen's gaze remained lowered.

"Yes. But you are the one he really misses. And of course, like the rest of us, he has his worries." For an instant Stephen thought the reference was to him, then, in a subdued tone, Caroline added: "Mother."

Carrie had always made it a rule never to discuss their mother, but now, softer, more communicative, she revealed, after a momentary hesitation, this added anxiety. Julia's eccentricity had lately grown to such an extent as to become a source of real concern. With housekeeping so difficult, imposing a restriction on her comforts, she was less at Stillwater than ever, often away for weeks at a time, leaving them ignorant of her whereabouts. Previously, she had seemed at home only in one of the inland spas where, indulging her indolence, she could drink the waters in the morning and, in the afternoon, wearing a plumed hat and many strings of beads, sit statuesque and unruffled in the palm court of the Grand Hotel close to the orchestra, listening to Strauss, Bizet, and Amy Woodford-Finden. But now her hypochondria, like her oddity, had progressed, so that from orthodox physicians who, while they humoured her whims and caprices, had at least kept her within reasonable bounds, she had passed, step by step, to chiropractors, osteopaths, and faith healers. Now apparently she was installed at Shepherd's Bush in the curative establishment of an Eastern mystic who expounded some form of theosophy centring—Caroline believed —upon the word "Karma". It was all dreadfully worrying. Julia, of course, had a small income of her own, yet this surely must be quite inadequate to sustain the varied extravagances of such a mode of life. But no one could discover the truth—she had become more secretive, at least more serenely detached, than ever. She lived in her own dream world . . . from which the war, Stephen's absence, the Rector's difficulties, even Davie's death had not moved her for a single moment.

A bell tinkled as Caroline concluded. It indicated lunch. During the meal, which, as predicted, was simple and bad, served without ceremony by the raw-boned Sophie, and later, when they went round the garden and she showed him how she had managed to keep things going with only a part-time man in summer and a boy who came on Saturdays, Stephen exerted himself to win his sister from her depression. Since their early childhood there had never been much love between Caroline and himself. Her jealousy, resentment at their father's fondness for him, had stifled such overtures as he had made. But now, adversity had worn her down, given her need of support.

At four o'clock in the afternoon the Rector arrived. He greeted Stephen quietly, looking at him closely, then away, as though he scarcely ventured to assess the effect of these years of absence. He asked no questions, but silently led the way into the library, where, before a wood fire, Caroline had ready the tea and toasted muffins.

"How good to have a fire these wintry days." The Rector held his hands to the blaze which brought out lines of sadness, hitherto undisclosed, upon his face. "I trust you had a pleasant journey down."

"Very. I walked over from Gillinghurst."

"Indeed." After a pause: "We are perhaps not so well equipped as of old, but we will do our best to make you comfortable."

His conversation, unnaturally stiff, disclosed the strain under which the Rector laboured. The meeting, indeed, was terrible for him. Torn between paternal yearning and the fear of fresh misfortune, he longed to take Stephen to his heart, yet, warned by past experience, he dared not. Even his son's appearance, the beard and clothes, and that set expression, like a mask over the face, aroused his apprehensions. Hope continually frustrated had left only a dull anticipation of some new and unforseen development which would bring further discredit upon them all.

Yet he was resolved to be calm and natural. When the tea-tray was removed he swept his fingers along the mantlepiece, emptied the blue vase that stood there.

"We haven't had much chance to excavate lately but these came to light the other day."

Stephen examined the coins handed to him.

"They look very early."

"The Harrington farthing isn't worth much but the other two are quite good."

"One's a long-cross penny?" Stephen suggested recollecting something of his youthful instruction. "Thirteenth-century?"

"Precisely." Pleased, the Rector leaned foward. "Henry the Third . . . around 1250. You see how they extended the arms of the cross to the edge to prevent clipping. And this"—he handed another coin—"is my latest find. Rather a good one . . . from the North Barrow. Can you place it?"

Stephen studied the paper-thin disc, hoping to be right.

"Might it be a rose noble?"

"Very near to it. An angel. It came shortly after the noble. You can just make out the ship on reverse, and the angel is St. Michael. This was the piece given to those touched for the king's evil. It was struck for this purpose down to the reign of Charles the First."

Stephen with a display of interest, returned the coins. Then, recollecting, he plunged his hand in the deep pocket of his jacket and produced the two wrapped packages which, impelled by something inexplicable within him, he had brought from London. He gave one to his father and the other to Caroline.

"What is this?"

"Nothing much, Father. But I hope you'll like it. Yours too, Carrie. It's so long since I've seen you both I wanted to bring back something. . . . propitiation of the Saxon gods."

Bertram, with suppressed misgiving, glanced at Stephen, then at the packet, which seemed to scorch his palm. Carrie was already opening hers and, with an exclamation of pleasure and surprise, drew out from its bed of cotton wool a brooch of aquamarines and antique gold.

"Oh, Stephen, how lovely. I haven't had such a nice thing for ages."

The Rector's gaze was glued to the brooch which Caroline was pinning to her dress. Slowly, as though dreading what he might discover, he unwrapped his gift. It was an illuminated Book of Hours, genuinely of the tenth century, almost certainly a work of the Winchester school, the most original and attractive in the whole range of mediæval art, a prize he had coveted all his life.

"It's . . . it's Carolingean . . ." Bertram stammered, then, speechless, gazed at his son.

"Don't look at me like that, Father." Stephen's smile, tinged with irony, was almost bitter. "I assure you it's come by honestly."

"You . . . you purchased it?"

"Naturally. I found it at Dobson's."

"But . . . how?"

"I'd been lucky enough to sell two pictures at the exhibition."

"My dear boy . . . someone has actually bought your paintings?" A wave of colour, pitiable in its intensity, flooded the Rector's face. His eyes filled, glistened. This unthought-of success, even in that field of art which had always invoked his disapproval, salvaged the battered remnants of his pride, gratified him beyond words. Several times, to himself, he repeated: "You have sold your pictures." Then, gazing at the gift, he added, in a voice that shook: "I am deeply . . . deeply touched by your thoughtfulness."

He would have said more but did not—he could see that Stephen wished the subject dropped. Yet many times that evening, after the brief supper, he took up the little book, turned its vellum pages with a fondling, meditative touch. Could it be that things might still come all right in the end? No doubt Stephen had strayed far from the decent ways of his upbringing. These dreadful stories of his dissipation, brought back by Hubert, his past perversities and deplorable behaviour during the war—all made it hard to place reliance upon him. But there must, there must be good in him. He had always been open-hearted and generous and he was older now, surely at last he must think of "settling down".

Hopefully, almost, the Rector studied the prodigal, now just concluding a game of chess with Caroline. How good that he should think of playing with his sister and not, as had been feared, seek distractions in the taverns of Charminster or Brighton. The clock showed ten o'clock. Quietly, Bertram rose and locked up—the back, side, front doors—returned to the library.

"You must be tired after your journey."

"Yes, I am rather. I think I'll turn in. Good night, Father. Night, Carrie."

"Good night, my boy."

Upstairs, Stephen stood in his own room, so lit by moonlight he needed no other illumination. Motionless under the sloped ceiling, he glanced round—at the shelves above the desk, still holding his first books, in the far corner the battered botanical cabinet, his early water-colours, and the map he had made of Stillwater Parish upon the walls—conscious even of the same musky odour, springing from a source always undetected, which had greeted him like a friend on his return from school. Slowly, he picked up a photograph, a snapshot taken by Caroline, of David, playing stump-cricket on the lawn. He looked at it steadily, enduring the solemn eyes, the nervous tensity of the boyish stance, more slowly put it down, then, turning with a set face, threw wide open his window, braced to the shock of the frosted air.

Bathed in moonshine, an angelic peace lay upon the Downs. Through the leafless beeches the fluted spire of the church was visible, rising from the dark yews whose shadows stretched still as death on the cropped turf, like fallen bowmen. A deep longing, unformed yet unsupportable, overcame him. This downland was his home, his inheritance, yet he had thrown it wilfully away. For what? He thought of the past eight years, the pinching and poverty, subterfuges, makeshifts, disappointments, the work and more work, the wild elations, the ghastly stretches of sterility . . . what a life, what a hell he had chosen. Abruptly he swung away, began to undress, throwing his clothes upon a chair. In bed he closed his eyes, as against pain, shutting out the moonlight and the still, sweet night. No matter how he thought or felt, he was in the power of forces that moved, predestined, to inscrutable and irrevocable ends.

CHAPTER IV

DURING THE DAYS which followed, Stephen spent most of his time working in the Rectory garden. He had always enjoyed manual labour, and with so much to be done, was able to indulge his passion for order. He pruned the orchard, removed the fallen tree—it was, alas, not an apple but the greengage that in his youth had borne such luscious purple-yellow fruit—and split it for firewood. He raked the leaves and made tremendous bonfires from which the blue smoke spiralled upwards, as from signal beacons. He painted the barn. With Joe, the boy who came out of school hours, he mended Caroline's poultry run, which had fallen into disrepair and was periodically raided by a fox from the Broughton coverts.

On the few occasions when he went to the village he became conscious of some queer looks directed at him. He was used to being stared at in the streets—his bare head, hollow cheeks, cropped beard, and long striding steps, to say nothing of his careless dress, his moleskin trousers and knotted scarf, made him a conspicuous figure—and he treated such scrutiny with complete indifference. But these local attentions were more marked. Several times abusive remarks were shouted after him by the gang of youths who habitually stood at the corner outside the cinema. And one afternoon, as he was leaving the yard of Singleton the carpenter, where he had gone to purchase nails and boarding, a lump of mud from an unknown source flew past his head, accompanied by the taunt "War hero!" He judged therefore, with tightening of his lips, that word of his return had gone the rounds and that his standing in popular favour was not high.

This was a strange fallow period for him. He had no wish to obtrude his painting on the household and his only brushwork had been upon the barn's stout oak beams. But occasionally, after lunch, when the weather was fine, he took the long walk upon the Downs as far as Chillingham Lake, where, partly sheltered from the keen wind by the sedges which fringed the lake, he sat upon a stump and filled his sketch-book with studies of ruffled water and stark, wintry trees.

Late one afternoon, returning from such an excursion, he came out upon the country road at the old turnpike known as Foxcross Corner which occasionally served as a gathering place for the hounds. Indeed, since it lay midway between the Rectory and Broughton Court, it had often been used in his youth as a starting point for picnics and expeditions involving both houses. Now, as he approached, he became aware through the gathering twilight of a woman, bareheaded, wearing a loose coat, coming towards him. It was Claire.

"I thought I might meet you here!" If her greeting held a trace of self-consciousness, it was more than offset by an animation, a flow of spirits, altogether unusual in one so habitually reserved. She smiled. "Don't look so surprised. Caroline told me you were at Chillingham. I walked over on the chance."

They fell into step along the road. A soft mist was rising, an exhalation of earth and fallen leaves, faintly mingled with the tang of distant wood smoke, subtle, intoxicating, the very breath of the Sussex Weald.

"Hasn't this been a perfect afternoon?"

"Wonderful," he agreed. "But the light gave out very early."

"You've been working?"

"Yes . . . can't keep away from it, you see."

"You've made it your career," she said warmly. "One can hardly blame you for putting your heart into it."

As he was silent she continued, in that same impulsive manner.

"We had so little time to talk the other day. But now we are neighbours. Are you happy to be home?"

He nodded. "One can't come back after years abroad without falling in love with England all over again."

She glanced at him quickly, but his face was expressionless. There was a short pause.

"And you can paint here?"

"I could anywhere. Perhaps in England best of all. It's a youthful delusion to think one must go abroad to paint. The best of the Impressionists painted in the suburbs from their own back yards."

"This is your back yard, Stephen."

He smiled at her sombrely. "I'm not exactly *persona grata* in the neighbourhood. Haven't you heard lots of gossip . . . interesting tittle-tattle?"

"I haven't listened. Seriously, the Rectory would be such a . . . such a haven for you."

"How could I ever go back to the shelter of the fold?" His voice, though restrained, was hard. "I've broken too far away from the beliefs and—thank God—the prejudices of my class. I wasn't made to hold the three percents and be a pillar of society. I'm too odd a bird ever to roost here again."

The look in his eyes as he glanced at her, sideways, pained her, made her hold determinedly to her point.

"I think you're mistaken, Stephen. You might find it difficult at first. But if you stay on, something may turn up to convince you . . ."

She broke off, sharply, awkwardly, leaving her words unexplained and a long silence fell between them.

In the train, on the day when she had met him at the exhibition, the inspiration of the Memorial Institute had come to her. For years past, in nearby Charminster, the chapter of the cathedral had been collecting for a hall which would meet the needs of the many church societies and ecclesiastical committees in the diocese and, at the same time, serve as a reference library and reading-room for the people of the district. The war had inevitably delayed such plans and subsequently the scheme had taken on a more grandiose significance. With commemorative shrines springing up all over the country, it was decided to make the new institute a war memorial which, while fulfilling its original practical purpose, would be also a monument dedicated to peace. New specifications were drawn up for a handsome stone edifice in the Gothic style. Within twelve months the structure was completed, and at a recent meeting of the committee suggestions for the decoration of the interior were discussed. Since the Dean had ruled out the use of mosaic and stained glass in favour of a more spirited treatment, murals were at first considered. But the architect of the building had advised against these on the grounds that the interior lath and plaster was unsuited to the reception of permanent frescoes. The vote therefore had fallen unanimously upon a series of panels, appropriate in theme, richly done in oils on canvas, and framed in Sussex oak, which would hang upon the five main walls of the building. The names of various painters had been tentatively suggested, but since local knowledge of the subject was limited, so far nothing definite had been decided.

All this Claire knew, and not only because her mother, a close friend of the Dean, had contributed largely to the original fund, but also from her own friendship with two members of the sub-committee, she felt herself, with a sanguine thrill, in a position to influence the choice of artist. Her eagerness for this self-imposed task brought her up for an instant, caused her a temporary qualm, but she shook it off sharply, shut her ears to the faint note of caution that discretion sounded. Was she not a sedate wife and mother, securely settled, in fact quite an old married woman? Her interest in the matter was purely disinterested, her feeling for Stephen no more than sisterly regard. And so, fortified and reassured by these reflections, on the very next day she had motored to Charminster.

The Dean was aged, a bent and desiccated figure, a tremendous Sanscrit scholar, but one upon whom growing deafness and a chronic arthritic infirmity had pressed an increasing withdrawal from all but his most essential duties—there had lately been rumours, uncontradicted, of his early retirement. But Claire's name was, even during this period of afternoon repose, an unfailing passport. He received her with affection, listened with cupped ear to the case which she diplomatically presented. Perhaps the half-heard sound of Stephen's name struck a mixed chord of recollection, evoked a faintly dubious echo, but it was quickly lost in the Dean's benign senescence and the desire to resume his nap. The young man may have erred, but he was clearly talented, a recent exhibitor in London, and one in whom ecclesiastical tendencies must still predominate. The Reverend Bertram was, like himself, graduate of Trinity, an excellent archæologist, a worthy worker in the vineyard too, and recently, in a material sense, not overly fortunate. And besides, who had more claim to suggest a candidate than the daughter of Lady Broughton? The Dean, patting her hand, promised to discuss the matter with the chairman of the committee.

From the Deanery it was, indeed, the chairman whom Claire immediately approached, for she drove directly to Crows' Nest, a large red-tiled villa on the outskirts of the city, residence of Rear-Admiral Reginald Tryng, R.N. retired. Reggie was at home and delighted to see her, his blue eyes twinkled in his ruddy face, his bald head glistened, his short stocky figure seemed to radiate a briny welcome as he bustled her to the library fire, insisted on giving her tea.

No one in the county was heartier, more jovially public-spirited than Reggie Tryng. Member of half a dozen committees, he was unfailingly at the disposal of a good cause, a loyal servant of church, state, and the local cricket club. For a man of sixty he had inexhaustible energy. Needless to say, he was a thorough sportsman, played golf and tennis, danced, shot, fished, skated in season, and although to his sorrow his limited means—he had no more than his pension—did not permit him to hunt, he followed the hounds energetically on foot, up hill and down dale in all weathers for miles around.

While one so genial could not properly be called a snob, he prized above all those gilt-edged cards which bade him occasionally to the great houses of the county, enabling him to remark casually next day, in the smoke-room of the Mid-Sussex Clubhouse: "Last night . . . at Ditchley Castle. . . ." Not only did he like and admire Claire as a woman, as a hostess her invitations were extremely flattering to his self-esteem. When, after some introductory small-talk, she mentioned the decoration of the Memorial, her interest puzzled him, as did her plea that he treat the matter in confidence. But he was the last person in the world to seek out hidden motives and, after a moment of perplexity, he thought: "That Desmonde fellow . . . Geoffrey's cousin . . . rather a dead weight upon the family . . . doing her best to give him a lift." Further reassured by the mention of her visit to the Deanery, he promised to confer upon the matter with his colleagues, refilled her cup and pressed her to Bath Oliver biscuits.

Surely she had done enough. Yet on her way home Claire made one last call—at the Cathedral and Southern Counties Bank, a staid and reputable institution which had handled the Broughton account for over a hundred years. Mark Sutton, the manager, who sat with Tryng upon the sub-committee, was easier to canvass. A slight, anæmic, clerkly little man in starched collar and stiff cuffs, unfailing model of respectful deference, he grasped immediately at the chance to oblige so distinguished a lady and so valuable a client. He was not "promised" in any way, he would be more than happy to support her nominee.

How simple it had all been! Bowed out of the bank, Claire drove home in a glow of accomplishment. Now that the seeds were sown, she could scarcely wait to see if they bore fruit. Ten days passed without result, then, early this very afternoon, Tryng had telephoned her. Everything had gone satisfactorily—the other two members of the sub-committee, Sharp and Cordley, had proved rather difficult, but Sutton and he had carried the day. Desmonde was to have an interview with the committee and, subject to its approval, would receive the appointment.

Immediately, Claire experienced a surge of triumph at the success of her diplomacy. She must tell Stephen at once. And here, after a wait at Foxcross of almost half an hour, during which she paced back and forth in the crisp, aromatic nightfall, with anticipation sweet as that of a country maid keeping tryst—here she was, walking by his side, unable to speak one word of her momentous news. She had acted from the highest motives, no improper thought had ever entered her mind, yet now, eager and tremulous, she could scarcely move for the softness of her body, the growing languor in her limbs. The beat of her heart almost stifled her. The abrupt appearance of a car, swinging round a bend, headlights flashing full upon them with dazzling intensity, made her gasp absurdly for breath and catch at Stephen's arm.

"Someone isn't driving too well," he commented.

In the succeeding darkness they reached the lodge gates which gave entrance to the Court, and here Stephen paused.

"I shan't come any further, Claire."

"Won't you?" She hesitated. "Geoffrey's been in town today . . . but he should be back quite soon."

Stephen shook his head.

"We're early people at the Rectory now. Six-o'clock supper."

His excuse, so palpable, intensified the irregularity of her position. She recollected a remark of Geoffrey's: "I won't have that fellow in my house. And if I meet him I'll cut him dead. The whole county knows he's an out-and-out rotter." Perhaps because of this she felt that she could stay no longer.

"Good night, then, Stephen," she murmured. "Remember that I have faith in you. The tide may turn, sooner than you think." The next moment she was lost to view in the shadows of the drive.

An hour later, hurrying lest he be late, Stephen arrived at the Rectory. Unusual lights were showing, and in the hall, impatiently awaiting him, was Caroline.

"At last!" She greeted him excitedly. "I thought you'd never come. Father wants to see you right away."

In the library, as Stephen entered, the Rector ceased his restive movements and, advancing with humid eye, took his son by the hand.

"My dear boy, today, in Charminster, I was given great and wholly unexpected news." Deeply moved, he almost broke down. "You are being considered, and may well be chosen to paint the panels of the new Memorial."

CHAPTER V

On the following day at some minutes after three o'clock, the four members of the Memorial sub-committee, Rear-Admiral Tryng, Sutton, Joseph Cordley and Arnold Sharp—the Dean was not present—had assembled in a small office of the Chancellery, and Stephen, waiting in a side room, was summoned before them.

Tryng, the chairman, cast a quick yet searching glance upon him as he entered and, having feared something worse, was at once appreciably relieved. He did not care much for the close-cropped hair and beard nor that independent air, but the fellow looked a gentleman, was neatly and quietly dressed, and on the whole seemed not half bad. Stephen, in fact, had been induced to shed his nondescript corduroys, and Carrie had laid out for him a white shirt and one of his old dark grey clerical suits which still fitted reasonably well.

"Good afternoon, Mr. Desmonde. Won't you take a chair?" At a gesture from Tryng, Stephen sat down, conscious of the united gaze of the committee bent upon him. "You know why you're here, of course, so we needn't beat about the bush. It's the Memorial. We want five panels, approximately six feet by four, which will suitably express the feeling, the dignity, the heroic yet tragic purpose for which this building stands. Now I understand that you have been painting for a number of years, have won several international distinctions, exhibited in various important cities and, in short, seem well qualified for the work we have in mind."

"I should certainly do my best."

There was a pause during which Stephen took a guarded look at the four men seated behind the long table. So acutely keyed were his sensibilities, he recognized immediately that two were favourable to him and two opposed. Of these latter, one now cleared his throat —sure preliminary to speech. He was Arnold Sharp, solicitor of Charminster, a thin, bleak-looking man with an elongated head and small, shrewd eyes set close together. Aware of Tryng's interest in Stephen, he strongly resented it, mainly because, having risen from the humblest beginnings—his father had been a poor "hedger and ditcher" on a nearby farm—he hated the gentry, beneath a manner that, from long practice in the County Court, remained always as expressionless as his face. Moreover, he guessed that Stephen was sponsored by some higher source and, while he could not from policy openly dissent, he intended to make things as difficult as possible for him.

"I suppose you have brought samples of your work to show the committee?"

"I'm afraid not."

"May we ask why?"

"Most of my recent paintings are in the hands of my London agent. I'll gladly have several sent down if you wish."

"I think," Tryng cut in, "I can vouch for Mr. Desmonde's competence. And so will the Dean."

"But is he competent for this particular task," the solicitor demurred, with an air of reasonableness, "dealing as it does with the recent war?"

Sharp's neighbour, stout Joe Cordley, churchwarden and cornchandler, bursting the seams of his black-and-white checks, cocked his blunt red face towards Stephen.

"You wasn't in the war, Mr. Desmonde?"

"No."

"Exempted?"

"No."

"Not a conchy, I 'ope?"

"I was abroad."

"Ah!" Cordley sighed, let his bulk sink back in his chair. "Abroad . . . but not in the trenches."

"I believe"—Sharp was speaking again, politely, as though in commendation, with no expression in his ferret eyes—"I believe your young brother was in the army, though?"

"Yes. He was not really fit for service but he enlisted in the first month."

A pause.

"He was killed, wasn't he?"

"Yes."

"In action?"

"Yes."

"Ah!" Cordley, who had doubled his capital selling forage to the forces at Chillingham Camp, drew down the corners of his mouth and turned up his eyeballs. "Brave feller! Gave 'is all for 'is country."

The pause which followed was more awkward than the first. Stephen compressed his lips. He had come to the interview eager for many reasons to obtain the commission; now, in the face of this hostile interrogation, his determination hardened.

"If I may speak . . . while I took no part in the war, and was, as you have so accurately pointed out, a mere spectator, I have, perhaps because of this, ideas on the subject which might qualify me for this particular work. It seems to me that, to justify its purpose, your Memorial should stand not only as a tribute to those who gave their lives, but as a deterrent to all future conflicts. These panels which I might do for you should serve to point out the essential tragedy of war, and through stressing the element of sacrifice and suffering, help, perhaps, by influencing those who view them, to prevent another world calamity."

"Bravo, Mr. Desmonde," Tryng said heartily. He liked that brief speech and the way Stephen looked straight at Sharp as he made it. Pity the fellow was such a deuced funk!—but there, he'd seen it in the service, once in a while even the best families would turn out a white rabbit. "And now about dates."

"Would you be prepared," Sharp interrupted, "to submit designs for our approval, bearing out what you've just said?"

Stephen glanced towards Tryng.

"That is quite contrary to the usual procedure."

"You mean we have to take you on trust?" put in Cordley.

"Every artist must be taken on trust," Stephen answered warmly. "A painter isn't a travelling salesman touting with a bag-load of samples. He has only himself to offer. I am prepared to submit designs if you insist, but since this represents at least half, and the most difficult half, of the work, only if you commission me beforehand."

"We've no time to waste on that." Tryng spoke definitely. "Not with the official opening planned for March."

"March fifteenth," Sutton murmured precisely, opening his lips for the first time. "Three months from today."

A short silence.

"Could you complete the work by then?"

"I think I could."

"Thinking's no good," Sharp interposed. "We must be sure."

"It isn't a lot of time for five large paintings. But when I'm interested I work very quickly."

"Good. And now about payment. The fee we propose is five hundred guineas."

"'Adn't we agreed on pounds?" muttered the corn-chandler.

"Guineas, my dear sir, is surely the more gentlemanly currency. Would our figure be satisfactory, Mr. Desmonde?"

"Quite."

229

Tryng looked at his fellow members. "Then I suggest we pay our artist one hundred guineas down. As a retainer. The balance on completion."

"I disagree." Sharp fixed his gaze on a corner of the ceiling. "We should pay on delivery."

"But Mr. Desmonde will have considerable outlay in providing canvases and other material," Sutton argued, "to say nothing of frames."

"That's his look-out," Sharp answered sourly. "Who's to say that he won't fall ill, or walk out on us, or for some reason fail to complete in time? All sorts of contingencies might arise. I say payment on delivery."

"Ah, that's sound business, Arnold. I seconds the motion."

Before Tryng could speak, Stephen intervened:

"I haven't always been in a position to get canvas and colours. But now, luckily, I am. I accept your conditions. I should, however, like your permission to work in the hall itself. I have no studio here, at present."

"I think that can be allowed. You'll want to have a look at it in any case. We'll get you the key." Tryng paused and, as his remarks encountered no opposition, he concluded: "That's all then, gentlemen. I congratulate you, Mr. Desmonde. And I know you will give us a magnificent job of work."

With the key in his pocket, Stephen walked directly to the new Institute, which stood on a slight eminence in Church Meadows, backed by a row of elms whose top branches harboured an ancient rookery, not far from the cathedral close. Immediately he saw the building he was favourably impressed, not only by its situation and the admirable manner in which it harmonized with the line and colour of the prevailing fourteenth-century stonework, but by the simplicity and purity of its design. When he entered by the arched doorway he could not repress a shiver of satisfaction. The interior, in shape an exact pentagon, lit by a high clerestory which made no break in the plain, whitewashed walls, was superb for such a sequence as he could plan. How his colours would burn and glow against that dead-white background—he saw them already in his imagination—and how perfect was the spacing, these five identical walls, for panels of precisely similar dimensions. For a long time he remained in the completely empty hall, squatting on one knee, amidst the plaster dust left by the builders, then, rising, he locked up carefully, walked along Church Road to the corner of High Street. From the Blue Boar, he telephoned Maddox in London to send him, immediately, canvas, colours, everything he would require. Then, bareheaded, with hands thrust in the pockets of his narrow parson's jacket, he strode off towards the Downs, oblivious to everything but the forms that were already swirling into the screen of his sight.

During several days he refrained, though with difficulty, from starting work. He wanted to reflect deeply on this subject, so painfully near his heart. The loss of his brother, all the arid hardships of his years in Spain undoubtedly shaped his thoughts. At the back of his consciousness, a source of vivid inspiration, were the *Desastres de la Guerra* which had so profoundly moved him when he stood, entranced, in the long galleries of the Prado. Within him stirred the revolt of a wounded spirit against the eternal tragedy of human violence.

Towards the end of that week he began to paint. And, as his designs took shape, more and more was he carried away by the fervour of his theme, by his burning desire to express not only the heroism but also the dreadful wastage of war, so that, if the world might only look upon his pictures, it might never yield to such madness again.

So intense was the flow of his composition, he often did not leave the Institute from his arrival in the early morning until the light failed him in the evening. Every day Caroline placed a packet of sandwiches in his pocket, yet he did not stop for lunch but, standing at the easel, snatching an occasional bite of bread and cheese, would still press on with his work. The quiet and seclusion of the empty hall suited him to perfection, for he could never bear to be watched, and after he had firmly dealt with several interruptions at the outset he was left in peace. At night he returned to the Rectory, exhausted from creative effort, but with a sense of growing accomplishment.

For the Rector, this sustained and Spartan application by his son was not only a staggering surprise—he had never dreamed that an artist, whom he pictured, mainly from the pages of Murger and du Maurier, as a shiftless and indolent bohemian, could display such unsparing industry—but also a source of satisfaction which, at first uncertain, strengthened as the days went on. Despite the disillusionment, the defeats and disappointments he had suffered, hope, which he had thought dead, was rekindled. His son was at home, leading a regular life, decently dressed, actually working at a project connected with the cathedral. To what might not this lead in the end!

There had been—he was forced to admit—a markedly unfavourable reaction when the news of Stephen's appointment was made public—much of it malicious gossip in the village and surrounding

231

country—but also a genuine note of protest which Bertram could sense in his daily contacts, even in the faces of his little congregation at Sunday service. Several letters had appeared in the local press, most damaging of all a communication signed "Pro Patria", prominently featured in the *County Gazette*. Worried, the Rector and Caroline consulted over it in low voices.

"It's a cruel attack." Bertram's brows were drawn in a harassed frown. "Most vicious. And unfortunately true."

"But quite unfair, Father. Why should it bring in all this about Stephen's not being in the army? He should be judged on his merits as an artist."

"I daresay, Caroline. At the same time, for a war memorial . . . there's justice in the idea that they might have chosen an ex-service man."

"Who might have been a very poor painter."

"Yes . . . yes, that's so. Caroline, who do you think sent in this letter?"

"Can't you guess, Father?"

"Not Albert Mould?"

"Who else? You haven't an enemy in the world . . . except him."

"But my dear, he's not sufficiently educated to have composed such a letter. And the signature, 'Pro Patria'."

"Someone has written it for him. He's in with lots of people who could!"

The Rector shook his head, as if bewildered by such a possibility of conspiracy.

"To think that dear old Mould, who worked here faithfully, man and boy, for over fifty years, should have . . . God forgive me . . . such an upstart son."

"It's the age of upstarts, Father. Even old Mould is starting up. He has his own wireless, gets better heating and more hot water than we have, he goes to the cinema twice a week and when I asked him in the village the other day if he'd like his usual Christmas leg of pork he said: 'No thankee, miss. Albert just 'ad a whole side of venison gave 'im.' Then he looked at me slyly. 'Shall us send 'ee a bit?'"

There was a brief silence.

"Well," said the Rector, "we must keep this letter from Stephen. He deserves all the encouragement we can give him."

"He was greatly encouraged the other day, Father. You remember his friend Richard Glyn . . . oh, I know you never quite approved of him but he has shown at the Royal Academy . . . anyway, he

232

came down to Charminster the other day, Stephen and he had lunch at the Blue Boar . . ."

"Yes?"

"Well . . . Stephen outlined the entire plan of his work, showed what he had already done . . . he'd completely blocked out his panels. And Glyn was quite carried away."

The Rector, a little lost, nevertheless looked pleased. A pause followed, while he meditated. Then, looking up at his daughter:

"Caroline, don't you feel that, if he makes a success of this, it might reopen for him a true spiritual field . . . church decoration . . . stained-glass windows . . . and the like? He would be much at home in the sphere of ecclesiastic art. He is still young. Who knows but that one day . . . under such influence . . . he might even yet . . . take orders?" He broke off, rose and reached for his hat. "I shall be back in a little while, my dear."

From the window she watched him go up the lane, slowly, slightly bowed, hands clasped behind his back, a long black figure under the flat shovel hat. She knew he was going to the church to pray.

CHAPTER VI

Amongst the many excellent and decided qualities which characterized General Desmonde's wife, that milder virtue, sweetness of temper, was less obvious than the rest. Brought up in a military atmosphere, toasted in her maidenhood as the daughter of the regiment, the blood of many pukka-sahibs flowed in her veins, and during her years of marriage, her long sojourn in India had intensified this natural firmness, strengthened—perhaps through some action on the liver—her capacity to rule. And this January morning there was about her a certain aura of asperity—a tightness of the lips, an imperceptible dilation and pinkish coloration of the well-bred nostrils, which boded little good for anyone who might cross her. To her staff her orders for the day were more than usually curt. She rated the country maid who—admittedly with noise—was filling the wood-box. Seated at her walnut bureau, her admirable figure taut in tweed and jumper, her still graceful neck clasped by a single string of pearls, she gave attention to her mail, which dealt mainly with her functions as patroness of the Red Cross, Girl Guides, and the local hospital. Then, immobile, gazed at the Benares brass-bound blotter before her.

What should she do about it?—that was the question which, since she awakened, had, like a persistent mosquito, increasingly beset her. After breakfast her husband had pulled on his Wellingtons and gone out to the stables, reminding her that he must spend the day in Gillinghurst arranging for the winter feed—in any case she had decided against consulting him; this was a matter best left in her own capable hands. But how . . . how should she act?

Upon that soft and ghostly evening, some weeks before, when a car drove beyond the entrance to the Court, illuminating momentarily, yet with incandescent brilliance, the figures of Stephen and Claire, she had been the driver, the startled witness of the incident. She had, in fact, called at the Court only a few minutes before, had found that her son was in London and Claire not at home. And then, that photographic flash . . . how close together they had been, upon that deserted country road, and with Geoffrey absent . . . the sequence, added to the notorious reputation of "that fellow", was most alarming.

In fairness, the General's lady acknowledged that Claire was of irreproachable character—at least so far as one could judge; in India she had seen some queer breakdowns in her time—and she had decided, while keeping her eyes open, to say nothing of the matter for the present. Yet the recollection of Claire's youthful predilection for Stephen was not easily dismissed and, recurring frequently, made more ominous this disloyalty—for that it was, even in its most innocent aspect—to Geoffrey. Product of the barrack square, imbued from infancy with the tradition of restraint, all the softer manifestations of maternal fondness curbed by the clipped word, the controlled gesture, the curt exactions of good form, Adelaide Desmonde nevertheless was devoted to her son. His marriage into the Broughton acres, which raised him from the status of obscure army captain to that of landed proprietor, had caused her greatly to rejoice. Yet there had been subsequent dissatisfactions. The bulk of the estate was entailed, which, though admirable in itself, impaired the gloss of Geoffrey's sense of ownership. Moreover, a major portion of Lady Broughton's fortune had been settled in trust on her daughter, a fact that afforded Claire a considerable private income. This more than wifely independence, despite the docility of Claire's nature, had often irked Adelaide, and now, after the events of the previous evening, she thought it positively dangerous.

They had been to dinner at Gresham Park, and her neighbour on the left was Reginald Tryng. Adelaide entertained for the ruddy Rear-Admiral, with his spinsterish gossip, his limited income and semi-suburban villa, a sort of patronizing tolerance. His jokes amused her less than the beads of perspiration which, after hot soup, burst like miniature water-spouts upon his rosy baldness; prejudiced by nature against the senior service, she considered him well-meaning and harmless but rather a fool. Bored, she had at first failed to understand his genial reference to Claire. Then, stung to attention, she listened while he preened himself, relating in strictest confidence his diplomacy in managing the little "family commission" with which he had been entrusted. It was, he concluded, extremely handsome of Claire to put herself about for Geoffrey's cousin!

Speechless, Adelaide took a convulsive sip of water. For once she had not a word to say. This naval idiot had brought to a head all her worst suspicions. Claire, interesting herself surreptitiously, yet with blazing indiscretion, in this despicable cad. It must be stopped, and at once, before it became an outright scandal in the county.

Now, in the cold light of morning, she was inclined to lay the blame entirely upon "the renegade". Without doubt he had again wormed himself into Claire's confidence, completely indifferent as to how he might compromise her, and cadged her aid. Useless, naturally, to go to him and appeal to his sense of honour. On the other hand it was always dangerous to intervene between husband and wife. Yet this was the only course open to her. She had confidence in her tact, would be delicate and discreet. Today, she knew, Claire would be in London. With decision, she went to the telephone, and enduring with forbearance the delays of the local exchange, got through to Stillwater, asked Geoffrey to drive over that afternoon for tea.

He came early, about four o'clock—having nothing else to do—and since the General was still at Gillinghurst, Adelaide had him to herself. She fed him well, with newly baked Sussex griddle cake, and hot buttered toast spread with Patum Paperium—a relish which had always been particularly to his taste. Then, erect and knitting, on a leather pouffe, while he stretched his legs before a glowing fire and let the smoke from his cigarette drift across his nose, she led the conversation into channels which she knew would please him—his bag at the final Stillwater shoot, the chances of a good run at the next meet of the hounds, his prospects in the gentleman riders' steeplechase at the forthcoming Chillingham point-to-point.

Time passed agreeably for Geoffrey in the sound of his own voice. The Mater really bucked a chap up, knew as much about a horse as anyone, and of course she was deuced fond of him. The clock struck six. Extinguishing his last cigarette end, he heaved himself out of his chair.

"Jolly decent tea, Mater. Quite enjoyed our little pow-wow."

"I, too, Geoffrey." She accompanied him to the hall, helped him into his heavy, lined ulster, then, standing with him in the sub-aqueous shimmer cast by the green-tinted gaselier, she added casually: "By the way, I hear that your cousin is at the Rectory."

"Yes, worse luck. I shan't have anything to do with him."

"That's wise, Geoffrey. And I should warn Claire to keep out of his way if I were you."

Geoffrey looked at her, knotting his bird's-eye scarf.

"What d'you mean?"

"Simply this . . . you know you cut him out with Claire . . . it must rankle frightfully. And after these years in the lowest haunts in Paris . . . he's not to be trusted."

"Tell me something I don't know. The fellow's capable of anything."

"Then do set my mind at rest and say a word to dear Claire."

He completed the adjustment of the scarf, viewed it in the small hall-stand mirror.

"Oh, very well. Good night, Mater."

"Good night, Geoffrey."

She stood at the open door while he raced the engine of his sports car and, with a crunch of wheels on gravel, shot off down the drive. Then, well satisfied with her afternoon's work, she turned back into the house.

Geoffrey drove at great speed and with extreme skill. He thought well of himself as a driver, and when he was single had often toyed with the idea of racing at Brooklands. Perhaps it was the swish of fresh air which induced in him a degree of cerebral activity beyond that which Adelaide had anticipated. At any rate, as he swung round corners, nursing the thin wheel of his machine, he kept asking himself "what the old girl had been after".

Obviously he had been asked to tea for a specific reason. In the past, at school and Sandhurst, when his mother had written to him she would convey the crux of her letter casually, as a sort of after-thought, in the postscript. Could it be, then, that the real purpose of the afternoon was contained in these final remarks concerning Claire? Beneath his checked cap Geoffrey grinned. Hampered by conceit and an expensive schooling, which had taught him nothing but the art of striking balls of various sizes, he was not especially intelligent, but long association with the sporting fraternity, with touts, bookmakers and horse-copers, had given him a species of astuteness, sharp awareness of what he called "a put-up job". His immediate reaction, therefore, was a decision to take a course exactly opposite to that suggested by his mother—he would not speak to Claire but remain mum and investigate the situation at his leisure.

When he got home it was only twenty minutes past six, and Claire, who normally travelled down by the five-thirty from Victoria, had not yet returned from London. Upstairs, as he went along the corridor to bath and change for dinner, he paused outside the small sitting-room that adjoined his wife's bedroom and which, because of its general convenience and sunny exposure, she used a great deal. An exploratory tap upon the door produced no answer and, after a second's hesitation, Geoffrey went in. The room was charming, done in pale grey with curtains and chintz covers of a delicate pink, and Geoffrey was quite familiar with it—often, indeed, in Claire's absence he would wander around, touching this and that, a letter on the desk, a card on the mantelpiece, in the manner of a solicitous, if inquiring, husband for whom his wife's affairs, and particularly her finances, held a natural and considerable interest.

Now, however, his inspection was less desultory. He went directly to the desk, which was always unlocked, and began systematically to search it. For a full ten minutes he examined the papers in the drawers and pigeon-holes. There was nothing, simply nothing; the innocence of what he found—there were even early snapshots of himself as a cadet at Sandhurst—brought a faint colour to his brow.

Half ashamed, he was about to turn and go when, from the top receptacle, he uncovered a single folded sheet. It was a bill in the amount of £400, stamped and receipted, from the Maddox Galleries, 21C New Bond Street, for two paintings: *Charity* and *Noon in the Olive Grove* by Stephen Desmonde.

CHAPTER VII

ON AN AFTERNOON in early March the monthly meeting of the West Sussex District Council was droning to the end of a lengthy session whereat discussion had flowed and ebbed on the advisability of supplying sewer-pipes for the hitherto earth-bound hamlet of Hetton-in-the-Wold. Amongst the fourteen members then present, Albert Mould sat unusually silent, gnawing at a thumbnail, his seal-like head sunk in the upturned collar of his greatcoat, which he wore against the chill spring draughts edging through cracks in the ancient wainscoting of the council room. Next to him sat his friend and colleague Joe Cordley, and across the table that assiduous public servant Rear-Admiral Tryng.

The gavel banged for the last time, the district clerk mumbled the customary formula announcing the closure, with date and time of the next meeting, and amidst a scraping back of chairs and a murmur of conversation the committee began to disperse. Not so Albert Mould, however. With Cordley at his elbow he stationed himself by the door and, as Tryng approached, buttonholed him.

"I'd like a word with you, sir, if it's convenient."

It was not at all convenient, Reggie was bent on bustling to the Mid-Sussex links for a brisk nine holes, but before he could bring out an adequate excuse Mould went on:

"I 'ate to take this up with you, a most unpleasant duty. But I 'ave to do it. It's about them panels that's being done for the Memorial Hall."

"Well, what about them?" snapped Tryng, pointedly looking at his watch.

"Just this, sir. It's pretty near three months now since them paintings was started and to the best of my knowledge and belief nobody 'as ever even seen them. I understand that several parties did make the attemp' and was refused, the panels being kept permanent under lock and key. Well, sir, what with the official opening drawing near that didn't seem right and proper—at least not to two members of your sub-committee. So, to put it plain, they asked me to accompany them to inspect the pictures."

"How the devil could you inspect them if they were locked up?"

"Mr. Arnold Sharp 'ad me get a duplicate key."

Tryng stared his displeasure. He had never liked Mould, less for breaking out of the limits of his class than for retaining its servility and using this as a sort of inverted sneer against his betters.

"Well, sir, to cut a long story short, we got into the 'all latish yesterday evening. And it's my painful duty to tell you we did not like wot we saw."

"Come, come now, Mould." Tryng took a patronizing tone. "You're no judge of art."

"But it ain't only my judgement, poor though that may be." For no more than a second Mould's mud-coloured eyes met the Admiral's gaze. "Lawyer Sharp and Joe Cordley 'as the same opinion as well."

"That we 'as," said Cordley with decision. "I'll take my Bible oath."

"Far be it for me to advise you. But if it was me was chairman, I'd 'ave a look at them at once."

Tryng was conscious of a twinge of concern. There was in Mould's eye a suppressed gleam which he did not like at all. Reluctantly he put away his pleasant thoughts of golf, reflected, then said:

"You have your key?"

"We 'ave, sir. And Joe and me are both free now."

"Let us go, then."

They left the council offices, took to the road in the Admiral's Morris-Cowley. At Charminster, on Mould's suggestion, they picked up Sharp and Sutton. Time was consumed in this operation and darkness had fallen when the five members of the sub-committee approached the Memorial. In silence Mould admitted them. The hall was empty—Stephen had left almost an hour before. With a portentous air Cordley switched on the lights. And there, before them, were the panels.

The first to attract Tryng's eye was that named by Stephen *Offering to Peace*: a young woman in the foreground holding out an infant against a background of golden wheatfields and fruitful countryside, richly peopled with reapers, harvesters, and cheerful rustic figures; and as he gazed he was conscious of an alleviation of his anxiety, a warm flow of relief. Why, the thing was good, in fact altogether excellent in a striking, unusual way—he really liked it. But when he turned to the second panel, *Hail, Armageddon*, with its deadly massing of guns and uniformed men, while, amidst cheering crowds, bands played and flags were waved under a darkening sky, all his misgivings were sharply reawakened. And they deepened, became shot with horrid certainty as, hurriedly, with sickening apprehension, he scanned the third canvas, *The Rape of Peace*, and the fourth, *Aftermath*, which, with stunning power, seemed to portray on the one hand, as far as his scattered wits could discern, an interwoven pattern of the dreadful incidents of war, and on the other the frightful consequences which follow it—famine, pestilence, burned-out houses, ruined villages, decimation of that fruitful countryside first portrayed, the whole surveyed by the nude, weeping figure of a woman. The final panel, *Resurrection of the Slain*, made his eyes start from his head. In the name of heaven, what the devil did the fellow mean with these strange human forms, corpses actually, disfigured, unclothed, some without limbs, women too, bursting out of their graves beneath a wildly trumpeting angelic host? He had never, in his wildest dreams, expected such a shattering debacle. And it was he, Rear-Admiral Reginald Tryng, who had sponsored it, practically forced this accursed Desmonde upon the members of his committee.

They were watching him now, waiting for him to speak. He squared his shoulders—he had never lacked courage.

"Well, gentlemen . . . this is extremely disappointing."

"Disappointing!" Cordley was apoplectic with indignation. "It's an outrage, a damn outrage."

"You see this 'ere." Mould jerked his head towards the figures in the final panel. "Naked, all of 'em . . . stark naked. And what's more, both males and females, their private parts showing."

Tryng averted his gaze, looked towards Sutton. But the meek banker, more than ordinarily pale, was in no mood to support him.

"Yes, gentlemen . . . this is obviously regrettable. I must see the Dean about it at once."

Sharp, who had been subjecting the paintings to an intensive scrutiny, now broke silence.

"May I call your attention to this particular item?" He pointed to a detail in the intricate composition of the third painting. "What are these soldiers up to? Perhaps someone more artistically inclined than I am could put a name to it."

"Good God!" said Tryng, in spite of himself.

Amidst a general murmur Mould added softly:

"That's what made us bring the whole thing up."

The Admiral, very tight about the lips, took control of the situation. He said abruptly:

"I call a meeting for tomorrow. Nine o'clock sharp. I'll have Desmonde there. In the meantime kindly refrain from all public comment. Good night."

On the following morning, at the time specified, with no premonition of disaster, Stephen came before the committee. Unaware of the reason for this summons—over the telephone Tryng had told him nothing—he was in excellent spirits, tired and somewhat tense from weeks of sustained application, yet permeated by a deep sense of achievement. His work was almost finished and he knew that it was good. He would show the panels to the committee in a few days' time. Doubtless they wished to ask him about that very matter.

"Mr. Desmonde, I must inform you that we have seen your paintings. We are profoundly shocked by them."

The unexpectedness of the attack caught Stephen completely off guard. He had been unable to control a sudden start and now stood there, very pale, his eyes grown sombre and almost hard. Before he could speak Tryng continued:

"I, personally, am at a loss to understand how you could have interpreted our wishes in so outrageous a fashion."

Stephen took a long, pained breath.

"What is outrageous about my work?"

"An undertaking of this nature calls for something noble and heroic. A united service group striding forward with the flag . . . a wounded man, supported on his comrade's arm, or by a Red Cross nurse." Stephen winced. "Instead you have given us a . . . a series of outlandish ideas . . . and a portrayal of human suffering that is, to say the least of it, morbid and degrading."

"I outlined my ideas to you before I began. You seemed to approve them then."

"No one in his senses could approve these panels."

"Are you competent to judge?"

"You thought us competent enough when we engaged you."

A flame of anger had begun to burn in Stephen.

"In that case perhaps you would be good enough to specify exactly how my paintings fail you."

"Ah'll give ye specify!" exclaimed Cordley, provoked to his broadest accent. "Did ye think us wanted cripples, and blinded men . . . naked wimmen . . . Jezebels . . . to say nowt of b——y lechery . . . ?"

"That's enough," Tryng interrupted sharply. In the intervening hours, since the previous afternoon, he had carefully considered his position and the means by which he might best extricate himself from it. Although his sense of personal injury remained acute, he had come to the conclusion that only by hushing up this unfortunate affair could he minimize the damage to himself. He was determined, above all, to prevent at this meeting all particularization of the objectionable features in the panels, since such discussion would, he well knew, be repeated at every dinner-table for miles around. He therefore fixed a cold blue quarter-deck eye on Stephen.

"The committee's position is perfectly clear and quite unalterable. We cannot accept your paintings. In my judgement to make them presentable one would require major alterations and three complete repainting. Will you do this?"

"No, I won't," Stephen answered without hesitation. "It's absurd of you to ask it."

"In that case I must ask you to desist from all further work upon the panels. In due course the decision of the committee cancelling your engagement will be formally conveyed to you."

A brief pause. Then the voice of the law was heard on a point that had escaped the chairman.

"I'd like to put on record," Sharp said, "that as these pictures have been unanimously rejected, under the terms of the agreement no payment, not a penny, is due on them."

Stephen remained completely still, struggling with the tumult in his breast. Never before, in all the bitter moments of his life, had he known such bitterness as this, such a suffocating sense of injustice. He wanted to cry out: "Keep your damned payment . . . your thirty pieces of silver. Do you think I poured my soul out for the sake of filthy money?" But he knew that such an outburst could only confirm their worst opinion of him. Silence was his only refuge. His eyes dwelt, in turn, upon each of these faces, so blurred he could barely distinguish them, then without a word he swung round and left the room.

Though his head was spinning, his steps led him instinctively to the Memorial. He was fiercely determined, despite the injunction laid upon him, to finish the panels straight away. Not much remained to be done, he would be ready for the final varnishing after two days' work. By a fortunate omission they had not forced him to give up his key.

But when he arrived at the Institute, he found the door secured by a bar and padlock, new, solid, resisting all his efforts to shake it loose. Again a moment of straining silence. And again he turned away. Through the town he went, all unseeing, with those hard and sombre eyes, out upon the Downs, where, striding forward, a dark and lonely figure against the skyline, he seemed, though extinguished by the vastness of the landscape, obliterated almost, beneath the great grey dome of sky, still to defy the universe that stood arrayed against him.

CHAPTER VIII

THAT SAME AFTERNOON news of the rejection of the panels was in the public domain. But as Tryng kept a firm hold on the committee, and indicated in the strongest terms how damaging to all of them would be a disclosure of the "unsavoury" nature of the paintings, since after all they must be held responsible for Desmonde's selection, it was announced simply that the work submitted had not attained the requisite standard and was therefore unacceptable. Nevertheless, the bare fact of rejection was enough to provoke a mild sensation, and a chorus of self-justification from those who disapproved of Stephen. To Adelaide, at Simla Lodge, it brought a pleasurable sense of vindication. Geoffrey, nursing his grievance, watching and waiting, but saying nothing, experienced a moody satisfaction intensified by a rumour, now circulating, that Stephen had disappeared and could not be found. No doubt the blighter was lying dead drunk in a Brighton pub!

Two days later, on the Thursday evening of that same unhappy week, a prevailing silence lay upon the Rectory of Stillwater. After delaying as long as she could, Caroline entered the library. In his usual chair the Rector sat, staring into the fire, with Bishop Denton's *Commentaries*, from which he now took his sermons, unopened on his knee. For a moment she stood, hesitant, as though unwilling to speak.

"I wondered, Father . . . if I should lock up."

Bertram did not move.

"There is still no sign of him?"

"No, Father."

The Rector straightened, blinked the film from his eyes.

"He's not in his room?"

Caroline shook her head.

"I've looked."

"What time is it?"

"Almost eleven. Perhaps if I bolted the front door and left the side door on the latch . . ."

"No, my dear . . . leave everything as it is. And be off to bed. You must be very weary."

"Let me sit up."

"No, no. I have work to do. And I'm not in the least tired. Good night, Carrie."

His use of her diminutive name—a rare event—plucked at her heartstrings. But she had no gift of showing tenderness.

"Good night, Father."

Reluctantly, with a lingering look, Caroline went upstairs to her chilly bedroom while Bertram, erect in his chair and with a careworn expression, began to wait for his son. As though to deceive himself, in a pretence of application he turned, from time to time, the pages of his book. But his mind was not on it. Continually he glanced at his watch, his ear tensely attuned for a step upon the drive outside the window.

Even now he could scarcely believe that Stephen, for weeks a model of propriety, could have plunged into a round of dissipation

243

in the effort to drown his sorrows. Yet such was the general opinion. And how else could his prolonged absence be explained? In extenuation, it must be acknowledged that the blow had been a cruel one. He had himself built so high an edifice it was anguish to see it dashed in ruins to the ground. He sighed heavily and laid his hand upon his brow.

Slowly the minutes dragged on; eleven struck on the grandfather clock; then the single chime of the half-hour. At midnight the last ember of the fire flickered and died. Useless to wait longer. The Rector got up, turned out the lights, and slowly mounted the stairs.

The following afternoon, towards three o'clock, Caroline, upon whom domestic pressures enforced an early rising, and who had scarcely closed an eye all the previous night, was resting, partly undressed, in her room. Bertram had gone out on a parochial call. Suddenly the sound of footsteps, brisk, familiar, alerted her, hurriedly drew her to the window. Her heart bumped. It was Stephen, approaching with an alacrity which quite dismayed her. Quickly she threw on her old pink dressing-gown, met him as he came into the house.

"Get me something to eat, Carrie, there's a dear." He spoke with a directness that angered her. "As soon as you can. I'm starving."

"Where have you been?" Though her voice wavered, it held an accusing note.

He smiled—at least his fixed expression broke.

"Don't look at me like that, old girl. Sorry if I've upset you. I've been busy."

"How could you be busy . . . for three days and nights?"

"Very easily . . . I had a screwdriver."

Had he gone crazy? Her tone changed.

"Don't joke about it Stephen . . . we've been worried. Where did you sleep?"

"Where d'you think? My natural habitat. Ground level. And in my clothes. I'm going up for a wash and a change."

She sighed, relieved to see him, yet mystified and full of misgiving. But she made him bacon and eggs herself—Sophie had so far become democratized that she never appeared in the kitchen between three and six o'clock—and brewed a pot of strong tea. Seated opposite, still in her robe, chin propped on her hands, she watched, doubtfully, while he made a hearty meal. As he ate and drank he parried all her questions, then, relenting, sat back in his chair and looked at her.

"It's really quite simple, Carrie. I had to finish my paintings. And as they'd padlocked me out, I broke in."

"Broke in?"

"I tried a ladder at first but it didn't work . . . so I unscrewed the bar."

"And you've been there . . . in the Institute . . . all this time?"

"Practically."

"With nothing to eat . . . for three days and nights? And sleeping . . . on the floor?"

"I assure you, dear Carrie, that didn't bother me in the least." His voice hardened. "I wanted to get my work done . . . and now it is . . . varnished and complete."

She was silent. While his cheerfulness helped to allay her uneasiness, yet she could not but observe how this last effort, imposed upon long and unsparing creative work, had physically reduced him. And there was a burning in his eye which frightened her. The candour and gentleness that were his better qualities had gone, replaced by what seemed to her a terrible perversity.

He glanced at the clock.

"I must be off."

"Oh, no, Stephen." She started up in protest. "Not again. Father will want to see you."

"I shall be back quite early," he assured her. "Certainly before ten. I promise you."

His words carried conviction, yet there was something behind them which she could not comprehend. The next minute he had left the house as abruptly as he had appeared.

At the end of the lane, after a brief delay, the "hourly" Rural District bus loomed up and Stephen hailed it. The antique vehicle was almost empty and, as he took his seat, moved off along the highroad in the direction of Charminster.

All the stubbornness in Stephen's character had risen against the treatment meted out to him. Six years ago he might have questioned the quality of his work. Now, he was convinced that the panels were of the highest quality, not only as the expression of a universal theme, but also as a work of art. That they should have been dismissed so arbitrarily, in such objectionable terms, and without recourse to expert opinion, made the blood surge within him. Worst of all was the manner in which the committee had sought to suppress the affair by impounding his work, for which they had paid nothing, forbidding him access to it, and in general stifling, before they could begin, his attempts to secure redress. Once again, as he sat in the lumbering bus, the recollection of all that he had poured out so willingly and in such good faith made him bite his lip and clench his hands. He could

245

not, he would not submit, but, in spite of everything, would bring the matter into the light of day. Carefully, he went over the arrangements he had made—though far from perfect they were the best he could improvise and he felt they would serve. How fortunate that he had, for once, adequate spare cash. He had never wanted it more.

As the bus entered the outskirts of Charminster he felt his nerves tighten. The market clock, illuminated against the encroaching darkness, showed a quarter to six o'clock. At the stop before the square he got off and, taking the short cut through Oat Lane, walked rapidly towards the county railway station. He reached the main platform and took up his position at the barrier just before the six-twenty-five from London drew in.

Few passengers descended from the train, and amongst them he immediately made out the youthful figure of Thorpe Maddox advancing towards him, carrying a handbag.

"Good of you to come," Stephen said as they shook hands.

"Only too glad to help, Mr. Desmonde. Uncle sent his regards."

"I'm putting you up at the Blue Boar. You ought to be comfortable there," Stephen continued as they walked towards the station exit. "But first we have some work to do."

"You did get the premises?"

"I've rented them for two weeks, beginning tomorrow. We're going there now."

In the centre of Charminster, just off Market Street, there was situated a shop, originally a stationer's and circulating library known as Langlands, which, through a succession of failures, had become a sort of local "let-out" on short-term leases for such diverse purposes as Boy Scout rallies, electioneering headquarters, and sales of work by the various charitable organizations of the district. Opposite this establishment Stephen drew up.

"This is the place. Not much. But it will do. Good wall-space, and a desk and chair for you. Come round the back way. There's a hand-cart in the yard."

Five minutes later, pushing the hand-cart between them, they trundled off, by a quiet, circuitous route, to the Institute. Charminster, known as a city only because of its cathedral, was actually little more than a small country town, seldom given to nocturnal gaiety. Few people were in the streets at this hour, and Stephen observed with satisfaction that their passage went unnoticed. In less than twenty minutes they had transferred his panels from the building to the barrow, where, having assured himself that the varnish had set hard, he covered them with a strip of sacking. After locking the door, as a final refinement which he felt the committee might appreciate, he screwed back the bar and padlock tightly, in its original place.

Proceeding towards the market-place with due discretion, they presently got back to the Langlands establishment, brought their vehicle alongside, unloaded the cargo, carried it into the empty shop. After drawing all the blinds they began to set up the five pictures. One, the *Rape of Peace* panel, Stephen placed in the front window; the second, *Armageddon,* directly opposite the entrance; the remaining three were hung in the large room which had once housed the library. It was not an easy undertaking—the frames were heavy and required to be strongly wired—but at last, just after nine o'clock, it was completed to Stephen's satisfaction. He turned to his companion.

"Well, what's the verdict?"

With an intent expression, young Maddox answered:

"You know how I've always been keen about your work, Mr. Desmonde, from the very first. I'll swear these surpass anything you've done. They are tremendous . . . they simply bowl one over."

"Then you won't mind sitting with them for a couple of weeks?"

"I'd say not. It'll be . . . exciting." He paused. "Uncle hasn't seen them?"

"No. Why do you ask?"

"I'm just wondering, Mr. Desmonde . . . whether he would think you wise in exhibiting them in Charminster."

"Damn it all, Thorpe, it's in Charminster I must show them. And why not?"

"Well, sir . . . this is a small, backward sort of place. I'll bet they don't know a work of art from a turnip."

Something was on young Maddox's mind. Stephen waited.

"If these panels were in the National Gallery or the Louvre, people would take them at their worth. But, Mr. Desmonde"—he made a gesture which expressed his artistic valuation of the whole rural neighbourhood, and his young eyes had turned oddly serious—"what on earth will they think of them down here?"

CHAPTER IX

Next morning dawned crisp and clear. At the Blue Boar, Thorpe Maddox rose early, breakfasted, then set out for the shop known as Langlands, which, at nine o'clock precisely, he opened, placing the panels on public display. Almost at the same moment

Mark Sutton, a punctual man, came along Market Street on his way to the bank, which stood at the corner only a few doors away. He saw the great painting in the window, recognized it, and almost had a fit. Four minutes later he was in his office telephoning to Tryng. Inside the hour the Admiral had joined him, and with a helpless gesture, declared that he washed his hands of the whole affair.

"I did my best, Sutton, to straighten out a very nasty situation. Not in my own interest, but because of persons for whom I have a high regard. Everything was taut and ship-shape. And now this damn fellow has scuttled us by pinching the pictures and throwing them right in the public eye."

"Of course they are his paintings . . . he was entitled to take them . . ."

"Isn't that just the trouble? Otherwise I'd have burned the lot long ago."

A pause, during which Tryng rammed tobacco into his pipe.

"Hadn't you better see the Dean?" Sutton suggested unhappily.

"I tried to on my way down. But he has a chill and isn't available. In any case he's beyond all this. It's we who must stand the rub."

"You think there will be . . ." nervously he balked at the word "scandal" . . . "a reaction?"

"Are you mad? Good God, man, these cursed paintings will cause a bigger commotion in Charminster than anything since the fire in Bailey's brewery. But I've taken my stand. I was let in for this in the first place. And now I'm done with it."

And Reggie stalked out of the bank.

In the ordinary way an exhibition of paintings would have had no more impact on the life of this country town than a snowflake falling upon a tombstone. Indeed, there had been few such exhibitions, the last, so far as memory served, before the war, a display of flower pictures by the paralysed daughter of old Major Featherstonhaugh, whose vases of primroses, pansies, and the like, priced at a guinea each, were really quite first-rate, when one considered they were done by a cripple.

But this was not the same kind of exhibition, nor were these floral pictures. The sequence of events which preceded their public presentation, linked to the known reputation of the artist, was enough to enwrap them with a horrid fascination. Briefly, they attracted because they repelled—and all Charminster went to view them, as a crowd might gather at a morgue. In so doing, the gentry, whatever they reserved for privileged conversation, maintained fitting hauteur —though distasteful mutterings were occasionally heard and it was observed that as she stepped into her Daimler the lady dowager, present incumbent of Ditchley Castle, wore a look of marked severity, thus increasing her likeness—a resemblance which she prized—to the late Queen Victoria. The lower orders, on the other hand, mainly workers of both sexes from the surrounding farms, were regrettably underbred. Some gaped in silence, but for the most part their comments were noisy, loud and vulgar, interspersed with gross humour, and a bawdy interpretation of certain phases of the compositions which provoked amused giggles from the younger females. It was left to the intermediate section of this cathedral town, the solid, respectable, God-fearing, law-abiding middle class, to assume a proper attitude towards this untoward presentation, and to weigh seriously its effect upon the community.

At the outset the reaction of these citizens was one of stupefaction. The panels, in theme and execution, contradicted everything they had expected, offended against the ordinary, set the normal at defiance, rode rough-shod over all their inherent ideas and traditions. They were scandalized, at a single glance. Then gradually, as they peered into the compositions, elements were discerned which seemed unquestionably to violate the decencies of patriotism, religion, and above all, morality.

Objection was concentrated upon a detail of that panel flagrantly exhibited in the window. Too late staid shopkeepers and sober merchants forbade their wives and daughters to view the soft flesh tints, drooping breasts and braced limbs of a peasant woman who, half stripped of her clothing, struggled ineffectually against the erotic embraces of a band of soldiers.

The sense of outrage grew, civic conscience was aroused, and the press—always the guardian of the people—went into action. Two news-sheets served the district: the *County Gazette* and the *Charminster Chronicle*. In the *Chronicle*, published on Wednesday, an editorial appeared, its caption: AN OUTRAGE ON OUR FAIR CITY. Three days later, the *Gazette* outdid its rival with a front-page leader under the title: SALACIOUS ART.

Observing the rise of public feeling which, though he had predicted it, far surpassed his expectation, Tryng experienced a mixed emotion. He had been well treated by the press, indeed, the committee, through influences which he clearly recognized, was represented as a board of upright citizens whose confidence and magnanimity had been sadly betrayed. But though personally exonerated, he was conscious, as the storm grew, of a sense of compunction towards Claire, who, after all, was an equal victim in the affair. Then, on the Monday following the *Gazette* article, at a forenoon meeting of the Rural Council, where the topic of the hour was freely discussed, a word let drop by Sharp alarmed him. He went home to his cutlet in a mood of concern, and meditating while he stripped the bone, decided to act. At two o'clock he took up the telephone, got through to Broughton Court.

"Hello, hello. Might I speak to Mrs. Desmonde?"

"Who is speaking?"

"Admiral Reginald Tryng."

"I'm afraid my wife is engaged at present."

"Oh, it's you, Geoffrey. Nice to hear your voice, my dear fellow. I should have recognized it. Are you well?"

"Quite. What can I do for you?"

"Well . . . as a matter of fact it was Claire I rather wished to have a word with . . . over this, er, matter of the exhibition. But if she's not available, may I speak with you?"

After the barest pause:

"Naturally."

"Then I do feel, seriously, in the light of something I heard today, that it's imperative your cousin be made to close the exhibition and clear out with his confounded daubs . . . without a moment's delay. I don't wish to say more over the telephone but . . . you get my meaning . . ."

"I think I do."

"Good. And you might convey my best regards to your wife. I quite realize that when she asked me to get your cousin the job, she had not the slightest idea what we were in for . . . poor girl."

A silence.

"Well . . . I'm ringing off, then, Geoffrey. Good-bye, and good luck."

Geoffrey came away from the telephone white with rage. Hadn't the week been damnable enough without this! While his suspicions had undoubtedly been active, they had never envisaged anything so damaging to his self-esteem. Still, he must keep cool. In the hall he stood collecting himself, then, with an expression carefully blank, went slowly upstairs. Usually he tapped upon the door of his wife's sitting-room—now he went directly in.

Claire was sitting idly by the window, her favourite seat, with an open book upon her knee, and there were circles under her eyes as though she had not slept.

"You're busy?" he asked casually.

"Yes . . . no, not particularly."

"What's this you've got?" With a sweep of his arm he took up the book—it was entitled *The Post-Impressionists*. "Ha! You've shown quite an interest in art lately!"

"Have I?"

"So it would appear." He lounged on the edge of the sofa. "By the way, when are we to see your new pictures?"

"What pictures?"

"The two you purchased in London."

She had turned even paler and now she glanced away and did not answer.

"Don't you remember? *Charity*, wasn't it? Charming title. And *In the Olive Grove*?"

Knowing that he was baiting her, she forced herself to look at him. "They are being kept for me at present."

"But why deny us the delight of seeing them? After all, they must must have cost you quite a bit." His tone lost its heavy satire, hardened suddenly. "Why did you subsidize that fellow?"

"I liked the paintings."

"I don't believe it. The blighter can't paint for little apples. Yet you flung away four hundred on him, when I—we need every penny we've got for . . . for the upkeep of the place. And not content with that"—his temper got the better of him, he stood up, the words came with a rush—"behind my back, you cadged and touted around to get him this Memorial job, which of course he promptly botched, letting down the people who had backed him, and making you the talk of the county. Why the devil did you do it?"

"I merely wished to help him," she answered in a low voice. What could a man like Geoffrey know of the cravings of the heart?

"Have you been seeing him?"

"Only once . . . for a few minutes in the public street."

"I don't believe you. You're carrying on with him."

"No, Geoffrey."

He did not know whether or not she spoke the truth. Actually, he had little doubt as to her body, but he wanted, also, to preserve the ownership of her mind. He took a swift turn up and down the room, then came and stood before her.

"I suppose it was you encouraged him to set up this damned exhibition."

"I did not encourage him. But I can understand why he did it."

"Indeed." He glared at her.

"Don't you see, Geoffrey, that if an artist believes in his work he must stand up for it? That's why the Salon des Refusés was started

. . . and painters like Manet and Degas and Lautrec whose work was jeered at in the beginning but who afterwards were recognized as great . . . they all exhibited there.''

"You're well primed," he sneered. "At least these fellows didn't set off a blasted scandal."

"But they did," she said quickly. "When Manet, Gauguin and Van Gogh exhibited their early works, there was a dreadful outcry. People mobbed round the paintings, shouting that it was an outrage, an insult to the public . . . there was almost a riot. And now . . . these pictures are acknowledged masterpieces.''

Her quiet tone, her use of these foreign and unfamiliar names, infuriated him. He went forward and gripped her arm.

"I'll give your precious genius masterpieces. When I get my hands on him I'll break his neck."

"Would that help?"

Her eyes, resting on him with a strange look, made him relinquish his grasp.

"So you're in love with him."

She did not answer but got up and moved slowly towards the door. As it closed behind her, inexpressibly goaded, he called out: "What you need is a good beating."

She gave no sign of having heard.

Alone, Geoffrey stood with clenched fists, his face dark with anger, thinking. One thing was clear—something must be done, and soon, if the name of Desmonde were not to be dragged further in the mud. Frowning, he repressed an impulse to wreak immediate violence upon his cousin—he would reserve that satisfaction for another day. Should he go and try to put some backbone into Bertram—induce him to post his blackguard son to Canada, or some other distant colony? No, they were too far under the weather there, the Rector was no better than a broken reed; as for Caroline, he had already suspected that she was hand in glove with Claire. Finally, he decided to confer with his parents, and, going again to the telephone, he called the number of Simla Lodge.

It was his father who answered and, cutting across Geoffrey's preliminary remarks, abruptly declared:

"I was on the point of ringing you. Shall you be in this afternoon? I want to see you."

"Is it about a certain matter?"

"Yes."

"Then I'll definitely expect you. Bring the Mater along."

"Your mother cannot come. But I shall be over within the hour."

Waiting in the billiard-room, in a flurry of impatience, Geoffrey smoked endless cigarettes, tried a few shots, missed, cursed, and gave up, went to the window a score of times. At last the little Standard, with the Union Jack upon the bonnet, swung round the tall rhododendrons that masked the curve of the drive. General Desmonde entered quickly, wearing, to Geoffrey's surprise, his garden clothes, long mackintosh, and gum boots. His blue eyes were frosty, the very raindrops on his moustache had a glacial gleam.

"It's good to see you, sir. Let me take your wet coat. Can I get you a drink?"

"Yes. A stiff whisky and soda, my boy. Pour one for yourself."

At the tantalus Geoffrey mixed the drinks, handed a full tumbler to his father, who took it off, standing, at a draught.

"Claire is well, I trust."

"Yes . . . quite all right."

"That is a relief."

His father's manner was puzzling, but Geoffrey drove straight ahead.

"This art show of that fellow is getting out of hand. We must have it closed."

"The exhibition is already closed, Geoffrey."

"What . . . ?"

A bar of stillness throbbed in the room. The General put down his empty glass.

"The Chief Constable of the County called on me after lunch. He was quite sympathetic about it, apologetic actually . . . the Charminster authorities have taken the matter out of his hands . . . but he felt that they had no other course than to confiscate these 'works of art'."

"I should think so!"

"He also indicated that he would do his best to spare your wife the worst of the publicity."

"What publicity?"

"Your cousin," said General Desmonde, dropping every word as though it polluted his clean-cut lips, "was taken this morning to the Charminster Police Station and formally charged with exhibiting an obscene picture."

"Oh, no sir . . . my God!"

"He is to be brought before the justices on Monday week"—the General's voice was hard as stone.

CHAPTER X

THE CHARMINSTER SESSIONS HOUSE, where the case was to be heard, was filled to the point of suffocation. Seldom before had that ancient building with its semi-circular gallery and high domed ceiling been so crowded, not only with the solid citizens of the community, but also the rank and quality of the County. To Stephen, standing in the court with a kind of sick impatience, a stolid sergeant beside him, it seemed as if he were surrounded, enclosed by a wall of faces. Impossible to recognize anyone in that misty assembly. He knew, thank Heaven, that none of his own family were present, but Richard Glyn was there, and the knowledge gave him a sense of support.

Suddenly, at an order, the hum of conversation ceased. The magistrates entered, and with appropriate solemnity took their seats on the bench. Then, after a moment's pause, Stephen's name was called, the sergeant led him to the dock, and the proceedings began. Stephen felt his nerves quiver as the clerk of the court, in a flat, rather sing-song voice began to read from the paper in his hand.

"Stephen Sieur Desmonde, you are charged with committing a public nuisance in that you did on March seventeenth on the ground floor of premises situated at 5 Cornmarket Street in the city of Charminster, being at that time the lessor and occupier of the said premises, wilfully exhibit three obscene pictures or panels; and you are further summonsed under Section 1 of the Obscene Publications Act 1857 to show cause why the said pictures or panels, which, upon a complaint being made to the justices, were seized and brought before the court upon a warrant issued under the said Section of the said Act, should not be destroyed."

As the clerk concluded, every eye was directed towards the three panels conspicuously displayed in the well of the court.

"Do you plead Guilty or Not Guilty?" the clerk asked.

"Not Guilty," Stephen replied in a low voice.

For a moment, the public's gaze turned upon Stephen, but almost immediately the focus of attention switched to the figure of the prosecuting solicitor rising to address the bench. It was Arnold Sharp.

"Your worships," he began, in a subdued, almost regretful tone, "if I may at the outset inject a personal note, I need not say with what distress, under the circumstances, I undertake this present task. But in my position as solicitor to the City Council, I have no alternative but to accept and carry out my duty."

"Proceed, please." The remark came, briefly, from the bench.

Sharp, holding the lapels of his morning coat, bowed.

"The facts, your worships, relating to the commissioning of these panels are too well and widely known to require recapitulation. Upon certain recommendations and the most solemn personal assurances, perhaps, also, because of the esteem in which his family has always been held, the work was entrusted to the defendant. It was, considering the object of the Memorial, a sacred trust. I pass over the feelings of the committee when they discovered in what manner the commission was executed, or how their wise and well-intentioned efforts to hush up the catastrophe were opposed. I simply ask you to examine, without prejudice, how despicably that sacred trust has been betrayed. The evidence is there, in open court—these so-called works of art—confronting all of us."

Sharp paused and gazed frowningly at the panels.

"In the interests of decency it is not my purpose to dwell intimately and at length upon the nature of these pictures. Nevertheless, since justice must be served, I am obliged to indicate the essential features which have led this charge to be professed."

Taking up the pointer with which he had previously armed himself, Sharp stepped forward. A ripple of anticipation went over the spectators as he tapped the panel *Aftermath*.

"Here," he said, "amidst a scene of destruction that is far from edifying, is the naked, full-length form of a woman, which, we are informed by the accused, represents the figure of Peace. Now we are neither prejudiced nor narrow-minded. In its proper place, such as the old historical Italian paintings, we have no objection to the nude, especially if it be, as in the work of the great painters, suitably draped." Stephen, listening with compressed lips, checked a bitter smile. "But this particular female is not draped, and is done with such voluptuous intent, and such intimate detail in the particular parts, it is enough to raise the blush of shame on the cheek of the innocent beholder."

Sharp paused and turned to the adjoining panel.

"In this next atrocity—and I think the word is justified, your worships—we are presented with what purports to be a field of battle, with our troops, their uniforms are quite distinct, engaged in combat with the enemy. Although we are concerned with the question of indecency, in passing let me draw your attention to the manner in which our own boys are depicted as lying dead and wounded in the trenches, as if, in effect, they were losing the war, instead, thank God, of winning it. But let that go—what I want you to look at first of all is these three great foul-looking creatures, half human and half bird,

255

hovering over the troops on our side. Now we all know about the Angels of Mons that appeared, clearly visible, to our gallant boys and helped them to victory over the Huns. If we had been favoured, here, with the reproduction of this beautiful celestial vision, showing the angels, shimmering in white, with their outspread wings, it would have been a glorious and edifying spectacle. But instead, we get these horrible freaks. And my point is this, your worships. With that same indecency that marks every stroke of his brush, the defendant has turned the human half of these vultures into naked women, with that identical definition of bare bosom and torso, right down into the feathers, that can only spring from a prurient and decadent mind. Why, I ask your worships, if it was not through sheer moral perversion, did the defendant have to invent these meaningless female monstrosities?"

At this point, from the gallery, a loud voice, which Stephen recognized as Glyn's, was raised in sudden, angry protest.

"Have you never heard of the Harpies mentioned by Homer in the Odyssey, you ignorant ass?"

Sensation. The chairman of the bench rapped angrily, and, failing to discover the offender, declared:

"If any such disturbance occurs again I shall immediately order the court to be cleared."

When order was restored Sharp, somewhat out of countenance at the interruption, resumed more acidly than before.

"I have not yet finished with this picture. Here, your worships, in the background, but still plainly visible—if you can bear to observe it—there is depicted three individuals, two male, one female, in the process of being shot by a firing-squad. A hideous subject at any time, though sometimes necessary in time of war, and in this instance made more revolting through the fact that the three potential corpses, barring a few rags, are practically in a state of nature. So much so, that although done very small, it is possible to determine the sex to which they belong."

Sharp took his breath, modestly wiped his moustache with a clean handkerchief as though the mere mention of these words had polluted it. Then he went on:

"As though what I have described were not enough, the most damning evidence, your worships, is contained in this same panel. Indeed, as you can see, from its lacerated condition, it has already provoked the righteous indignation of our citizenry. And well it might." He pointed ominously. "We are not done with the obscene by any manner of means. Once again we are presented with yet another semi-garbed woman. And how do we find her? Being assaulted, licentiously, by members of the armed forces. In one word, though I hesitate to use it, your worships, it is rape. Incredible though it may seem to a Christian country, this shocking act is openly depicted, and to make it worse there is a child, watching, while they are struggling with her, on the ground."

A murmur went through the court, and supported by it, Sharp switched his pointer adroitly to the last panel.

"I have neither the wish nor the need to press this unsavoury demonstration, your worships. But consider, if only for a moment, this final saturnalia of noodity. Look at these male and female forms rising in a shameless, and shameful, state of nature from what apparently is a graveyard. Look, I beg of you, and before you look away, ask yourself if this ghastly portrayal does not in every sense of the word reek of corruption."

Sharp laid down the pointer, drew himself up by his lapels.

"Your worships, surely it is apparent that from first to last there exists in these works an attack, sometimes subtle, sometimes crude, but always diabolic, upon morality. Whether this arises through decadence, perversion, sheer malice, or barefaced pornography on the part of the defendant, it is not my position to say. I simply reiterate that the paintings are not only coarse, gross, hideous and unlovely, but under the meaning of the Act, are clearly indecent and obscene. The test of obscenity is whether this matter is of such a character as to corrupt those whose minds are open to such immoral influence, such as our children, young men and women, our wives and mothers. I submit, your worships, that you cannot have the least difficulty in coming to the conclusion that these productions satisfy in all respects the meaning of the legal word 'obscene', that they should be destroyed forthwith before they further pollute the fair air of our city, and their perpetrator punished to the full extent of the law."

Amidst a murmur of applause, quickly suppressed, Sharp concluded his opening address. The sergeant who had seized the panels was then called, and gave formal evidence of what had taken place. When he had finished, the chairman of the bench, after consultation with his clerk, directed his gaze towards Stephen. He was a conscientious man, upright, precise, fair-minded, a local churchwarden and father of three unmarried daughters, who, while a stickler for procedure, prided himself upon the impartiality of his attitude upon the bench. And in this case, because of the public bias against the defendant, he was resolved to be more than usually considerate in his treatment of him.

I

His tone was moderate and helpful as he said:

"You are not, I understand, legally represented and propose to conduct your case yourself."

"That is correct."

Now that the moment was upon him, Stephen, who had endured the vicious attack of the prosecution with a pale and quivering cheek, gripped the guard rail of the dock tightly. If only because of his paintings, so unjustly maligned, and of all the desperate work he had put into them, he was resolved to offer a good account of himself.

"Now, I must tell you that you are entitled to give evidence on oath in which case you may cross-examine; on the other hand, if you prefer, you may make a statement from where you stand."

"I will give evidence, sir," he said.

The sergeant led him to the witness-box, and with a peculiar tightness at the back of his throat and a heavy thumping about the heart, Stephen took the oath and faced the justices of the bench.

"Be good enough to proceed."

"In the first place I wish to deny, with all the emphasis of which I am capable, the charge that has been brought against me. I have never painted with such a base object as to titillate obscene-minded people. My approach to art has always been serious. And in this instance it was more serious than ever before. The definite animating purpose of these panels was a sincere and profound desire to symbolize one of the greatest tragedies affecting mankind. It was a major effort attempted on the grand scale. And how has it been judged? By taking little pieces from each picture, as one might take words out of their context in a page, and assuming them to be representations of the whole. No method of evaluation could be more absurd, more unjust. If you would come with me round the National Gallery I could assemble various component parts from the masterpieces there into an entity which I have no doubt would shock you to the core. I must therefore submit, with due respect, that the ordinary standard of taste, whether of a police sergeant or of a common informer, is not a competent one. Perhaps my work is difficult to understand. Nevertheless, there are those whose critical faculties and personal achievements enable them to interpret and properly appraise such new movements in the plastic arts. In support of my case, I propose to call Mr. Richard Glyn, an exhibitor at the Royal Academy, who is now in court."

Immediately, Sharp jumped up.

"Your worships, I protest. If it were permitted to call such witnesses as Mr. Glyn, will you consider what volume of evidence I might have called from eminent persons who might hold contrary opinions? Clearly such a hearing would extend for weeks."

The magistrates considered, then, after talking with their clerk, slowly nodded agreement.

"We cannot allow Mr. Glyn to be called," the chairman ruled. "The calling of evidence on purely artistic grounds is quite inadmissible."

"But," exclaimed Stephen, "how else can you judge a work of art?"

"It is perfectly immaterial whether or not these are works of art," the magistrate said reprovingly—he did not like to be interrogated. "The most beautiful picture in the world could be obscene."

Staggered by this masterpiece of logic, Stephen for a moment was speechless.

"Then I may not call Mr. Glyn in evidence?"

"No."

At this point a massive figure rose from the front row of the gallery and leaned over the rail, chin thrust pugnaciously forward above the knotted red scarf.

"If I am not to be called, at least I will be heard."

"Silence in court."

"I will be silent only after I have spoken. In my considered opinion these panels are æsthetic creations of the first rank. In their realism and breadth of treatment they rival the work of Daumier. In their rhythm and dramatic form they are fit to be compared with the finest creations of El Greco. Only a vulgar and dirty mind could regard them as indecent."

"Officer, remove that man."

"I'm going," said Glyn, moving up to the door. "If I stay, I'll say something obscene." He went out.

The sensation produced by this outburst lasted for several minutes. When it subsided the chairman, seriously provoked, looked up at the gallery.

"If such a disturbance occurs again I shall immediately commit the person creating it to prison for contempt of court." He turned to Stephen. "Will you continue?"

"If I am not permitted to call witnesses in support of my contention, I can only repeat it."

"Is that all?" Suppressing his irritation, the magistrate again proffered assistance. "Surely you have something more to produce in your defence?"

"No."

When Stephen said this, Sharp got to his feet, without haste, as though he meant to be upon them a considerable time.

"With your permission, your worships." Anchoring one hand on a lapel, he bent his head reflectively, then raised it abruptly, fixed his gaze on Stephen.

"In all that you have said, you have not once told us why you felt obliged to incorporate in these panels no less than six stark-naked figures, four of which are female."

"I did so for various reasons, one being the beauty of the nude human form."

"But surely you don't contend that the naked figure should be completely revealed?"

"If it is to be naked, it must be revealed."

"Don't deliberately misunderstand me. Doesn't modesty demand that certain parts should always be kept covered?"

"If that were so, how could we take a bath?"

Sharp's eyes sparked.

"Ill-timed humour won't help you."

"I assure you I feel far from humorous. I am merely attempting to show how ridiculous is your attitude, which seems to me nothing more or less than a survival of Victorian prudery. It is the same spirit that caused Manet's *Déjeuner sur l'Herbe* to be spat at and execrated because it depicted two nude women seated on the grass. All the supreme artists have painted from life. Goya's great painting *La Maja* shows the Duchess of Alba reclining on a couch without a stitch of clothing. No doubt it would horrify you. *Olympia* would be to you a shocking nude. You forget that it is the lightly draped figure that is lewd and suggestive. Nature pure and unadorned is never obscene. The symbolism, the dramatic content of my panels demanded this nudity. But it is a chaste nudity and not the salacious, half-hidden variety that you seem to prefer and which I regard as fit only to adorn the walls of brothels."

The chairman, thinking of his three daughters, frowned his disapproval.

"I must ask you to moderate your language."

"No doubt, your worships, it was the voice of experience referring to such places." Sharp's sneer faded, his tone was grim as he turned again to Stephen. "I will not admit that it is pure and modest to portray for public exhibition the private parts of the human anatomy. I suggest to you that it is obscene."

"Then why are they so exhibited in the great galleries of the world? In the Prado alone you will find a score of statues, by masters such as Michelangelo and Donatello, in which what you are pleased to call the 'private parts' are publicly displayed."

Sharp did not pursue the argument, but went on to his next question. "I believe a moment ago in describing your work you used the word 'chaste'. Now tell me, would you consider the violation of a woman a chaste act?"

"Not for the violator."

"Yet you must admit that in your paintings you have portrayed the act of . . . rape . . . if I may use the word . . ."

"So far as I am concerned you may use the word."

"Thank you for your kind permission. It is, however, an unpleasant word."

"It is in the dictionary."

"And has a most unpleasant meaning. Will you be good enough to tell the court why you chose to use this quite unmentionable subject?"

"It may be that I was guided by precedent."

"What precedent, sir?"

"The old Italian painters, as you have so classically defined them, and for whom you entertain such admiration and respect—they used it constantly."

"Do you expect us to believe that?"

"I expect nothing from you but ignorance and prejudice. Nevertheless, it is the truth. Titian, for example, one of the oldest of the old Italians—he lived to be ninety-nine and, although he was an artist, received a magnificent funeral—used the subject repeatedly, most notably of all in *The Rape of Europa*. Then there is *The Rape of the Sabine Women*, one of the world's most famous paintings. And again, *The Carrying Off of Psyche*, by Prud'hon. These canvases hang in the Louvre, which, since doubtless you have visited there, you may agree to be a fairly reputable gallery. If one takes the subject of *The Ravishment of Danaë* alone, this was treated by Titian, Correggio and Rembrandt, who, while not an old Italian, was nevertheless a painter of some distinction and who painted Danaë as a woman lying, undressed and completely uncovered, on her bed."

There was a silence. Sharp looked uneasy and, with a spot of colour in his cheek, glanced towards the bench for support. The chairman, after conferring with his fellow-magistrates, looked across his spectacles at Stephen.

"Who is this Danaë to whom you refer?"

"The daughter of King Acrisius."

"And she was the victim of . . . er . . . such a violation?"

"Yes."

"By whom?"

Unfortunately Stephen saw a chance to score. With a chilly smile he answered:

"Jupiter . . . descending in a shower of gold."

A titter arose from the back of the gallery, but Glyn, now positioned in the crowded doorway and watching intently, did not smile. He saw the magistrate redden with displeasure and knew that Stephen was prejudicing his case. Sharp was quick to seize advantage.

"Your worships, I submit that such historical tomfoolery has nothing to do with the present case. To get back to the point," he turned to Stephen, "you admit you painted this particularly scene deliberately?"

"Deliberately? Do you imagine it got there by accident?"

"Mr. Desmonde," the chairman interposed severely, "I must warn you that I find the tone of your answers most unseemly."

"Then I am in character, your worship, for that apparently is the charge against me."

"Proceed, Mr. Sharp."

"Your worship, I am trying to get from the accused a direct reply as to why he brought in this particular scene of rape."

"Will you answer, sir?"

"Because I wished to emphasize the brutalities and horrors that are inseparable from any war, yet are glossed over and forgotten, or worse still, glorified in the name of patriotism."

"Am I to understand that you blame such enormities on our own men?"

"Are they any different from other men? Is it always the enemy who is the butcher and barbarian?"

"You mention the enemy. But you didn't get too near them in the war?"

"No."

"Didn't have the plain guts, I suppose?"

"To be an artist one must have some courage."

"Courage for what?"

"To sustain the world's universal contempt."

"Is this relevant, Mr. Sharp?" One of the magistrates intervened. "Mr. Desmonde is not on trial for cowardice."

"Your worship," exclaimed Sharp, "the defendant's war, or should I say peace, record is well known and speaks for itself. At your behest I will not further impose it upon the court. However," to Stephen again, "I will ask you this. What right have you to impose on our quiet, God-fearing community this perverted attitude of yours?"

"It is not only mine. Many others have created works that were protests against war—Callot and Delacroix. In literature, Tolstoi, Vereshchagen, Zola. The same essential viewpoint was expressed by Goya in his *Desastres de la Guerre*."

"Goyer, a French painter, I presume?"

"Spanish, if I may correct you."

"It amounts to the same thing. You seem devoted to these foreigners."

"That is because unfortunately there have been so few great British painters."

"You except yourself, naturally."

"I believe I have considerable talent. Otherwise I should not have undertaken the supremely arduous life of the artist, with all its despairs and privations, nor for that matter placed myself in the position where I have to suffer your cheap sneers."

"Cheap? They may cost you more than you think. Instead of attempting to make a martyr of yourself, try to keep to the point. You mentioned the word 'horrors'. Why did you introduce such things?"

"Why?" Stephen, weary and harassed, like a hare hemmed in by a pack of hounds, was growing careless. "I wanted to shock people into a permanent resistance to war."

"And you adopted very shocking means. Were you surprised at the reaction you got?"

"When I was working I was oblivious to all but the effort of creation. Now, however, I am not surprised. Every period of æsthetic innovation and endeavour has suffered from public malignity. All the greatest and most significant changes in the history of art have been ushered in through mass demonstrations of ridicule and ignorance. But I regret nothing that I have done. I would do it all over again."

Sharp smiled grimly.

"Your worships, I will leave you with that unrepentant statement from the defendant. I think I need not add to it."

He resumed his seat amidst applause which was immediately suppressed. The chairman shuffled his papers, and looked across his glasses at Stephen in a manner now far from sympathetic.

"Have you anything more to say? You may address the court, if you wish."

263

"There is much that I could say. But it would be futile. I shall not say it."

Suddenly exhausted, with a splitting headache, he felt he must rest, but as he made to sit down the sergeant, with a tap on the shoulder, indicated that he must stand.

After consulting the notes on the bench before him, and exchanging a few words with the other members of the bench and his clerk, the chairman, in dead silence, gave judgement.

"We have," he said, "listened with extreme attention and, bearing in mind the unseemly interruptions that have occurred, with extraordinary patience, to the arguments put before us. We have also studied the relevant pictorial evidence with unusual care. Now, we cannot regard it as cogent to reason that because these productions are magnificent works of art they cannot be, under the meaning of the Act, obscene. In the first place, who shall finally determine whether or not they are magnificent? Their creator is an obscure artist, quite unknown in his own country. He is no Constable, no Landseer. He is not Sir Joshua Reynolds. And so far as ordinary taste is concerned, the taste for instance of an ordinary citizen like myself, these works are not masterpieces. Indeed, in their general violence of colour and composition, in their lack of elegance and refinement, they fall, in my opinion, lamentably short of masterpieces. And in the second place, as I have already been at pains to indicate, even if they were masterpieces they could still be obscene. For a picture, though it be painted with the most consummate skill, could, if it related to a lewd or lascivious subject, be an offence against the Act. To coin a phrase, it would be a masterpiece of obscenity.

"Again, from first to last the whole history of the production and defiant exhibition of these works is prejudicial to the defendant. Instead of gratefully falling in with the wishes of his sponsors, consulting with them from time to time, and striving to achieve a result which would be definitely acceptable to them, and to the decent people of this city for whose benefit and edification those paintings were primarily designed, he wilfully conceived and gave effect to a production which, he now admits, did not surprise him by immediately occasioning a public outcry. In plainer terms, he set out to shock and revolt and he succeeded.

"Nor is it a valid defence to argue that the motive behind all this was serious, honest, and sincere. If a person be inherently decadent and depraved, he might still, with the best intention in the world, produce a vicious and depraved picture.

"Lastly, the attitude of the defendant has not impressed us. Instead of evincing a due sense of respect and contrition, he has been by turns contumacious, ironic, and defiant. We have, I may say, the most acute sympathy for his family, in particular for his father, who bears, and despite the heavy burden of today's proceedings, will continue to bear, a reputation untarnished and undimmed. Nevertheless, justice must be served, and in whatever light one may regard this case, making every allowance, the fact remains that in actually delineating and thereafter publicly exhibiting the intimate parts of both male and female, the defendant has committed a public nuisance. We therefore find you, Stephen Sieur Desmonde, guilty of the charge brought against you. As this offence is a misdemeanor, we have the power to imprison you. Despite the seriousness of the offence, we are reluctant to impose the full penalty of the law. Instead of imprisoning you, we therefore fine you the sum of fifty pounds. In addition you will pay the costs of the prosecution. I need hardly add that it is our duty, under the Obscene Publications Act, 1857, to order the three panels here displayed to be destroyed forthwith."

This judgement having been given, the bench rose, and amidst tumultuous applause, which could not be controlled, the court recessed.

CHAPTER XI

WHEN HE LEFT the police office, Stephen went directly to the railway station. Glyn had arranged to wait for him at the Blue Boar, but in his present mood he wished to see no one, nothing could suppress his almost frantic impulse to escape. In the raging fury and despair that filled his soul, his one desire was to lose himself in some place where he would be unknown and unseen. Never would he return to Stillwater. This Sussex, and all that it contained, had suddenly become hateful to him.

The clock indicated four o'clock as he entered the booking-hall. It seemed deserted. Then, as he made his way towards the grille, he felt a light touch upon his arm.

"Stephen."

So overstrung were his nerves, he spun round with a visible start. It was Claire, in a costume of dark grey, with a dark hat and veil, beneath which her face showed pale and her eyes unusually luminous. She spoke hurriedly.

"I thought I should find you here. I . . . I had to see you."

"Yes?"

"Stephen . . ." Although keyed to an unnatural pitch, she was striving to keep her voice calm. "You must need something . . . coffee and a sandwich . . . let's go to the buffet."

"No, Claire, I couldn't."

"Then sit here for a moment." In that strained, uncertain manner she indicated a corner of the bare and dingy waiting-room. "You must be dead-tired."

He hesitated, then went with her to the bench.

"I am tired," he said.

"Oh, no wonder. It was frightful for you."

"You were there?" He gazed at her in weary surprise.

"Yes, yes . . . from the beginning to the end. Did you imagine I could have stayed away? Oh, Stephen, it was all so stupid and cruel . . . so beastly and horribly unfair. I longed to be able to help you."

He glanced away.

"Haven't you helped me too much already?" His voice was flat, yet free from bitterness. "From the beginning . . . when you bought my pictures."

"So he came over and told you . . . Geoffrey?"

"It was part of our interview. Before he knocked me down. He indicated that you'd done it out of charity."

"It was not that . . . I liked the pictures." She spoke passionately. "I wanted them."

"No, Claire. Let's stop pretending. You simply gave me an alms of three hundred pounds. How could you like the pictures when you admitted you didn't understand them?"

"But I do," she protested, a little wildly. "I've studied, read ever so many books . . . tried to educate myself in art. I do know what you're striving after, and what you have to contend with in the way of ignorance and prejudice. That's why I suffered so much for you today."

"Yes, they had their fun." His lips drew together. "I don't care for myself. I almost wish they'd sent me to prison. What really hurts is the loss of my work. To think of it . . . that they'll actually burn my panels."

"Never mind. You'll go on painting."

"Yes, even if they burn me . . . I'm not finished, though I am clearing out like a beaten dog. But I swear to Heaven I'll never give anyone the chance to do this to me again."

She drew a sharp, agitated breath as though summoning all her

266

strength. Her gloved hands were tightly clenched, her figure, bent towards him, was taut with the effort to speak these tremulous and unexpected words.

"Stephen . . . take me with you."

He turned his head slowly and looked at her. She had raised her veil and he saw that she had been crying, that her eyes were again filled with tears. He was shocked by the pallor of her ravaged face.

"Don't, Claire. You've been compromised enough."

"What do I care?" She caught hold of his hand. "Oh, Stephen . . . dear Stephen . . . I'm so unhappy. I should never have married Geoffrey. I never loved him. Never. And now . . . I can't go on."

The wild abandon in her tone startled him. Knowing her natural reserve, the inveterate restraint which, by reason of temperament and breeding, distinguished all her actions, he realized the intensity of feeling which swayed her. And, in his mood of savage bitterness, he was tempted momentarily by an impulse to accept this offering of herself, to revenge himself on Geoffrey, to justify the ill opinions he had earned and place himself beyond the pale. He had been hurt, had suffered an almost mortal wound, why should he not strike back in return? He did not love Claire, but she was sweet and docile, had always made an agreeable companion. They could travel the length of the world together, he could paint to his heart's content.

But almost before the thought was born it died within him.

"You're sorry for me, Claire." He spoke sombrely. "Pity is a dangerous emotion. It's thrown you off balance. But you'll get over it. You have your children, your home, lots of things you couldn't give up."

"But I could, Stephen . . ." A sob shook her.

"Besides," he went on as though he had not heard. "I'm too fond of you to let you wreck your life. You don't really know me. I'm not your kind. I'm a queer sort of throwback. We'd never get on together. After six months with me you'd be eminently miserable."

"I'd be happy . . . just being with you."

"No, Claire, it's impossible."

But she was moved beyond all caution, all self-respect.

"Everything is possible when one is in love."

He averted his gaze.

"You don't know what you're saying. No love could survive the kind of life you'd have to lead with me . . . hacking around in poor lodgings, spending whole days alone while I'm hard at work, enduring my disreputable friends, putting up with hardships you've never dreamed of."

"I have the means to change all that, to make you happy and comfortable."

He looked her directly in the eyes with a finality she could not fail to understand.

"That would be the certain death of my art. And if you killed that, Claire, I could only hate you."

There was a quivering silence. All the supple erectness went out of her figure, her swan-like neck drooped and her face, shadowed by her long fair lashes, was desolate. Huddled there, on the bare waiting-room seat, she had the look of a wounded bird, broken and pitiful. Presently she took a square of cambric from her bag and dried her eyes. He broke the long silence, stroking her sleeve.

"One of these days you'll thank me."

"I wonder," she said, in a queer, far-off tone.

The bells of the cathedral began to peal for Evensong, the chimes coming soft and clear. Sighing, as though recalled, she replaced her handkerchief, got up and, moving like a woman in a dream, with a strange look, no longer filled with longing, but shamed and defeated, went out of the waiting-room.

He sat a long time after she had gone, crushed by an overpowering sadness. Then, as the sound of a train broke into his painful meditation, he rose and, with a glance through the window, hastened towards the opposite platform.

CHAPTER XII

As he came from the waiting-room the train was pulling out of the up platform. Heedless of its destination, he swung on to the footboard and flung himself into an empty compartment. The meeting with Claire had taxed him more than he had realized, and now, alone, wave after wave of wretchedness assailed him. His brain was spinning, he pressed his hand against his eyes in anguish. He had reached the furthest limit of endurance, the point from which, surely, there was no return. His spirit was dead within him. Would he ever succeed, meet anything but neglect, or the same brutal misinterpretation which had reduced him to this extremity? He stole a dazed and fascinated glance through the window. In this section the embankment ran high, across a series of narrow culverts, with a bed of broken metal a sheer seventy feet beneath. But quickly, with a shudder, he looked away.

What then was he to do? Clear out of England altogether—seek immunity in a sunnier and less biased land? No. He could not. Sick to the heart of Continental journeyings, he felt physically unable to face the pinchbeck shifts and complications of a further European adventure. The tension of these last weeks, broken like a snapped string, had left him in a strange lassitude. The palms of his hands were damp with sweat and when he breathed he left a stitch in his side. Sunk in his corner, he studied a pale and unfamiliar image in the fly-blown mirror fixed, amongst advertisements for laxatives and beer, on the opposite partition of the compartment. I'm not well, he thought, with a stab of realization. If only he could find a quiet room where he might lie up and rest. But where? Not for anything would he impose further upon Glyn's friendship and support. Richard would expect him, the studio would be available, an admirable refuge. But he could not accept it. He must, at this juncture, be hidden and alone. He was like a child, sick for the darkness of the womb.

As the train dragged its way, with many stops and jolting starts, he saw from the wayside stations that it was bound for London—a local. And through the interminable journey, which seemed exactly to symbolize his own uncertainty, Stephen grappled, in a growing mental haze, with the problem of his immediate future. His brain would not work, he could find no solution, then, as they reached the suburbs and Clapham Junction fell behind, he recollected his meeting with Jenny Baines. Had she not told him she had a room to let? Yes, he was sure of it. If it were still available, what could be more suitable as a temporary lodging? No one would ever dream of looking for him there. The river district was one he had always liked, and now especially, in his recoil from Stillwater, its appeal was intensified.

His drawn face lightened somewhat, and as the train, with a prolonged hiss of steam, clanked finally to rest at Victoria, he came down the platform and boarded a number 25 omnibus at the depot outside the station. A fine rain was in the air as the bus started off and moved towards Whitehall and the Strand. Traffic at this hour was heavy, the streets were greasy and darkness had fallen when, almost an hour later, they swerved and skidded into Stepney. Gazing through the beaded windows at the narrow streets, lined by flare-lit costers' barrows, teeming with obscure humanity, Stephen felt already a soothing loss of his identity. Here, at least, he would not be recognized, abused and vilified. Rousing himself, he got off at the Good Intent, mingling immediately with the crowd, and, at a

269

pace inexplicably sluggish, made his way to Cable Street. Number 17, he remembered, and presently he was standing on the doorstep of the narrow brick house, one of the long low row of workers' dwellings sweeping the length of the street.

In sudden agitation Stephen raised his hand to the brightly polished knocker, feeling, with a deepening of his exhaustion, that if this should fail, he scarcely knew where to turn. Had his knock been heard? He was about to try again when the door opened and, framed against the yellow gaslight, Jenny stood before him.

"Good evening." How difficult it was to make his words sound casual. "I wondered if you had a vacant room."

She had been peering at his shadowed figure with the dubiety of a householder subject to the aggravations and importunities of beggars, tramps, stowaways, and those loose-robed Orientals who came straight from the docks with rugs to sell, but now she gave an exclamation, surprised, perhaps, yet full of warmth.

"Mr. Desmonde! Well, I declare! Do come in, sir."

She shut the door behind him and faced him in the warm little passage, bright with chequered wallpaper varnished to a prevailing yellow, made smaller by an antlered hat-stand of formidable design. Through a prevailing blur he was conscious of the reddish veins on her cheeks and the brown mole, which he had first noticed nine years ago, on her cheekbone.

"It's an odd thing, sir. You'll never believe it." Smiling, she shook her head. "But since we had our chat in the tea-room I felt in my bones, with all respect, you might want to come painting Stepney way again."

"So you have a room?"

"That I do, sir. Old Mr. Tapley, my regular, him I told you of, has the downstairs front permanent. But my upstairs back—and I only let the two—is vacant. Would you care to have a look at it?"

"Yes, please."

What a relief, he thought, as he followed her up the almost perpendicular wooden stairs, that she knew nothing of what he had been through, but accepted his sudden appearance, without luggage, in the wet darkness, with that matter-of-fact calmness which had always distinguished her.

The back bed-sitting-room, though of box-like dimensions, was neat and decently habitable, with a fumed-oak wardrobe, washstand, cushioned cane chair, and two hand-hooked rugs on the waxed linoleum.

"There isn't a deal of space," she remarked, with a practical proprietary survey. "But it's cosy—with the gas fire—and clean. I never could abear dirt, Mr. Desmonde."

"It's very nice indeed. I'll take it, if I may."

"Would you want board, sir? I give Mr. Tapley his breakfast and supper. He's out mostly midday and I daresay you'd be too. The room would be ten shillings without and a pound with."

"I think . . . with board."

"Very good, sir. Now, if you'll excuse me. Then I'll just pop round to Lipton's for something tasty for your supper. Would you fancy a nice breaded veal cutlet?"

"Yes . . . anything, thank you." Shaken by a sudden chill and a tightening of the stitch in his side, Stephen all at once felt so queer he had to steady himself against the wall. "I'd like to wash now."

She made a gesture of understanding, added, with tactful gravity, as she moved to the door:

"The bathroom is at the end of the landing. It's a good geyser, sir. Penny in the slot."

When she had gone he sat down heavily in the armchair, making an effort to gather his disjointed thoughts. How lucky he had been to find this decent little place. And Jenny was such a good sort. At a time like this she would be the last person to get on his nerves. It was a nuisance he felt so seedy, but naturally, after these past weeks, he couldn't expect to be fighting fit. And, come to think of it, he'd eaten nothing since breakfast—he'd be all right after supper. But this tightness in his chest was rather bothersome—he recognized it as the old bronchial trouble which always seemed to crop up in-opportunely when he least expected it. Perhaps if he had a trifle more air it might help his shortness of breath. He rose and went to open the window. The sash, however, was tight, slightly warped, and as he strained to tug it upwards, a salty warmth, fluid and familiar, came into his mouth. He pressed a handkerchief to his lips, then, already knowing what to expect, looked at it with revulsion. Oh God, he thought, not that again!

Before the bubbling uprush could escape from his clenched jaws he sought for the bathroom, bent hastily over the wash-basin, turned on the cold tap. It was, at least, some satisfaction that he had not made a mess. But the hæmorrhage, frothing scarlet into the blue-patterned china bowl, while less than the last attack he had ex-perienced in Spain, was more severe than that which had preceded his illness at Garonde. Recollection of that event, the sharp subse-quent fever and delayed convalescence, made him burn with a weak rage. He would not, he must not, be ill here. What a return to make for the unpretentious, unsuspecting hospitality with which he had been received. Compressing the wet towel which he had placed on the back of his neck, he willed desperately that this untimely infliction should pass.

At last the flow slackened and ceased. He straightened, took a careful, sparing breath, sighed with relief when no further uprush came, cleansed the basin, wiped his numb mouth with the towel. For some reason his movements were incredibly slow, as though performed by another person, seemed to come from a long way off. His streaked, earthy face confronting him in the mirror had, he noted in weak exasperation, that greenish colour with which the earlier Spanish painters delighted to invest their corpses. He washed it laboriously. His head felt empty, light as air; his feet were heavy as lead. Yet his mind was clear, dominated by the imperative need that he return to his room. Yes, if only he could reach his room, lock the door and get to bed—he could refuse supper on some pretext—then no one need know of this disgusting mishap. In the morning he would be quite recovered. Holding himself together, he started back. The sense of his own weakness as he slowly clawed his way along the passage was so ludicrous it brought a feeble grimace to his blanched lips. It seemed that he might do it. But when he was almost there, stretching out his hand towards the knob of the door, everything wavered, whirled in a dazzling arc, and finally retreated, leaving only a black void into which he fell, noiselessly, as though slipping into the well of soft eternal night.

When he came to himself, after what might have been æons of oblivion, he became aware that he was in bed, undressed, with a warm stone jar at his feet. And gradually, as his eyes resumed the power to focus, there took shape before him the forms of Jenny Baines and an old man in a striped shirt and braces, with a celluloid dickey about his neck.

"He's coming round." The traditional remark, uttered in an undertone, gave Stephen a sickening sense of embarrassment. Oh God, he thought, what a damned fool I've made of myself, what an insupportable infliction I've landed on this poor woman, and his gaze turned to Jenny in apology.

"I felt rather dizzy . . . I think I must have fainted."

"I should think you did, sir." The tremor in her tone showed relief at his recovery. "If I hadn't had Mr. Tapley by me, I don't know how I should have got you to bed."

"Sorry to have been such a nuisance," he muttered. "I'll be up and around tomorrow."

"We'll see about that, sir." Jenny spoke with a warning tilt of her head. "It's well seen you've had a nasty shake. I'm just wondering if you shouldn't have the doctor."

"No, no. I'll be perfectly all right."

"What do you think, Cap'n Tapley?"

"I think we can 'andle him. His colour's coming back. Have you 'ad these spells before, my lad?"

"No . . . not really," Stephen lied. "I've been overdoing it lately, that's all."

"Then a mite of rest won't hurt you. And a mite of summat in your stomach."

"Yes, indeed," agreed Jenny eagerly. "I shan't offer you the cutlet now, sir . . . lucky I didn't have it on. But you only have to tell me what you fancy."

"Could I have some milk, please? Cold."

"That you can, sir. And I'll start some beef tea for you straight away."

At that, they both left him. But in three minutes Jenny was back with a small japanned tray, on which stood a tumbler and a flowered jug covered by a glass-beaded lace doyley. Placing the tray at his bedside, she poured him a glass of milk, watched him while he slowly sipped it. Then she went out with the glass, returned with it washed and dried, set it on the tray beside him.

"Shall I leave the light?"

"No. Turn it off, please." His head was beginning to throb but the cold milk had made him feel less dead. He added, untruthfully: "I think I'll sleep."

"Sure you'll be all right?"

"Quite sure."

"Good night, sir."

"Good night, Jenny."

The light was off, the room in darkness, but he still sensed her presence. Then, in a low voice, she said hurriedly, respectfully, losing something of her grammar in her determination to speak her mind:

"You ain't no trouble, Mr. Desmonde. Don't even think it for a minute. You was very good to me, at Clinker Street. I haven't never forgot it. And I'm more nor glad to have the chance to pay you back."

The door closed behind her. He lay there, flat on his back in the strange little room, his breathing shallow and uneasy, and though he held all his depleted body rigid in a frantic effort to stifle feeling, two meagre tears welled from his shut eyelids and rolled slowly down his cheeks.

CHAPTER XIII

DESPITE HIS ANXIETY to be up and about, under the pressure of his own weakness and the insistence brought to bear upon him, almost a week passed before Stephen was able to leave his room. Through the apathy which bound him, he again blessed the chance that had brought him to this obscure Dockland house. How often in the past had he known the bondage of miserable lodgings—the dirt and discomfort of ill-kept apartments, the lack of privacy, of linen and hot water, the abominable food, the greasy breakfast tray left outside the door, and all the pinchings and meannesses of mercenary landladies for whom he existed merely to be despoiled and endured. But here, the place shone with cleanliness. And Jenny herself had always the untroubled face and active limbs of one quite untouched by moods, depressions, or the dreadful state of the world, whose nature, though fiercely independent, seemed perpetually content, and who, ignoring his embarrassed protestations, was bent on doing everything within her power to serve him.

Every afternoon Joe Tapley came in to visit him and, as far as his deafness and taciturn disposition permitted, passed the time of day. Old Joe had worked most of his life on the Thames, for many years as part owner of a coal-barge, then as skipper of a canal boat making a weekly run to Hampton, on the Cut. Now he had retired, invested his savings in a small wharf where he let out moorings, maintained an odd skiff for hire, and in general kept in touch with the water-front. The river was, indeed, the core of his existence, and every morning after breakfast he would depart for his jetty, where, ensconced by the stove in the wooden shanty at the pier-end, he would absorb slowly, word for word, the arrival and departure columns in the *Greenwich Meridian*, looking up, every now and then, to observe, over steel-rimmed spectacles, the passage of craft, both foreign and familiar, and to answer, more by instinct than audition, the hail of a friendly skipper.

On Stephen's first day downstairs—he had tried his legs with a short and rather uncertain afternoon walk the length of Cable Street —the Captain had returned from his maritime avocations. Companionably, his door stood open, and as his fellow lodger went slowly upstairs, he called him to his room, where, seated by the window, darning a sock, was Jenny.

"Well," Joe said, "how does it feel when you're out?"

"Pretty well, thank you. A trifle shaky."

"You've had a shake all right. Take a chair."

Stephen sat down, glanced from the one to the other, sensing an unusual, even a disturbing air of complicity.

And indeed, after a prolonged pause, Jenny, still too obviously darning, broke the silence.

"I have to go to my sister-in-law for a couple of weeks, Mr. Desmonde—Florrie Baines, you know, my poor Alf was her brother. I always do this time of year while she's setting up her stall. And Mr. Tapley thinks you didn't ought to stop here." She hurried on, as if in explanation. "He always fends for himself when I'm away. But it's different with you . . . being ill like . . . you'd never manage."

"I see." Stephen, with a sudden weariness, now saw what had been arranged. He did not blame them for wanting to be rid of him.

"So," Jenny resumed, in the same breath, before he could speak, "Mr. Tapley thinks you ought to come along. There's no place like Margate to pick a person up. The sea air is wonderful."

"Dr. Margate," the Captain confirmed with a sententious nod. "He'll put you on your pins in no time."

A sudden warmth replaced the chill around Stephen's heart. But he was still oppressed and melancholy, borne down by hours of bitter brooding—in no mood for such a project. He shook his head.

"I couldn't think of troubling you. I've abused your kindness enough."

"It's no trouble, sir. Florrie'll be glad to have you." Suspecting a reason for his hesitation: "You can pay her for your board . . . just what you pay me."

In his weak and pliant state, there was no withstanding their joint persuasions, so well-meant, so bent on getting him back to health. And indeed, his brief, erratic sortie into the raw Stepney afternoon had rudely qualified his hope of starting work at once—if, for that matter, he could ever work again. He realized he could do nothing till he was stronger, he must take this friendly advice.

That evening a letter was written to Florrie Baines, and on the following Monday, after lunch, Stephen and his landlady took train from Charing Cross for Margate. Jenny, who did not have many treats, was in a gay holiday mood and unusually talkative as they rolled through Dartford and Chatham, across the salt marshes of the estuary into the flatlands of Kent. Her chapped cheeks had a more than ordinary scrubbed look, they glowed, and her eyes held a vivacious sparkle. She had on a dark green velvet coat, its pile rather worn at the seams, but becoming, with a braided cape collar. On her feet she wore neat black button boots, and her small work-roughened hands were encased in freshly laundered white cotton gloves. Her hat, however, was a tragedy of shiny satin and incredible plumage which sat on the top of her head like some fabulous bird upon its nest. Stephen could not keep his eyes from it, indeed, so fascinated was his stare that Jenny smiled, gazing at him half confidentially.

"I see you like my toque. Such a bargain—the January sales. Red always was my colour.'"

"It's a really remarkable hat, Jenny. But do take it off. A cinder flying through the window might ruin it."

Obediently she complied, her newly washed hair was revealed, with its crinkling fringe, and she was herself again, natural and vivid, a small woman, stoutish, in a white cotton blouse, yet somehow little different, he thought, from the trim young girl who had swept his room and sewed on his buttons at the Settlement. Covertly, he watched her as, presenting in profile her short upper lip and tilted nose, holding in her lap for politeness, but unread, the woman's magazine he had bought her at the bookstall, she gazed with thrilled interest at the swift succession of windmills, oast-houses, and mellow brick barns flashing past.

"Look, Mr. Desmonde," she exclaimed, "these rows and rows of poles. They're for the hops."

"Are you interested in hops, Jenny?"

"I do occasionally fancy a glass of mild and bitter. That I will say," she answered seriously, then threw him a glance and laughed. "Nothing stronger, though."

In her cheerful Cockney accent, she kept the conversation going. Presently she got up, and taking her string bag from the luggage rack, unwrapped, quite unmindful of the two other occupants of the compartment, a packet of ham-and-tongue sandwiches.

"Come now, sir. You've no call to be shy," she insisted. "I promised the Captain I'd make you eat. Florrie will anyhow. One thing I will say of her, she keeps a good table. I hope you like fish."

"I do, Jenny," he answered, through a sandwich. "On that subject I have no anxiety. What does rather worry me, however, is whether the fishmonger, I mean Florrie, will like me."

"Florrie's all right. Got her head screwed on properly. Independent too. Manages everything, with a boy—Ernie Wood, her nephew. 'Ad a bit of sadness in her past. Suffers terrible from the cold. Her feet and all. You'll get along."

"I hope so."

"Of course, you mustn't expect too much . . . it's a small house."

"I hope I shan't strain the accommodation."

"Oh no, sir," she answered innocently. "I'll bunk in with Florrie. You shall have my bed."

As she gazed at him, her remark seemed to strike her oddly—a sudden violent blush overcame her. She averted her head and gazed out of the window in constrained silence.

But they were almost there. They drew into Margate at three in the afternoon, and immediately Stephen stepped on to the open platform he felt, like an electric shock, the tang and tingle of that magnificent air which, blending the rich ethers of river and ocean, of sand, shells, ripe seaweeds and healthy mud, provides for the humble visitors from London's East End an ozone, plebeian, doubtless, yet unsurpassable in all of England. As Jenny had hoped, Ernie, a small but smart-looking boy of fifteen, was at the station to meet them with the pony-cart. The baggage was bestowed between two empty haddock boxes and, mounted three abreast in front, they drove off to the old town.

Florrie's place was directly on the harbour, in the Row, a broken sweep of ancient and rather tumbledown buildings which smelled of tar and brine and faced, across the cobblestones, a confused vista of masts, rigging, cordage, barrels, boxes, and tidal silt, with the long stretch of the pier and the tumbling grey of the North Sea beyond. The shop, Number 49, though low and slanting, was painted bright blue, with a marble slab behind the pulled-up window, and a gilt sign which read FLORENCE BAINES: WET FISH: SHRIMPS AND COCKLES A SPECIALITY, while above, approached by a side stone staircase, were the living quarters of the establishment.

The visitors were shown by Ernie to the front parlour, snugly furnished with a moquette suite, and already set for a formal high tea, but containing no living occupant but a fine yellow cat. Ernie, however, immediately dashed below to relieve his aunt, who soon appeared, a spare and angular woman of forty, rolling down the sleeves of her cardigan over her bare, chilled arms. When she had kissed Jenny affectionately on the cheek, she examined Stephen across her prominent nose, offered a hand limp and cool as a fillet of sole.

"I expect you're ready for tea. Sit in and I'll infuse."

Moving actively, she brought from the back regions a large tray holding toast, teapot, and a sizzling platter of fried fish, then, seated erect at the table, began to serve her guests with a composure which plainly indicated that she, at least, had all her wits about her.

"And how are things, Florrie?" Jenny asked, having tasted her tea with a sigh of appreciation.

"Mustn't grumble. The stall is a worry."

"Always is, Florrie."

"Always."

"The silly old Town Council, I suppose?"

"And their permits. Think they can do anything with a woman."

"Still, you shall have it fixed in a couple of weeks."

"Nearer three, dear."

"Never mind. It's worth it, Florrie."

"Sometimes I wonder."

Florrie shook her head, despondent over her conflicts with official-dom, deploring the unjust domination of man, seeming, indeed, to brood darkly over all the misfortunes of her sex suffered and endured since the fall of Eve.

Jenny smiled at Stephen, bent on bringing him into the conversation.

"The summer trade is wonderful. And Florrie rents a pitch near the promenade. She's famous for her shrimps and cockles."

"I did think I had a name for flounder." Florrie looked hurt at the omission.

"Of course you have, dear."

"This we are having is most delicious," Stephen said, politely.

"Plaice," Florrie corrected gloomily. "Help yourself. Plenty more in the sea."

The meal was rich and ample, the room comfortable, the coal fire crackled cheerfully, yet it was apparent to Stephen that he was, and had been from the first, the object of his hostess's sharp suspicion. This caused him slight concern, yet for Jenny's sake, rather than his own, he felt he must try to dispel it. Mere politeness would, he guessed, never do this—rather the contrary in fact. But he had observed Florrie's fondness for the yellow cat, which as it sat on the arm of her chair she fed from time to time with morsels from her plate, and taking his sketch-book and a crayon from his pocket, he began, while the two women continued their terse yet intimate exchanges, to sketch the tawny animal.

Ten minutes and the thing was done. He removed the sheet, handed it in silence to Florrie.

"Well . . . I declare . . ." Surprise, indecision, fear of being taken in, doubt, incredulity, all these shades of feeling were reflected in her keen features until finally she yielded to her satisfaction. "It's as like Ginger as two peas. So you are an artist, after all."

278

"If it pleases you I hope you'll accept it."

"You'll never make a living if you give your things away."

Although reproving him with slight acidity, she was plainly pleased. Indeed, after tea, when he said he would go out for a brief walk alone, she called after him:

"Be careful of the wind. Margate looks straight out to the North Pole."

This geographic fact was accurate, but unlike Florrie, Stephen enjoyed the cold—it had always suited him. And now, on the sea-front promenade which, since the season had not begun, was deserted of trippers, he felt, through the lassitude of convalescence, the springs of vigour stir within him. The tonic air, stinging as iced champagne, filled his lungs without effort, brought a faint blood to his cheeks, braced and stimulated him. In his first flicker of optimism since the trial, he decided to attempt no work during the next two weeks—he would not even sketch or make colour notes, as he had intended, but would concentrate on clearing up once and for all this absurd bronchial condition which had plagued him at intervals during these past years. On the darkening promenade, alone in that universal greyness of sky and surf, with the wind humming and sighing in his ears like a great sea shell, the loose sand swirling and eddying about him, his pulse quickened, and raising his head he thought, brokenly:

"Perhaps . . . I'll still prove . . . that I am not beaten . . . after all."

CHAPTER XIV

In the days which followed, Stephen's spirits lifted further. How happy he was with these simple people whom the members of his own class would doubtless have looked down upon as "common". He, on the contrary, was at home with them, felt indeed that he was one of them. The salty life around the harbour, the comings and goings of the smacks, the unloading of the catch—all this interested him, diverted his mind from the bitterness of reflection. Early in the morning he accompanied Florrie to the fish market, noting the sharp success with which she made her bids by merely catching the eye of the auctioneer, whose hoarse voice fought a perpetual battle with the chatter of winches. He increased the length of his walks along the cliffs, slept with his window wide open to the breeze. Best of all was the bathing. Although this early in the year the water still reflected those polar influences to which Florrie had scathingly referred, Stephen was not deterred. Every forenoon he went in from the pier, joining those hardy natives who had formed an All the Year Round Club and who, one friendly member informed him, even took their swim when the snow lay on the beach. It was the brusque tonic of these briny immersions which, more than anything, accelerated Stephen's recovery, restored in him not the desire to paint alone but, most glorious of all, the surging knowledge and conviction of his own creative powers.

He was much alone—Florrie, when not occupied in the processes of securing her concession from the Corporation, was supervising the erection of her stall, Jenny had her hands full in the shop, while Ernie, every afternoon, made the "caller" round with the cart. But on Wednesday an excursion was proposed, *en famille*.

"Can you get away?" he inquired of Florrie.

"All work and no play makes Jack a dull boy," she answered cryptically, then, taking pity on his ignorance: "We close half-day Wednesday. So we'll go shrimping."

"Shrimping?"

"You heard me the first time. Aren't you always pestering me about them blinking shrimps? Well, now I shall show you where, when, and how we catch 'em. For your further information we shall boil a kettle and make tea. And if you want to freeze to death you can have one of your North Pole bathes. That suit you, Michael Angelo?"

"It sounds delightful, Florrie," he agreed amiably.

Florrie, at his tone, almost smiled in return. In a cautious manner, she had slightly softened towards him. She could not forget the drawing of Ginger, which, although studiously avoiding all reference to the matter, she had privately taken to W. H. Smith's to be passe-partouted. Moreover, Stephen's repeated offers to do duty in the shop had, though firmly rejected, inclined her to the view that he was not "stuck-up"—a view reinforced when, one evening, she had come in to find him in his shirt sleeves, washing up the supper dishes.

Wednesday arrived, overcast but dry. Punctually at two o'clock the shutters of the shop were put up and the party set off in the pony-cart, driving out of the town and along the east shore road towards Cliftonville. After about five miles, Ernie turned from the main highway to a lane which wound between hedges of budding hawthorn and ended in a grassy track passing through an osier gate into a field of burdock and rough sea-grass. Here the pony was unharnessed and turned loose to graze while Florrie, with an air of cicerone, led the way down through the tufted dunes to a small secluded sandy bay guarded by rocky promontories and open only to the sea.

"What a lovely spot!" exclaimed Stephen.

"Tide's on the turn, just right," noted the practical Ernie. "That's when you get them."

"You'll have a dip with me, boy?"

"Got to gather sticks and dig the cockles." Ernie excused himself, hastily moved off.

"I'm game," said Jenny, and at his look of surprise, burst out laughing. "Race you first in."

They undressed behind two not too adjacent rocks. Despite the supposed complexities of feminine attire, she reached the water before him and struck out through the surf.

"Where did you learn to swim?" With an effort he had made up on her.

"Joe Tapley's wharf. As kids we were off it all summer long."

She turned and floated with eyes closed. Rounded and young, she seemed quite unchanged by those years which had passed since first he knew her. He saw in her a freshness, a natural attractiveness which made him marvel that she had not found another husband. A sudden curiosity overcame his natural reserve.

"Jenny . . . why have you never married again?"

She sat up with a splash and a splutter, gazed at him, then shook her head.

"Never had the chance, I suppose. Well, yes . . . I'll admit. A few fellows have come messing around. But I couldn't fancy none of them." She smiled suddenly. "You know how it is, Mr. Desmonde. Once bitten twice shy."

Before he could speak she darted off towards the shore.

When they had put on their clothes, except for shoes and stockings, they walked barefoot to the sheltered side of the cove, where Florrie and Ernie were waiting with the shrimp-nets, each attached to a long pole with a wooden end bar, like a rake.

"Better late than never," Florrie greeted them caustically. "Take your net from Ernie. And if you're actually ready we'll begin."

Resting the wooden cross-bar on the serrated bottom, she started off through the shallow water, pushing the net before her, raising a smoky cloud of sand. Ernie and Jenny ranged themselves in line moving slowly behind, and a little further out, Stephen followed. In the clear water just ahead he could discern faintly the outlines of the

281

shrimps, gelatinous shapes almost invisible, with delicate antennæ. Quite translucent, transmitting only the mottled colour of the sand, each had a tiny jet-black eye which gave the frail organism substance, seemed to attune it to this common danger, which sent the whole school scurrying hither and thither in desperate mobility. Many escaped, but at the end of the drag, when the poles were upended, the nets held a reasonable haul.

"Bring the bucket, Ernie," Florrie commanded. "Only keep the biggest ones, turn the tiddlers back. And you three carry on. I'm going by the rocks for cockles."

The wind blew soft, the sun came out like a shiny orange, ankle-deep they ploughed their primal furrows, in the space of an hour the bucket was filled. Then, from the rocks, where a drift-wood fire smoked and sparked, came Florrie's shout. They joined her. A white cloth had been spread on a smooth dry ledge, weighted at the corners with round, streaky pebbles, the tea was made, and on the fire stood an iron pot of boiling water.

"I shall have chilblains after this," said Florrie, holding her blue toes to the blaze. Then, with a nod towards the shrimps: "In with them."

"Shame," murmured Jenny, with a little shiver as the squirming crustaceans disappeared in the steam. "Poor things."

"They don't feel nothing," Ernie reassured her. "Ain't got nerves like us. That so, Mr. Desmonde?"

Stephen, staring at Jenny, scarcely heard the question. All unconscious, she stood there, shrimp-net still on her shoulder, bare legs planted apart, slightly foreshortened, skirt tucked back, showing a clean flounced petticoat, blouse open at the throat, sleeves rolled back, her cheeks stung by sea and scudding sand to a bright vermilion, wind-tangled hair a deep blue-black, her figure, short and sturdy, bent slightly forward, turned against the dull and disappointing sunset. He had neither pencil nor paper, but he thought to himself, with an ache of desire, My God, if only I could paint her like that, with those fierce reds and blues and that smudged madder sky.

The tea was strong, dark as over-cooked meat, scalding hot. Florrie insisted they drink a mugful to take the chill off their stomachs. Then, with her eye on Stephen, she served the cockles, noting with a knowing compression of her lips the surprise which he evinced on tasting them.

"Never thought they'd be so good, eh?" she chided him. "Swallow the juice as well."

"Beats oysters hollow," agreed Ernie, laying in.

They were delicious—each in its white fluted shell, delicate and saline, a fresh sea-fruit, holding the essence of the ocean, perhaps the first act of creation.

Next came the shrimps, straight from the pot, a tender pink, shedding their armour without a murmur, crescentic, succulent. They ate them with thick slabs of cottage loaf spread with country butter. More tea. Then a cheesecake which Jenny had baked the previous evening. A silence followed, intensified by the slow, rhythmic rustle of the incoming tide. No one seemed to want to move—in a strange and glowing mood of indolence, watching the pale moon take substance in the still clear sky, Stephen wished this lovely hour might not quickly end. But at last Florrie stirred.

"Getting dark. Better make a bend."

The picnic things were gathered up, the pony re-harnessed, the lamp-candles lit, Florrie and Ernie took their seats in front. Stephen, already in the cart, held out his hand to pull Jenny up to her place beside him in the back. He clasped her fingers tightly, drew her towards him. And in that simple act, as by a lighting stroke, he experienced the liberation of an emotion that had burgeoned within him throughout the afternoon, a physical sweetness in the pressure of her dry, warm skin, a flooding tide of intoxication which made his heart turn over with a tremendous throb and—so unexpected was its onset, so violent its intensity—left him speechless.

Ernie jogged the reins, they set off at a steady amble. Because of the basket, which restricted space, Jenny and Stephen were obliged to sit close together. From the soft contact of her thigh and side, waves of warm vitality seemed to flow into him. Not for years, not since his futile pursuit of Emmy Berthelot, had he looked at a woman with desire. It had died within him; self-discipline, perhaps, had killed it, destined him to an existence of perpetual celibacy. But now, not to save his life could he have spoken a coherent word. Was she conscious, he wondered blindly, of the longing which had suddenly stricken him? Could it be that she shared the same emotion? She too was extremely silent, perhaps over-consciously still. And that throbbing pulse, where their limbs met in the darkness, was it from the pounding of his blood? Or was hers pounding too?

They drew into the town, which welcomed them with a glitter of lights, reflected on the oily water of the harbour. And as they approached the quay Florrie exclaimed prosaically:

"These there shrimps do give you a thirst. Shall we stop at the Dolphin for a mild and bitter?"

283

"Let's," said Ernie. "I'll have a mineral."

"You ain't allowed in such places, not under eighteen."

"But Aunt Flo . . ."

"No," said Florrie firmly. "I'd forgot about you. We shall have something at home."

They drew up at the end of the Row, where the stable was situated, and as Ernie, somewhat peeved, pressed Jenny to stay while he unharnessed the pony, Florrie and Stephen set out for the shop alone. As they walked slowly along the quay, Stephen, still deeply disturbed, was conscious of his companion's sidelong scrutiny.

"Been a real good day," she began conversationally.

He gave a murmur of assent.

"Jenny's a nice little thing," Florrie resumed, without apparent continuity. "She's wise, yet she's simple. Works hard . . . had a bit of a struggle too. As for kind-heartedness! I do hope she'll make up with a fine steady fellow one of these days . . . I should hate to see her make a mistake. Someone with a good regular wage, as would take proper care of her."

There was a pause. Then again, in that same detached voice, as though thinking aboud:

"For instance . . . there's a local feller by the name of Hawkins, half owner in a brand-new trawler . . . worth a tidy bit. We'd p'raps have met him if we'd went to the Dolphin. Sociable feller. Throws a beautiful dart . . . he's pretty gone on her."

He kept silence, not knowing how to answer. Although her tone was casual, he sensed behind it a note of warning. At any rate, her meaning was clear, he could not dispute it.

They went up the stone stairs and into the house. In the kitchen she turned to him with a brightness which convinced him that her remarks had been deliberate.

"How about a sandwich? And a drop of ale?"

No, at this moment he could not remain to face Jenny in a false, convivial atmosphere. He forced a smile.

"I'm rather tired, I think I'll turn in. Good-night, Florrie."

He went to his room, closed the door and stood for a long moment in perturbed thought, from which, almost automatically, he tried to rouse himself, reaching for his sketch-book, telling himself he must record that beach impression while it was still fresh in his mind. Using crayon, he made, during the next hour, several pastel drawings, but none of them pleased him and, in the end, with a kind of nervous exasperation, he put the book away, began to undress.

In bed, he switched off the light, stretched at full length in the cool sheets. Through the wide, open window, lit by an invisible moon, he could see a swathe of milky sky in which the Dog Star hung, low and placid. But there was no placidity in him. His skin, smarting from the strong air, seemed on fire.

Presently, footsteps sounded next door, and through the thin wall he heard the quiet movements, the low-toned conversation of the two women as they prepared to retire. Abruptly, he covered his ears with the pillow. Yet if he could occlude the sounds of Jenny's disrobing—the click of corsets unhooked, the snap of an elastic, the tap of heels as she stepped from her petticoat—that sunset vision which by some strange alchemy, fusing with wind, sea and sand, had made an image, clear and shining as Venetian glass, that was less easy to dismiss. At last, drugged with air, his mind clouded, he fell asleep.

CHAPTER XV

His two weeks' stay would end on Saturday, he was due to leave in three days' time. And he believed that, by an effort of will, and the exercise of some self-control, he might get through this brief period without making a fool of himself. So he set himself to work on a series of marine impressions. On Thursday he took a block of handmade paper, matt-surfaced and of a soft yellow shade, which he had found in a second-hand book-shop off the Row, and went to the inner harbour. He began a gouache, showing a low line of tied-up smacks, two trawlers beyond, and on either side, leading the eye inwards, nets drying on weathered wooden piles. But his heart was not in it, even before it was half done he knew he had something as insipid as a Christmas calendar. After wasting two sheets of his precious paper he went moodily to the Dolphin and, sitting alone in a corner, lunched on bread and cheese and a pint of shandygaff.

The afternoon was no better—the sun kept dodging amongst the clouds, his touch was not swift enough to catch the fleeting play of light, and just as he began his fourth attempt the trawlers cast off and steamed out of the pool, leaving a gap in the composition like an extracted front tooth. He gave up in disgust. Yet he would not go back to the shop, but instead, with the block under his arm, hands in his pockets and shoulders hunched, he hung around the old town, staring into the windows of marine stores, presumably appraising the stock-in-trade of ships' chandlers, rope-and-tackle-makers, purveyors of heavy-duty kerosene motors, simply killing time.

Was he seriously in love? The situation seemed so manifestly impossible, he was forced to reject it, telling himself that he was thirty, temporarily fit, perhaps, but subject to a recurrent weakness of the chest, disowned by his family, with scarcely a shilling in his pocket, bound irrevocably to that profitless mistress, art. And Jenny? . . . she herself was no longer a girl, however much his fancy might deceive him, but a working-class woman approaching middle age, short of stature, blousy-cheeked, quite uneducated, with no more knowledge of painting than an Esquimo, and a hideous taste in hats. Besides, hadn't he been warned off, with tactful insistence, by Florrie? Then in the name of sanity, let him put her from his mind. But for all his show of logic, he could not.

In desperation, he set out for a brisk walk along the front. As he was passing the Grand Hotel, which occupied a central position on the promenade, a man in a bowler and a seedy overcoat with a velvet collar, carrying a square black bag, emerged from the swing doors and came towards him. Something in the figure, in the swing of the shoulders, was vaguely familiar, and indeed as they approached each other there came an instant of mutual recognition.

"Dash it all, if it isn't Desmonde! What a surprise. Fancy seeing you again, old boy."

It was Harry Chester. Seizing Stephen's hand, he shook it effusively, expressing his satisfaction at the encounter and remarking on the strangeness of chance and the smallness of the world.

"I was in the Grand having a quick one, thought I'd have another, but didn't. If I had, I should never have run into you. Providence, old boy. Nothing else."

He had put on weight since their last meeting, there was a roll of fat at the back of his neck, and his tight waistcoat, of a sporting check, failed to conceal the beginnings of portliness. His face, though still quite handsome, was coarsened, and while his eyes beamed with that same heartiness, they held a shiftiness that would have been suspect even to a stranger.

"Come along back in. You must have one with me."

They went into the bar of the hotel, where Chester smiled at the barmaid and, his foot automatically seeking the brass rail, tilted back his hat.

"What'll it be, then? Glass of bitter. I'll have a Scotch and splash."

"What brings you to Margate?" Stephen asked, when, at last, he had an opportunity to speak.

"Business, my boy. The south coast is my beat. I do all the hotels on that circuit."

"You've given up painting?"

"Good Lord, yes. Long ago. There comes a tide in the affairs of men . . . Shakespeare, old boy . . . I have a job . . . and a damned good one. . . ." He delivered the fiction with an affable smile, stroking his unshaven chin. "Promoting the cleanliness of the nation."

"In what way?"

"I sell soap, old boy . . . for Gluckstein Brothers. Damn good firm. I'm well in with them . . . in line for a partnership, in fact." Glancing in the mirror, he adjusted his tie, which, Stephen now observed, openly advertised the improvement in Harry's position—it bore the old Etonian pale-blue stripes. "It's nice work. I enjoy travel."

There was a silence. Despite the jollity, the oozing good-fellowship, there were lines at the corners of Chester's eyes and his charm, like the nap on his velvet coat collar, had worn a trifle thin. His nails, for a man with the country's hygiene at heart, were lamentably dirty.

"Do you hear anything of Lambert?" Stephen asked, after a pause.

"Philip?" Chester looked portentous. "He's come rather a cropper. Elise left him, you know. Went off with an Australian officer in the war. Last thing I heard of Philip he was designing wallpaper for some potty little firm in Chantilly." He paused, and shook his head. "Of course . . . you know about Emmy?"

"No."

"Good God, man. Don't you read the newspapers? One night, about six months after you left, she went up for her act. They said at the inquest that the track was wet, not well enough lit, but she'd been out to supper and in my opinion it was she who was too well lit. In any event she flubbed the take-off, lost her balance in the air, landed on her head, and broke her neck."

Stephen was silent. Although he knew Chester as a sensational liar, he could not doubt but that this was true. Yet the news, while it shocked him, had a strange remoteness, as though it merely marked the closure of an episode so long forgotten it was already dead. Nor had he time to dwell upon it, for at once Chester had resumed talking about himself, less with outright deceit than with that curious undaunted self-deception that ignored his position as a cheap commercial traveller working on commission, forgot the unpaid debts, the cadged loans, the drinks sponged from friends, glossed over the one-night stands in cheap hotel rooms, the jobs he had already been thrown out of, and almost gave reality to his bogus assumption of the superior old-school tie, his sham of high prosperity. Beyond a few perfunctory inquiries he had no apparent interest in Stephen's doings. In a fashion there was something almost to admire, a quality near to the heroic, in this breezy charlatanism, never for an instant yielding to depression or the bitter shafts of truth. But suddenly, with a glance at the clock above the bar, Chester broke off.

"Good Lord," he exclaimed. "Half-past six. I've only seven minutes to catch my train for Folkestone. I must run. Good-bye, old man. Been wonderful seeing you. Thanks for the drink." Resetting his bowler to a more rakish angle, he shook hands, nodded to the barmaid, and swinging his black bag of samples, went off with a swagger.

In a thoughtful manner Stephen paid the reckoning and made his way through the falling darkness to the Row. This accidental meeting, with its reminders of that early period in France, brief perhaps, yet filled with self-delusion, had thrown into more vivid relief his present reality. After Chester's shallow dash it was a relief to contemplate the cheerful ordinariness that he would find in the warm kitchen of No. 49. His indeterminate mood had gone, he mounted the steps with sudden briskness.

Within, Ernie sat at the table—Jenny was busy at the stove.

"Thank goodness," she greeted him with a cheerful face. "I been keeping your supper and was just worrying it would spoil. We've had ours a good half-hour."

The warmth of her welcome, the glow in the homely little room, touched him like a blessing. He sat down beside Ernie, who was bowed studiously over the weekly periodical known as *Comic Cuts*.

Tipping open the oven door with her foot, Jenny took a dish-towel, brought out a deep platter of shepherd's pie, placed it on the table, one half of which she had kept covered with a cloth.

"Mind, it's hot. Move over, Ernie, with your Latin and Greek."

When he sat down and began to eat—the pie was steaming and savoury, with a thick russet crust of toasted potatoes—she took the chair opposite, observing his appetite with approval.

"Been working?"

"Trying to . . . then I went round the harbour."

"It's done you good. You have picked up down here."

"I'm a new man, Jenny. And owe it all to you."

"Garn. Try these pickled onions. Florrie has her permit. Old Councillor Stick-in-the-Mud finally obliged."

"That's good news."

"She came in at four. Let me off minding the shop for the evening. That's why I come up and cooked you the pie. Like it?"

He answered by passing his plate for a second portion.

"I'll help you with the dishes."

"There's nothing to do. Only yours. Won't take a minute."

As she cleared the table he went into his room, washed, came back into the kitchen. She had finished drying the dishes and, with a steaming vapour rising from her hands, now hung the wrung-out cloth on the side of the sink. Her gaze fell upon the chuckling Ernie.

"You'll have brain fever, Ern, if you study so hard. How's Weary Willy this week?"

"Perfect scream. I'm reading slow to make him last."

"I thought you was going to the pictures?"

"Not me. It ain't a cowboy this week."

There was a pause. A sudden idea came to Stephen as he sat with his hands in his pockets on the edge of the dresser.

"You wouldn't care to come to the cinema, Jenny?"

She gave him a quick smile, but shook her head.

"Oh, do come."

"I'm not one for the pictures really. Especially a beautiful night like this." She glanced through the window. "It is lovely out. Clear and mild."

Following her gaze, he saw the round silver moon rising over the harbour pool, and sensing her inclination, he said:

"Then let's take a walk."

Her smile deepened, she looked really pleased.

"Would be nice, a stroll, after being cooped in all day. I'll have my coat on in a jiffy."

She kept him waiting barely a minute, then, enjoining Ernie, who paid not the slightest heed, to keep the stove in, and let Aunt Florrie know they'd be back in half an hour, she led the way downstairs and they set off along the quay towards the promenade. The night was superb, warm and clear, the moon, enthroned by glittering planets, at its dazzling full, the milky way a path of lambent silver. As they passed the Dolphin he glanced at her inquiringly.

"Like a spot of something?"

But again, she made a gesture of negation.

K

289

"I couldn't fancy it somehow. Too nice out. Such a moon . . . and stars."

Indeed, when they reached the promenade the string of lights seemed a pale necklace in competition with the stellar brilliance. On the benches, lovers sat no more than holding hands, as though bedazzled and bemused by the lack of shadow. The sea moved in a shimmer of sequins, a great sea-serpent rustling its scales. Too quickly they came to the end of the esplanade and, hesitant, yet unwilling to cut short these miraculous moments by turning back immediately, Stephen said:

"It's so light, shall we go along the sands?" She made no objection and as they stepped out on the wide waste of sand exposed by the receding tide, he reflected aloud: "You know, Jenny, this is the first time we've ever been out alone together."

"Funny." She laughed uncertainly. "Haven't had the opportunity. Chance is a fine thing."

"Yet I feel as if I'd known you all my life."

The words, expressing the comfort he derived from her companionship, were wrung from him. She made no reply. And in silence they continued over the smooth firm beach upon which white shells, half buried, gleamed like fallen stars. Behind them, the town receded distantly, bathed in liquid light; they were alone on the deserted shore.

At last, reluctantly, he felt they had gone far enough. Yet he could not bear the thought of going back. He turned to her.

"Let's rest a little, and look at the moon."

They found a sheltered hollow in the dunes, protected by rough grass, but open to the singing sky and the sighing sea.

"You should have your overcoat," she said. "It might be damp. Take shares of mine." And, solicitously, she opened her coat and spread out half of it for him to sit on.

"It is a shame we have to leave day after tomorrow," she murmured presently. "Margate is nice this time of year."

"I have certainly enjoyed it."

There was a pause.

"I suppose you've made your plans."

"Well . . . in a way."

She did not look at him, her gaze was straight ahead.

"I shouldn't wish to seem pushing, sir, and you know it's not for the money, but I was hoping you'd keep your room on for a while. You did say you was going to paint the river. With you and Captain Tapley in the house there's such a nice settled feeling."

"I should like to stay a bit. But I ought to be on the move again."

"It's terrible the way you've lived, alone, no house, travelling about, no one to look after you." There was distress in her voice. "Do you really have to?"

He did not answer. The warmth of her body, so near to him, and so alive, was more than he could endure. All at once an irresistible wave of feeling burst over him. Unable to resist, he passed an arm under her coat and firmly around her waist. Immediately her flow of conversation ceased, he felt a sudden strained tension in her figure.

"You shouldn't do that, sir," she protested, in a low voice.

"For God's sake don't call me sir, Jenny." He could scarcely speak the words. And suddenly he kissed her, with a fierce hard pressure of his mouth. Her lips were full and dry, slightly roughened, warm as a plum on a sunny wall. Under the unexpectedness of his embrace, she bent away, lost her balance, and fell upon her back. There she lay, on the soft sand, as though defenceless, looking upwards, the moon reflected in her eyes.

His heart was beating like mad, never had he felt such a surge of wild emotion. Anything he had known before, those moments of fondness for Claire, his senseless infatuation for Emmy—all were nothing compared to this sweet intoxication. He had believed himself a strange, unnatural being to whom the happiness of requited love was eternally forsworn. It was false. Leaning on his side, he slipped his hand inside the open neck of her dress, cupped in his palm one soft breast. Warmer than her lips, richly veined, it seemed to flutter beneath his fingers like a pinioned bird. His touch was gentle, yet, with the movement of his wrist, the buttons of her bodice had opened and, with a sigh, almost of anguish, he placed his cheek against the smooth white cleft as though beseeching her for solace. Oh, God, he thought, this was what I wanted, needed, longed for, this is the remedy, the eternal Lethe, to pillow one's head upon this woman's soft, dove-like breast, to find oblivion in her arms.

Now he could feel the trembling of her body, sense with answering joy the yielding weakness of her limbs. Supported by his elbow, anguished himself, yet draining to the full this foretaste of delight, he looked downwards, saw that her breath came quickly, that her eyes were tightly shut. Her face seemed small, contracted as by pain, her lashes cast moon-shadows upon cheeks suddenly pinched and careworn. When he touched her lips again she fiercely returned his kiss, then, with a shiver, in one last faint futile protest, tossed her head aside.

"No . . . not fair," she muttered. "Not on a night like this."

In answer he held her close. And now her arms reached out and twined themselves about his neck. Her lips sought his, opened, invited. The earth spun, the moon went out. An instant, inevitable as death. And then peace, warmth, and silence . . . a long silence, wherein they lay, not moving, in each other's arms.

At last, a tear trickled from her cheek to his, made him raise his head, pillowed in her neck, look into her eyes.

"Jenny, what's the matter?"

Her voice, conscience-stricken, muffled by his shoulder, reached him faintly.

"That's twice now, in my life. And this time I can't even blame it on the drink."

"You don't regret it? You do care for me?"

"You know I do." She clung to him with renewed fierceness. "I always have. Always . . . from the first. Even with Alf I used to think on you. Oh, I shouldn't have then, nor now either . . . serve me right . . . me that's not even married."

He had to stifle a wild, frantic desire to laugh. He took up her small hand, gritty with sand, and held it tight.

"Don't worry, Jenny. If you'll have me, we'll get a certificate tomorrow at the registry office. We're in for it now, for better or worse, you and I together."

PART FIVE

CHAPTER I

On that autumn morning in the year 1928, before the first pencil of light had penetrated the darkness of the back ground-floor bedroom in Cable Street, Stephen awoke. For a while he lay still, conscious of the solid form of his wife beside him, of her regular breathing, then, without disturbing her, he got up and dressed silently, knowing by instinct where his clothes lay on the chair, his flannel undervest, serge trousers, and the thick blue woollen jersey she had knitted for him. Then, in his stocking feet, he went out and along the passage, knocked sharply three times on Joe Tapley's door, and entered the kitchen.

The gas-ring exploded mildly under the kettle, already filled, upon the stove. On the table, everything was prepared, as usual. In ten minutes, when the Cap'n joined him, they sat down to a breakfast of hot tea, bread and dripping, and sausage. They ate without speech until they had almost finished. Then Tapley said:

"Wind's from the west."

Stephen nodded, and bent forward to the old man's ear.

"We ought to get that cloud effect this morning."

"There'll be a chop on—hope that outboard behaves. I don't hold with them things at all."

"It spares your lumbago."

"Bah, I'll take oars any day."

Stephen rose, filled a fresh cup of tea and took it to the bedroom, where, covering the cup with the saucer, he placed it on the table by the bed—sometimes the catch on the front door awakened her. Back in the kitchen, he put on his boots, looked warningly at Tapley, who was beginning to trifle with his pipe.

"We'll have to hurry."

"I'm ready."

Closing the tricky door with only the lightest slam, they went out together, walking free and unencumbered—all the gear was in the shed at the wharf.

The house remained silent behind them. But at half-past six the alarm clock whirred, Jenny opened her eyes, blinked at the cup of

293

tea beside her, felt it to be stone-cold. Reproachfully, she shook her head, and immediately got up. The room was still bathed in crepuscular greyness—the wooden lean-to which Stephen had built for a studio blocked some part of the early light—and as she dressed, slipping her arms through her camisole, stepping into her pink woollen drawers, briskly, yet deftly and, despite her short, thickened figure, with unconscious grace, she hoped he had got down to Greenwich before dawn.

Quickly, she "got the house going"—her own phrase—and by eight o'clock she had breakfasted, aired the two ground-floor beds, lit the fire beneath the scullery boiler, and taken up Miss Pratt's morning tray. At a quarter to nine Miss Pratt, now the permanent occupant of the upstairs back room, went off to her infants' class at the Stepney Board School. Jenny tidied up, made all the beds, and putting her head out of the back door in exploratory fashion, noted with personal satisfaction the fresh drying breeze. Today, Monday, was her wash-day.

As she sorted out the linen and popped the things into the copper boiler, without knowing it, and quite without skill, she began to sing. It was her nature to be happy. But beyond that, she counted herself a lucky woman to be privileged to love and serve this extraordinary man who had married her. She did not, and never would completely understand him. She did not try, but watched him in all his moods, in his silences, exaltations and depressions—so different from her own balanced common sense—with tender and possessive wonder. His carelessness in respect to meals, clothing, and conventional obligations made her shake her head. To think that a man for whom she had packed a nourishing lunch would forget about it, then, driven by hunger, dash into a baker's shop, buy a loaf of bread and break off and eat pieces of it as he walked along, passed all understanding.

Yet his desire to paint she looked upon with kindly tolerance. It was a gentlemanly occupation that befitted him, gave him pleasure and relaxation—it was "something for him to do". His especial preoccupation with the river she thoroughly approved, since it took him out of the house into the good fresh air. For if she had a worry— and at certain moments she would pause in the middle of her work, while an anxious wrinkle gathered between her brows—it was the condition of his health . . . she did not like that cough, now so permanent it seemed a part of him, and which indeed he completely ignored.

But today she was too busy to worry. When her washing was

294

pegged out and blowing lustily on the clothes-line in the yard, she made her lunch—toasted cheese on bread, and that indispensable, a strong cup of tea. Then she took off her wrapper and put on her second-best dress, picked up a basket and went down the street. The Glyns were coming to supper; she had fixed on a nice vegetable stew and, after some discussion with the butcher and the rejection of several cuts, she secured a piece that satisfied her. Afterwards she visited the grocer's and the dairy, enjoying the shop windows as she went, examining from fresh angles a three-piece suite in the East London Emporium she had long had her eye upon for the parlour. Presently she was back in her house, had cut up the meat and chopped the vegetables. The thought of the evening's entertainment pleased her—she liked Anna, who was just "her sort", and who managed like a proper housewife the little house in Tite Street that Glyn, lapsing into respectability, had bought four years ago after he had regularized their relationship and married her. She knew, too, that it did Stephen good to see Richard, who, apart from Cap'n Tapley, was now his only friend, indeed, the only person for whom he would consent to break his fixed and solitary routine.

Thus far, the day had followed a normal pattern—quiet, agreeable and supremely ordinary. But towards two o'clock, as she made to take in the dry clothes, the front-door bell pealed. For a moment she thought it was the afternoon postman with a letter from Margate— Florrie had lately been a regular correspondent, with news of young Ernie, about to be articled to a solicitor.

However, when she answered the summons, a taxi was disappearing round the corner and before her stood a spare, clean-shaven man in a somewhat worn fawn trench-coat. He raised his hat.

"Is Mr. Desmonde at home?"

"No," she said, studying him. Then she added: "He'll not be back till evening."

"I wonder if I might talk with you for a moment. My name is Maddox. Charles Maddox. You, I am quite sure, are Mrs. Desmonde. I am, or rather I used to be, your husband's agent."

She hesitated. It was far from her custom to admit strange gentlemen to her house, yet his manner, open and direct, was not that of one desirous of selling unwanted articles.

"Please come in," she said.

In the little front parlour, spotless and chilly, with its moquette furniture, upright piano, and potted fern in the window, she faced him guardedly, though predisposed in his favour by the thoroughness with which he had wiped his boots on the outside mat.

"Can I get you a cup of tea?"

"I should appreciate it, if it is not too much trouble'"

Without flurry, she brought him tea and hot buttered toast.

"This is good of you. I've been on the go all the forenoon and missed my lunch." He paused. "Won't you join me?"

"No thank you." She declined a little primly, thinking that such informality would be going a little too far. "The weather has turned fine at last."

"Yes, it's a beautiful day."

There was a pause.

"Mrs. Desmonde." He spoke with sudden resolution, after he had accepted a second cup. "You seem to be a most sensible person, and I particularly want your help. I have come here this afternoon to ask you to persuade your husband to permit me to handle his work."

"But you said you was his agent."

"A nominal title, I am afraid. I have not in eight years had a single Desmonde canvas in my gallery. While I am sure"—he threw a quick glance of interrogation—"in his studio there are scores."

"Yes," she answered mildly, still rather at a loss. "They're all out there. But he won't part with them. He's told me so. After they used him so bad, he vowed he'd never show another picture in his life."

"That was long enough ago, and since then there's been a lot of water under the bridges. Mrs. Desmonde"—he leaned slightly forward—"art is a curious affair, it proceeds in a straight line for a certain number of years, then strikes off at a tangent. At one time your husband's paintings were practically unsaleable. Now, because of information I have from Paris, I have good reason to believe that they would find a select and discriminating market."

He had hoped to evoke from her a start of pleasure and surprise. Instead she smiled equally, not in the least impressed, least of all by the mention of the foreign city, which struck her as ridiculous.

"Would that make such a difference?"

"But of course. Why, financially . . . it might make a very considerable difference."

"My husband," she articulated the word with a kind of tender pride, "my husband don't care a button for money. And bar what he needs for his paints, he never spends a penny on himself."

"Yet as an independent character, and I well know he's that"—Maddox floundered slightly but went on, bent on making his point—"surely it must be rather humiliating for him to . . . well . . . if you'll forgive me . . . to be supported by you."

"He don't never give it a thought," Jenny answered firmly. "And

I shouldn't never hope he would." She drew herself up. "What I have is as much his as mine, Mr. Maddox, and it's quite enough for both of the two of us. There's this house, bought and paid for, and our two steady lodgers, to say nothing of as good as thirty pounds what we have in the Building Society. We couldn't be more comfortable if we tried."

"Nevertheless," he still insisted, though rather lamely, "a larger income could make things much easier." He glanced round the frightful little parlour, wondering at the same time how a person of Desmonde's taste and susceptibilities could bear to live in it. "You could have a . . . a larger home. Then, I'm sure you work terribly hard. You could have help in the house . . . a good servant."

She laughed outright, mirthfully, charmingly, as though he had made an excellent joke.

"I *was* a servant, Mr. Maddox, and I hope a good one. As for my work, I'd be miserable if I didn't 'ave it. I tell you straight, I shouldn't be 'appy if we lived any different than we do now. And what's more, I promise you, we shouldn't be one half so cosy."

Completely floored, he gazed at her in silence and, despite his defeat, with growing respect. The hideous black imitation marble timepiece on the mantelpiece indicated twenty-five minutes past two o'clock.

"In the meantime," he ventured, "I suppose I couldn't look round the studio?"

Her refusal was a masterpiece of kindly diplomacy. Indeed, his diffident manner and unprosperous appearance, which made her regard him as someone trying rather hopelessly to make a living by means so impractical as to verge on the fantastic, had already aroused her sympathy.

"It might p'raps be as well to speak to Mr. Desmonde first."

"I have spoken to him." His manner indicated how unproductive that approach had been. After a short silence he picked up his hat and rose. "You might be good enough to tell him that I called."

"I certainly shall. But I shouldn't build too much on it if I was you."

When he had gone Jenny returned to the kitchen, stood for a moment in puzzled thought, then, with a shake of her head, dismissing the matter from her mind, she went to take in her washing.

At five o'clock the door-bell rang again and, changed and ready, she hurried to admit her visitors.

"I'm so sorry," she said, when she had greeted them. "Stephen isn't home yet."

"We're ahead of time." Glyn hung his hat and scarf on the hall stand. "By the way, did you have a call today from the agent, Maddox?"

"Yes," Jenny said guardedly. "A Mr. Charles Maddox."

"You let him have a couple of Stephen's paintings, I hope?"

"Good gracious, no. I couldn't 'ave done that without permission." She smiled. "It would 'ave been as much as my place was worth!"

"I see," said Glyn and paused. "Well, you two women can get together and gossip. I'll go into the studio."

He went directly through the kitchen and across the flagged back area, found the key under the mat and entered the ramshackle wooden shed where Stephen worked. Completely bare of furnishings, except for a broken-backed Victorian horsehair sofa along one wall, without even a stove, the place was uncomfortably chilly, but it was dry, and had an excellent north light. On an easel in the centre of the floor was a large incomplete painting of the river, while at the further end a stack of canvases of assorted sizes, all unframed, stood untidily together.

Richard took a good look at the unfinished work, meanwhile charging his pipe with plug tobacco, then, having lit up, he removed the painting, placed another from the stack upon the easel and sat down on the broken sofa to study it. After five minutes he again changed the canvas, re-seated himself, and resumed his meditative inspection—a process he repeated several times.

In all of Glyn's movements there was a thoughtful deliberation, an air of maturity intensified by his heavy frame and massive head. At fifty, that earlier fiery intensity, the untamed Bohemian spirit that made him flout orthodoxy and snap his fingers at authority, had been subdued, or rather mellowed, by a genuine and well-merited success. His work in its sureness, its combination of freedom and dignity, had been accepted, rightly, as a worthy contribution to English art. No longer a vagabond, but a settled householder in Chelsea, married, a member of the Academy council, who had come to enjoy his position, he was, in a sense, in conflict with himself. Yet now, as he pondered over Stephen's work in its opulence and audacity of colour, its prophetic disregard of the conventional rules of anatomy and perspective, its richness and subtlety of texture—the hard bone of the compositions hidden by a masterly execution of scumbles and glazes—in its sense of mystery, of something implied, always withheld, he knew that whatever the change in himself, at heart he was still the champion of the outlaw, upholder of the banner of revolt. The paintings in this wooden shack were, he realized, calmly, and without jealousy, not only far superior to his own, they were fit to hang, in their magnificent execution and originality, in company with the great. And as he considered how, during these past seven years, Desmonde had laboured without ceasing, unknown, unheard of, leading the life of an ascetic, a recluse, buried in this East End Dockland slum, refusing all contact with the world, nursing a sense of persecution that even with its basis of reality was dangerous in the extreme, he felt that it was time to act, to break at last this sustained complex of withdrawal. He had come today with the fixed intention of making this decision, and because of the pattern of his own later years, the solidity of his present position, his thoughts inevitably moved in one direction. Recognition—that was the solution. It had done much for him. It would do everything for Desmonde. Useless of course to speak to Stephen. He had tried that more than once without success. He had known of Maddox's visit this afternoon—had been in consultation with the agent beforehand —and now that it had obviously failed in its purpose, he saw that he must act upon his own initiative.

With a frown of determinaton he rose, picked up a painting he had already singled out—*Hampstead Heath*—then, with brown paper and a piece of string, wrapped it up. Moving with unusual lightness, he went out, locked the studio and, using the area door, stepped into the back alley. In three minutes he was at the corner pub, the Good Intent, and after drinking a glass of ale, asked the barman to hold the package until he returned later that evening. It was not quite six o'clock when, quite unobserved, he got back to the yard and entered the kitchen.

Stephen, who had just arrived, came forward to meet him. As they shook hands, Glyn could not help thinking how great was the change in his friend since the days when he had first known him at the Slade. It was not his thinness alone, which emphasized all his facial bones and made deep hollows in his temples. Standing there, erect, as by an effort of will, in his rough paint-stained clothes, an old scarf draped across his shoulders, with his long bony hands and one cheek smudged with soot from a river tug, he conveyed the impression of a man supported by nothing but his own intensity. But the high colour on his cheekbones and the extraordinary brightness of his eyes saved him, gave to his expression a vivid sense of life.

"Had a good day?" Glyn asked.

"Not bad. I've been down at Greenwich since morning."

"How is old mother Thames coming along?"

"I'm having trouble with her—as usual. What have you been doing lately?"

Richard hesitated, fingered his watch-chain—no longer a frayed length of picture-cord but a gold Albert of admirable solidity, weighted by a cornelian charm, the gift of a satisfied sitter.

"As a matter of fact I'm starting a portrait of Lord Hammerhead."

"You're doing lots of portraits now. Is this another commission?"

"Yes."

"I seem to remember the name. Isn't he the brewer?"

"Well . . . that is one of his interests."

"And art is another? These are the fellows who keep painting alive."

From under his brows Glyn glanced sideways, a trifle suspiciously, wondering if there was not the slightest irony in the other's tone, but Desmonde's expression had remained open and cheerful. A pause followed, then Jenny, her face reddened by the stove, came forward with a steaming dish and, placing it on the table, cheerfully bade them be seated.

It was a plain but satisfying meal, the savoury stew served with potatoes in their jackets, a home-baked plum cake and a deep bowl of stewed apricots adding variety to the main course. Glyn, whose enjoyment of good food had increased with the years, and who showed evidence of this in his growing corpulence, set to heartily, yet despite his preoccupation he could not but remark how indifferent was Stephen's appetite. He seemed neither to know nor care what he was eating, and only Jenny's attentiveness kept his plate supplied. But his mood was unusually light-hearted, the beauty and life in his eyes were irresistible as he described in detail how, after a barge had almost run him down in mid-stream, he had engaged in argument with the skipper.

"It was a good slanging match," he concluded gaily. "After it I completely lost my voice."

"What!" exclaimed Jenny, with a glance towards him.

"It was nothing. When I'm working I've no need to talk." Stephen turned to Glyn with a smile. "Tapley is almost stone-deaf. Often I don't open my mouth from the time I leave this house till I get back."

Glyn, with a sweep of his fork, made a gesture of disapproval.

"It's unnatural," he said. "You're like Anna. Sometimes I scarcely get a word out of her all day."

Anna looked up, subdued, as always, and serious, but with an enigmatic upturn of her lips.

"That was the first condition you made when I came to live with you."

"Came to live!" Glyn protested. "Can't you ever remember you're a respectable married woman now?"

"Sometimes I think we have become too respectable."

"What d'you mean? Don't you enjoy your position a little? Look at the people you meet."

"Oh, we meet lots of people. We dress up and go to receptions where we stand all the time and can't hear ourselves talk. We attend public dinners, sit in a draught, listen to long, pompous speeches. We are very much engaged. But we had more fun in Paris when you used to throw your boots at me and tell me I was just a slut."

Stephen burst out laughing, but Jenny seemed a trifle shocked and Glyn himself looked distinctly put out.

"You're unjust, Anna. We're older now. We have a certain standing, duties to be undertaken, responsibilities that must be accepted." He turned to Stephen. "This kind of life you've fallen into . . . it isn't right. It's not good for you. We must get you out of it."

"Really?" Stephen smiled. "And how would you set about it?"

"By ensuring that you have the rewards you so richly deserve."

The pedantic tone of this remark made Stephen shake his head.

"If someone had said anything as stuffy as that to you twenty years ago, you'd have knocked him down. I don't want success. I've no time for it. Success, especially popular success, imprisons the spirit. Now that I'm free from the desire for it I can give myself unreservedly to my work."

"Now look here, Desmonde." Glyn spoke a trifle heatedly. "Let's be sensible about this, without affectation. We'll leave the public out of it . . . no one wants you to popularize your art. But do you mean to say that you're indifferent to what people who really know, your fellow artists for example, may think of your work?"

"No artist should paint for the applause or appreciation of his fellows. He should work only to satisfy himself."

"Indeed! So you propose never to show your work?"

"In my early years I wanted passionately to show my paintings, to gain recognition, renown. Now I simply do not care. I don't want to sell. I love my things, I like them around me, I enjoy taking them out and re-touching them. It's enough that I myself know their quality."

"My God! It's inhuman not to want some appreciation."

"Praise or blame has but a momentary effect on the man whose love of beauty makes him the severest critic of his own works. And don't blame me for that statement. It was Keats who made it."

Glyn seemed about to embark on an explosive harangue, but he checked it and began to fill his pipe. Yet as he struck a match, forcibly, he told himself that he would not be put off, he would carry out his intention more determinedly than ever. Presently, adopting a milder, rallying tone, he said:

"At least you'll admit that you've been a trifle too exclusive lately. It's not good for a fellow to be too much alone."

"But if one is working?"

"I work too. Yet I have to get about a good deal—it isn't always convenient but I do it and, frankly, I've got to like it. I meet my colleagues of an evening at Frascati's, look in at the Garrick Club, attend Academy committee meetings. I think it's high time you came out of hiding. Now, I have two tickets for Covent Garden. *Don Giovanni*. Thursday night. They were given me by Madame Lehman—you remember I did her portrait last year. Will you come?"

Slowly, Stephen shook his head. That word "hiding" which Glyn had used, and which he felt to be unjust, had hurt him.

"I haven't been to the theatre for fifteen years."

"You used to enjoy it in the old days."

"I'm too busy now."

"What rot! I insist. And you'll have supper with me at the Café Royal after."

"Yes, do go, Stephen," Jenny pressed. "It'd make such a nice break for you."

Desmonde looked from one to the other, a faint sign of strain appearing on his face, the look of one who must always be free, for whom in the mere hint of coercion, of constrained association with others, there could be nothing but disquiet. He knew himself so well, always fighting a vague apprehension, an unknown fear that seemed waiting round the corner, and saving himself by this very isolation which Glyn decried, finding forgetfulness in his work, in the happy obscurity of his life with Jenny. A refusal was on the tip of his tongue, but he had worked especially well that day. An unusual indulgence, the desire to please his wife and Glyn, caused him to relax his rule.

"All right," he said. "I'll come."

"Good," said Glyn, and he nodded, with a gratified air.

CHAPTER II

THE PERFORMANCE AT Covent Garden was over and the audience came from the opera-house into the cool, clear air. For Stephen, who went out so seldom, it had been an evening of mild diversion, due less to Mozart's effervescent melodies, for as a pure visual he was almost unmoved by music, than to observing its elevating effect upon Glyn, who, not unmindful of the glances of recognition directed towards him during the entr'actes, had maintained throughout an attitude which, while attractively Bohemian—his corduroy jacket, grey shirt and red tie were rather striking amongst the surrounding black and white—was yet shot with the dignity of an Academician who could command five hundred guineas for a half-length portrait and was always hung upon the line. The changes wrought by fame on Richard's robust personality were not too damaging, but they were there, nevertheless.

They stood outside for a moment, opposite the entrance to Bow Street Station.

"You're sure you won't even have a drink?"

"No thanks. I'll get along to Oxford Street for my bus."

"I shall be seeing you soon. And by then I'll have some interesting news for you."

It was the strongest hint that Glyn, during the course of the evening, had ventured to throw out, but, like the others, it seemed to pass over Stephen's head. Still, Richard felt that definite progress had been made.

They shook hands, Glyn set off for the Strand and Stephen turned away in the opposite direction. As he did so he almost collided with a woman emerging alone from the foyer of the theatre. Instinctively he stepped back, with an exclamation of apology, and in the same instant saw that it was Claire.

"You!" The word came from her in a whisper.

From her expression, startled, suddenly fixed, he knew how painful was this recognition, and in this position, on the almost deserted pavement, they remained motionless, gazing at each other in silence, rather like two wax figures in the not too distant establishment of Madame Tussaud. This thought, indeed, occurred to Stephen, but before he could end a silence that struck him as ridiculous, Claire broke into a nervous flow of words.

"Stephen. I can't believe it. Who would have imagined meeting you here? You've been to the opera?"

"Did you think I'd come from across the street?"

He could not resist that ironic reply, but the change in her expression, at once grave and subdued as she glanced towards the blue police lamp, caused him to add: "Yes, I have been, for once. I suppose you come pretty regularly."

"Every night, during the season. Music is a great joy to me."

Her tone did not suggest joy, but rather consolation, an emotion confirmed by her serious face, which, deprived of its youthful colour and contours, had become almost angular, the eyes shadowed, the nose more prominent, the chin a trifle elongated. Her black dress too, while in admirable taste, was devoid of all ornament and, worn with a black lace scarf drapped across her hair, produced an effect restrained to the point of severity.

"Are you alone?" she asked, after another difficult pause.

"Now, I am. My friend has gone."

She hesitated, gathered her courage.

"Then won't you come up to my place for a chat? We can't stand here in the street. I'm quite near, in Knightsbridge."

The invitation was issued in a matter-of-fact voice, and because of this, although he was anxious to get home, perhaps also because the change in her aroused his interest, he made a gesture of acquiescence. Her car, a dark-blue Daimler landaulette, was waiting a short distance down the street, and presently they were being driven west at a good pace through the empty streets.

"This is luxury, Claire." He spoke lightly. "Rather better than your old De Dion."

"It's a hired car," she answered. "I don't own one now. I get this from the mews. At night I can't quite face the underground. But during the day I take it . . . to and from my work."

Her suggestion of personal mortification, of grace acquired in braving the discomfort of the London tube, fell oddly on his ears. But he merely said:

"You have a job?"

She inclined her head.

"At the St. Barnabas Settlement for Destitute Girls. I am the honorary secretary. Under our dear vicar, Father Loftus."

"Loftus!" he exclaimed.

"Such a splendid person. He has been . . . " she hesitated ". . . a tremendous spiritual help to me."

He made to speak, but remained silent. And presently they reached her flat, situated on the top storey of a converted house in Sloane Street. She admitted him to the drawing-room, which was

304

long and somewhat narrow, but restful, softly carpeted, decorated in shades of silver, quietly furnished. And on the two end walls, framed in carved stripped pine, were his paintings which she had purchased seven years before.

"They look well, don't they?" she remarked, as he gazed towards them, and before he could answer ran on, with a vivacity which did not ring true but was, more likely, a cloak for some inner agitation: "Perhaps you recognize some of my old things. Most of them I brought from Broughton. I spend most of my time here. Except for the children's holidays. Nicholas is at Wellington, you know, and Harriet at Roedean. There they are on the bureau."

She indicated a silver-framed photograph, and while he examined it, removed her wrap and gloves, then moved to a small Pembroke table on which were set out a Thermos jug and a napkin-covered plate.

"Can I offer you a drink? Do sit down. There's hot milk here. But perhaps you'd prefer a whisky and soda."

He could have sworn she looked relieved when he indicated his preference for milk. Despite the briskness of her manner, he sensed that she was acutely nervous, inclined to be distrustful, desperately afraid of compromising herself. Unobserved, while she poured the milk, he studied her. There were lines of disappointment running down from her nostrils. She talked much more than of old and had a queer air of driving herself on. On the desk he had noticed files, note-books, a list of appeals, the miscellaneous papers of charitable effort, and above, beside the photograph of the children, a large studio portrait of a clergyman—handsome, high-browed, radiating a lofty serenity—indisputably Loftus. He went over and studied it.

"So this is the vicar of St. Barnabas?"

"You know Father Loftus?"

"I did once. He was hard on Jenny . . . my wife . . . when she worked at the Settlement." Absently, he added, "He looks well-fed now."

"Oh, how can you, Stephen? Just look at the nobility of that face."

"You can do anything with a photograph, Claire." He smiled, quite without malice. "If I painted him I'd get beneath that layer of fat." Suddenly he burst out laughing, a short spasm which ended in a fit of coughing. He wiped his eyes with a paint-stained handkerchief. "Sorry. I was just thinking how near I came to ending up like that."

As she did not reply, nor express the obvious thought that came to mind, he seated himself again.

"How is Geoffrey?"

She coloured painfully, but answered calmly.

"Well, I believe. We have not met for some months."

It was not difficult for him to fit the pieces together. If she were not actually separated from Geoffrey, at least she saw him as seldom as possible and, instead, filled her life, a little too desperately perhaps, with good works, committee meetings, well-bred philanthropy. Yet how many lonely moments had she known in this lovely room, so cool now after the heat of the theatre, and smelling of lavender?

The silence threatened constraint—which above all must be avoided. She came forward, offered him a sandwich, thin triangular white bread, the crusts cut off, enclosing cream cheese and chopped olives.

"They're not very substantial, I'm afraid."

"I'm not hungry," he answered. "I had a bowl of tripe and onions before the opera."

She glanced at him quickly with a faint flush. Why need he obtrude this unnecessary coarseness? Was it unconscious or deliberate? And with a queer interior sinking, a qualm almost of dismay, she asked herself why she had invited him to the retreat she had, with such difficulty, created for herself, so inviolate that no man, except Father Loftus—and he of course as a minister of religion need not be considered in the masculine sense—had crossed the threshold. Could this be Stephen Desmonde? In that dreadful ready-made suit and those cheap brown shoes—bought with care, though she knew it not, by Jenny at the East London Emporium—he was dressed exactly like a working man—a labourer out for the evening. His head, poised and erect, had a certain distinction, but the cropped hair, emphasizing the bony structure of the skull, held for her an intimidating quality, stressed by the ironic calmness of his eyes. His beautiful hands were roughened, the nails uncared for, ragged and stained with pigment.

Yet she mastered these feelings, conscious of a mission towards him. The desire to help, to succour, fostered by her work for the unfortunate, rose strongly within her.

"Stephen." She spoke impulsively. "Where have you been living all these years?"

"In the East End," he answered vaguely. "By the river."

"Down by the Docks?"

"Yes. Cable Street, Stepney. Why not?"

Shocked, she gazed at him.

"Don't you think it's time you made a change? I mean . . . what sort of life is it for you in such an environment . . . mixing with that class of people?"

"An artist belongs to no class. And I like the people."

"But you should be amongst beautiful things . . . in the country . . . even if it were only a little cottage."

"And paint the roses round the door? No, Claire, I get my inspiration from the good Thames mud. Please don't pity us. We have our amusements. Most Saturday nights we go for a pint to the local pub. Occasionally we have an outing to the Heath. Then in the summer we spend a fortnight at Margate with my wife's sister-in-law. She keeps a fish shop, her jellied eels are something to remember."

Claire bit her lip. Was he trying to provoke her, or had he really lapsed to these common standards and degraded tastes? The thought of him living in squalid intimacy with that low servant-girl of whom Father Loftus spoke in such scathing terms and whose abandoned instincts doubtless were responsible for dragging down Stephen and, yes, devitalizing him, roused in her a cold sickness.

"I would have imagined . . ."

He smiled in something like his old manner.

"Don't worry, Claire. It makes no difference where I live, so long as I can paint. Only one thing matters. I must be free to work when and how I like."

"Then," she said slowly, "you won't go back to Stillwater?"

"Never."

"Don't you ever think of them there?"

"It may shock you . . . I don't."

"You don't even know what's been happening . . . at the Rectory?"

He shook his head.

"Not a word."

"Suppose they wanted you . . . needed you?"

"Impossible."

"There have been changes, Stephen . . . great changes . . . and not for the better."

The solemnity of her manner—almost portentous—was too much for him, and at his quiet smile she flushed again, hurt and offended at his indifference. Was he proof against everything? Or was it that, in his submerged existence, living in this unnatural vacuum, communicating with no one, receiving no letters, reading no newspapers

—otherwise he must surely have come across some item relating to his mother's case—he was completely insensible, oblivious to everything but the act of transferring pigment to a square of canvas? For a moment she was tempted to strike back, to hurt him by revealing the full extent of the misfortunes that had fallen on Stillwater. But once more she restrained herself, less from a motive of Christian charity than from the feeling that it was not her responsibility and, indeed, that such action on her part might make matters worse.

A little French clock chimed softly on the mantelpiece, and at the sound Stephen stirred.

"It's late. I mustn't keep you up any longer."

She did not answer. He rose and held out his hand. As she took it, a sense of sadness, of something wasted, and of pity overcame him. Quite unexpectedly, he rested his arm on her shoulder.

"We are friends still, aren't we?"

The look on her face, which he had half anticipated, shocked, almost panic-stricken at his nearness, made his eyes spark.

"I'm glad, Claire. You don't care any more."

He released her. They went into the little hall.

"You must come again," she said weakly, striving for a semblance of normality.

He smiled without answering and the next minute was gone. She had the sudden conviction that she would never see him again. Slowly, with drooping head, she went into her bedroom, once again as white, as freshly virginal, as in the days of her maidenhood, stared unseeingly at her reflection in the mirror. He had looked so worn—bodily, emotionally and mentally over-worked—and in many ways so strange. Was it true that everything she had felt for him was dead? She did not know. Tears welled from her eyes, flowed slowly down her cheeks.

"At least I know where he lives. I must speak to Caroline about him. I really must."

CHAPTER III

For over seven years nothing of consequence had disturbed the tranquillity of Stephen's life, but now, set in motion by Glyn's visit, a sequence of unexpected events began to harass him. Some twelve days after his meeting with Claire a letter arrived at Cable Street bearing the Stillwater postmark. Jenny, who had a strong regard for family feeling and, being quite without pride, often wished privately that he might be reconciled with his relations, even though she herself should remain excluded, placed it on Stephen's plate to await his return from the river.

When he came in and had seated himself he took up the letter, thinking it came from Glyn—for Richard's insistent hints had prepared him for a communication of some sort—but observing the handwriting on the envelope, he put it down with a faint frown. However, when he had eaten his supper, he opened it, then, some moments later, observing her look of eager interest, he said:

"It's from Caroline. . . . She wants me to meet her."

"You will, won't you?"

"What on earth good will it do . . .?"

"Surely it's good to see your sister."

"But it's such a waste of time."

"She's your own flesh and blood."

His brows relaxed, he had to smile. Not only at the reproach, but at the earnestness with which she delivered it. He touched her hand with his. Her reasonableness, the open simplicity of her nature seemed always to bring him back from that strange country into which he strayed alone. Not for the first time, he deeply realized how much he owed not only to her abundant, cheerful, healthy good temper, her good humour, and self-control, but to her understanding, her instinctive knowledge of human nature. The sympathy, unspoken, that flowed from her when he was depressed, was like a healing balm. Her so modest tastes and ambitions, whether for a "nice strong cup of tea" or a new hearthrug for the kitchen, her lack of envy, her childlike interest, ungrudging, in those richer and more fortunate than she, as revealed in the picture periodicals, which she studied intently, were to him unutterably touching. And how splendid, too, were her calm, efficient activities in the house, her presence of mind in a crisis. She was the real romance, the romance of commonsense and kindliness, of a woman you could sleep with in a warm bed. The home she had given him, a refuge, fixed and stable, made all his wanderings and unhappy strivings seem stupid and futile.

"I love you, Jenny. And because of that I'll go." He added, to conceal his feelings: "It's what I deserve for going to that damned opera."

She smiled at him with a grave sympathy, comfortably, and sensibly.

On Wednesday of the following week, although with reluctance, he set out for Victoria, where, under the central clock, Caroline had said she would await him. The morning was wet and overcast, conditions which made work impossible and tempered somewhat his unwillingness to make this quite unnecessary concession to family sentiment. During the past few days he had felt unaccountably tired. The fog of the London autumn always upset him, and as his cough had kept him awake part of the night, his mood was not altogether effervescent as he approached the station.

When he got off the bus and pushed through the crowded platforms it was past eleven o'clock, and he asked himself if Carrie, the soul of punctuality, might actually be late. Then, by the bookstall, he saw a short, middle-aged woman, her hair streaked with grey, dressed in an ill-fitting brown tweed costume which touched a familiar chord of recollection. When she caught sight of him, her broad anxious face lighted up, she came forward and, with a little nervous gasp, greeted him. Although he scarcely recognized her, it was his sister.

"What a morning!" she exclaimed, finding safety in a remark about the weather. "Regular cats and dogs."

"I expect you had a wet drive to Halborough."

"Yes, it was wet. There wasn't a bus, so I walked. My brolly blew inside out." Again, attempting a deprecating laugh, she gave that slight gasp, demonstrating the umbrella, a wreck of tattered black silk and twisted frame, that she carried. She added: "It will mend, though . . . I think."

There was a pause, then he said:

"You'd be glad of a cup of coffee. Shall we go to the buffet?"

She seemed to shrink from the rush and bustle of the station restaurant.

"We couldn't talk in there. It's too noisy. There's a homemade place . . . the Copper Kettle . . . just across the road, near the Palace."

They went out of the station, through the bus terminal, and in a backwater off Victoria Street entered an establishment painted a watery apple-green where, in the window amidst some pots of jam and a wire tray of stale buns, a large black cat was asleep. Upstairs, in a little chilly room, empty at this hour, they sat down at a fumed-oak table on which stood an unsteady vase of paper flowers, a contribution box for Dr. Barnardo's Homes and a Swiss cow-bell. Stephen rang the bell, which emitted an unearthly tinkle, and presently a woman in a grey cardigan haughtily appeared, brought, after an interval, two cups of a greyish, tepid beverage and a stand of pallid cakes.

In the presence of the proprietress Caroline had brightly initiated a purely fictitious conversation relating to the weather, the condition of the crops, and the prospects of the cubbing season, but once they were alone her shoulders sagged, she stirred the fluid in her chipped cup mournfully.

"I suppose," she said, in a lowered voice, after assuring herself that they were not overheard, "I'd better begin at the beginning. You know nothing?"

"Nothing."

"Well . . . as if we hadn't had enough trouble," she gathered herself to sustain the pain of her communication, "we are leaving the Rectory."

He did not seem to understand.

"Leaving . . . Why?"

"We are forced to sell it."

He looked at her in surprise.

"But surely . . . as a church entail it can't be sold."

"The ecclesiastical commissioners have given Father permission . . . under the circumstances . . . provided we still live near the church."

There was a pause.

"Where are you going?"

"To a horrid little house on the warren. One of Mould's brick bungalows with no view, no garden, and only four rooms, all so small you couldn't swing a cat in them. Oh dear, oh dear, it's unbearable."

Even in her distress, as the words came tumbling out, reducing her anew by their frightful import, she could not fail to note how little the dreadful news disturbed him. He considered her in silence, with a strange calmness. Then:

"I thought you liked a small house. I've often heard you complain that Stillwater was far too large and old-fashioned for you to manage. It may well be that you'll find the bungalow more convenient."

"How can you say that?" she exclaimed with sudden heat. "Stillwater has been the home of the Desmondes for two hundred years. You know how proud Father is of it. How he loves it. The very ground is sacred to our family. Doesn't that mean anything to you?"

"No," he answered, after a moment's reflection. "At one time it did. But not now." He paused. "Who is buying it?"

"Can't you guess?"

"Mould?"

She nodded, bitter tears starting to her eyes.

"He's bought ever so much land near the village. There's talk of him starting a cement works on the Downs, just by the old limestone quarry, in front of the house. It's unbelievable . . . the view will be gone . . . everything. When I think how Sussex has changed I could sit down and weep. Beauty spots despoiled, estates broken up, ribbon development, cheap cinemas and dance-halls everywhere, not a maid to be had, and as for politeness, even common civility, in the village shops—it has simply ceased to exist."

He brought her back to the point.

"You haven't told me how this came about."

She choked down a dry mouthful of cake which, unknowingly, in her agitation, she had placed between her lips.

"It was Mother. You know how she always was . . . with no sense of economy, or caution, no idea of the value of money. When she went away on these holidays we always thought she had private means, a little income of her own that she had never mentioned to us. But oh dear, it wasn't so. Just twelve months ago we discovered that she was in the hands of moneylenders, two creatures from the City who appeared one day and threatened Father with a lawsuit if he didn't pay up. You see . . ." Caroline faltered . . . "over the last few years Mother had . . . had signed papers making herself liable for a large amount."

"How much?"

"Almost ten thousand pounds. Of course," Caroline rushed on, "she'd only received a small part of it, but with the exorbitant interest charged, that was the sum they made out she owed. It was sheer extortion, blackmail if you like, but rather than face the series of cases that would be instituted against her, Father decided we must pay. Better to be ruined with honour, he said, than to face another disgrace . . ."

"Like the one I inflicted on him." As she broke off, he mildly completed the phrase for her.

She averted her gaze, which remained, for some moments, distressed yet censorious, upon the panorama of chimney-pots grotesquely blurred by the blown-glass window-panes.

"Couldn't Hubert have done something? Or Geoffrey?"

She shook her head.

"They are quite hard put to it themselves. Taxes and high wages have hurt Hubert—the orchards aren't paying. And I believe Geoffrey has mortgaged Broughton." She added: "We scarcely see anything of them these days."

"Well," he said at last, "the old girl certainly had her fling. In a way I always admired her for doing exactly what she wanted. Where is she now?"

Caroline straightened, then, in a suppressed voice, with the air of one forced to disclose the final disaster:

"In a private asylum in Dulwich."

He stared at her blankly for a moment, then all at once burst into a shout of laughter. Stupefied, pale and distraught, she watched him, so paralysed with indignation she could not speak. What in Heaven's name had come over him to behave in this shameful manner? She remembered that Claire, in one of their long discussions, attempting to excuse him, had once told her that no artist was a completely balanced person. Could there be a strain of madness in him too? With nervous agitation, she bent forward and shook him.

"Don't! Are you out of your senses?"

"I'm sorry," he apologized, recovering himself. "It just struck me as the most wonderful finish to a thoroughly amusing career."

"Amusing! You're absolutely heartless. I . . . I'm ashamed of you."

"Oh come now, Carrie, don't be so sorry for everyone, yourself included. I've known people with far more trouble than you've had, or ever will have. In Spain I lived with an old blind woman who had less than nothing, not even enough to eat, who froze in winter and sweltered in summer, who knew not only absolute penury but the desolation of utter loneliness, and yet never once complained about it. You needn't be so cast down."

"How can I help it, when I think of the way things have gone? If you'd only been a good son, stayed at home, gone into the Church and helped Father, kept control over things, and over Mother, we'd still be all happy at Stillwater. You'd be loved and respected . . ."

"Instead of hated and despised."

"Stephen." Again she leaned forward, but it was to place an entreating hand on his arm. "Even now, it isn't too late. Father needs you. He still . . ."

"For God's sake, Carrie," he interrupted her harshly. "You know I'm married. Do you want us both down there in your four-roomed bungalow? Really, you have a genius for suggesting the impossible."

"Then there's nothing more to be said." She sighed, drew on her damp cotton gloves, picked up the ruin of her umbrella.

"By the way." A thought occured to him. "Isn't that place at Dulwich rather expensive? How do you manage?"

"Claire is helping. She is so kind." Carrie added, "I'm going out to visit Mother now. It may not interest you in the least, but she often speaks of you."

"Then shall I come with you? I'd quite like to see her."

As she stared at him, taken aback, wondering if he were serious or if this were merely some new iniquity of his incomprehensible nature, deciding finally that it was one action she must commend, he added, with a queer smile, destroying her faint approval even before she gave expression to it: "The light's no good for painting anyhow."

When Stephen had paid the bill at the counter downstairs they went out of the shop, crossed to the station and, after some waiting, boarded a train bound for the South London suburbs. It was not a long journey, and presently they emerged from the smoke and grime of central London into the fresher atmosphere of Dulwich, where fortunately, it was dry. The asylum, situated in an open stretch not far from the station, was a weathered grey-stone mansion in the extreme baronial style, with twin towers, castellated pediment and pointed windows in the Gothic taste, apparently a conversion from an early Victorian country house, set in extensive grounds and enclosed by a high brick wall surmounted by a fringe of broken spikes. At the gate lodge, where Caroline produced a visiting-card, they were admitted by an attendant who directed them up a gravelled drive, flanked by beech trees, towards the house. Along another avenue a procession of inmates, dark-coated figures profiled against the grey sky, could be seen taking their daily walk, quietly, and quite at ease. Others, apparently of a humbler category, were occupied in a leisurely manner in the vegetable garden. To the right, distantly, on a strip of lawn outlined against a hedge of yew, an underhand game of tennis between two middle-aged gentlemen was lazily in progress, over a sagging net. Adjacent, some ladies with croquet mallets were in the process of propelling balls through a variety of hoops. And in the foreground, from a group of both men and women seated with a nurse in a red-tiled shelter, there came little recurrent wafts of laughter. A sense of remoteness and repose permeated the air, which, with the odour of decayed leaves and vegetation, the formal box planting, the dark shrubbery—enclosing a derelict grotto where damply, amidst ferns, stood a Grecian statue, broken unfortunately—and, overlooking all, the turrets of the mansion, gave to the place a character not of the world, unreal, sedate, stately.

At the main doorway they rang the bell and were ushered through the vestibule, tiled in black and white marble, to a curtained waiting-room, ornate and old-fashioned perhaps, but furnished with dignity, mainly in buhl, with a row of four chairs against each wall. Here also there was evidence of animation, from next door a murmur of voices, the cheerful clink of crockery, and from upstairs the sound of a Strauss waltz played with considerable *brio* upon a piano so mellow and dulcet that Stephen could almost see the broken yellow keys flashing under that animated attack. And it was to the tuneful strains of *The Vienna Woods* that Julia, gently prompted by hands from behind, entered the room.

There she stood, looking from one to the other, smiling at them with the same blank detachment that, even in moments of the most acute domestic crisis, had all her life distinguished her. Dressed in one of her flowing frocks, to which she had added some pieces of lace, adaptations of her own conception, with a length of tulle about her neck, and on each of her wrists a bow of pink ribbon, her hair frizzed *en pompadour*, her features floury with powder, a mask of white in which her velvet eyes were ringed with black, she had an appearance admittedly eccentric, yet both striking and elegant.

"How are you today, Mother?" Caroline asked.

"I am well, naturally. As I am every day under Sagittarius."

"Stephen has come to see you."

"So you have made the trip from Paris." Ignoring Caroline, she advanced and took a chair beside him in the most cordial manner. "How do you find the French?"

"Very nice. And it's nice to see you again."

"Thank you, Stephen. Are you still living with that woman over there? The one your father was afraid of?"

"No. I'm leading an almost respectable life, for a change."

"Don't you remember, Mother?" To prevent further indiscretions, Caroline intervened, in a pained and helpful voice. "Stephen returned from France a long time ago. And since then he has been in Spain."

"Ah, Spain. I remember as a girl when I was in Madrid with Father, we had great trouble with a waiter who refused to boil the water. . . ."

"And now," Caroline persisted, "he is working at his painting, in London."

"Of course," Julia answered brusquely, and again presenting a shoulder towards Caroline, addressed herself to Stephen. "Your painting. Only the other day I was recollecting how when you were a very small boy you used to go round the gallery at Haselton with my dear father, before he sold our pictures and took to helicopters. There was an afternoon when we thought you were lost, drowned in the lake perhaps, a great outcry. And you were found alone in the gallery, seated on the floor, before one of the paintings."

"Yes," He nodded. "A really lurid Teniers, *The Butcher's Shop*, full of the bloody carcases of bullocks. It fascinated me."

"And it was after that," she pursued with animation, "that your father gave you the box of water-colours."

"Perhaps that was my undoing." He laughed.

Julia did not respond. She could be deeply serious in the presence of laughter, her own came unexpectedly when others were grave.

"No, no, my dear." She shook her head, raised one finger in a regal gesture. "What is in us, we will do, in spite of others."

He did not answer, but he thought: That is the most sensible remark I have heard all day. A silence followed, then, moved less by curiosity than by an unusual solicitude, he asked:

"Do you like it here?"

"Very much. It does not interfere with my comfort or bring extra fatigue upon me. It seems to combine the qualities of a spa, which I have always appreciated, with a more intimate and selective atmosphere. We have an excellent physician, a young man well versed in the therapeutics of elimination, whom I find most attentive. The nurses are willing, poor things, they do their best for one. The life is restful, I enjoy my walk in the morning, in the afternoon we sit a great deal, then in the evenings we have quite a social life, with concerts, occasional dances, a visiting conjurer, and our own orchestra of twelve pieces. Believe it or not, I have actually been approached, quite correctly of course, by one of our gentlemen guests to see if I would not consent to sing. I used to think when I was a romantic young girl and passing through a religious spell under the late Canon Pusey, that I should like one day to retire to a monastery . . . I should say," she corrected primly, "a convent. Now, since it appears that I must be confined, this, I assure you, is considerable improvement."

Stephen nodded in sympathy, impressed by Julia's spirit, realizing more clearly than ever before how much he had in common with this strange woman who was his mother. From her, unquestionably, came his disregard of convention and contempt of the banal, his complete indifference to what went on around him, and also, no doubt, that strain of singularity, self-recognized, which made him feel himself an oddity, someone apart from the rest of the world. Yet, while he would not have minded a lively aberration such as

316

Julia's, unhappily all the queer tendencies of his nature took him in precisely the opposite direction. Her head was serenely in the clouds, his bent resolutely towards the abyss.

As he reflected in this manner, Caroline, in lowered, serious tones, had engaged her mother in conversation relating to more practical affairs. Questions of linen, laundry, and the need for warm winter underwear were brought up, lightly considered by Julia and airily dismissed. Messages from Bertram were then communicated and accepted with an air of benign amusement. Presently a bell reverberated through the building, and a moment later there came a tap on the door, which opened partly, discreetly, to admit a cajoling voice.

"Lunch time, Mrs. Desmonde, dear."

Julia, with a confiding glance as though to say, complacently, you see how they attend to us, rose and, having smoothed her skirt and arranged the ribbons on her wrists, assumed a modish attitude.

"How do you like my gown?" She touched the extravagant flounces coquettishly, inviting their admiration. "Nurse was rather against the lace but I think it quite becoming."

"It's a superb dress," Stephen said. "It suits you. And if you are not careful I'll come back one day soon and paint you in it."

"Do come, Stephen dear," she murmured, in her old, charming manner, as she swept from the room. "Any day . . . in Sagittarius if you can . . . never in Scorpio."

Outside, dark clouds had blown across from the city, it had begun to pour heavily—a considerable disadvantage, since Stephen had no coat, merely the scarf he wore always on his shoulders, and Caroline, of course, was bereft of the protection of her umbrella. On their way down the drive, bent forward against the slant of the rain, neither of them spoke. Stephen, for the life of him, despite his disturbed mind, could not help regretting that he had been unable to make a sketch of Julia as she stood there in the bizarre dress, gracious, charming, and absurd. What marvellous and fanciful effects he could produce against the background of this strange place, this refuge of unreality, vibrating still, it seemed, with the tap of croquet balls, the echoes of light laughter, the giddy rhythms of that tinkling Strauss waltz. At last, as they turned towards the shelter of the tube station, he broke away from his thoughts.

"She didn't appear too bad," he said, trying to inject a note of encouragement into his words. But Carrie would have none of it.

"You haven't seen her when she's really outrageous."

He bit his lip, annoyed.

"At least she's not unhappy."

"No," sighed Caroline. "I suppose not. But the doctor says her mind will get progressively weaker. Softening of the brain, he called it."

In the train, as they rattled through tunnels, intermittent flashes of daylight affording wet-roofed vistas of the suburbs, of traffic-clogged streets and streaming umbrellas, moving like tortoises, over wet pavements, she kept her head turned from him. A surreptitious glance revealed that, pretending to look out of the window, she was weeping quietly, her handkerchief clutched damply in one hand. Although he despised it, this perpetual lamentation affected him. Already it had worn down his earlier cheerfulness, now it left him wretched and subdued, attacked by pangs of self-abasement, a sudden realization of his uselessness in the material world. After all, was there not there reason in Caroline's attitude?—in this family crisis she must naturally look to him for help. Yet he could not, or would not, give it. Now, more than ever, no human attachment, nor force on earth could divert him from the course that he had chosen and which, like a man obsessed, he must follow to its bitter end. Abruptly, he shook off a sudden sense of giddiness. His habit of forgetting about food—for he had a few coins in his pocket and could easily have stopped at Dulwich to take a meal with Carrie—undoubtedly contributed to his lowness of spirits. Yet beyond that he felt confoundedly seedy—his wet feet were icy, his head throbbed, and he was more than ever aware of that strange, recurrent numbness in his throat.

At Victoria they got out of the train and crossed to the main station. The departure board indicated that a train would leave for Halborough in three minutes' time.

"If I rush, I'll get it," Carrie exclaimed nervously. "Thank you for coming, Stephen. Good-bye."

"Good-bye."

They shook hands hurriedly and awkwardly. Already out of breath, she scuttled like a floundering duck through the barrier on to the platform. He watched until she boarded the train, then turned away. As he came out of the station the newsboys were calling the early editions of the evening papers. Intent on getting home as quickly as possible, he paid no attention to their shouts, but despite his preoccupation, a word here and there intruded upon his moody absorption, and broke through, finally, upon his consciousness. He stopped short and, as in a dream, stunned, yet with a shocked and sickening sense of dismay, read the headlines in the placards:

ACADEMY SENSATION

SCANDAL OF THE CHARMINSTER PANELS REVIVED

R.A. Resigns

CHAPTER IV

THE TRAM WOULD not go fast enough as, bent over the newspaper with contracted brows, he read and re-read the wavering print. It was five o'clock when he reached Cable Street and there, pacing up and down at the corner bus stop, was Glyn.

"I thought I might catch you here. Jenny told me you were away." Glyn paused, his eye, restive and disturbed, touching the other, then moving away. "Let's have a drink."

"I'd rather get home," Stephen said stiffly.

"No, don't go up there yet." Glyn glanced significantly over his shoulder along the street. "I must talk to you first."

Stephen hesitated, his face hard, unresponsive, then without a word he accompanied the other across the road and into the bar of the Good Intent. The low, sanded room was empty, and in a corner, beneath the model rigged barque that gave the tavern its name, Glyn ordered two double whiskies served hot. His manner, though it held a hint of awkwardness, was taut and truculent. His face was flushed, something of the old fire sparked in his eye. When the grog arrived he said:

"Drink that up. I had a couple while I was hanging around for you. I'm a little tight, but don't let that bother you."

Stephen gulped down a mouthful of the steaming liquid. Choked by bitterness, he was struggling to keep his nerves under control.

"So now you know," Glyn said suddenly. "I took your *Hampstead Heath* and sent it to the Academy."

"Without consulting me."

"If I had, would you have let me have it?"

"No . . . never."

At the violence of the reply Glyn shot a quick glance at Stephen.

"Well, I did take it. And it was not an unconsidered act. I had already spoken to three members of the committee, Stead, Elkins, and Prothero, all good fellows, and damn good painters. Don't look at me like that. At least have the decency to let me explain what happened."

"Go on then, for God's sake."

Glyn, also on edge, reddened more deeply, and with an effort controlled an angry reply.

"Blame me as much as you please. But remember that I acted for the best." He paused for a moment, then resumed. "The meeting of the selection committee took place at eleven o'clock this morning. You probably know the procedure. The members sit in a semicircle of armchairs, with the president in the centre, in one of the galleries of Burlington House. As the paintings are brought in one at a time, by the janitors, and placed on a throne, they vote on them Acceptance is indicated by raising a hand or a finger, rejection by keeping the hands down. Well, it was an extra poor lot this year—apart from a dozen canvases nothing outstanding, the usual run of muddy landscapes, flower arrangements, and dull portraits. Under the circumstances the voting was particularly lenient, it had to be, otherwise there wouldn't have been any exhibition."

Glyn broke off and ran his fingers through his hair. "We were getting down to the thin end of the submissions when your *Heath* came in—as a matter of fact I'd arranged it that way. And I can tell you, after what had gone before"—he struck the table with his fist—"it really hit the spot. There was one of those pauses that rarely happen in that room. Everyone sat up and took notice. I could tell at once that the men around me were impressed. When I raised my hand the three fellows I told you of followed suit. Then another hand went up, and a fifth . . . all from the new group coming on in the Academy, members who don't spit at modern art, who admire Matisse, Bonnard and Lurcat, and know a fine thing when they see it."

In spite of his determination to remain detached, Stephen felt a tremor go through his limbs. His eyes were strained as Glyn went on.

"There's another group that sits together at the head of the room —old Sir Moses Stencil, Dame Dora Downes, Carrington Woodstock, and Munsey Peters. They're the old, old guard, and that's the understatement of all time. Stencil paints nothing but cows, he's painted more cows than Cooper, more than Harpignies ever painted sheep, they say he keeps a pet Holstein in his Bloomsbury studio. Woodstock, on the other hand, is a dog man, the hearty squire type, he's painted every pack of hounds in England and comes to the meetings in breeches and a white stock; Dame Dora does those

Kensington interiors—you must have seen them reproduced in the Christmas supplements; as for Peters, he's just Peters—I couldn't say more than that. I hadn't expected this lot to like your picture. Who the hell would want them to? And it was obvious they didn't. However, that didn't worry me. There's a convention that if even one R.A. votes for a painting the others automatically agree. I felt sure you were in, when Stencil suddenly got up, hobbled over to the easel, shook his head, then slewed round.

" 'I sincerely hope the committee will remember its responsibilities to the nation before passing favourable judgement on this work.'

"Actually it is most unusual for anyone to comment on a painting, and there was an odd silence. Then Dame Dora put in her word.

" 'It is certainly outrageously modern.'

" 'And why not?' I said. 'We're badly in need of new blood.'

" 'Not this kind,' said Woodstock. 'It's entirely the wrong strain.'

"This exchange had created a diversion which stopped the voting, and Stencil, still standing by the picture, looked across at me.

" 'Do you like this painting, Mr. Glyn?'

" 'Very much.'

" 'You don't find it obscure and unintelligible?'

" 'Not at all.'

" 'Then be so good as to tell me what these innumerable black tongue-lickings in the lower part of the picture represent.'

" 'Those are people walking about.'

" 'Do I look like that when I walk along Piccadilly?'

" 'Perhaps not. These people are younger than you.'

" 'Indeed. Thank you for reminding me of my antiquity. Then what is this conveyance in the left foreground?'

" 'That obviously is a coster's donkey and barrow.'

" 'Impossible,' Woodstock cut in. 'Never saw such an animal. Its pasterns are all wrong.'

" 'It is certainly not a coloured photograph, if that is your taste. But it conveys its meaning absolutely, and with great feeling.'

" 'By out-of-line drawing?'

" 'Executed deliberately and with infinite skill. Isn't that better than the servile rendering of nature which so many of us repeat year after year?'

"Stencil must have thought that I was referring to his cows. He glared at me.

" 'I will not be persuaded to renounce the grammar of design which has been accepted since Giotto.'

L

" 'Surely that is a reactionary view. When someone gets away from the commonplace you condemn him.'

"The old boy was losing his temper, and although I had determined to keep mine, it was going too.

" 'I certainly condemn this. There is not one simple, honest presentation of the natural human form in it. This is not a picture, it is a mere spattering of colours.'

" 'Nevertheless, it is art?'

" 'I don't know anything about art,' Stencil shouted. 'But I know what I like. Blood and thunder, we are not here to be made a mock of or to allow some artistic adventurer to throw a pot of paint in the public's face. No normal Britisher would be attracted to this picture.'

" 'I agree. And you could not pay it a higher compliment.'

" 'Indeed, sir. So you impugn the national taste?'

" 'Naturally. After a diet of your cows and Woodstock's hounds they must obviously be suffering from chronic indigestion.'

"I knew I was going too far, but my blood was up, I couldn't help myself. The president intervened.

" 'Order, order, gentlemen. All this is most irregular. If we are to have a discussion on this work, let us keep it within bounds and without personalities, please.'

"But Stencil was out of control now, he banged the floor with that ebony stick he uses, I thought he was going to have a stroke.

" 'Mr. President, and gentlemen of the committee, I have been a member of the Royal Academy for more than thirty years. During that time I have tried with all my strength to preserve the fount of British art at its source. By setting my face sternly against all foreign influence and innovations, new experiments, expressionism, and all forms of exoticism, I have, I submit, in all modesty, helped to keep our heritage undefiled. I have always been able to look my conscience in the eye and say that here, at the Royal Academy Exhibitions, the people of our country will see only works which are solid, honest and wholesome.'

"There were protests at this from our end." Glyn paused and took another swig of grog. "But Stencil went on."

" 'What is this so-called modern art? I will tell you. Nothing but a lot of damned nonsense. Some upstart the other day had the insolence to declare that Renoir was a greater painter than Romney. I tell you, if I had been there I would have taken my stick to him. What is all the fancy daubing of these Frenchmen but a cover up for bad technique? If we are to paint a meadow, for God's sake let us make it look like a meadow, and not like a patch of verdigris. Don't let us have this affected juggling with form and colour which no sensible man can comprehend. You all know that a certain modernistic statue was recently erected at the taxpayers' expense in a public park of this city. It was presumed to be the figure of a woman, and God help all women if they look like that, indeed it so angered and disgusted the decent ordinary people of the neighbourhood that one night some honest citizen smeared it with tar and feathers and by the mercy of Providence it had to be removed. Now this picture is clearly in the same unwholesome category. It offends one's eye immediately as unreal, distorted and pernicious. It is no more like Hampstead Heath than my foot. It is, in every detail, a dangerous outbreak from orthodox tradition. It is rank socialism. Gentlemen, we cannot support a decay of elegance and good taste which can only confuse and corrupt our younger generation of artists. One never knows when a revolution may break out. It is our responsibility to crush it in the bud.'

"With a final tattoo, Stencil sat down. By this time I was boiling mad. There, in front of me, was your beautiful painting and here was this . . . this cow-fancier, who didn't comprehend even the first stroke of your brush, with the other die-hards leaning over to congratulate him. I got on my feet.

" 'You say that our responsibility is to suppress. I say it is to support and encourage. Good God, we are not policemen. Why should we set out to kill all provocative and venturesome art? Every original artist of the past hundred years has been the victim of this assassination. Courbet and Delacroix were both stabbed in the back —while the Barbizon school, turning out its traditional tripe, was exalted to the skies. Ridicule and abuse smothered the Impressionists. Cézanne was called a clumsy dauber, Van Gogh a psychopathic mutilator, Gauguin a half-baked amateur whose work gave out the odour of a dead rat. The Fauves were hooted at, Braque reviled, Seurat and Redon stigmatized as madmen. You can look it up, it's in the record. There was always some damned traditionalist who felt himself attacked, insulted and undermined, standing there, eaten up by jealousy, with a sneer on his lips and a brickbat in his fist. But in spite of that their work lives, and the man with the sneer is not even remembered. And I'll wager this—however much you may snarl at it—the painting before us now will still be alive when every damn one of us gathered in this room is dead and forgotten.' "

Glyn, losing a little of his violence, drank again, then shook his head. "It was the wrong line to take, Desmonde, but before Heaven, I couldn't help it. There was a kind of hollow pause. Then, as nobody seemed to have anything to say, the President, who is a good fellow and wanted to end the squabble, proposed that the vote be taken. Then an odd thing became apparent. I began to sense that in general the attitude of the committee was favourable. Yes, I'll swear to it. They were for you. The hands were ready to go up when all at once Peters, who hadn't opened his mouth during the entire rumpus, suddenly said:

" 'One moment please.'

"Everyone looked at him as he bent forward, with his pince-nez on the end of his nose, peering at your signature on the canvas. Then he settled himself back in his chair.

" 'Gentlemen, I have so far abstained from this controversy because I had a vague suspicion that I had come across work of this nature some years before. And now I am certain of the fact. I must inform you that the painter of this picture is none other than the man responsible for the notorious Charminster panels, who was convicted in open court of producing and exhibiting obscene art.'

"There was a sensation, of course, and, my God, I wish you had seen the look of justification on Stencil's face.

" 'I told you it was degenerate. And it is.'

"Peters continued: 'How can we assume the onus of sanctioning work from such a source? If we do so, we set the seal of our approval on it.'

"I had realized what was coming, and I jumped up again.

" 'Are we judging panels that were burned through crass ignorance over seven years ago, or this painting before us now?'

"I can't remember all I said, I was so angry at the time I scarcely knew what I came out with, except that it was hot and strong. But it was no use, and I knew it. Even those who would otherwise have supported you were afraid to risk a scandal. There was only one thing for me to do. I wanted to do it and, by God, it gave me some satisfaction. I resigned on the spot. And I'm damned glad I did. I've been getting soft in these last years, Desmonde, flabby and stodgy, my work isn't near as good as it used to be. I'm sick of turning out made-to-order portraits for Hammerhead and his kind, fed to the teeth painting strings of decorations on the pigeon chests of peers of the realm. I'm going to get out the old caravan and push off to North Wales with Anna. Maybe I'll do some real work there. And now that's off my chest, I hope you're not too mad at me. I admit now that I was wrong. You can't ram a masterpiece down the throat of a committee. Rembrandt found that out with the Insolvency Chamber in Amsterdam. And El Greco with the Spanish Ecclesiastical Commission. I only hope you won't take it too much to heart. After all, what do we care what the ruddy world thinks of us? Let's have another drink."

Stephen gazed at the other in silence, his features pale and impassive. The long recital which Glyn, perhaps in self-justification, had been at pains to present in detail, had carried him through anger and distress to a final indifference. But the hurt was deep and he knew he would feel the pain of it again. If only Richard had left him alone, without interference, simply left him alone. Still, he could bear no rancour in his overshadowed heart, nor would he reveal the fresh anxieties that had been created for him. He held out his hand.

Glyn now tossed off his grog and, more than a little elevated, clapped Stephen fraternally on the shoulder.

"Let's go, Desmonde. I'll see you home. And if there's bloody well trouble ahead, by God, we'll stand up to it."

CHAPTER V

ART, IN THE national sense, must always be regarded as a serious matter. Coming at a season when copy was scarce, with no more than a dull murder in Glasgow and a somewhat unenterprising society divorce to appease the public appetite for news, this startling incident at the Academy was a windfall to the popular press. After the Charminster trial the reaction had been local rather than general. Now, however, the affair was given wide circulation—in particular by those Sunday papers whose duty it is to safeguard the decencies of England by presenting in full the more succulent misdemeanours of the day. Under this leadership the new scandal rekindled the ashes of the old. Files of the *Charminster Chronicle* were combed for tasty tit-bits. A drawing of Stephen, standing in the dock, was reproduced from the *County Gazette*. Archibald Dalgetty, whose articles in the *Universe News* were read by millions and who, perhaps more than any other man, could be regarded as the protector and upholder of British morality, who, indeed, had just added to his lustre by flagellating an unfortunate woman novelist for her book *The Lonely Heart*, seized sternly upon the affair. Under the withering heading of ART RUN AMUCK, just indignation flowed from his pen. What, he asked, had happened to Old England when such an insult could be offered to one of her most cherished, revered, and dignified institutions, when, under duress, its æsthetic bastions were threatened by obscure and revolutionary works from a brush already proven to be putrid and debauched? Not all the outcry was so elevated in tone. There were snickers in the livelier publications, jokes on the vaudeville stage, and in one of the picture weeklies, a cartoon appeared which showed a furtive-looking individual accosting a dignified top-hatted Academician outside the steps of Burlington House: "Want to buy a spicy postcard, mister?"

During the days that followed, Stephen went on working with that disregard of exterior events which was now so strong it took the form of disdainful contempt. Once again, through no fault of his own, he was in the pillory of publicity, held up to general contempt. How did it come about that he, by nature quiet, unassuming and retiring, who all his life had desired nothing more than to pursue his art in peace, should have so violently drawn upon himself this outburst of condemnation? An enterprising journalist had found it necessary, in the public interest, to present a brief sketch of his career, and it was as though this record of his years—his defection from the Church, from his family, and above all from his country—revealed him as unnatural and despicable, deserving fully the odium of his fellows.

Because he felt so deeply, he had learned to impose upon himself a rigid self-control that enabled him to sustain misfortune with at least an outward calmness. Bruised by adversity, whipped so often by mockery, he had striven to achieve such liberty of spirit as to care nothing for what was said, or done to him. Yet there were moments when he felt completely lost, when a kind of dread came down upon him and life seemed so unreal, so frightening, he felt he could not face it. He realized, too, that he had lost something he greatly prized, the sense of anonymity, of being unnoticed and unknown in the common flow of humanity. However he might conceal it, the strain told upon him, and even when the hubbub began to slacken, left him physically worn down and with an unusual feeling of foreboding.

He had taken to staying late in the shack on Tapley's jetty. Here he would sit, with bent brows, gazing out at the black river, a sharp breeze ruffling the tide, a tug coming through the bridge with a tail of barges making red and green eyes in the night. The lapping of the waters, the beauty, the invisible essence of the night, softened him, but he forbade himself pity, thinking only of the work he had done that day and would resume tomorrow. Then, in the darkness, he would walk home, holding to the shadows, as if striving to remain unseen, to Cable Street.

One Saturday, towards the end of the month, he was later than usual. When he got home at six o'clock he felt thoroughly done up and his throat, which had troubled him off and on all day, was peculiarly numb. Jenny had his supper ready, cottage pie, kept hot in the oven, and while he ate the comforting meal she sat at the table opposite him, watching in silence. She saw that he did not wish to talk. His look of exhaustion worried her, but she was too wise to mention it.

When he had done he took his usual chair by the kitchen hearth and, with his sketch-book on his knee, stared into the fire as though evoking from its red glow noble and heroic forms. She washed the dishes, removed her apron and picked up her knitting. After a few minutes he raised his head and became aware of her. It was the hour when they usually talked together, avoiding the painful issue of the moment, often of nothing more important than domestic matters, yet with an intimacy which he knew she enjoyed. Tonight he felt near to her. Something in her, a simple quality of womanhood, of homely warmth, drew him. He began to relate the events of his day. But he had not gone far before his voice cracked unexpectedly and, instead of speaking in his usual tones, he found his words coming in a husky whisper. The experience was no novelty to him, but in this instance came so suddenly that his wife's eyes lifted sharply from her work. He saw her face change, then compose herself. After a momentary pause, articulating with difficulty, he said:

"There it is again. All day I've felt I was going to lose my voice. And now I have."

"You've caught cold." She spoke logically and with the mild accusation of one who continually reproved him for neglecting himself, yet this was no more than a screen for the anxiety that gripped her.

He shook his head.

"My throat isn't really sore."

"Doesn't it hurt when you swallow?"

"No."

"Let me have a look."

He submitted while, with a spoon from the table drawer, she depressed his tongue, and from various angles inspected the back of his throat.

"I can't see anything wrong. It's not swollen or inflamed."

"It's nothing."

"Maybe not," she answered firmly. "But you're not going out on

327

that river tomorrow. Not if I know it. That's where you've had the chill. I shall tell the Cap'n tonight.'

"Well . . . I have enough to go on with in the studio."

"Only if you're better. And now you ought to have a good hot drink."

She made him, with boiling water, a mixture of rum and her own black-currant preserve—which she knew to be a panacea for afflictions of the throat—a scalding tumberful that brought him out in a grateful sweat. Then she persuaded him to go to bed.

Next morning, his voice had returned and he worked at his *Thames* all the forenoon. But after lunch he had another attack of hoarseness, and when he came out of the studio at four o'clock he had to admit, with a self-conscious gesture, that the trouble, whatever it might be, had completely silenced him.

"That settles it," said Jenny with determination. "We must have advice."

Handicapped as he was, he did his best to protest, but she was firm.

"No," she reasoned. "We must know where we are. It's different with something we understand, but this we don't, so I shall just go round to Dr. Perkins now."

Her growing concern made her seize this opportunity to have him examined by the local panel practitioner, something she had wanted for a long time and which he had always put off. Resolutely, therefore, she slipped on her raincoat, went out, and in a remarkably short time was back with the information that Dr. Perkins had gone off on a brief vacation. However, his housekeeper had promised that the locum would call as soon as he returned from his afternoon round of visits.

No sooner had she concluded than, without warning, he was again able to speak in a perfectly normal manner.

"You see," he said, really put out, "you've made a fuss about nothing. It's just a simple chill, or nerves, or something equally futile."

Distressed, she gazed after him doubtfully as he again went to the studio to work, wondering if indeed she had not been too precipitate in her action. In this uncertain frame of mind she began to cut up some vegetables for the soup she was preparing for supper. An hour passed and still the doctor had not arrived. The attendance at Dr. Perkins's surgery on Saturday night was always large, and she began to wonder if he would come at all. However, just at that point the doorbell rang and, answering it, she found on the

328

threshold a young man who immediately and without ceremony stepped into the hall.

"I'm Dr. Gray. Where is the patient?"

Jenny took him into the kitchen and, having called Stephen, left them together. The doctor put down his bag, removed his hat but not his overcoat, with the air of one sorely pressed for time. He was less youthful than had at first sight appeared, about thirty perhaps, and his blunt though not unpleasant features wore the harassed and irritable expression of one thoroughly overworked in an environment supremely distasteful to him.

"So it's you," he said, in a marked Northern accent. "What seems to be the trouble?"

"Something quite absurd and trivial. But it has rather worried my wife. I keep losing my voice."

"You mean there are periods when you can't speak at all?"

"Yes, at least when I can't make myself heard."

"Is your voice normal between these times?"

"I think so. Perhaps a little hoarse."

"Have you any pain?"

"None at all."

"No other symptoms?"

"No. I have been conscious of a slight numbness in my throat. Imagination, no doubt."

Dr. Gray made an impatient sound with his tongue. Always imagination, another damned neurosis, he suspected, probably hysterical aphonia. Yet this man didn't look like a hysteric, and the fact that he minimized his symptoms supported that view.

"Let's have a look at you." Then, as Stephen bared his throat, he added brusquely: "No, no. That's no good. Strip to the waist and sit down."

With a heightened colour, Stephen did as he was bid. Meanwhile, the doctor had taken from his bag a round mirror which he now adjusted upon his forehead, and directing a beam of light upon the reflecting surface of a laryngoscope held at the back of the patient's throat, he made a considered inspection. Then, without a word, he put on his stethoscope and examined Stephen's chest. Finally, he evinced a certain interest in the ends of Stephen's fingers. The entire investigation, although it was thorough, took not more than fifteen minutes.

"You may dress now." The doctor returned his instruments to the bag, snapped it shut. "How long have you had a cough?"

"A cough? Well . . . I've been bothered with bronchitis off and on for quite a number of years."

"Bronchitis, eh?"

"Yes. I always had a weak chest."

"Always? Can't you remember the first time you had a particularly bad cold, with a pain in your side, that kept on for a while and just wouldn't clear up?"

In sudden recollection Stephen's thoughts went back to the drenching day of the Channel crossing and the weeks at Netiers that had followed it.

"Yes," he said, "about fifteen years ago."

"Ever had any bleeding subsequently?"

"Yes."

"How often?"

"Twice," he answered, suppressing the attack he had suffered in Spain.

"How many years ago was the first? Could one say around fourteen?"

Again, a vivid picture of the past came to Stephen's mind—Dom Arthaud bending over him in the bare, whitewashed monastic room.

"Yes."

"I see." The doctor, having rinsed his hands at the kitchen sink, was drying them on a dish-towel. "You've had chest trouble all that time and a couple of hæmorrhages? And you mean to tell me that you never bothered to find out what was causing it?"

"I never regarded it as serious. And I was always too busy."

"Doing what?"

"Painting."

"You're an artist?"

"Yes."

"Ah!" Dr. Gray, from solid industrial Manchester, compressed into that exclamation a wealth of ironic comprehension.

Suddenly a thought struck him.

"Good God, you're not the fellow that's been in the papers?"

"Does it makes any difference?"

A pause.

"No . . . no . . . of course not."

He gazed at Stephen curiously, and despite his professional insensibility, not altogether without feeling. What chain of circumstances, what careless, unheeding, persistent self-neglect had brought this queer-looking chap, obviously a gentleman, to such a pass without his knowing it? What was one to make of such a case? Worse still, what could one say of it?

The doctor, who was both skilful and ambitious, had undertaken this East End locum simply to raise enough money to enable him to sit for one of the higher medical degrees. He had no interest in this type of practice and conducted himself in it with almost brutal frankness. At present he could not forget that ahead of him was a steamy waiting-room, choked to suffocation with panel patients. Also, he had eaten nothing since one o'clock. Yet, in this instance, something restrained his habitual asperity. He sat down on the arm of a chair.

"You know," he remarked, "I have to tell you that you're a pretty sick man."

"What is wrong with me?"

There was a short pause.

"Advanced pulmonary tuberculosis."

"Are you serious?"

"I wish I were not. You have an old-standing lesion in the right lung. And now the left is acutely infected. Your larynx has become involved . . . an extension . . ."

Stephen had turned pale. He steadied himself against the table.

"But, I don't understand. I've always been able to get about . . . I've felt all right . . ."

"That's the curse of this cursed thing." Gray shook his head in a kind of gloomy rancour. "Insidious. The toxins even induce a sense of well-being. *Spes phthisica*, we call it. Can be quiescent, too, then suddenly goes on the rampage. That's what has happened with you."

"I see. What is to be done about it?"

The doctor fixed his gaze upon the ceiling.

"You ought to get away to a suitable environment."

"Where exactly?"

"To be precise, a sanatorium."

"I couldn't possibly afford it."

"There are ways of fixing up these things . . . it might be arranged . . . through one of the hospitals . . ." There was a forced note of encouragement in the doctor's voice.

"How long should I be away?"

"At least a year, probably longer."

"A year! Should I be allowed to paint?"

Abruptly Dr. Gray shook his head.

"Far from it. You'd be in bed, my dear sir, flat on your back, in the open air."

Stephen was silent, staring straight ahead.

"No," he said, "I couldn't."

"For your own good . . ."

"No, Doctor. I must paint. If I can't go on with my work it'll kill me."

"I'm afraid, if you do go on. . . ." He broke off, shrugging slightly, and with a serious expression looked directly at Stephen.

Again there was a pause. Stephen moistened his lips.

"Tell me the truth. If I stay here and go on working, what is the outlook?"

Dr. Gray started to reply, then stopped. It was not his nature to equivocate, compromise was not in him. Yet something prevented him from bluntly communicating the truth. He said:

"One can never tell. With luck you may go on for quite a bit."

A silence followed. With a start the doctor seemed to recollect himself. He pulled a prescription pad from his overcoat pocket, wrote briskly, tore off the slip and handed it to Stephen.

"Get this made up. A tonic, and a creosote spray for your throat which should effect a local improvement. Take care of yourself, drink as much milk as you can, and push down a tablespoonful of cod-liver oil three times a day. By the way, you're married, aren't you?—ask your wife to come in and see me at the surgery in the morning. The fee is three and six."

When Stephen had paid him, he nodded, picked up his bag, put on his hat and, remarking that he would let himself out, left the room. The front door closed behind him, his footsteps could be heard on the pavement outside. Afterwards a strange stillness fell. Stephen stood quite motionless. Then, as Jenny came in from the scullery, he turned his head.

She entered slowly, and from her expression, fixed and frightened, her desperate striving for control, he knew that she had overheard everything. They looked at each other.

"You will go away, won't you, Stephen?"

"Never."

"You must."

"No, I hate hospitals, I won't leave you, and I can't give up my work."

She came close to him. She could not think clearly, the suddenness of the blow had stunned her. Yet had she not all along had an obscure premonition of this calamity? Fiercely she blamed herself for accepting with such docility his casual glossing over of symptoms now revealed as the manifestation of a serious malady. Holding back her tears because she knew how much he hated them, she begged him to be sensible. But to all her appeals he shook her head.

"If I've got this thing there's not much they can do about it. But these doctors don't know everything. Perhaps I'm not half as bad as he makes out. In any case, he says it's only fresh air I need."

As he said these words he lifted his head as at a sudden inspiration. Margate! It had always done him good. There he could get wonderful air, and all he wanted of it. Indeed, when he was so ill before, had it not completely cured him? He liked the place, had the happiest memories of it—and he could go on working there, in a quiet way. All at once, that optimism so characteristic of his condition caused his spirits to rebound. While she looked at him, rent by the deepest anxiety, wondering what he was about to say, he gave her the shadow of a smile.

"I'll tell you what, we'll pack up here, let Miss Pratt and Tapley fend for themselves for a few weeks. And if Florrie'll have us, we'll go to Margate."

CHAPTER VI

IN THE LATE afternoon, in the little back kitchen above the fish-shop, under a green-shaded lamp already lit against the autumn twilight, Florrie sat warming herself at the stove with the cat upon her knee, gazing towards Jenny, who occupied a seat by the table, with passive yet penetrating inquiry. A pot of tea and a plate of cut bread and butter stood on a tray between the two women. Except for the slow tick of the clock, the room was strangely still. At last, as with an effort, Jenny roused herself.

"Puss is shedding," she said.

"Always does this time of year." Florrie stroked the quiescent animal, then flicked the soft yellow fluff from her fingers. "She's a lovely coat."

"How long now, Flo, since we've been with you? Near seven weeks, isn't it?"

"Near enough, I suppose. Time does fly."

"You are good about it. It's an imposition really. Only, the air does seem to help him." Jenny paused. "Do you see an improvement, Flo?"

"I see a change . . . and a big one." Florrie took a slow sip of tea, then put down her cup. "And the sooner you face up to it, the better for you, my girl."

"His voice is better. It don't fail so often."

"That's the least of it."

Jenny lowered her head, compressing her lower lip with her teeth —she had fought hard in these past weeks and would go on fighting harder. Yet as she remembered all the ineffectual remedies she had tried, all the care she had lavished so unsparingly and with so little result, it was difficult to keep an overwhelming discouragement from settling upon her. What anguish she had endured, night after night, listening in silence to his deep, hollow cough—she would not take another bed, nothing could shake her splendid health, she only wished she could give some of it to him.

Courageously, she tried to shake off her depression.

"I wish he'd come for his tea . . ." she said, looking towards the door. "But it's no use to fetch him."

"Why a man in his condition should want to go on paint, painting in that front room. . . ." Florrie turned up her eyes, a gesture that indicated a supreme lack of comprehension. "Here, you haven't 'arf drunk your tea. Let me give you some fresh."

"No, Flo."

"Come along, my girl, you must keep up."

"I don't fancy it, really."

"But you always was a one for your tea," Florrie exclaimed, surprised. "Remember our elevenses in the old days?"

"I've turned against it, like."

Florrie held the teaport in mid-air, studying her sister-in-law curiously, then she set it back, under the cosy. After a moment she said:

"Don't you want no bread'n butter?"

Jenny shook her head.

"You have gone off your feed. Why, at breakfast this morning you didn't more'n touch your kipper. And come to think of it . . . these other mornings . . ."

She broke off. Jenny had coloured painfully, then slowly, under the other's searching scrutiny, she turned pale and her eyes crept guiltily away. A brief ominous silence followed, during which Florrie's expression registered a range of emotion that passed from sheer incredulity to shocked suspicion.

"It ain't that?" she said at last, slowly.

Jenny, still with averted head, did not answer.

"Oh, no," Florrie said, in a suppressed voice. "As if it wasn't bad enough. How long 'ave you missed?"

"Six weeks." The reply came, barely audible.

"My God, when I think on it . . . when I . . . oh, it makes me boil. After he's lived off you all them years. Never doing a hand's turn, the perfect gentleman, letting you work and slave for him, while he mooches around, pretending to slap paint on a piece of canvas. And now, when he's just about done for, to leave you in this condition . . ."

"Don't, Flo," Jenny interrupted fiercely. "Don't blame him. I'm the one what's responsible. It was . . . it was that night the doctor told him . . ."

She broke off, inarticulate, striving to keep back the tears. How could she explain that emotion, transcending any she had ever experienced, wildly passionate, yet intermingled with pity and despair, which had seemed to soften all her being, to surrender everything that was her. She had known, even at that moment, that she had conceived.

"Well, I wish you joy, I'm sure." Florrie spoke in a stiff, inimical tone. "But how you'll manage, my gel, is quite another question."

"Don't be hard, Flo. I shall manage. You know I 'ave a good pair of 'ands."

" 'Ands, yes," Florrie agreed gloomily. "But oh, my gel, where was your 'ead?" She paused. " 'Ave you told him?"

"Not yet. And I shan't till we get home. He'll be more like himself then."

With an effort that went against all her nature, Florrie cut off the exasperated reply that rose to her lips. Jenny's stubborn refusal to admit what, in Flo's own words, was "staring everyone else in the face", was to her the supreme exacerbation of a lamentable situation. At the time of his arrival Stephen had seemed, in Florie's phrase, "no worse than usual", but soon he had begun to deteriorate and now, in fact, his decline had become so rapid as to be precipitous. Her own doctor, whom she had called in a fortnight ago, had told her in no uncertain terms—pronouncing the fatal words "galloping consumption"—that his condition was hopeless and that another hæmorrhage, which might occur at any moment, must immediately prove fatal.

"Have it your own way." She shook her head resignedly. "But why you should go on sacrificing yourself fair beats me."

"There's some'at about him that you, nor nobody else, won't never understand."

Florrie exhaled a long aggravated breath.

"I won't never understand what 'e's ever done for you."

"He's made me happy."

A sound in the passage abruptly terminated the conversation. Both women had adjusted their expression as Stephen came into the room.

"Am I late for tea?" he said, and smiled.

To see that gaunt smile on the tight-skinned, bony face drove a lance into Jenny's breast. Now he would scarcely let her speak of his illness, it was something he preferred to ignore utterly. It was this inveterate detachment, his heroic failure to complain, that most of all cut her to the heart. Yet, knowing how he hated it, she forbade herself to express the least emotion. Instead, in a matter-of-fact voice, pouring him a cup of tea, she said:

"We would have called you. But I thought you might be finishing up."

"As a matter of fact, I have finished. All but a few details. And it rather pleases me." He rubbed his hands together and, accepting a slice of bread and butter from the plate she handed him, sat down at the window.

"You mean the picture's done?" Florrie asked, stroking the cat.

"Yes. It's as good as I can make it. And it is rather good, I think."

"But will it do good *for* anyone?" Florrie's glance rested significantly on Jenny.

"Who knows?" he answered lightly.

Jenny, as she watched him, her face in shadow, could sense the contained excitement of his mood. His eyes, deep in their orbits, showed spots of light, his fingers trembled slightly as he held his cup. She said sympathetically:

"You've been a long time over that one."

"Six months. It was difficult, technically, to convey the sense of elemental things . . . the background of the river . . . earth, air, and water . . . and still preserve a harmony with the central theme."

He did not as a rule talk about his work, but now, suffused still by the thrill of creative achievement, he went on for a few minutes, giving expression to the thoughts that were in his mind.

"And what's to happen to it now?" Florrie asked, tight-lipped, when he concluded.

"Heaven alone knows," Stephen replied indifferently.

"I hope it don't start such a nasty mess-up as you 'ad with that there last one."

"I hope not, Florrie." He smiled, determined not to take offence.

"This seems quite a respectable painting. And to reassure you completely, I promise it won't be exhibited."

Instead of pacifying, his answer provoked her further.

"Well, I must say, you really 'ave me beat. What use can it be, I ask you, what earthly use to stand in that parlour, and make a shambles of it too, paint, paint, painting the livelong day with nothing to show for it? Don't it matter to you that you won't make a single penny on this picture?"

"No. All that matters is that I've done it." He got up. "I'm going out now for a bit of a stroll."

"You shouldn't," Jenny said quickly, protectively. "It's cold outside. And getting dark."

"I must have a walk." He looked at her kindly. "You know that fresh air is good for me."

She did not argue, but came with him into the hall and helped him to wrap up in the thick coat she had bought him, gave him from the stand the stick he now used. Then, at the door, while he went down the stairs, she watched him with that ever-present anguish, yet still revolving in her mind with unquenchable devotion, though a little desperately now, projects for his recovery.

His progress along the street was slow. An incline, so slight as to be almost imperceptible to the eye, made him comprehend the extent of his own debility. Each foot seemed weighted as, avoiding the busier part of the town, he made his way towards the sea-front. At the entrance to the esplanade there stood a circular rotunda, with mirrors in the windows, and as he passed he saw his reflection in the glass, the drawn face, incredibly emaciated, eyes dark and staring, the shoulders stooping as though with age. Instinctively he grimaced and withdrew his gaze. No one knew better than he how preposterous it was that he should be up and about in such a fashion, but he had firmly resisted all attempts to keep him in bed and would continue to do so. He could not bear the thought of being confined.

Presently he reached his objective, a bench at a curve of the bay beyond the pier, usually unoccupied, which afforded an open prospect of the sea. Here he sat down, breathing quickly, but feeling the cool, clear air about him with a sensation of relief.

It was a superb pale sunset, a streak of salmon upon the western horizon, merging to primrose and faint green, the colours, and all their varying merging tints, clear and delicate against the dove-grey sea, and cold with the approach of winter. Not one of Turner's sunsets, he reflected, watching it with sensuous appreciation, sunk down into himself, chin buried in his chest, and for a moment his thoughts turned to that painter of visions, supreme colourist, secret, cantankerous, eccentric, in his old age hiding himself in a filthy Thames-side house, known to the children of the neighbourhood as "old Admiral Booth". We're all mad, or half mad, he told himself, a band of lost souls, cut off from the rest of the world, perpetually in conflict with society, the predestined children of misfortune. At least, he added, with a mental reservation, all except the ones who compromise. He had never done that. Ever since his boyhood he had been obsessed by the desire to grasp a beauty which he felt imprisoned beneath the surface of things. In solitude, through his own struggle, he had pursued his destiny, yet who would ever understand the loneliness, the hours of hollow sadness—broken only by fits of momentary exultation—he had endured in its fulfilment? He had no regrets; indeed, there was a strange peace upon him. Only out of pain and distress and unhappiness, out of all the hostility of the world, could he have created beauty. It was worth the price that he had paid.

While the colours faded from the sky, the different phases of his work passed, in slow review, before him, culminating in the great canvas he had now completed. This final creative mood, or rather its consummation, product of the strange nexus between his sickness and his art, gave him an exalted sense of being above time and death, partaking of the eternal. The more ill he had become the more mysteriously his powers had been renewed. Yet he knew that he was doomed, the fount of physical energy within him had ceased to flow, an ultimate weariness lay upon him. He thought: I shall speak to Jenny tonight . . . it's time we were home . . . we'll leave for Cable Street at the end of the week. . . . And again: Raphael died at thirty-seven . . . why should I complain?

He shivered slightly and, as it was now almost dark, he got up and started back towards the Row. As he did so, he heard a brisk step behind, and a cheerful voice hailed him. He turned, saw advancing the short, active figure of a young man. It was Ernie, looking quite professional in a dark suit and bowler, with a rolled umbrella in his hand.

"Well! I fancied I might find you here." He slowed his pace, adjusting it tactfully to Stephen's. "How are you doing?"

"Oh, fine, Ernie. You on your way home from the office?"

"No, I've been and had my tea. I'm off to my night class now. But Aunt Florrie asked me to look out for you and fetch you back."

Good God, thought Stephen dully, am I so decrepit that they have to send someone to lead me in? Indeed, his companion at this moment, with the best will in the world, had taken his arm and was helping him down the promenade steps. But apparently his suspicion was ill-founded, for almost at once Ernie exclaimed:

"It's not often you have a visitor. And they didn't want you to miss him."

"A visitor? Who is it?"

"Search me. Regular toff by the look of him. Came in a swank car too."

Stephen's brows drew together with a nervous constriction. What next? he asked himself. Had his father or Hubert come to see him? No, that seemed most unlikely. Was it perhaps an emissary from Claire, bringing, misguidedly, some charitable offer of assistance? The possibility dismayed him.

"Maybe it's a posh doctor come to examine you," Ernie speculated optimistically. "A specialist. 'Strewth, 'e ought to do you a real bit of all right. You do 'ave connections what could have arranged it. Good enough! Why, with a bit of luck we'll be digging cockles on the beach next summer, just like old times."

While Ernie rattled on, with purely fictitious enthusiasm, bent ingenuously on raising Stephen's spirits, they passed through the town, quiet now, since most of the stores were closed. Then, as they turned the corner at the harbour, he saw the car, a large black landaulette, standing outside the shuttered entrance to the fish shop.

"There you are!" Ernie drew up, with an air of justification. "Now in you go. I'll be late if I don't rush."

When Stephen had climbed the stairs, he paused to recover his breath, but at once the door opened and Florrie let him in.

"There's a man to see you. A foreigner." Her manner, startled, yet filled with an odd import, confirmed his premonition of the unusual. She added: "In the parlour."

He did not speak, although evidently she expected a question and was prepared to answer. He took off his coat, a slow process, though for once she helped him. When he had hung it on a peg with his hat and scarf, he turned and went into the front room. This was a small apartment, seldom used except when "company" was entertained, and at present completely disarranged by Stephen's easel and the large canvas upon it. A fire, hastily lit, sparked damply in the small black-leaded grate. Occupying the one easy-chair, with his legs crossed, engaging Jenny in conversation, was a short sallow-faced man who, as Stephen appeared, rose quickly to his feet.

"Mr. Desmonde, I am happy to meet you."

His manner, polished yet serious, had a restraint that matched his impeccably severe suit, the dark pearl in his cravat, his shoes of a perfect gloss. In that small front parlour he conferred upon it, without effort, a distinction that almost shattered the cheap china dogs— won by Ernie at the Margate Fair—upon the mantelpiece. Stephen had recognized him at once and barely glanced at the crisp engraved visiting-card which the other presented to him as Jenny, with a murmured word, excused herself and left the room.

"You know, my dear Monsieur Desmonde, it is so good to make your acquaintance at last."

"Haven't we met before?"

"But where, my good sir?"

Stephen considered the dealer calmly.

"In Paris, fifteen years ago. I was broke, starving in fact, hadn't a centime. I tried to sell you my paintings. You wouldn't even look at them."

Tessier's eye flickered slightly, but his manner was proof against any embarrassment. He threw out his hands in charming apology.

"Then I assure you the shoe is now on the other foot. For I have come all the way to London to seek you out. And I may say I had enormous difficulty to find you. First I wrote to Charles Maddox, and received no satisfaction. Then I called upon him. We went together to your house in Stepney but you were not there. Only by the greatest perseverance did I obtain your address here, from Monsieur Glyn. So you see how extremely anxious I have been to achieve this meeting."

"I wish you had not put yourself to so much trouble," Stephen said.

"My dear sir, it is not a trouble, but a pleasure."

Tessier resumed his chair and, balancing his hat on his knee, studied Stephen critically, yet at the same time managing to convey a veiled sense of admiration.

"Even if I had not seen this magnificent canvas"—he made a gesture of reverence towards the painting on the easel—"I should have known you anywhere as an artist. Those hands ... your head. But let us not waste time." He took himself up abruptly. "Monsieur Desmonde, it is my privilege to inform you that in recent months there has been in Paris a growing interest in your work. Some time ago one of your paintings, *Convent Sisters Returning from Church*, belonging to the colourman Campo, was shown in the window of Salomon et Cie—a relatively unimportant dealer. Here, however, it was seen by Georges Bernard, perhaps the most distinguished art critic in France. Bernard greatly liked your painting—forgive me, that phrase is inadequate—moreover, since something of the recent animadversion against your work, coupled with certain derogatory comments upon the French Impressionists, had been reported in the Paris papers, he recognized your name. The following Thursday in *La Revue Gauloise*, in a full-length column, he praised *Sisters* in the highest terms. The very next morning the picture was sold.

"Now Campo, for an obscure little merchant over seventy years of age, is not altogether a fool. He had, of your works, no less than twenty canvases, mostly your early French period, some of your circus compositions including a glorious study, *Horses in a Thunderstorm*, and several of the early Spanish period, which apparently you had pledged to him when you were working with Modigliani. He took all of these to Bernard, permitted him to select one as his own—he chose the frieze of horses—and asked him to sponsor an exhibition. This was held two months ago, again, unfortunately, at Salomon's. I use the word advisedly, for as a result, every one of the pictures was immediately sold—at prices which in a few years will seem to you derisory. Moreover, with the appetite of connoisseurs stimulated to a high degree, there remained not a single Desmonde canvas in the whole of Paris. No," he corrected himself, "I am wrong. Just after the initial *frisson* there came into Paris from, of all people, a country *épicière* in Normandy, a delicious pastel of two young girls, unsigned, but obviously from your hand." He looked inquiringly at Stephen. "You recollect the work?"

"Perfectly . . . they were the Cruchot children."

"Such was the name. And the pastel, it may interest you to know, sold for no less than fifteen thousand francs."

"Good," Stephen said in a flat voice. "That would please Madame Cruchot greatly."

"Now, Monsieur Desmonde, I don't wish to bore you by stressing a situation which is so obvious. You have come into your own at last. The collectors are asking for your work, demanding it. And you . . . with practically every one of your paintings in your own hands, you have, in a phrase, cornered the market. So if you will honour me, and I think my position in the world of art is pre-eminent, by permitting me to act for you, I can guarantee that you will have no cause to regret it."

Stephen had listened to these admirable remarks standing, supporting himself with his elbow against the mantelpiece. He felt faint and breathless, on the verge of one of those prolonged bouts of coughing after which his voice would leave him, and so expose the extremity of his condition. But he straightened, by an effort of his will alone.

"I appreciate your interest. But I have neither the need nor the desire to sell my paintings."

Taken unawares by this quite unexpected reply, Tessier nevertheless recovered himself quickly. He spoke soothingly.

"Naturally, Monsieur Desmonde, one does not speak exclusively in terms of money to an artist such as you. But there are other considerations. For example . . . reputation. It is high time that you should be known."

"To be known is not my concern. Such a vanity can gratify only a very mediocre talent."

"But surely . . . you must desire fame?"

"Would that serve as a gauge of my worth any more than my present obscurity? I have never sought to please the public, but only to please myself."

"Monsieur Desmonde . . . permit me to call you *cher maître* . . . you seriously distress me. You have something of great value to give the world. You cannot bury it. Remember the parable in the Scriptures."

At the Biblical allusion coming from the shrewdist dealer in Paris, Stephen, still fighting to suppress that cough, could barely repress the flicker of a smile, transient, and so weary it distorted the drawn, haggard features. He said quietly, without rancour:

"I gave the world something of value years ago. They burned it."

"Forget that. The market—that is to say," he drew himself up, "the time and circumstances are much more favourable. Come, *cher maître*, give me the opportunity to gather laurels for your brow."

Stephen's eyes rested on the other with a sort of contained irony, but his face remained impassive—the stiff muscles of expression, beyond a twitching of the pale lips, seemed unable to relax.

"No. I have conceived a certain manner of painting. There is a certain interpretation of beauty which I wished to achieve. If my work is good it will one day find its place—as with most artists, after I am no longer here. In the meantime, having lived with my paintings, I propose to die with them."

A pause followed. Tessier sat swinging one foot in circles; Desmonde's expression, strained yet indifferent, was strangely disconcerting. Is it pique, he asked himself, a form of revenge because I once refused his work? Most artists, in his private opinion, were more or less unpredictable. No, he thought finally, this man is sincere. He simply does not care whether I, Tessier, take his paintings or not.

And, becoming more and more aware of the signs of illness and extreme fatigue in Stephen's face, a sudden understanding came to him.

"Monsieur Desmonde," he said at last, slowly and without affectation. "I need not say how profoundly you grieve me. I have no wish to importune you. It may be that you suspect me as a man of commerce. I am that, it is true. At the same time, I know beauty, and love it. This painting here, which I examined wih excitement and delight before you came in—permit me to tell you it is superb. And if you will allow me to have it, at the price which you name, I give you my *parole d'honneur* that within three months I will donate it, through the Ministre des Beaux Arts, to the Luxembourg. Come now . . . you see that I am serious, that my motives are not altogether unworthy."

While the other was speaking, Stephen's look had softened, but the sad intensity of his posture did not relax. With unmoved stillness and sadness he shook his head slowly.

"You must permit me the final luxury of refusing you. At the same time," he stilled the other's protest, "I will make you a promise. You have spoken of three months. Come back then . . . come to Cable Street, in Stepney . . . I don't think you will be disappointed."

There was a long silence. My God, thought Tessier, he is really ill, he is going to die . . . and he knows it. A shiver went over him— he was a man who loved the pleasures of life, to whom the very thought of the grave was distressing—but he concealed it, smiled and exclaimed:

"Very well. I accept. It is an arrangement clearly understood. And now, you have been working all day . . . you are tired . . .I have already taken up too much of your time. . . ." He saw indeed, with deeper intuition, that his visit must not be prolonged another moment. He picked up his portfolio, rose, held out his hand. "*Au revoir, cher maître.*"

"Good-bye."

With a last look at the painting, Tessier swung round, and, involuntarily, with a sudden display of emotion, theatrical perhaps, yet strangely dignified, embraced Stephen on both cheeks; then, in silence, he went out.

When the dealer had gone, Stephen, still standing, let his head drop upon his hand, and allowed his cough to have its way. The spasm lasted several minutes, after which, bent double, he struggled to regain his breath. Then he leaned back against the mantel. It was in this attitude that Jenny found him as, a moment later, she came quietly into the room.

"Who was it, Stephen?"

He found his voice.

"A man I once knew in Paris."

"I never saw such a swell. What did he want?"

"Something he might have had a long time ago. He's coming back again, Jenny . . . in three months' time . . . to buy my pictures. You can trust him. He's not a bad sort. . . ."

There was a pause. She studied his face anxiously.

"Oh, my dear, you are dead-beat." She put a supporting arm around him. "Let me get you into bed."

He was about to submit, then, by a superhuman effort of the will, he forced himself erect.

"I think . . . first of all . . . I'll finish varnishing my *Thames* . . ." He took a step forward, put his arm round Jenny's waist and stood looking at his work. A smile barely touched his lips. "You know . . . he really meant it when he said it was superb."

CHAPTER VII

On an April afternoon in the year 1937 a man, to be exact, an elderly clergyman, and a boy in a long blue coat, yellow stockings and buckle shoes, descended from a bus at the north end of Vauxhall Bridge, turned off into Grosvenor Road, and by way of the Embankment entered the quiet precincts of Millbank. It was a lovely day. The air, fresh yet mild, smelled deliciously of spring. In Westminster Gardens daffodils waved and tulips stood gaily at attention; upon the trim green lawns the chestnut trees, in snowy flower, had spread a soft white carpet. The Thames, shimmering in the sunshine, glided beneath its bridges, silent and stately, as from time immemorial. Against the blue, flecked by a fleece of clouds, the Abbey stood out in exquisite tracery, beyond were the Houses of Parliament. Glinting in the distance, amidst a constellation of Wren churches whose spires and steeples ennobled the skyline of the city, was the major orb, the dome of St. Paul's. The Palace, though not visible, lay within bowshot. The standard flew, the royal family was in residence. Slowly Big Ben chimed the hour: then three deep notes. And the Rector, walking with young Stephen Desmonde, strangely stirred, lifted, despite the weight of years, by the beauty of the day, the vagrant primrose-scented airs of spring, a prey to many memories, thought to himself, Here beats the pulse of England, less strongly than of old perhaps, yet still it beats.

As the two came along the Embankment, at a leisurely pace, for Bertram, although his tall spare figure held fairly erect, was slowed by rheumatism, one sensed in their movements an air of custom, made manifest more particularly by a suggestion of polite sufferance on the part of the boy. Some fifty yards from the end of the street they crossed over and climbed the steps of a large building that stood behind railings and a small ornamental garden. Removing his hat, Bertram turned, stood for a moment at the entrance recovering his breath and viewing the sweeping panorama of sky, river and majestic edifices. Then the turnstiles clicked and they were both inside the Tate Gallery.

Few people were about, the long, high ceilinged rooms held that echoing quietude which pleased Bertram most, and, making their way, still with that sense of habit, through the central gallery, past the glowing Turners and silvery Whistlers, the Sargents, Constables and Gainsboroughs, they bore to the left and finally sat down in a room, fretted by sunshine, on the west side. Upon the wall, directly opposite, exquisitely framed and hung, were three paintings. At these, silently, the boy as in duty bound, his elder with remote and meditative vision, gazed. Presently, without removing his eyes, Bertram spoke.

"You are settling down quite well at Horsham?"

"Quite well, thank you, sir."

"You like the school?"

"It's not at all bad, sir."

"Of course, the first year is always difficult. But afterwards you'll get into the swing of things. You've made some friends, I hope?"

"Yes, sir. There's a couple of boys, Jones minor and Piggott, that I'm chummy with."

"And you're not bullied?"

"Oh, no, sir. You have to look smart when the monitors tell you to do something, but if a fellow keeps on his toes and doesn't josh they're rather decent on the whole."

"Good."

The conversation, hauntingly reminiscent of his talks with David and the other Stephen, so many years ago, brought a strange pain to Bertram's heart. Yes, so long ago—and yet it seemed like yesterday when they first went off to Marlborough, nervously intent on the ordeal ahead, only half listening to his good advice. What an old man he was getting to be, an old fogey so given over to dreaming back that he mixed up the present with the past and sometimes, looking at this Stephen, fancied himself in company with his own dear son. The two were certainly alike—the living Stephen had the other's delicate colouring, open brow and deep blue eyes, the same proud set of the head upon the still narrow shoulders. He looked a gentleman, thank God, a regular Desmonde. And Christ's Hospital, while he would naturally have preferred Marlborough, was a fine sound school and would make a man of him. Under the circumstances, he could count himself lucky to have got the boy in on a foundation—they were hard to get these days, with everyone feeling the pinch. The uniform, too, was fetching—today, when they had taken luncheon at Simpson's, in the Strand, the looks directed towards them, interested, amused, all flattering, had warmed him, more, much more than the pint of Chablis which, as a treat, he had permitted himself. For that matter, none of the vintages were half as good as they had been in the old days.

The desire to plant the good seed, the feeling that it was his duty to do so, drove him, rather against his will, to a little homily.

"We expect fine things of you, my boy. You must stick in and do credit to your name. Are the lessons coming along?"

"Pretty fair, I think, sir. We had a test before we broke up for the holidays."

"How did that come out?"

"I did all right in English and arithmetic."

A shadow crossed Bertram's mind, he scarcely could bring himself to ask the question.

"Do they give you drawing?"

"Yes, sir. But I did badly in that. It seems I can't draw at all." Unconsciously, Bertram gave out a little sigh of relief, glanced towards his grandson, who continued, "But Mother said I must tell you I got full marks for Scripture knowledge."

"Well done . . . well done," Bertram murmured. Who could tell? Perhaps even at this late hour the great hope of his life might be fulfilled, if the good Lord would only let him survive to realize it. He laid his blue-veined fingers on the boy's hand and patted it approvingly.

Under the caress Stephen flushed and glanced round to see if they were observed. Although his grandfather aroused in him that mixture of constraint and awe, with an occasional flicker of amusement, which it is the sad lot of the aged to occasion in the young, he rather enjoyed these not infrequent expeditions which they took together, especially during term time, when a slap-up lunch of his own choosing, followed, if the programme were suitable, by a cinema, and ending, inevitably, by their pilgrimage to the Tate, constituted a thoroughly agreeable break in the routine of classes. But today, the beginning of the Easter vacation, after having been away from her for nine weeks, he was eager to see his mother, who would meet them at Waterloo Station and take him home with her. Several times in the last hour he had tactfully inquired of Bertram what the time might be, and was, indeed, about to do so again when a party of schoolgirls entered the room, under the escort of their mistress.

There were about a dozen of them, in dark green skirts and blazers of the same colour with a badge on the pocket, straw hats with a green ribbon, kept on by an elastic under the chin. All wore brown kid gloves, black stockings and shoes. The mistress, in restrained tweeds and flat-heeled shoes, was pale and earnest, bareheaded, bespectacled, and carried a little sheaf of notes, to which, as the cicerone conducting the tour, she referred from time to time. Exactly opposite Bertram and Stephen, but without taking any notice of them, she drew up.

"And now, girls," she announced, "we come to the Desmondes, three representative paintings purchased in 1930. The first, entitled *Circus*, distinguished by a marvellous sense of colour and composition, is of the artist's early French period. Note in particular the grouping of the clowns in the foreground and the manner in which a sense of movement is given to the figure of the young woman on the bicycle.

"The second painting, *The Blue Wrapper*, which I am sure you have seen reproduced many times, is a portrait of the artist's wife. Here you will find the freedom of arrangement and unconventionality of design which characterized all Desmonde's work. As you see, the subject is neither pretty nor young, yet by subtle colouring and a rhythmic flow of simple lines, an extraordinary feeling of beauty is created. Observe, too, that through the window at which she sits, there is an exquisitely suggested vista of the street outside, with some poor children engaged in a game of ball. This, incidentally, was the subject of another well-known Desmonde known as *Children at Play*, which may be seen in the Luxembourg, Paris.

"The third, and largest painting, was the last work accomplished by the artist, and is considered to be his finest. It is, as you see, a large composition of the estuary of the Thames, showing all the crowded, turbulent movement of the river." She began here to consult her notes. "Observe, girls, that it is no mere pictorial representation. Note the skilful deformations, the audacity and subtlety of the colouring, the expressive divided tones, the projection upon the canvas of an interior drama of the spirit. See also how the light seems to emanate from the canvas, gleaming and vibrant, a luminosity that gives great intensity to the work. In a way it is reminiscent of the radiance of expression found in the great paintings of Rubens. Desmonde was not altogether a revolutionary painter. Just as the Impressionists drew from Turner, he drew, in his early years, from Manet, Degas, and Monet. There are some, indeed, who have contended recently that the Spanish period of his art stems from the painter Goya. But although he studied the masters, he went beyond them. He knew how to recognize beauty in all its forms, and his conscience forced him to reject any technique but his own. He was in every sense of the word an individualist whose work, even when most specialized, seemed to cover the whole span of life, a great original artist who, resisting every temptation to be repetitious, opened up a new era of expression. When we look at these works we know he has not lived in vain."

Here the mistress discarded her notes and became human again. Looking around her pupils, she asked briskly:

"Any questions, class?"

One of the girls, who stood close to the teacher, spoke up, in the manner of a favourite pupil.

"Is he dead, Miss?"

"Yes, Doris. He died as quite a young man, rather tragically, and almost unrecognized."

"But, Miss, didn't you just tell us he was a great painter?"

"Yes, Doris, but like so many others he had to die to become great. Don't you remember what I told you about Rembrandt's poverty, and Hals, buried in a pauper's grave, and Gauguin, who could scarcely sell a single picture when he was penniless, and Van Gogh . . ."

"Yes, Miss . . . people didn't understand, were mistaken about them."

"We can all make mistakes, dear . . . Gladys, do stop sniffing."

"Please, Miss, I have a cold."

"Then use your handkerchief . . . as I was saying, Doris, England may have erred over Stephen Desmonde, but she has made up for it handsomely. Here are these paintings in the Tate for all of us to admire. Now come along, follow me, don't lag behind, girls, and we'll take the Sargents."

348

When they had gone, clattering down the long gallery, Bertram, still immobile, maintained his baffled contemplation of the pictures. How often, in these last few years, had he heard from its small beginning, yet ever growing, and swelling to a chorus, that panegyric on his son, the same fulsome words and phrases used a moment ago by the young art mistress to her class. All the evidence of failure that had seemed so certain, the cut-and-dried opinions of those who presumed to know, finally disproved; Stephen, his son, a great artist . . . yes, even the word genius was now being used without reserve. There was no pride in him at the thought, no belated triumph, but rather a strange bewildered sadness, and thinking of the pain and disappointment of a lifetime crowned too late, he wondered if it had all been worth it. Was any picture worth it—the greatest masterpiece ever wrought? What was beauty, after all, that men should martyr themselves in its pursuit, die for it, like the saints of old? It seemed to him that the conflict between life and art could never be resolved. Peering hard at the canvases, he tried to discern virtues in them not apparent to him before. Slowly, regretfully, he shook his head. He could not do so. He bowed again to the opinion of the experts as he had bowed before, yet in truth they remained to him indecipherable, as great an enigma as had been his son in every action of his life, most of all, in the utter, incomprehensible, careless unrepentance of his end. That last scene of all, he could never contemplate without a dull ache in his heart, when, in the grey morning, summoned by Glyn to the small back bedroom in Cable Street, he had found his son *in extremis*, ghostly pale and barely breathing, his speech completely gone, the larynx so destroyed as to make swallowing impossible, but still with a pencil and a sketch-block at the bedside and, as if that were not enough, a long cane tipped with charcoal, with which, while supine and helpless, he had only the day before been tracing strange designs upon the wall. Bertram had tried, his breast rent, to speak words of affection and consolation, striven, at the eleventh hour, to lead this wayward soul back to the Lord, but, as he was uttering a prayer, Stephen, writing weakly, had handed him a note: *Too bad, Father . . . I have never drawn you . . . you have a fine head.* And then, incredibly, sunk in the pillows, he had begun to outline Bertram's profile on his block. A final portrait . . . for presently the pencil slipped from his grasp, the fingers sought it feebly, instinctively, then, like all the rest of him, were still. Then, while Bertram sat bowed and broken, Glyn, with a hard, set competence, had begun immediately to make a death mask of the gaunt, passionless face.

"For God's sake," he had cried out, "must you do that?"

"Yes," Glyn answered, sombrely, "for art's sake. In the future this will be for many a source of faith and perseverance."

At least the funeral had been at Stillwater, and Stephen was at peace there now, within the church, lulled by the Downland winds, beside his ancestor the Crusader.

With an effort Bertram roused himself . . . the past was past, there was no profit in mourning it.

"Come, my boy. You shall have an ice at Buszard's before we meet your mother."

They took a bus to Oxford Circus and, seated at a little marble-topped table in the old-established confectioner's, the Rector watched his grandson eat a strawberry ice.

"Good?"

"Awfully." He looked up. "Won't you have one too, sir?"

Touched, Bertram shook his head.

"I liked them when I was your age. There's a coconut sweet they make here which is quite excellent too. I used to be given it when I was a boy." He smiled faintly as he added: "They've been making it for almost a century."

When they went out he paused at the mahogany counter and bought a pound box of the pink-and-white confection. Wholesome stuff, he reflected, taking the neatly wrapped box—it wouldn't do the boy a bit of harm.

It was not far to the station. And there, well ahead of time, waiting for them under the clock, was young Stephen's mother, neat and unobtrusive in her black serge costume, a figure one would scarcely notice in the crowd. But the boy saw her and went towards her quickly. She bent a little, held him closely in her arms.

Standing a little distance off, the Rector discreetly looked away. Yet he couldn't help noticing. . . it was a loving reunion. And his son's widow . . . she was really a modest, decent little creature, living now with her sister in a detached house in Cliftonville, quite the better part of Margate. There was a steady, indeed, an increasing income from the sale of Stephen's pictures. He felt sure the black she wore was still a sign of mourning—she must have cared more, yes, much more than he had believed. They were coming towards him now.

"I do hope Stevie's been a good boy."

"Very good." But he wished she would not so abbreviate the name. "We had a nice time together."

"It's kind of you to take him out."

"And good of you to let me do so."

They talked amiably for a few minutes. Then a pause. Jenny looked meaningly at her son.

"Thank you very much, sir, for a splendid time."

They shook hands. He saw them go off together, arm in arm, watching until they were quite lost to view. He sighed. Although the clock was above, he consulted his watch. His train was due to leave in fifteen minutes. Caroline most probably would have been to the Halborough market and would meet him at the junction, come home with him in the bus. Since Julia's death two years ago she had seemed to worry less. She made him comfortable in the Little Rectory and had done it up so nicely, he rather liked it now. Although only a bungalow, it was most convenient, and warm in the winter. Yes, a good soul, Carrie. Why, she had looked almost cheerful the other day when Claire had given her that cocker spaniel pup. Ah, Claire . . . Claire . . . If only . . . but no, he must not wander into that land of might-have-been. At the bookstall he prowled around—nothing worth reading now, all sensational rubbish; in the end he took the *Cornhill Magazine*. Perhaps he might find something in it for his Sunday sermon. He had rather used up Bishop Denton now, been over the old chap once too often, and ideas did not strike one quite so sharply or so easily as they once had done.

He found a third-class corner seat—gone were the days of travelling first—and when the engine started off, settled himself to read. But the daylight was fading, his eyesight enfeebled, the illumination in the compartment poor. He suddenly felt tired, and the lunch which the boy had chosen, a mixed grill, though he had partaken of it sparingly, or perhaps it was the Chablis, he had never been a drinker, gave him a slight sense of heaviness. Leaning back, he closed his eyes. Was he asleep? Or listening to the pounding of the wheels, which seemed to repeat, over and over again, the name of his dead son?

Night fell, the train went rattling on, through the dark landscape of the night.